# KEEPING MY FOREVER

## The Pennystone Series

Sierra Hebdon

*To all the girls waiting for your soulmate, partner, and best friend: he's out there, but he might not be ready for you just yet. Give him time—he will become the person you deserve.*

# CONTENTS

# PROLOGUE
## - SAGE

Me: Tonight is the night! I think Matt is finally going to seal the deal.

Brooklyn: WHAT?! Are your nails done? What are you going to wear? Why didn't he tell us so we could prepare!!

Gracie: Wait, I feel like he would have told someone or asked for help with the ring. Are you sure it's tonight?

Me: I really think it is tonight! Earlier this week he got a confirmation text from Roscos for tonight at 7pm.

Brooklyn: You definitely don't make a reservation at Roscos unless it's something big. That place has reservations for months ahead of time!

Gracie: Oh. My. Goodness! It could be finally happening!!! Has he dropped any other hints?

Me: Actually the opposite. I feel like he's been a little distant the past couple of weeks but figured he was just stressed at work with his new promotion. Maybe he is just anxious about tonight and keeping it a surprise.

Brooklyn: Go get ready for your man! Send us pictures before you leave.

Gracie: You're beautiful no matter what you wear Sage.... But send pictures! And call us ASAP after!

I jump off the couch and run to my bedroom. If the reservation is at 7pm, I have about two hours before I need to leave my apartment to make it on time. Easily enough time for a shower and to get ready while freaking out about what tonight is going to bring. Now that I have confirmation from my girls that tonight could very well be the night, I need to get ready.

Matt and I met my junior year of college in a children's literature class. He was one of those guys that I didn't think would ever notice me. You know the type, football starter, at all the parties, and very well known with the ladies. At 5'10 with dirty blonde hair and blue eyes, he was the epitome of an All American wide receiver. Matt and I ended up being paired up for our midterm project. We were assigned to strategically choose 5 children's books to take to the nearby children's hospital and spend an afternoon reading to the kids and their families.

Matt quickly learned my passion for working with children and I learned how Matt has the ultimate soft spot for kids.

Some of the kids at the hospital recognized him

from his football career and were immediately starstruck. I loved sitting back and watching him read those books to the kids with patience and care.

That was 3 years ago and we have been together ever since. We enjoyed graduation together, moved into an apartment together immediately after, I got my dream job as a kindergarten teacher at one of the best schools in Knoxville and Matt settled into his job returning to our university as an assistant football coach.

About a month ago, Matt got promoted to offensive coordinator and we have begun looking at houses to make some permanent roots.Taking some time to reminisce in the shower ate up some precious time and now I need to hurry. I quickly towel dry my hair and wrap it up while running to the closet. This night calls for the best dress I have and I know just the one.

Matt's mom spoiled me this past year for my birthday and bought me a very expensive and very gorgeous Roberto Cavalli black cocktail dress. It is a beautiful off the shoulder long sleeve dress that hugs my body just enough and stops midthigh. My favorite part is that it has a subtle amount of sparkle to it throughout the entire thing to make it look like you are shining no matter the lighting.

I have been saving it for a special occasion just like tonight. After slipping on the dress that fits like a glove and is already making me feel beautiful for tonight, I run back to the bathroom to finish getting ready. A quick dry of my long blonde hair and add some loose wide curls, my hair is ready to go. Now onto some makeup, applying more than I typically would but it's a special night so what the heck. With a little spritz of Matt's favorite perfume and my favorite strappy black heels, I check myself out in my tall mirror and give myself the final approval.

Giddy about tonight and how I have pulled myself together, I FaceTime my girls. "Hey guys! I'm about to walk out the door but wanted your final approval" I say to their smiling faces. I flip the camera showing them the full mirror.

Brooklyn immediately gushes "Sage. You look incredible! Is that the dress that Matt's mom bought you?"

"Yep! I was saving it for a special occasion since you know it costs more than my monthly salary." Gracie looks more tentative. "Have you heard anything from Matt?" .

"Not yet but I'm sure he is just stuck in traffic on the way from work. He always forgets to check his phone before hopping in the car"

"So what's the plan? You show up looking like a freaking trophy which makes him drop to his knees and instantly asks you to be his wife". It is obvious that Brooklyn can barely contain her excitement.

"I honestly don't know. I'm going to show up

and kind of surprise him I guess. Then we will have a nice dinner and see where it goes. I'm sure he has it all planned out."

Gracie gives a small smile. "Sage you are beautiful inside and out. Matt would be extremely lucky to one day call you his wife." Barely containing my excitement and love for my girls I know I need to get on the road if I want to make it in time with traffic. "Alright ladies, I better head out so I can make it on time. I will give you updates once I get that ring on my finger. Love you guys. Couldn't imagine this night without the two of you."

"We love you! Now go get yourself a fiancé and maybe just update us in the morning after the full celebration." Chuckling, I end the call, grab my keys and race out of the apartment to the parking garage.

By some miracle I don't hit any traffic and not a single red light. As if it is a sign that tonight is going to be one of the best of my life. I pull into a parking spot at Rosco's right at 7pm and give myself a minute to take some deep breaths and calm my nerves. Tonight is the night that I will go from girlfriend to fiance.

I still haven't heard anything from Matt by the time I get to the front door and am greeted cheerfully by the hostess. "Good evening, do you have a reservation with us tonight?"

"Yes, my boyfriend made the reservation. His name is Matt Holmes and it was for 7pm" The hostess looks confused for a second which makes me wonder if maybe I read the date wrong on the confirmation message. That would explain why I haven't heard anything from Matt.

Now feeling silly for possibly getting all dressed up when he could be walking into our apartment as we speak, the minute the hostess takes to look up the reservation feels like hours. "Oh yes. Here it is. It looks like the party has already arrived so I can take you back to your table now"

The party has already arrived? That's weird. It should only be Matt. Plus the look the hostess is giving me puts my nerves on end. Something doesn't feel right. As we round the corner of the restaurant I am stopped in my tracks. Matt is already at the table. The problem? During the time it took to walk through the restaurant with the kind and tentative hostess, another woman was also beelining it to Matt's table. The second I stopped walking was the second that Matt stood up, gave this beautiful woman a hug and a kiss before pulling out her chair for her.

At this point the hostess has realized that I have stopped walking. She also saw the scene unfold in front of us and since I told her that "my boyfriend" made the reservation, she must understand what exactly just happened.

Glancing back at me with unsurety and pity in her eyes, we are both stuck. My eyes bounce back to the table at the exact time that Matt's eyes finally find me. Looking shocked, he quickly composes himself and returns to the woman, his apparent date. Mortified and embarrassed beyond belief, I turn as quickly as my heels will let me and flee from the restaurant. I jump in my car and break possibly every speed limit to get home.

Anger has now settled in and I am determined to pack my things as quickly as possible and get out of the apartment before Matt shows up. I may have all night depending on his plans following his date with the beautiful woman, especially since he knows that I am very aware of what just occurred. But on the off chance he chooses to rush through dinner and come back here, I need to hurry it along.

I have my car packed to the brim within 30 minutes and nothing is left behind besides probably some old hair ties in random places. Because I am not completely perfect and definitely not in a forgiving mood, I leave a note on the refrigerator for Matt.

*Thank you for showing me your true colors tonight. Next time be sure to not schedule a reservation that your girlfriend can easily see. My key is under the mat. Have a good life.*

I run to my car to avoid any embarrassing moments with any of my neighbors. The weight of the night has finally started to catch up with me. Knowing exactly who I need at this moment, I call my twin brother Stanton. With how my night is going I shouldn't be shocked that he doesn't answer so instead I'm stuck leaving a voicemail.

"Hey Stanton. I'm coming home."

# CHAPTER 1
# - SAGE

We made it. The last day of the school year is finally about to be over. This past year has been a rollercoaster for me. After the night at Roscos that changed everything for me, I ended up back in Pennystone Georgia, the small town that I grew up in living with my parents.

Thank goodness the local elementary school was in need of a kindergarten teacher and since the principal Mrs. Applewood has known me since I was in kindergarten myself, I had the job the second I walked into that interview. The year was long and lonely.

While juggling learning a new curriculum and school culture, I was also forced to live with my parents while waiting for my house to be built. One of the perks of living with Matt straight out of college, I was able to build up a good savings. Due to material delays, 6 months soon turned to 8 months which turned to 10 months and counting. Not that my parents would ever complain about me there with them. My mom cried the day I rolled into town with nothing but all the things packed in my little car. My dad didn't say much but I could see the anger in his face when I told him what occurred with Matt then he gave me a long tight hug.

Now don't get me wrong, there are some perks of living back at home. My mom constantly makes sure that I not only have a home cooked meal every night but that there is enough for me to have lunch the next day. I will get home from work to find my clothes washed and folded on my bed. And on days where the loneliness really sits in, my parents will pop on one of my favorite romantic comedies on the tv after dinner and throw a bowl of ice cream at me.

There are also some negatives of living with my parents. Beyond the obvious of feeling like a child again, my mom also is constantly checking in on me to make sure my heart is healing and my dad often looks my way with concern. I have grieved and healed the past year over my relationship with Matt. Where I once thought he held my future, I now realize that I was naive to put my happiness in the hands of a man.

Now? No chance in hell. Now I have my family, still have my girls, and have the best students in the world. Plus I am about to have 8 weeks of summer to move into a brand new home and reset before getting a new wave of kindergarten kiddos next fall.

Today has been a long and busy one. Whoever thought that it would be smart to have a field day full of water games on the last day of school never had to deal with exhausted, wet, and hyper 6 year olds. By the time 3 o'clock comes around, I am ready to be in my bed with a book in my hand. Not even wanting to clean up and pack my classroom today, I walk to the front office to tell them that I will pop in sometime during the summer to set up for the new school year.

Before I am able to leave Mrs. Applewood pops out of her office, "Hey Sage! Did you stay dry today? It seemed pretty crazy out there".

"Good afternoon ma'am. I tried my best. My students however are probably crashing at home right now. I've never seen those kids more tired climbing onto the bus"

"Field Day seemed to be very successful. Sage, do you mind chatting with me for a minute before you head out?"

"Yes of course". I immediately forget how exhausted I am and start worrying about what Mrs. Applewood needs to talk about. I know I am one of the newest teachers here so I really hope that my job is still available for next year. With the new house being built, I was excited to start building real roots here. "Alright Sage, how did you like your first year here at Pennystone elementary?"

"It's been a great year. I feel lucky that I had such a great class. I'm confident that they are ready for the first grade. I am sad to lose them but that is the worst part of teaching. I love the culture you have built here. I feel like the admin team really cares and are willing to help out in any way that they can. The parents are great and involved but I am not surprised since everyone has been in this town for most of their lives." Heat crawls up my neck and into my cheeks as I have realized that I have been caught rambling.

"I am really glad that you are enjoying your time here. That will make this next question easier." Of course sweet Mrs. Applewood chooses to take a dramatic pause. Okay maybe it was just to take a breath but felt like it took forever.

"We would like you to become the department head for grades kindergarten to third grade. You're responsibility will be to help them with teaching strategies and be their go to person if they need guidance or help. We know this is a larger responsibility and can require more time but we feel that you are the best person to fill the role. We have been very impressed this year."

"Oh wow. Thank you for the opportunity. I am a little speechless." I can't believe that this is how the conversation turned. While I'm here stressing about if they are going to take away my job, they see more potential.

"I know it is a change of pace from only worrying about the students in your classroom. If you need more time to decide on whether you would like to take it, I would completely understand."

"No ma'am, that won't be needed. I would love to take the opportunity. Thank you again for thinking of me." Smiling, Mrs. Applewood looks very satisfied with my answer. "You're a great teacher Sage and we are lucky to have you. Now go home, get some rest, and enjoy your summer. I'll reach out before the school year starts to discuss more about this role moving forward."

Standing up I shake Mrs. Applewood's hand. "Thank you ma'am again for this opportunity. Have a great weekend" Walking out of her office with a new smile on my face I say goodbye to those still in the office and head outside. The Georgia heat is coming in strong this year and it's been dry lately. We haven't been getting our typical afternoon showers that cool the temperatures down.

Jumping in my car and blasting the air conditioner as soon as possible, I pull out my phone while waiting for the cool air to hit and see five missed notifications. Four of them are from the girls.

Brooklyn: Summer starts TODAY! You made it Sage.
Gracie: holla! When does your house finish? Do you have a closing date yet?
Brooklyn: we HAVE to have a girls weekend once you get your house keys.
Brooklyn: no but for real. Tell us the weekend and

we will make it happen.

I shoot off a text quickly to them before leaving the parking lot.

Me: Summer has officially started! I am supposed to find out about the house by Monday with an exact date. I'll keep you posted when we can plan a weekend together! Maybe a painting weekend?

With the new house on my mind, I decide to take a little detour to drive by the house and check if it looks finished. Last time I drove by there were not any windows so hopefully they made progress. With Taylor Swift playing and the air conditioner chilling the air, it is starting to feel like summer. I stop in front of the house and get excited when I realize that there are now windows AND a front door. Hopefully this means it will be finished soon. Remembering that I still have another text, I pull out my phone to see a text from my brother.

Stanton: Hey sis. You made it to summer! Meet me at The Diner at 6pm so we can celebrate.

It's now 4:30 so I better get home and get ready. Time to celebrate and start enjoying my break.

# CHAPTER 2
# - SAGE

The Diner is one of my favorite places to go. I was not surprised when Stanton told me to meet him here for dinner. Stanton and I grew up going to this diner with our parents, continued coming with friends especially for milkshakes after the football games on Friday nights, and now as adults have continued to spend evenings here. I'm running a little behind but texted Stanton on the way. He also may be late with his life being even more hectic than mine.

Stanton has always been the guy that everyone goes to for support and advice. It only made sense that he used that in deciding what he wanted to do with his career. Stanton was an all american football wide receiver who could have chosen the football career path. He chose to stay close for college at the University of Northern Georgia. This did mean he was a big star in a smaller named football program. While he loved his time playing, he knew it wasn't going to be his passion for life. He graduated with top honors and became a licensed mental health therapist. He returned home to Pennystone to work with his lifelong mentor John Ward.

His life turned upside down when his high school sweetheart, Jessica, ended up pregnant shortly after they returned to Pennystone. Stanton was already planning on proposing before they got the news but decided to wait until after the baby was born to drop the big question. Unfortunately he never got the chance to ask because 6 months after Miles was born Jessica decided that she needed to experience more out of life. Jessica handed over her parental rights to Stanton and moved to Europe to "explore the world and find herself".

Honestly, as hard as it was on Stanton I believe this was the best thing that could have happened to him. He is the best dad to Miles and he loves that little boy with everything he is. I mean, Miles is the cutest kid I have ever seen so it's not a hard task. And if Jessica is dumb enough not to see what she is missing out on, good riddance.

Running into the diner, I immediately am greeted by Susie Myers, the owner of The Diner. "Hey sweetie Sage" the nickname she has called me since as long as I can remember, "Stanton is already here at the usual table. Go ahead and head over and give an extra kiss to Miles for me".

"Thank you Susie" smiling at one of the sweetest ladies in town, I make my way to the table that Stanton and I always sit at. As I get to the table I immediately squeeze Miles while he is in the high chair. Now that he is almost a year old, he has become more animated but also wiggling. His excited squeals fill the diner as I attack his chubby cheeks in kisses. Once I get my fill I release him and he goes back to playing with the sugar packets.

Looking up I find Stanton's tired and dim eyes. "Hey Stants. How has the week been?" Sliding into the booth across from him, I grab a menu even though we both know that we will order the same thing we always have, a bacon cheeseburger with sweet potato fries and a peach lemonade.

"It's been a long one. We have officially opened the doors of the private practice and it seems like we are barely keeping our heads above water these days with a wait list that would make you nauseous"

"A waitlist is good right? It means that the practice is doing what it is supposed to by increasing mental health awareness throughout the community"

"It's great until you realize that there are so many people that need help and only one of you. Plus theres a little boy that is in the middle of teething so neither of us are getting much sleep." Stanton sighs heavily but seeing the concern on my face quickly shifts the conversation. "But we will figure it out at the practice and Miles' teeth will pop through and all will be okay. We are here tonight to celebrate you not talk about the woes of my life."

"I know you are trying to change the conversation on me but first I need you to know that if you ever need help, I am here and would love to steal Miles from you anytime. Especially this summer while I am off, please use me to help."

He gives a small nod at that. I am hoping that he actually will take me up on my offer this time. Stanton is an amazing dad, he just doesn't see it which means he suffers a lot of dad guilt and doesn't put himself first ever. Saving Stanton from furthering the conversation, our waitress swings by for our drink order. But like I said we already have our order memorized. We place our order and she skips off to the kitchen to get it started.

Allowing for the subject change I tell Stanton about my day. "Today was field day which meant a lot of wet and wild kids. And by a lot I truly mean A LOT. Just imagine Miles a little older but even more busy with a bunch of water activities" Stanton grimaces at that thought and I continue, "It is safe to say I am going to sleep hard tonight after that. But before I was leaving Mrs. Applewood called me into her office"

"Well that probably was a different feeling for you. I don't think you were ever called to the principals office growing up. Me? If I wasn't in there for something at least once a month we weren't having enough fun." The thought finally got a small smile from Stanton as he considered the pranks and mischief his childhood brought.

"That's why we are the perfect set of twins. We balance each other. Me the responsible one and you the fun one." This must have been the wrong thing to say because that small smile slowly slips away from Stanton. "Anyways, I got called into her office and she tells me that she wants to make me a department head to oversee the teachers from kindergarten to third grade for next year."

"Wow Sage. I honestly don't know what that entails but it sounds like they recognized how amazing you are and all the potential you bring" Stanton has always been my biggest cheerleader and the greatest friend. Maybe it is a twin thing or maybe it's just a brother thing. Either way I am lucky to have him.

"I would try to explain it to you but I am not going to bore you to death. The main responsibility is that I get to help other teachers be the best teachers they can be. I feel like my life is finally coming together."

"Sage, I know this year has been hard on you with all the change you have faced but I am really proud of you. You not only left that scumbag and came home, but you have really put your heart on your sleeve for your students. They are truly lucky to have you." Not being great at taking praise, heat rises to my cheeks but I smile down at Miles and imagine him in 5 years in a little kindergarten class and feel that passion for teaching in my heart. I grew up knowing that I would only be happy if I was working with kids and teaching soon became my dream.

"Thank you Stants. I honestly could not have pulled my life together like I did without you, mom and dad."

Our waitress swings by with not only a refill on our lemonades but also our hot and juicy burgers. The exhaustion of the day is starting to set in again and drool instantly fills my mouth as I see this burger. I am going to destroy this meal with no shame."Speaking of the old folks, how are you doing living with them? It's been 10 months now. Are you ready to pull your hair out or are you still loving all of moms cooking?"

"I am not going to lie and tell you that I am not dying to have the house complete. I actually swung by it again after school today and it is looking great! It has windows and a door now so we have to be getting close." Stanton was the one that told me to buy a house in that neighborhood. The area has been growing like crazy and he was right in that it was a great time to invest in my own property instead of thinking of an apartment. He even drove me to the construction site to meet with the builders to make sure that I loved the area and had the support to make this decision.

"That's great Sage. I want to be the first one to know when you get the official closing date. Maybe we can swing up and grab burgers and have a picnic on your living room floor to celebrate." Glancing over at Miles who is now chewing aggressively at his gums on the table, thank goodness for the clean tablecloth, I smile at his big blue eyes. "Yeah this little one would probably love to crawl around in that large empty space."

"You know, Lucas mentioned that I should consider changing the loft in my house from an office into a play room for Miles now that the practice is open. He showed me a bunch of pictures of indoor kids jungle gyms that we could put together in that space." At the mention of Lucas, I fight the urge to roll my eyes. Oh Lucas, the golden boy of Pennystone. If you ask the older ladies in this town they would call him "the yummiest bachelor in town". Granted you put any 29 year old, very fit and toned male in a cop uniform and women's ovaries start to sing but thats besides the point. Lucas may be seen as the biggest sweetheart by the town members, but me? I know Lucas as the competitor who always tried to one up me. "Oh is that what Lucas said? Because he knows SO much about kids and their developmental needs."

"Come on Sage. When are you going to stop trying to beat Lucas in your little who is the smartest contest you two always had going on?

I thought that ended in high school when you won Valedictorian and he was Salutatorian." Honestly, I should be more mature about the situation with Lucas. He is my brother's best friend and from what it sounds like, is supporting Stanton as a single parent. He is also the only person to ever get under my skin with simply a look on his face. Lucas knows how to push my buttons and enjoys doing so.

Trying to steer the conversation away from Mr. Perfect, "A playroom in the loft sounds like a great idea for Miles. He has gotten so big so fast and is a busy little guy". As if on cue Miles starts to realize that the table isn't giving his gums the attention they need and starts getting fussy. Stanton hurries to dig through his diaper bag for something to help calm down Miles. "Dang it, I forgot his favorite teething toy at home."

Sensing Stanton's anxiety starting to rise, I quickly slip Miles out of the high chair to play with my wiggly fingers in my lap. This helps distract Miles for about two minutes until he gets fussy again. "Sorry sis but I think I better head home and get him in his bath before his fussing becomes screaming."

"It is totally fine!" Glancing down at Miles I give him a smile which he returns. "Taking a bath sounds like the perfect way to end my day. Thank you little man for going on a date with Aunt Sage tonight" I bop his nose and kiss his cheek which gets me a giggle in between fussing and chewing on his hands. This poor baby must be getting a good chunk of teeth soon.

Handing over some cash, Stanton swaps me for Miles. "Here is money to pay for dinner, and don't even try to fight me on it. We are celebrating the end of the school year so it's on me". "You didn't need to do that but thank you."

Standing up, I quickly give him and Miles hugs before they dash out the door to head home. I slink back into the booth right as the waitress probably witnessing my brother and Miles leaving comes over with the check. Handing over the money and telling her to keep the change, I grab my bag and head out to the car. Miles was right, a bath is definitely needed to end out this long and exhausting day.

# CHAPTER 3
## - SAGE

June went by in the blink of an eye. I ended up returning to the school to clean up my classroom and begin preparations for next year during the first week. The next week I spent the week in Knoxville with Brooklyn and Gracie. Don't worry we avoided any place that we could have ran into Matt. That week was one of the best as I was able to forget all my worries and enjoy time with my two best friends.

I also finally got the official move in date for my house. On July 6th I will officially own my first house. These last two weeks have been filled with packing (not that I have much to begin with), shopping for furniture to fill the house, and designing the interior so that when I get those keys, I'm ready to go.Lucky for me, my parents are letting me take my entire bedroom set with me so it's one less thing I have to worry about. Now everything is in boxes and ready to go for moving day, two days from now.

Today however is all about family. The 4th of July has always been one of my moms favorite holidays. She says nothing beats spending time with family while my dad grills and later sitting around the fire pit making s'mores. I know that this year will be even better for all of us with the addition of Miles to join in on our traditions.

Hearing my mom already downstairs working on breakfast, I slip out of bed, throw on my sweatpants and head to the kitchen. I can hear my parents talking in the kitchen so I slowly sneak around the corner. They don't see me right away. My dad is trying to convince my mom to stop mixing the pancake batter and to dance with him first. He has George Straight playing from his phone. Rolling her eyes at him, she wipes her hands off in her kitchen hand towel and takes his hand.

It may be a little creepy to be watching their moment but this is one of the things I admire the most about my parents' relationship. They are teammates, best friends, and partners. They will also make sure to take time to show their love especially on busy or stressful days. Knowing my dad, he saw how stressed my mom was this morning about making today perfect for the family.

I continue watching my parents slow dance in the kitchen until the song ends. Now making my appearance, I see that my mom now has a smile on her face and some redness in her cheeks.

"Good morning. I hope I am not interrupting anything."

My dad gives me a large grin. "No honey, I was just making sure my wife knows that I love and appreciate her". My stomach tightens at that statement. Not upset by the love my parents have but the longing for that myself. My mom must have seen that emotion pass through my face, "morning Sage. Do you wanna come help me with these pancakes? You can have your usual job of getting the strawberries and blueberries ready for me." Did I already mention my mom is obsessed with this holiday? Everything has to be red white and blue today. "Of course. It's one of my favorite jobs"

"That's because you eat half the fruit in the process, baby girl." My dad heads to his station working on the bacon while my mom continues on the pancake batter. Smiling down at my fruit, I begin washing and cutting the strawberries.

Tentatively, my mom asks about my week in Knoxville, "we haven't heard much about your trip with Brooklyn and Gracie. Did you enjoy your time back in Knoxville?"

"It was really great to see the girls. We spent the week doing all the things we loved doing during our summers in college. When the girls had to go to work, I would see places in the city that I have missed."

"I know that it was hard on you to leave Knoxville. I am glad it's still close enough for you to visit and I bet Gracie and Brooklyn loved having you back for the week." She gives a small sigh indicating she is unsure if she should ask the next question. "You didn't run into Matt while you were there right?" You can feel the tension coming off my dad and see his eyes snap to mine at that question.

"No Matt sightings thank goodness. The only times that would have been possible is when I was with Gracie and Brooklyn so I know they would've had my back."

"That's good. He hasn't had any more contact with you right?" When I first moved here, Matt tried calling almost daily. Apparently the guilt finally set in when he returned to an empty apartment. I don't know what else he expected when he made eye contact with me at that restaurant and refused to acknowledge me. He must have thought that I would be at home licking my wounds until he returned. He did not expect me to be long gone by the time he made it back home.

After not answering any of his calls or texts and deleting voicemails as soon as I got them, he stopped his daily efforts. He then went to only a text a month typically with a memory attached like he is trying to remind me of the good times we had together. "I did get a message on my social media after I posted about my trip to Knoxville with the girls. But I did not respond and I haven't heard from him since."

Not loving the answer, my dad continued to look angry. "You tell me Sage if his messages escalate in any way or make you uncomfortable. I refuse to let him hurt my baby girl anymore than he already has."

"Dad, I can handle Matt. He is probably still grieving the fact that he not only lost the best thing he had in his life but that he got caught as a cheating asshole in the process. I am honestly not worried." Still with that protective look on his face I add, "but I will come to you if I ever find a reason to worry about it."

"I know you can handle it Sage but it doesn't mean you have to. We just want you to be the happiest version of you."

"I am happy. I have the best family in the world, especially with Miles, he is my favorite" I say with a wink that finally gets my dad to smile. "Plus I am about to move into my new home, have an amazing job with a new opportunity, and have amazing best friends. I promise I am happy"

With that we finish up making breakfast, enjoy it outside on the back patio as I give them the run down on my new responsibilities at my job and how excited I am to be able to help more teachers and students. While my mom and I are cleaning up breakfast, my dad picks out a movie for us to watch. Before I know it we are watching How to Lose a Guy in 10 Days which I know my dad only picked because he knows it's my favorite.

Mid-afternoon Stanton and Miles pop by bringing chips and soda with them. "Hey y'all. Sorry, we would have come sooner but Miles actually had a good nap which is hard to come by with his teeth pain. I wasn't willing to wake him up and I may have also dozed off in the process." My mom comes flying around the kitchen island as soon as she sees Miles smiling his gummy smile at us. "Don't you dare apologize for putting this little man first. We would've waited all night for him." My mom is the picture perfect grandma. While she wishes that Stanton didn't have to wear the burden of being a single parent, she wears her grandma title with honor and love. She scoops Miles out of Stanton's arms and pulls his high chair over so that he can "help" her with the food. She gives him a teething cracker and he is perfectly content chewing away while watching her zoom around the kitchen.

"Hey Stants, glad you got a nap. You probably needed it. No emergencies at the practice for today?"

"Nah. Fourth of July seems to be a holiday where people enjoy themselves. Now Christmas? I may be fielding clients dealing with mother in laws and unrealistic expectations." Stanton may not see it but he makes such a difference in so many people's lives.

Chuckling a little imagining the chaos of Christmas and him and John trying to calm down their clients, "I'll keep that in mind for Christmas this year. Maybe your gift will be a vacation for you and Miles on a paradise beach."

"You know I'll never say no to a good vacation and some pina coladas." Smiling we head out to the backyard to find my dad at the grill. "Hey son. Where is my cute grandson?"

"Hey dad. I'm good thanks for asking." My dad gives him an eye roll for that one. "Miles is inside with mom helping her cook while munching away on a cracker"

"Still no teeth popping through?"

"Not yet but I am thinking soon with how miserable he is." My dad becomes serious all of the sudden. "I don't say it enough but we are very proud of you Stanton. You are an amazing dad." My heart swells at the love my dad has for us kids. We have never once wondered if we were loved by our parents.

"Dad you literally tell me every time you see me." He may be told all the time but it breaks my heart that Stanton still doesn't believe that he is an amazing dad.

"It's still not enough." Stanton is saved as my mom calls from the kitchen "hey someone is at the door and my hands are covered in Miles' slobber. Can one of my kids come get it for me?"

Stanton turns to me while walking backwards,

"I'll go grab it, it's probably Lucas." My dad sees my eye roll at that. "Sage you have to cut that boy a break. He is a good man. He is one of the best cops this town has, is a great friend to your brother and honorary uncle to Miles" ugh I hate that about him. If only Miles didn't love him.... "And he is constantly checking in on his mother to make sure she isn't too lonely". Lucas's father died right after I moved away for college. I don't know much more than it was an unexpected heart attack and now his mom is on her own. Lucas ended up staying in Pennystone after high school so she wouldn't be left alone.

"Yeah yeah he is perfect, I am very aware."

"Cut the sass with me baby girl or you are on dishes duty all week" I know my dad is teasing me since I already help with dishes each night so I stick my tongue out at him which causes him to chuckle.

Soon we hear Stanton coming our way with Miles in his arms followed by Lucas and another cop who must be his partner. And since life isn't fair, Lucas is looking real good in his cop uniform. His dark brown hair is perfectly gelled but not too gelled that it looks stiff. He fills in his uniform almost perfectly with it enhancing his bicep muscles where he has his sleeves rolled up slightly. And can I just say thank you to whoever designed cop pants? The fact that they accentuate their butts so perfectly is straight *chefs kiss*. I can dislike the guy and still admire the gift he is to women everywhere okay?

James is a good looking guy too. He's a tall and bulky African American man. If I were to guess, probably in his early thirties with short hair and a short beard. His deep brown eyes seem to tell a story. I'm more of a sucker for green eyes. Caught in a little trance, I don't realize that the guys have made it across the yard until I see Lucas and hear "Hey Blue".

# CHAPTER 4
# - LUCAS

I don't know how Sage and I have not crossed paths since she has been back but it seems like today is the first time I have been able to speak to her since she moved back home. The last time I truly saw Sage was the summer after our graduation before we both went off to college, her going to her dream university in Knoxville and me choosing to stay close so I could stay near mama.

Sage was a beautiful girl in high school, but now? She's stunning. The kind of stunning that makes you weak in the knees. Today she is wearing frayed jean shorts with a rolling stone tshirt and vans. Think girl next door meets every guys dream girl. Her long blonde hair is curled and held back by a red bandana headband, making her blue eyes pop with the small amount of makeup she has on.

While I can easily admit that Sage is gorgeous, she is also the person that brings about the worst side of me. Something about her just makes me want to push her buttons. And by the way she is looking at me after I called her Blue, tells me she still finds me irritating and that brings a smile to my face.

With fire in her eyes she finally acknowledges me. "Hello Lucas. Aren't we lucky to have the 'yummiest bachelor in Pennystone' gracing us with his presence?" Next to me, my partner James chokes while taking a sip of his water. "Did you just refer to Lucas as the yummiest bachelor in Pennystone?" James glances at me with a cringe.

Sage grins at James, "yep, that's what Susie Myers from The Diner told me all the ladies refer to Lucas as." I give Sage a smirk I know she will hate. "Aw Blue, have you been asking around the town about me?" If looks could kill, I would be six feet under with the look Sage is giving me. "Nope, turns out those little old ladies are just as obsessed with you as you are."

Rolling my eyes because we all know that is the exact opposite of the truth. For some reason, ever since my dad died and I chose to stay close to home for college for my mama, the older ladies in town think it's their personal mission to find me a wife. The problem with their little plan? I don't want to be involved in it.

Forgetting that there are more people here than just Sage and I, I hide my shock when Stanton comes to my defense. "Come on sis, it's not Lucas's fault that women love handsome cops". I can see blush coming up Sage's neck and into her cheeks. Maybe it has something to do with the way she was staring as we made our way over to her earlier. My gut tightens as I look towards James and see him chuckling at Stanton's statement.

Miles becomes fussy and Sage snatches him from Stanton and heads inside ending our conversation. I see James watching Sage leave and while I can't blame the guy, it is also hard to ignore the pit in my stomach as I watch it happen. I glance back over to see Mr. Calloway looking my way. "Sage is a spitfire. I sure do love my baby girl but sometimes she forgets a filter." With a smile he looks back at the house then back to us, "Lucas, James, thanks for coming over for some dinner tonight. Lucas, you know how much Sandy loves the Fourth of July."

"Thank you for having us Mr. Calloway. We are technically still on call since holidays get busy for us but we are hoping to be able to enjoy the meal before anything comes up."

"Lucas, you have known us since you were a little boy. You don't need to call me Mr. Calloway, call me Shawn." Mr. Calloway has never once made me feel like an outsider but always a member of their family, no matter how hard Sage tries to prevent it. "James, it's great to meet you officially. Lucas has always talked highly of you as a partner."

James is one of the best cops out there. After returning home from a tour in Afghanistan with the army, he decided he wanted to settle down in a quiet town. His family once visited Pennystone while heading to South Carolina, so when he made it back to the states with the goal to find something simpler, his feet brought him to Pennystone. "Thank you sir. And thank you for letting me join your family for dinner. I typically am at the coast with my family but we have been busy here lately so it was harder to slip away this year."

Speaking of being busy, at that moment I get a call from the station. Picking up the phone, it's our dispatcher on the other line. "Hey Lucas, I'm sorry for doing this to you but we have a three car accident near the Calloway's house. I know you guys were looking forward to dinner but everyone is already out on patrol and unavailable. Do you mind taking this one for us?"

"We are on it. Don't even worry about it Karen. Can you text me the closest address to the accident and we will head over now."

"Will do, thanks again"

Stanton looks over with a knowing face, "duty calls again?"With disappointment for leaving earlier, I nod my head and explain to James the details of the call. We head towards the house to say goodbye to Mrs. Calloway, Sage, and Miles. We can hear them before we see them.

"Mom I know. Everyone loves Lucas. I get it, he

is just SO perfect" I can hear her sarcasm and can see the eye roll from here. James gives me a look asking if we should be hearing this. I shrug to him but make no movement towards the kitchen or away from our spot.

"Sage you sound just like you did in high school. I don't understand what it is between you two that makes you bicker back and forth so much."

"He just pushes my button and loves doing it." Miles lets out a giggle which tells me that Sage still has him. That little boy loves all the attention he gets here at the Calloways and I can't blame him. I envy that little boy for growing up with so much love. Deciding we can't hang out in the hall forever eavesdropping, I clear my throat to make our presence known as we walk into the kitchen.

Sage whips her head towards me with a glare. "Excuse me Mrs. Calloway, unfortunately we just got a call about an accident and we are going to have to head out."

"Oh Lucas, that is absolutely okay. You have lives to protect and serve. Never apologize for that."

"Yes ma'am. We are just sad to miss out on your famous strawberry shortcake." Mrs. Calloway quickly glances back to Sage but she is too busy chasing after Miles as he crawls around the kitchen.

"Don't you worry about that. I actually made

an extra for the station. I know this day is one of the busiest so I wanted to make sure the station still has a moment to celebrate."

"I am sure everyone will love that. We will just need to make sure to get some before it is completely gone."

"Here how about you take it with you so that way you and James definitely get a slice." Smiling, she goes to her refrigerator and pulls out the extra cake and walks us to the door. "Make sure you stay safe out there tonight boys. And Lucas, tell your mama that we say hello."

"Yes ma'am. Thank you again for having us even though we had to leave earlier than expected and for the cake." Hurrying off to our patrol car, we quickly jump in, turn on our lights, and speed off to see what accident is in store for us.

Turns out that accident was a fender bender between neighbors. Could they have handled it without us? Probably. But on the plus side, it didn't take too long so we are headed back to the station to deliver the strawberry shortcake.

"So what's the deal between you and Sage?" James looks over from the passenger seat with genuine curiosity.

"What do you mean what's the deal between us?"

James gives me a knowing look. "Well for someone who I have never seen be sarcastic with anyone, you sure loved teasing Sage."

"Stanton and I have been friends since forever. You know how things got with my dad so I was over at the Calloway's often. At first it was always the three of us together but as we grew up Sage started going off on her own with her own friends. Stanton and I remained best friends and like any boy, we would tease her and her friends. By the time we hit high school we started to compete with each other more and more academically. Sage hated that school came easy to me and was worried I would take the number one spot from her in school. She's brilliant so I was never able to get past her GPA."

"Ah gotcha so you guys had a little rivalry growing up. And you push her buttons because....?"

"I honestly don't know, it's just what I have always done. It is fun to see her reaction. When she gets annoyed her eyes spark a little and her eyebrows crease causing her nose to crinkle slightly."

James stares at me for a solid minute after that comment and I'm left driving and thinking about what I said that would give him that look. Finally breaking the silence but bringing a new tension, "Why? Are you interested in Sage?" For some reason I am extremely curious on his answer.

"No, I don't think I'm up for dating right now. I'm still settling into the new house and getting used to the station." I let his answer settle in and try to ignore the relief from hearing that he is not planning on pursuing Sage. "Speaking of new houses, don't you move into yours soon?"

"Yep, finally. Move in date is in two days."

# CHAPTER 5
# - SAGE

Moving day has finally arrived! I stayed up late last night to finish packing up and had to wake up early this morning. My dad and Stanton had a fishing trip planned for today so we needed to get the move done early this morning. Luckily, I don't have much since I will need to buy furniture once I move in. My things should easily fit in one truckload. Walking downstairs I can hear my dad getting his fishing gear together. He looks up when he hears me coming into the room. "Good morning baby girl, are you ready for your big move?"

"The real question is are you ready to have me out of your hair and have an empty nest again?" My dad gets a serious look on his face. "You know you are always welcome in this home Sage. Your mom and I have loved having you here with us. Who else is going to watch rom-coms with me?"

Rolling my eyes I don't even try to hide my smile. "We can still have movie dates dad. We will just rotate houses for them now."

"Just tell me the day and time and I will be there baby girl." He comes over and gives me a kiss on my forehead before heading towards the front door. "The truck is all ready to go for you. How about you carry the boxes downstairs and Stanton and I will start with the bigger items?"

"Sounds great Dad. Thank you again for helping me. I don't have much so you, Stanton, and Miles should be headed to the lake in no time." My dad and Stanton try to get out on the lake at least once a month if possible. It has always been their own special thing between the two of them and I have seen multiple times them come back with no fish but lighter after their day together.

"We will head out whenever we get finished up with your house. This may work out better so that Miles can get a morning nap with your mom before we head out." As if on cue Stanton pulls up to the house at that moment. My mom already went over to his house after waking up this morning to help watch Miles while we move.

My mom sat in my room last night and got teary eyed when talking about me moving out again. I had to remind her that I am a ten minute drive and that we will still see each other often. She told me that she is happy for me since I have waited so long for the house to be done but now that it is here, she is realizing she will miss having me around. I am lucky to have such amazing parents. But I also need my own space again and they need to be able to live their best retirement life.

The three of us work quickly and efficiently. Within 30 minutes, all of my items are loaded up in my dads truck and we are headed to the new place. Driving into the neighborhood we see a couple of other moving trucks for people in the neighborhood. Looks like there are lots of us that are excited to finally be getting keys. One of the reasons I picked this house was the potential of a family style neighborhood.

My house sits at the corner of a cul de sac so it still feels a little more secluded compared to the rest of the neighborhood. Pulling up to my house, I realize that the houses next to mine both look empty. Maybe they haven't finished building those ones yet. My dad and Stanton pull into my driveway and I pull in next to them. We quickly unload the truck and before I know it I am sitting in the living room with all my boxes and my dad and Stanton are headed out the door to the lake.

"Thank you again! Once I get settled in and get all my furniture, I will have you two and mom and Miles over for dinner."

"As long as it is your cheesy lasagna and garlic bread you know I will be here."

"Come on son, we know you will be here no matter what your sister makes." My dad gives me a wink. We both know that Stanton loves a good home cooked meal. "I will make sure it is cheesy lasagna and garlic bread just for you Stants. I really appreciate the two of you."

My heart swells as I take a moment to reflect on how far I have come since leaving Knoxville. I would have never expected to be where I am today but am so happy I made it here. "Have fun on the lake and make sure to send me lots of pictures of Miles in the boat." This is the first time Stanton has decided to take Miles out to join the boys fishing trip. My dad is over the moon about having him with them but I know Stanton is nervous about it. "And make sure that he gets lots of sunscreen!"

"Grandpa is going to make sure Miles has the best day, don't you worry. But we should probably head out before the traffic on the lake gets too busy."

"Love you guys! Thank you again and have the best day." My dad gives me a quick kiss on the cheek on the way out and Stanton gives me a tight hug before heading out the door.

Once the door shuts I realize, I am finally in my first home.

In the middle of unpacking while belting out a song about a boy throwing pebbles at a window for Juliet, I receive a notification that there is movement by my front door. I guess this is one of the perks of a new house, a fancy video camera doorbell. Pulling out my phone I see that one of my neighbors must be moving in next door. Not thinking much of it I mute the notifications for the next hour and get back to work.

Lost back in the music, this time of a girl being enchanted, I don't realize movement by my backdoor until I hear barking. Jumping with a hand over my heart I whip around to see a beautiful Siberian husky with the bluest eyes at my back door with a tail wagging at about 100 miles an hour. Leaving my mess I walk to the back door and step outside. I make sure to allow the dog to sniff my hand but as soon as I get the go ahead, I make sure to give the dog all the lovins. "Hey beautiful, what are you doing over here?"

The dog stops attacking me with kisses and cocks its head to the side as if confused on why I am confused at its appearance.

"Aspen, where did you run off to now?"

"Oh beautiful girl I am assuming that is your dad looking for you." Aspen looks off into the distance of where the voice came from. Looking up, it is the last person I expect to see.

"Hey Blue. Looks like you have met my girl Aspen there." Lucas looks down at me kneeling with his dog with a small grin on his face. Turning back to Aspen, "well Aspen you are a beautiful girl but I am afraid your choice in men isn't the best. But neither was mine so maybe I just need to give you some more time to figure it out." Lucas looks very confused at that statement but doesn't get the chance to respond. "What are you doing in my backyard Lucas? Did Stanton send you over to see if I needed help unpacking?"

"Uh no. That definitely sounds like something Stanton would do but I am currently about to go back to my own backyard and finish moving myself" He hooks his thumb over his shoulder to the house next to mine.

"Nope, you don't live there."

"Yep Blue, I most definitely do. I just got the keys for it and my name is on the deed so sorry to break it to you but I definitely live in that house right there."

"Nope you can't. Because I now live here." I also use my thumb to indicate which house I am talking about as if he didn't already know I came out of my back door about five minutes ago.

For some reason Lucas looks way too happy about this. "Well, looks like we are neighbors now." I let out a large sigh, "You're kidding right? Because we can't even be in the same room without wanting to kill each other. How are we supposed to live next door to each other?"

Lucas gives a shrug, "Seems pretty simple, I will be right over there. And you will be over here. We will continue to go about our lives. I will go to work and strive to save lives. You will go to the school and change lives." We are not going to mention how my heart fluttered at the statement that he thinks I am changing lives at the school.

"Well what happens when I see the most eligible bachelor bringing home a new girl every night? It will ruin your reputation of being Mr. Perfect."

"Wow Blue I didn't realize that you were so hung up on my relationship status." Of course he gives me one of those grins that I know make the old ladies blush.

"I am just getting tired of hearing about it all over town. Maybe if you shave your head the old ladies will stop gushing over you. I wouldn't mind helping you out with that, neighbor." I smile my most innocent smile at him knowing he would never take me up on the offer. Honestly, it would be a crime to shave off his hair. It would ruin his model cop look.

"As tempting as that sounds, I am going to pass at the thought of you next to my head with a sharp object. But you don't need to worry about me, Aspen is the only girl in my life." At the sound of her name, her tail starts to wag and she finally leaves my side to prance over to Lucas.

"Well you are a lucky man to have such a beautiful lady at your side." Lucas bends down to pet the top of Aspen's head while glancing back up at me. I try to ignore how piercing his forest green eyes are in this midday sunlight. "I should probably head back and unload the rest of my things before it gets even warmer. Thanks for taking care of Aspen for me when she wandered off. I will make sure to keep a closer eye on her."

"I would offer to help but I have my own mess of chaos calling my name and you aren't kidding about the heat." Lucas gives me another smirk, "You offer to help me? Never."

Rolling my eyes at him, I glance back down to Aspen. "And don't worry about Aspen. She is welcome to stop by anytime. I don't mind seeing her beautiful face." I give her a smile and then look back to Lucas. "But your face? Yeah I can do without".

Who am I kidding? That is definitely a lie. Again, his face is model status. If only he didn't make me want to pull my hair out. Sigh.

"Well this has been lovely, as always Blue. I guess we will see you around the block. Good luck with your chaos and don't worry, I bet the other neighbors don't mind the personal Taylor Swift concert you are putting on for yourself." Heat rises to my cheeks as he breaks out in a grin then spins around to head back to his side of the yard with Aspen trailing after him.

# CHAPTER 6
# - SAGE

The next evening Stanton stopped by with Miles to check in on how I was coming along with unpacking. I was able to get a majority of the things put away. When you don't have much to begin with, it is easy to find them homes in a brand new house. Luckily for me, my bedroom is completely done besides maybe some decor but I haven't had time to shop around for that yet.

Since the master bedroom is the only thing ready to go, when Stanton brings over pizza with him for dinner we have to sit on the floor in the living room with my very effective box made table.

Miles loves all the room he has to crawl around and I quickly find an empty large box and some toys for him. We stuck him inside the box about 10 minutes ago and he is still playing away in his box fort. Stanton looks tired tonight. He may end up taking another one of my large boxes home with him for another time. "So how are you liking the new house Sage? You ready to move back in with mom and dad?

"As much as I am missing moms home cooked meals and dad always having a movie ready for me, I am really loving being back on my own." I smile as I look around the new house. My new house.

"You haven't ever lived completely by yourself though. Are you doing okay with it?" Thinking about his question I realize that I haven't actually ever been completely on my own. I left home to go to college where I ended up rooming with Gracie and Brooklyn, thank goodness for that. And then right after college Matt and I ended up finding an apartment together. This is the first time I have ever lived on my own.

"It is kind of weird but I also really like the freedom." Stanton still looks a little wary and concerned. "Plus, as you probably know already I am not completely alone since I have an annoying neighbor next door. Did you know this whole time that Lucas bought the house next to me?"

Now Stanton looks a little sheepish. "Uh... I did know that Lucas was buying in this neighborhood but I did not realize his house was next to yours."

"Wait, is that why you pushed so heavily for me to buy in this neighborhood? Because you knew Lucas was buying here?" The dots are starting to connect in my head. Stanton went with me to almost all my house showings.

We looked at resale houses and a couple of new build communities. When we got to this neighborhood, Stanton was obviously rooting for it. He kept telling me that he felt that I would be the safest here.

"Maybe" He gives me the same little grin that he gets when our mom catches him doing something. "I knew it would be your first time truly out on your own and I didn't like the idea of my baby sister being alone without someone close by." Stanton has always been protective of me but that comes with the territory of having your twin as one of your best friends.

"Okay first off, I am your 'baby sister' by like 10 minutes. And while that is sweet of you to worry about me I can take care of myself. Plus you are only 10 minutes away one direction and mom and dad are 10 minutes away the other direction." I can tell by the look on his face that this is an argument that I won't be winning. I can appreciate his worry for me but I wish that I wasn't faced with the consequences right next door.

"Wait, how did you find out that Lucas lives next door? Did he move in already? He was supposed to let me know when he was moving in so that I could help him."

"I found out when his dog Aspen showed up at my back door. I didn't realize he had a dog, and a beautiful one at that. When I was outside introducing myself to Aspen, Lucas came over looking for her. He said he was unloading a truck and she snuck away. He must not have told you because you were on your fishing trip with dad." I know how much Stanton hates when he isn't able to help people.

"Did both of you freak out when you figured out that you are now neighbors?" Stanton cringes at the thought of the interaction. It is no secret that Lucas and I are oil and fire, a destruction waiting to happen. "I was pretty shocked but Lucas was really calm about it. He told me we will just live our own lives and probably won't see each other. He wasn't even worried about me seeing all the girls he will end up bringing over there even though I can definitely use that as ammo against him with all these townspeople that think he is the greatest thing to walk the planet". I slightly grin at the thought of disrupting that image.

"Nah Lucas isn't like that. I haven't seen him with anyone since college. He mainly keeps to himself. He is typically either at home, at the station, or at my house. Especially since I got Miles, we don't really have time to go out. I think that's why he got Aspen when he did. He must have been feeling a little lonely." Since Stanton has the biggest heart I know that thought hurts him as he thinks of his best friend being lonely.

"Eh, I am sure Lucas is fine. He's a big boy, I am sure he can handle himself. Plus his mom is right down the road if he ever gets too lonely."

"That's true. But Sage there are some things that you don't know about Lucas." That statement makes my gut sink and I am not too sure how I feel about it. Before I can ask what he meant, Miles begins to get sick of being stuck in the box. When we look over he is rubbing his eyes, the biggest sign that it is time for them to head out so that Stanton can get Miles down for the night.

"Looks like that is my cue to leave sis. Thank you for letting us hang out with you tonight, even if you didn't have any chairs for us." He says it with a smile so I know he is just giving me crap.

"Furniture should be delivered this week, thank goodness. So next time, you should have something to sit on. Thanks for bringing the pizza."

"We both know how much you love pizza. When you get all the furniture, let me know and we can come over to help you put it together." Stanton may be a little down in the dumps right now with life, but he is never one to miss an opportunity to help his family. Really anyone.

"I will let you know" Even though we both know that I won't. I am way too stubborn for that. I am going to force myself to put it together all by myself. I go over to Miles' box fort and lift him out so that I can say goodbye to my favorite little man. "Wow Miles, you liked this little box. Maybe we need to cut a door in it for the next time you come so you can crawl in and out."

Miles giggles like he knows what I am saying and plants an open mouth kiss on my cheek. Man, I love this little boy.

Reluctantly, I hand Miles off to his dad. "Drive home safe. Thank you again for coming by. Love you Stants."

"Love you too Sage. Text me when that furniture comes in." Stanton jogs down to his SUV and buckles Miles into his carseat. Once he is backing out of my driveway I give him a small wave. At that same moment, Lucas drives down towards his house. Stanton slows down and rolls down his window to say hello. Wanting to avoid any interaction with Lucas, I slip back inside my house. Before calling it a night I clean up our pizza and can't help but think about what Stanton could have meant about Lucas's past.

By the time Friday rolls around most of my furniture has been delivered. The good part is that now I have lots of large boxes for Miles. The bad part? Thinking about putting it all together. While contemplating where to begin, I receive a notification on my phone that there is motion at the front door. Pulling up the app, because let's be honest I am not going to open the door for just anything especially since there have been so many solicitors with all the new houses, I see a delivery person dropping off a basket on my doorstep. Speaking through the camera I tell them thank you as they hurry back to their car.

Opening up my door, I see a large basket filled with new home items. Thinking that maybe it is a housewarming gift from the sales agent on the home, I bring it inside. It isn't too hard to find the note attached.

> CONGRATULATIONS ON YOUR NEW HOME.
> LOOKS LIKE PENNYSTONE IS GOING TO BE
> PERMANENT. -M

Ugh. Matt again. Looking over the basket I notice that it includes some really nice items. But since it came from the worst guy in the world, there is no way I am going to be keeping this. Thinking about what to do with it, I decide I am just going to sneak over and place it on Lucas's doorstep. He won't even know it's from me. He will probably think the same thought I did that its from the sales agent and then I don't have to deal with Matt's guilt driven present anymore.

I quickly pop my head out the front door and notice that Lucas's patrol car isn't there. Perfect. I run over super sneaky and drop off the basket. On the way back to my house I wipe my hands clean of Matt's gift. Now onto my furniture building.

Hours later, I am surrounded by various parts

that make up my table, a bookshelf, and a coffee table. In this moment I am so grateful that my sectional came in sections of the couch that just needed to be arranged. I feel like I have looked at furniture instructions so much that they are blending together.

I started on the table but got confused when I didn't seem to have the correct number of screws. Then went to the bookshelf and got it halfway up until I realized that I flipped the side pieces the wrong way. Frustrated with that one, I switched to the coffee table thinking since it is smaller it would have to be easier, wrong. This one may be the most complicated. So now I am laying on my new rug in the living room staring up at the ceiling fan wondering if I should pull the trigger and call Stanton to come help me or if I should just sleep right here on my cozy rug.

I am in the middle of a pros and cons list when I hear a dog barking out back. Popping only my head up, I can see Aspen and next to her? Lucas is standing there with the gift basket in hand and a scowl on his face. Oh brother. I don't know how he figured out that I gave him the basket but he does not look happy about it.

Reluctantly I get up off the floor, turn off the music on my phone, and walk over to the sliding glass door. When I open the door, Aspen becomes very excited so I make sure to say hello to her first. Turning to Lucas, he still has a glare on his face. His eyes roam my face before he asks, "Are you alright?"

# CHAPTER 7
# - LUCAS

Sage seems weirdly confused by my question. She was the one laying on the floor in the middle of her living room looking like she was about to give up on life. It doesn't seem that weird of me to ask if she is alright. "Uh, yes? I am fine. Can I help you with something?" Okay got it, she isn't in the happiest mood. I should have figured that out by the star stretch on the floor.

Peering around her, I now notice the chaos that is happening inside. There are instruction manuals scattered all over the floor with half built furniture lying around. "Ah, you must be building some furniture. You were in the black hole of regretting all your life decisions and deciding if it would be terrible to throw out all the pieces and make a bonfire with them weren't you?" I smirk because I have been there a time or two myself. When you have spent a majority of your life on your own, you come to know these moments often.

"Nope. No idea what you are talking about. I was just in the middle of resting because I was putting everything together like a pro and it made me tired for a second there." Sage says this with confidence but I notice the redness starting in her cheeks.

"Yeah sure Blue. Anyways, just wanted to pop over and say thank you for the gift basket? But I am also wondering if I should be concerned that some of the items could cause me physical harm." I was very shocked when I got a notification while on patrol from my front door camera and saw Sage drop off a gift basket for me. Seems like a very neighborly thing she would do for anyone but for me? There is no way."

"Oh. Um how did you know it was from me?" More and more redness stains her cheeks, it may be my new favorite thing to cause. For some reason she doesn't want me knowing that she dropped off this basket and now I am curious on why.

"Well you see when I get motion by my front door, my camera flags it and starts a recording. I am honestly surprised you didn't think about that since you also have one."

Rolling her eyes you can tell that she did not think that through as part of her plan, "should have added something dangerous to the basket after all" she mutters under her breath. I can't help but smile. Sage definitely thought she was being sneaky today and I may keep that recording forever.

"It doesn't seem like you to go out of your way for me so I am just curious on why." Now don't get me wrong, Sage has one of the biggest hearts and once upon a time I may have been on the receiving end of her kindness. It becomes obvious that she doesn't know what to say. "You can tell me the truth, Sage. I won't be upset."

"Okay fine." she lets out a long sigh before continuing. "I am not sure how my ex found my address but he sent me that gift basket to congratulate me on my new home. I personally want absolutely nothing to do with him so while the items looked nice, I couldn't keep it. The easiest option was to drop it at your house. I figured you would just think that your sales representative got it for you. Did not think about the fact that we all have cameras."

I can feel my jaw tighten as she continues in her story. Her ex dropped this off for her? He is probably still licking his wounds and hoping to get her back. You don't let a girl like Sage slip through your fingers without regrets. "Your ex dropped this off?" okay maybe that came out a little harsh. By the shock on her face I realize I need to cool it a bit. "Did you see him? Has he done something like this before?"

"Woah there tiger. No, I did not see him. A delivery person dropped it on my doorstep. And yes he once had a bouquet of flowers delivered to the school with a note that told me he was happy that I found a new beginning. But again it was through a delivery person. I am not sure how he got my new address but I am confident that he is still in Knoxville living his miserable life." I smile at that comment. Sage may be the only person in the world that keeps me on my toes but one thing is certain, she knows her worth. "Besides, if he did show up, I could handle him." That makes my smile drop real quick.

"No Blue. We aren't going there. If he does show up you do not open your door for him. You call your dad, you call your brother, or you call me. Hell, call the station and they will get to me. But you do not open that door."

If she wasn't shocked at my attitude before, she definitely is now. Recovering herself she looks down at the basket and then at Aspen sitting next to me staring off into the trees. "Well I will keep that in mind but there is no way Matt would show up here. He is not aggressive enough for that... But you can keep the basket if you want. Maybe there is a toy in there for Aspen."

While contemplating how I can safely burn this basket, I glance back over her shoulder at all her half built furniture and the state that she was in when I popped over. "I can go over and drop off this basket and Aspen at my place and come back to help you with that furniture."

"Oh you don't need to do that."

"Sage, I really don't mind and it seems like you could use some help." I smirk when she rolls her eyes at me.

"No, I meant you don't need to go take Aspen back. She can come in and you can leave the basket on the counter if you want." She must have been deep in the black hole of furniture if she is willingly taking my offer to help. "I wouldn't mind sitting on the couch with Aspen while we watch you struggle with the furniture if you think you can do it better than me." Ah, there's the typical Sage. She steps aside to allow room for me and Aspen.

Chuckling, I motion to Aspen to come and we walk into Sage's home. It is obvious that she still has to do a few things to get settled in but it instantly feels homey. I try not to overthink that thought and blame it on the vanilla coconut candle she has lit on the kitchen island.

Walking further into her house we make it to the living room where I can now see that she started and stopped multiple projects. Blowing out a breath I turn to Sage, "you were in deep weren't you?"

"I had everything under complete control. I just needed to take a little break." We both know that's a complete lie as we look at the damage before us. "Do you need anything before you start slaving away for me?" Oh she is going to really play into this isn't she?

"No I'm good. Aspen may jump on your couch especially if you sit there but if you don't want her up there just let me know and

I will give her the command to come down." Instead of acknowledging that, Sage sits down on the couch and pats the cushion next to her. Aspen carefully maneuvers around the pieces of various furniture before hopping onto the couch with Sage. Well I guess that answers my question. If Sage isn't careful she is going to steal Aspen's heart and for some reason I smile at that thought.

"Okay so I thought the coffee table would be the easiest since it is the smallest but that manual doesn't even have words. Then the table seemed straightforward but I think I did step 5 before step 3. And then the bookshelf was going to be perfect but I put the two outside panels on backwards." Yep, she was in deep and needed some help.

"Alright I'm going to start with the table since that is the biggest one to get it out of the way. Plus that seems like the most important since you need somewhere to eat." I go to grab the instructions and look down at what Sage has already done. This one seems like it'll be an easy fix.

Turns out the table was the easiest option and I'm glad we started with that. To my surprise Sage did not just lounge on the couch and watch me but hopped right in and we have been working side by side for the past hour. We are on the last project, the coffee table and Sage was right it is the most complex. "Okay Lucas, I have a question for you."

"I'm sure you have more than just one, knowing you." I smile as her eyebrows crease causing her nose to crinkle just slightly. "But go ahead. Unless it's about my relationship status which you seem extremely interested in." Sage scoffs but doesn't ask that. "Why Aspen?"

Glancing back to the couch I see that Aspen is passed out on Sage's couch. I cringe internally at the amount of dog hair that Sage is going to find on the couch once we leave. I'll need to buy her a lint roller for the times we come over.

Wait. This is a one time thing, what am I even thinking. Looking back at Sage who is still waiting for my answer I tell her about Aspen. "I got Aspe a couple of months after I joined the police force. It was around the same time that Jessica left Stanton for Europe. I saw the love that Stanton had for Miles and was a little envious of it. My mama had been talking to me about getting a dog so that I wouldn't be living completely alone."

You can tell that Sage's wheels are turning in her brain as she is processing what I have just told her. But she doesn't push for more, "and why the name Aspen?".

Pondering how much I want to share with her I pause for a moment. "I have an uncle that lives in Aspen Colorado, my mama's brother. Growing up my mama and I would go see him at least once a year. He is one of the best men in the entire world and someone I value highly in my life. Aspen was a place where I always felt safe so I told myself if I ever got a dog that I would name it Aspen to remember that you can always feel safe when you feel loved." Maybe I said too much because now she is looking at me with more questions. She glances back to Aspen and a small smile reaches her lips. In that moment I hope to one day be the reason she isn't glaring but smiling.

"Well it's the perfect name then for that beautiful girl." Sage and I continue working until late into the night. When we finish up I'm confused on why I am happy when Sage walks us not to the front door but to the back where we came in. "Well Lucas turns out we can be in the same room without destroying things." I look down at her with a smile. Sage isn't short, more average height but at my 6'3, the top of her head comes to about my shoulders. "Thank you for your help." She adds on a little more timid and quiet.

"Did you just say thank you to me Blue?" A small blush hits her cheeks.

"Yeah yeah I know, we might want to check the sky to see if pigs are flying." Aspen wiggles herself between us and looks to Sage longingly. Sage drops down to a crouch to make sure Aspen gets a goodbye. Once Aspen seems to be satisfied, Sage pops back up. "You'll have to apologize to whoever's heart you broke tonight for spending your Friday night with me."

"I was wondering when you were going to bring that up" I wink at her and she rolls her eyes. "Like I said before, Aspen is the only girl in my life and I would say she had a great night. I did too, Sage. I guess we will see you around."

Not waiting for her response, I spin towards my yard with Aspen trailing after me. I didn't lie when I said I had a great time tonight. And that thought confuses me as I think about the girl next door who also brings out the worst side of me, who is also my teenage rival, who is also my best friend's twin sister. I'm starting to realize that when it comes to Sage, I have always been in over my head.

# CHAPTER 8
## - SAGE

Lucas and I did not cross paths for the next week. I hardly saw his patrol car pull into his house, not that I was looking for it or anything. Since we are getting closer to the school year starting, I decide to pop over to the school to work on my classroom and lesson plans. I woke up this morning as the sun was coming up, went on a quick run, went home and got ready and now headed out the door. Since it is a Wednesday morning in the middle of summer, I don't worry about dressing up too much since I may be the only teacher there.

As I am pulling out of my garage I notice Lucas is headed out as well. We slowly back up at the same time and he waves for me to go ahead. Since this is our first interaction since the night we built furniture I give him a small wave before ducking my head and head out of our neighborhood.

That night didn't change everything for me

as I still find him arrogant and annoying. But, I was surprised at how comfortable it was putting furniture together and have been thinking about what he told me about Aspen. I grew up with Lucas. He was at our house all the time with Stanton for as long as I can remember. When we were smaller, the three of us did everything together until I decided I needed some girl friends instead and they became teenage boys constantly teasing me. But now? It feels like I hardly know him, like truly know him. That thought has been making my head spin.

Lost in another head spin, I realize that I went into autopilot going to the elementary school. There aren't many cars in the parking lot as I suspected. I head towards the front and get buzzed in by someone in the office. "Hey Sage. How has your summer been?"

"Good morning Mrs. Brown. My summer has been great. It is going by so fast! It is crazy that we already go back in three weeks. I am sad to see the end of summer but also excited to get to know the new bunch of kiddos. How has your summer been? How is Gabby doing?" Gabby is her granddaughter that she adores.

She is now beaming at me at the mention of Gabby. "Summer has been fantastic! I obviously am here some days but I also have more time to spend with Gabby. She is now in a dance program and she is extremely talented. Hold on let me show you a video!" She pulls out her phone and for the next five minutes we look at Gabby's last dance showcase. I have to break it to her, she is extremely talented.

"Oh my goodness I have trapped you here haven't I darling? I am so sorry. I should let you go get to the work you planned to do so that you can get out of here and continue enjoying your summer."

"Don't apologize ma'am, I love getting updates on Gabby and those videos were incredible." I give Mrs. Brown a smile and a small wave before heading down the hall towards my classroom. For the next few hours I am zoned in on getting everything done that I hoped to do today. I organize my lesson plans for the first month, when those lessons started to blur together I worked on my first week of school bulletin board, and now I am staring at my room deciding if I like how the desks are arranged or if I should mix it up.

Breaking me from going through seating options, I hear a soft knock on the door. I glance over and see Michael and Julie at my classroom door. Julie is a first grade teacher whose classroom is across the hall from me and Michael is the school librarian. Both of them became my instant friends when I first got here and made me feel really comfortable in the new school. I had my door propped open so they step inside when they see that they got my attention.

"Oh hey guys! I got lost there for a bit on desk

arrangement options." I laugh slightly at myself. "I should probably go home if I am to the point of staring endlessly at my desks. May be a task for another day"

Julie shakes her head with a smile. "Yeah I was getting to that point too. Thats why I went into the library and found him staring at the bookshelves with a blank look in his eyes. And now we found you. Sounds like we all need to either take a break or go home."

Sighing, Michael moves further into my classroom and drops to sit at the reading corner. "Sage, you know you can put your desks in any arrangement and it won't matter. Your kids will love you regardless of where you put the desks." He gives me a smile and then turns to Julie. "And Julie, I know you are worried about loving your kids as much as you loved your last bunch. It may be hard for the first little bit, but we all know by week three you will love your students just as much as last year."

Michael is one of those friends that is always there to cheer you on. When I first got to the school, I was feeling overwhelmed about learning a new culture. Since I had only taught at one other school in Knoxville, I wasn't sure what that transition looked like. He made sure to introduce me to Julie and made sure that we had lunch together in the library whenever our class schedules lined up.

"Thanks Michael. I really appreciate you. Also,

the library is crazy efficient with the new numbering system you put in last year. It sounds like we all need a little break." Julie sits down next to Michael while I sit on top of one of my kids desks near them.

"Julie, how was the Bahamas with your family?" Julie is about to start her second year here at Pennystone Elementary after coming here right after college. Unlike most of us she did not grow up here in Pennystone but grew up in a military family that moved around the world.

"The bahamas was really great. We ended up taking a cruise so that we could see more sites. My brother and his kids ended up getting sea sick which was terrible but I was able to sneak away from that madness and enjoy the shows on the ship." Julie is a social butterfly. She loves talking to anyone and everyone so I don't doubt that she was the life of the party on the ship.

"That vacation sounds like a dream." I promise myself that one of these days, I will go on a trip to a beach paradise. "What about you Michael? We didn't hear about your summer plans before the school year ended." Michael looks a little sheepish. He isn't the most social person and tends to stick to himself or his small circle. "My summer has been pretty low key. I spent some time up North and visited the DC area. I was reading a book where the character toured all the national monuments there so I thought it would be cool to go up and see them myself since we have all this time off this summer."

DC is one of my favorite places since going there on a field trip during high school. "Oh man, I love DC. The history that is there, and also just the entire vibe of the city, is awesome. I went on a trip my senior year up there with my debate class and loved it so much." Michael laughs slightly, "I also went on that trip." I forgot that Michael was in my class at the time. We went to high school together and graduated the same year but had different friend groups so never really crossed paths. Since it's a small town we knew of each other but didn't know each other much.

"Oh yeah! I am sorry I forgot you were there too. It was such a great trip." Feeling a little embarrassed that I forgot that Michael was on that trip. I realize that Lucas was also on that trip. We spent a majority of the trip bickering while Stanton tried to play peacekeeper until I ended up just avoiding the two of them and staying close to my friends.

Shifting the conversation so it doesn't get more awkward "Julie, have you ever been to DC?"

"Nope. But it sounds like it is a lot of fun. Maybe we could all go up one of these summers." Thank goodness for Julie because Michael's face shifts and he ends up smiling at that thought.

"Well not to be a buzz kill, but I am going to slip out of here. I have a pedicure calling my name." Julie wiggles her toes then jumps up and walks to the door. "See you guys around!"

"Alright Michael, lets be serious real quick." At that he gives me his full attention. "Do I move my desks around or keep them the same as last year?" His lips tip up at that being my 'serious question'.

"I truly do think that it doesn't matter where you put your desks. Actually you could put them all right next to your desk and your students would probably love it. You are an amazing teacher, Sage." Giving Michael a smile, "Thanks Michael. I don't know why I worry about it. I am going to keep it the way it is for now" I pause and walk over to my desk to grab my stuff. "I am going to head out for the day, are you headed out too?"

"Yep! You wanna walk out to the cars together?" Michael jumps up from off the rug as I nod. "Let me go grab my bag from the library." While Michael goes and grabs his stuff, I pack up my bag and head out my classroom door. By the time I am stepping out the door, Michael is back and we walk out to our cars saying goodbye to Mrs. Brown on the way. I ask her to make sure she videos Gabby's next dance showcase so I can see it again. Once in the parking lot, Michael and I say goodbye and head our own way. On the way home my mind drifts to the DC trip from my senior year.

❖ ❖ ❖

Later that evening, I am standing at the kitchen sink finishing up my dinner for the night when I see Lucas make his way into his kitchen. This is the first time I have noticed that both our windows above the kitchen sink face each other. Lucas is still in uniform and looks pretty exhausted. He makes it to the sink to wash his hands and glances up noticing me. Feeling a little embarrassed about getting caught staring across our yards to his house, I offer a little wave. Lucas's lips tip up at that and he gives a small wave back. I motion with my hands for him to wait one minute and leave the kitchen to find a small whiteboard that I know I have somewhere.

Finding the whiteboard next to some boxes in the guest bedroom, I come back to the kitchen window and am surprised to see him still standing there. With my whiteboard in hand I write out a message.

*Is Mr. Perfect exhausted? The old ladies in town said that they have seen you running around like crazy this past week*

Lucas looks to be laughing after reading my message. A minute later I hear my phone ding. Reaching into my back pocket, I pull out my phone and see a text.

Unknown: Blue, you need to stop asking those old ladies about me. They are going to start to think that you are obsessed with me.

**Me**: Um who is this?

**Me**: Also, how did you get my phone number?

**Lucas**: Stanton gave it to me once he realized I lived next door, in case you needed anything.

Before I have a chance to respond, I hear a bark at the back door. Knowing it is probably my favorite dog, I walk over to the back door with a smile. Sliding the door open I greet Aspen before looking up to Lucas. "I figured it would be more efficient to just talk to you instead of texting." Lucas is still in his uniform and leaning against the side wall. It is just unfair for someone to be that attractive even when they are exhausted.

"Yeah this does seem to be more efficient. You doing okay? Because you know the ladies in town are becoming worried." Lucas smiles down at me still petting Aspen. "Just them, Blue?" I roll my eyes at that and that just makes Lucas smile more. "Yes Lucas, just them."

"You can report to them that I am doing good. The station has just been busier this summer with more people visiting the town."

"I will make sure they get the message. I wouldn't want them to be worrying too much about their yummy bachelor." I stand up from Aspen after she has agreed that I have given her enough attention. She goes and sits next to Lucas's feet. "I am glad you think I am 'yummy' Blue. It really boosts my ego for the day." He winks at me and my face turns to a glare.

"I definitely don't think your ego needs any

type of boosting, seems to be just fine." Wanting to shift the conversation away, I make an offer that shocks both of us, "would you like to come in? I was just finishing up dinner and made more than I can eat." My cooking may not be as amazing as my moms but it still is good.

You can tell that Lucas is unsure of why I am offering but reluctantly agrees. "Yeah that would be nice Sage. I am not going to lie, I am pretty tired, so thinking of making dinner was not on my list of things I wanted to do tonight."

I step to the side and motion for him to step in. Aspen prances into the living room and hops up onto the couch. She looks over at the two of us with her tail wagging and tongue poking out. Well looks like there is no turning back now. I am going to have dinner with Lucas, the boy that would pull on my pigtails but the man that put together my furniture. This should be interesting.

# CHAPTER 9
# - LUCAS

Stepping into Sage's home I realize how much work she has done here in the past week. It looks like all her furniture is finished now. There is a small part of me that is disappointed that she didn't ask me to come back and help. She also has put out some decor as finishing touches and the house now feels very much like Sage. But why does it feel like home each time I step in? Before I can dive into that scary thought, I hear Sage coming up beside me. "You finished setting up your house. It looks really good, Sage." She glances over at me a little shocked for the compliment which makes me feel a certain way. Going back to our normal, "But you know that end table over there looks a bit lopsided."

She glances over to the end table and then whips her head back to me with a glare. "No it is not! It is perfectly level."

"Sure, Blue." I smirk at her as she walks away and into the kitchen. It's in that moment that I realize it smells like heaven in here. "Sage, what are you making that smells so delicious?" I round the corner to the kitchen and lean my hip against her kitchen island. Her cheeks go a little pink and I notice her eyes drift down to where I have my arms crossed across my chest before they pop back up to my face.

"Uh it's just lemon chicken with some roasted potatoes and a salad." I have never seen Sage shy but in this moment you can tell that she is a little nervous.

Trying to lighten the mood and shake her nerves I resort to what I know best with Sage. "Are you sure that it is edible and won't kill me? It would be pretty smart for you to act all sweet inviting us over for dinner to find out that you are slowly poisoning us."

Sage's eyes light up. "Come on Lucas, you know I would never harm Aspen like that. I like her way too much to poison her over dinner." Good. We are back into our comfort zone. "But if I am gone, who will the ladies around town talk about? All the gossip that you love would be gone."

"Oh I am sure they will find another handsome single man to fawn over during book club." A kitchen timer goes off causing Sage to spin towards the oven to pull out the chicken and potatoes and leaves me staring at her deciding how I feel about the fact that she just admitted that she finds me handsome and I don't even think she realizes she did it. Something turns in my heart at that but I push it away.

"Alright, it looks like it is ready. Let me just grab some plates and we can dive in." Sage turns towards a cabinet and pulls down two glass plates, then goes to reach up towards the top shelf for some cups. Realizing that it may be a little too tall for her, I go behind her. "Here I got it" Sage stiffens as she feels me at her back and when I place one of my hands at the small of her back I can see her head turn slightly and eyes glance up at me from behind her long thick lashes. Sage drops down from her tip toes and quietly says "thank you."

I snag the cups and place them on the counter before removing my hand from her back and taking a step away. Ignoring the heat that I can still feel on my hand, I wait for her to dish herself and then dish up a plate for myself. Sage then turns to me, "Do you want to eat inside or on the back patio? It rained this afternoon so it shouldn't be too hot."

"If you don't mind, can we eat outside so that will let Aspen run around in the yard? She has been inside most of the day while I was at work." Sage looks to Aspen with a smile, who has since hopped down from the couch and is laying on the cold kitchen tile. "Anything for our girl. Let's eat outside." She turns and heads towards the back door with Aspen following right at her ankles. I stand there and watch them walk out before I shake my head and follow them out.

Once we are sitting down and Aspen is running around the yard, I realize that we forgot drinks. "Here, can you hold this for me? I'm going to slip back inside and grab us some drinks. What would you like?"

"Oh you don't need to do that. I can go grab them."

"Sage, you didn't answer my question. What would you like to drink?" Sage rolls her eyes but continues "I will take a water, there is some in the door of the fridge. You are welcome to whatever you see in there." Jogging back inside I grab the cups that I grabbed earlier and fill them both with ice water. I carefully slip out the back door and see that Aspen found herself a stick and is running around the yard. I sink back down in my chair next to Sage and exchange her cup for my plate. While her eyes are watching Aspen she tells me thank you.

We eat in silence for a couple of minutes both watching Aspen run around the yard and enjoy the evening sky. I finally speak up when I am getting close to finishing my food, "Sage this meal is delicious. Thank you for asking me to join you. This is way better than the frozen meal that I was planning on heating up."

Smiling Sage looks down at her plate and then back to me, "Thank you. Cooking has always been something that my mom and I do together. I am nowhere near the level she is but the kitchen is one of my favorite places to be."

"I have had both your mama's cooking and now yours and I can confidently say that they are both amazing." The Calloway men are extremely lucky to have this type of cooking every day.

"Well thank you. My mom would be happy to hear that all her training didn't go to waste." Sage looks back down at her plate with another smile like she is replaying a memory of her and her mom in the kitchen together. I let her have her moment of memories.

"So Lucas, you did look pretty exhausted today. Has work been crazy busy?"

"It has been. A little more than usual, I am not going to lie. With summer coming to an end, it seems like we are getting a lot of last minute vacationers that are looking for a small town retreat. The only problem is that they bring their big city attitude with them."

"Oh yeah, that is definitely a thing. It is one of the things I miss the least about Knoxville." I try to visualize Sage in a big city and I can't picture it. She is just too perfect right here in Pennystone.

"Big city people bring more traffic tickets, more bar fights, and unfortunately more drinking and driving crashes." I think about my week of chaos. Between going to the bar about five times this week to handle assaults and the three different car accidents, I am feeling beat. Wanting to change the subject away from me, I shift the conversation. "You were pulling out pretty early this morning too. Were you headed to the school?"

"Yeah with summer almost over I have been stopping by every so often to get things ready for the new school year. It is nice because not a lot of teachers or staff are there so it's quiet and I can focus more." Sage grew up wanting to work with kids. She was always the girl that had a babysitting job each weekend because everyone knew she had a special gift when it comes to connecting with kids. It didn't surprise anyone when she headed to college for elementary education. She is a great teacher and she will make a great mama one day to some very lucky kids. "Today I had a couple of friends that were there doing the same thing so it was nice to check in with them and see how they are enjoying their summer. One of them is our librarian. Do you remember Michael Jones from high school?"

Thinking back to the people we graduated with that name doesn't ring a bell. "Uh I honestly don't remember him."

"Yeah I assumed, he is a little more quiet and reserved. He was in some of our AP classes with us. I honestly didn't remember him at first when I first started at the school so I assumed you wouldn't remember him since he wasn't on the football team or a cheerleader."

I notice her smirking so I roll my eyes at her. "Don't pretend
that I was some airheaded jock, Blue. We both

know that I wasn't like that. Now you? I am shocked you had your nose out of a book long enough to notice anyone."

"Hey, my nose being in a book led me to a full ride scholarship and if I do remember correctly passing you for that valedictorian spot." She's right. All her hard work paid off for her to go to her dream university and I remained in second throughout our senior year. "But anyways that's besides the point, I guess he was on that DC trip that we took with our debate class. I felt bad because I didn't even remember him being there."

Thinking back to that trip, I smile. "I think I remember him now. He was probably the poor boy that would follow you and your friends around like a puppy. You were so oblivious that you didn't notice that he had stars in his eyes around your group." You can see the wheels turning in her head at that. Sage is one of those girls that is truly beautiful but doesn't know it. Michael wasn't the first and probably won't be the last that will notice Sage.

"Honestly, the only thing I remember from that trip was how you and Stanton snuck away to that chocolate shop and he brought me back the chocolate hazelnuts. It was a rare moment where you weren't finding joy in embarrassing me." The memory of that moment comes back to me. Stanton was going a little stir crazy in our hotel room because Jessica was off on vacation with her family so she wasn't answering his calls. I mentioned to him that we could sneak out and walk around the city for a little bit. We passed by a chocolate shop and the smells coming out convinced us to step inside. I saw the chocolate hazelnuts in the display case and mentioned to Stanton that we should bring some back for Sage. He looked at me confused at first but got the chocolate anyway. Still lost in thought at that memory, Sage continues. "I still don't know how Stanton knew that they are my favorite chocolates but it was a nice surprise."

Deflecting away from the memory, I decide to go with a safer bet, teasing Sage. "What I remember from that trip was how you totally nerded out at the National Smithsonian Museum when we got to the education section."

"Hey, the educational leaders displayed there changed the entire education system for children. Between the Progressive Movement and No Child Left Behind Act, there were some monumental events that changed the entire nation." You can see the passion coming off of Sage. This is what makes her such an amazing teacher.

"I am shocked that is what you remembered and not the fact that your tongue was down Hallie's throat the entire trip." Well now I am the one feeling heat creep up my neck and into my cheeks. Hallie was a cheerleader our senior year. She was a girl that hinted that she was interested in me all throughout high school. Finally on this trip, Stanton convinced me to give her a shot. The bad part of that decision? Sage came into Stanton and I's hotel room looking for Stanton right when Hallie decided to stop by to say goodnight.

"Hallie? Hmm, doesn't ring a bell." I smirk as Sage rolls her eyes at me. "Yeah sure." Aspen saves me from any more embarrassment as she lets out a bark and prances over to me. With her tongue sticking out and panting, I look towards Sage. "We should probably head home and get this girl some water. Plus with how much she has been playing she will probably pass out wherever she lays down next."

A brief emotion flashes across Sage's face almost one of disappointment. As quick as it came, it is gone. "Of course. You are probably tired too after the start of the week you have had." We both stand up and head inside, leaving Aspen outside so she doesn't bolt to her spot on Sage's couch. "Can I help you with cleaning up before I leave? My mama would be disappointed if I received such an amazing meal and didn't help with cleanup.

"Uh sure. You can go ahead and rinse off those plates and throw them in the dishwasher. I will pack up the leftover food." I head over to the kitchen sink and roll up my sleeves before starting on the dishes while Sage deals with the leftover food. In no time, the extra food has been packed up, all the dishes are loaded in the dishwasher and the dishwasher is started . "Thank you again Sage for feeding me tonight and hanging out with me and Aspen."

"You're welcome, you know how much I love seeing Aspen. She brightens any day." My smile drops slightly at her focusing on only Aspen. It seemed like we had a nice evening together again. "Oh and here is a container with some leftovers. Wouldn't want you to have to resort to frozen meals when I have way too much food over here."

"Thank you. The boys at the station will be very jealous of my lunch tomorrow." Sage beams at that and my knees almost give out. If Sage isn't careful, her smile could do some damage.

Aspen barks at me through the sliding glass door as if to say that she also needs to say goodbye. We step out on the patio again and Sage makes sure that Aspen gets enough attention. Once Sage stands up we say our goodbyes. "Thanks again Sage. We will see you around." I motion for Aspen to come, which she eventually reluctantly does as Sage calls out "Have a good night."

We walk across the backyard and into my house. As I refill Aspen's bowls with food and water and then head upstairs to take a shower to end out the day, I am lost wondering how I can convince Sage to feed me again.

# CHAPTER 10
# - SAGE

Me: Are you guys all packed up and ready for tomorrow?!

Brooklyn: YEEESSS! I am SO ready for a good girls weekend.

Gracie: Yep! All packed and ready to go. As soon as we are done with work, we will make the drive to you. We are both taking a half day from work so we will probably be to your house around 6pm.

Me: YAY! So excited to show you guys the new house and to see the both of you.

Brooklyn: Finally! We know you needed to settle in and with our schedules this was the best weekend for everyone but we miss you.

Gracie: No one is allowed to leave the house all weekend until we leave on Sunday. We will cook or deliver every meal. We need to make up for lost time.

Me: Definitely. I already have all my streaming services loaded on my tv for our movie night and both guest rooms officially have beds now so we are ready!

Brooklyn: AHH!! SO excited. Okay, now I need to get back to work.

Me: Go change lives Ms. Big Shot Lawyer!

Gracie: Brooklyn, I get off at 1pm tomorrow so I will swing by and get you at your apartment around 2. See you then! And Sage we will see you tomorrow evening. Can't wait to spend the weekend with my girls!

The furniture delivery trucks just rolled out of my driveway as Lucas's patrol car pulled in. I wave to him before he pulls into his garage. It feels a little weird that we are now on a waving basis but seems right after the furniture night and him coming over last night for dinner. Speaking of dinner, I should probably go in and check on my casserole in the oven.

I peek into the oven and see that it probably needs another five minutes before it is ready to get pulled out. I head to the sink to get some of the dishes out of the way while it finishes cooking. Naturally, when I get to the sink I look across the yard towards Lucas's house. Lucas is at his own sink and it looks like he has changed out of his uniform into a tshirt. It is weird to see him without his uniform, makes him seem more like a normal human.

Lucas gives me a smile and man does that do funny things to my tummy. He gives me the same one minute signal that I gave him last night and disappears from the window. I return to my dishes as I wait for him to come back.

When he gets back I look up and see that he has his own whiteboard. On it he has a message,

*Anyway you have another yummy meal in the oven right now?*

I chuckle and pull out my phone.

Me: Lucas, you know now that we both have each other's number that we can text?

Lucas: Eh, that seemed too boring. This way I could see your smile when you read it.

I catch myself smiling at that message and look up to see Lucas staring. He gives me a shrug and a grin. Grabbing my whiteboard I write out my own message,

*Dinner is in the oven. Will be ready in 5. Should I get you a plate?*

I don't know why but I become anxious at his answer while he is reading my message. When he gets to the end his face breaks out into a big smile and he turns and walks away from the window. Feeling a little disappointed that he didn't answer back, I focus back on my dishes. Right when the oven timer dings, I hear a bark at the back door. I pull out dinner from the oven and find myself giddy as I walk to the back door and see Lucas and Aspen standing outside.

I was right, Lucas did change out of his uniform. He is now in what looks like an old college t shirt and sweatpants. Something about the way he is dressed so casual makes tonight feel a little more intimate.

Opening the back door, Aspen zooms past me towards the couch. Laughing as I glance to her, "Well hello to you too Aspen come on in and make yourself at home." Beside me Lucas gives a small chuckle as he walks inside. "Apparently she has claimed that spot on the couch as her own."

Smiling at the fact that Aspen loves to be here, "Good. Like I have said before, she is always welcome here. If you ever get called into the station and you don't want her over there by herself, let me know and she can come hang out with me". Aspen lets out a happy bark after that statement.

"Well it looks like she agrees to that plan." Lucas looks down at me with a smile. "Thank you, I will keep you posted." Trying to escape from being on the receiving end of one of Lucas's heartbreaking smiles, I head to the kitchen with him following after me. "What is on the menu today chef?"

"It is nothing crazy, just a taco rice casserole with some homemade guacamole and chips on the side."

"If this is your version of 'nothing crazy' please let me come over when you do get crazy." This man knows how to make my chest swell with pride over my cooking. I head to the cabinet to get the plates and cups again but stop when Lucas beats me to it.

"I got it." He reaches into the cabinet as I feel heat enter my cheeks as I remember how the same interaction went last night. Thankfully tonight I am on the other side of the kitchen where I won't feel the heat from his body against my back. But at the same time I feel a sense of disappointment and that confuses me. Seeing my confusion Lucas looks at me with uncertainty, "everything okay?"

"Oh yeah, I just was thinking of some of the things I need to do either tonight after dinner or in the morning" the lie comes out easy and Lucas seems to buy it. We start dishing ourselves up and end up walking outside without even discussing where we were going to sit. Aspen takes off in the yard. "I saw that you had some more furniture being delivered when I got home. Is that on the to do list?"

"Yep. I got some beds and mattress delivered today for my two guest rooms. So I need to get those put together." I don't tell him about Gracie and Brooklyn coming this weekend but I am sure he will be busy this weekend so he probably won't even see us.

"Oh well that's easy, after we finish up dinner we will go in and put them together." I would normally argue with him about not needing help but he looks so happy and satisfied with the thought of putting together more furniture.

"That would be really helpful. Thanks Lucas." I smile down at my plate as we continue eating our meal. "So was today a better day? You don't look as tired."

"Wow Blue, all these compliments may start to get to my head." I roll my eyes because he knows that isn't what I meant. "But yeah thankfully Thursdays are typically pretty slow. Now this weekend may be another story with it being one of the last before school goes back." See, he is going to be busy and probably doesn't even care about my weekend plans. "Speaking of summer almost ending, are you ready to go back?"

"Yeah I am. I love my summers but towards the end I get really excited to meet the new students. One of the reasons why I love kindergarten is because they come with such a light in their eyes excited for the new chapter of their lives. It's amazing that I get to be there during that." I can feel myself smiling big as I think about how much I love my job.

I look up from my plate over at Lucas and he looks like he wants to say something but doesn't so I continue "but I am going to miss the freedom of summer. Time goes a lot quicker in the school year with how busy everything is. Before we know it, we blink and it's summer again." At this point Lucas has already finished and I am feeling stuffed. "Alright handyman, you ready to go inside and build some beds?"

"As long as you don't poke me with the screwdriver again" Lucas winks at me with a smirk and I am grateful to be sitting because it is doing something silly to my head.

"I only poked you because you weren't listening. The instructions clearly stated to flip the table upside down but you went all scowly on me and decided you knew better than the instructions."

"I went all scowly on you?" Laughing a bit, "yes you were being so grouchy about it and not listening so I poked you. Honestly, I have zero regrets."

We both stand up to head inside and Lucas calls in Aspen. We round the kitchen island and Lucas naturally goes to the kitchen sink and starts rinsing off the dishes. I stare at him for a moment then shake my head and get the leftovers into tupperwares making sure to give him two this time since I probably won't see him this weekend. Why am I a little sad at that thought?

"You ready to go put these beds together?" Lucas turns towards me and I realize that he has all the dishes completed and the counters are also wiped down.

"Yep. Let me just go to the garage and grab my tools." I hurry off to the garage, grab my tool bag and we make our way to the first guest bedroom.

◆ ◆ ◆

We have been working on the first bedroom for about 10 minutes. I am again surprised at how efficient we work together. Where we would normally argue and bicker, apparently you give us a task with the same goal in mind and we become perfect teammates. Who would've thought?

"So Sage, Stanton briefly mentioned that you came home because of a break up and I know your ex has been sending you gifts which I am still not okay with but I honestly don't know the whole story behind you two." Lucas glances up to me from where he was screwing in the headboard to a leg of the bed.

I let out a long sigh before I begin. "Matt and I met my junior year in a children's literature class. We were partners for a project and that began our relationship. We continued dating throughout the rest of our time at University of Tennessee. I finished my elementary education degree and started at a top rated elementary school in Knoxville and Matt finished his sports studies degree with a job offer to return to the university as an assistant coach. We then moved in together after graduation and everything was going great. About a year later Matt received a promotion to offensive coordinator and I was still loving the school I was at. We began talking about engagement and buying a house."

Lucas at this point has stopped working on the bed and is sitting with his back against the wall.

We should probably keep working but I continue with my story anyways. "There was a night when I saw a text on his phone with a reservation confirmation for one of the nicest restaurants in Knoxville. He didn't know that I saw it and I thought that he wanted to surprise me and possibly propose there." I am assuming Lucas is starting to see where this is going because his jaw tightens. "Well that night I got all dressed up and went to the restaurant to find him there with a gorgeous woman. I saw as he hugged her and gave her a kiss before they sat down. This all happened while I was walking to the table thinking the dinner was meant for me. Matt looked up and made eye contact with me for a brief minute, then turned back to his actual date leaving me there shocked and mortified."

Now Lucas looks like he is about to have smoke come out his ears. Before he can respond and give me the pity that I don't want, I continue. "I rushed back to our apartment, packed all the things in my car, wrote him a note saying I was done and best of luck then drove straight here. I didn't find out until months later that the woman was a sport journalist that he met while at an away game. I'm sure he was hoping that she would do a piece on him to help further his career."

Realizing that I am done with my story, Lucas lets out a short breath. "Sage, no woman deserves to not only be cheated on but to be disrespected by not acknowledging your presence shows me that he never deserved you to begin with. You are a diamond and he was only tarnishing you instead of letting you shine."

Overwhelmed with how much emotion his response is bringing, I turn back to the bed. "Looks like we are just about done here. I can always do the other bed by myself if you need to head back home. Tomorrow may be the start of your crazy weekend." Lucas can probably sense that I am trying to deflect away from talking more about Matt and how much that night broke my heart but he doesn't let it go. "Blue. Look at me." I turn back to Lucas and his eyes spark. "You deserve to be loved the way your dad loves your mama, the way the boys in all those movies you love love their woman, and the way your future kids deserve to be loved by someone one day. Never settle for anything less than that."

Now there is no sense in hiding how much his words are impacting me as a single tear slips from the corner of my eye. Lucas reaches across and wipes it away before it can fall to my chin. "Let's get the mattress on this bed and go work on the other. Are you okay putting on the sheets and making them in the morning?"

Composing myself I give him a small smile. "That sounds like a perfect plan. Let's go to the other room." We flip the mattress onto the bed that is now fully assembled and head to the next room. We finish putting together the next bed quicker than the first since it is the same bedframe so we know what we are doing. While we work, we keep the conversation much lighter as Lucas tells me about what moves his favorite football team did this off season. Once we are done we head downstairs where we find Aspen fully asleep on the couch.

"You are welcome to leave her here if you want. Looks like she passed out from all that running around in the yard." Lucas smiles when he looks over at Aspen. "She would probably love that but her food and water are over at my house so if she wakes up she will be hunting for some." Lucas heads over to the couch and as soon as he sits down next to Aspen, her head slowly pops up. "Come on beautiful girl, it's time to go home."

Lucas and Aspen make their way to the back door and we say goodnight. As I watch them walk across the yard to their house, I think about how I need to go to the store and get some dog bowls to keep by the backdoor for when Aspen is over.

# CHAPTER 11
# - SAGE

**Brooklyn:** on our way! ETA is a little after 6pm.

I've spent the day running around making sure everything is ready for the girls weekend. Since Lucas and I were able to put together the beds last night, I only had to put the new bedding on them before they were ready to go. I then went to the store to get some movie snacks, things for dinner, and then went to the pet store. I may have gone a little too crazy at the pet store. Aspen now has dog bowls, a dog bed that will go next to the couch, some dog toys and a basket for the toys, and some treats to put in a new jar that will live on the corner of the counter closest to her dog bowls. I didn't know what dog food to get so I figured Lucas could give me a baggie next time they come over.

A month ago I would've laughed at the thought of Lucas coming over to my house. Now? The thought makes my heart feel a certain way and I'm not sure what to do about it.

Now as I am headed back to my house I notice Stanton's car in my driveway. Since he has one of my extra keys, I assume him and Miles are already inside. Pulling into the garage, I park and grab my groceries as I head in. "Hey Stants. I am back home." Peering around the corner I see Miles in a large box with some toys and Stanton laying on the couch asleep. I am grateful he didn't wake up to me yelling.

I put my groceries away and set up Aspen's new items before going over to Miles' play box. Looking in I see Miles in his own little world playing with some teething toys and books. Once he notices me he gives me the cutest little gummy smile.

I scoop him up out of the box and give him a squeeze that makes him giggle. "Ssh Miles we are gonna let your dad sleep a bit." He smiles at the idea and I take him upstairs to check one more time to make sure the bedrooms are ready for Brooklyn and Gracie.

Me and Miles do a sweep of the upstairs before I get a notification that there is motion at the front door. Jogging downstairs I notice the couch is now empty and Stanton is just about to open the door. He is greeted by a smiling Brooklyn. "You aren't Sage but close enough. You going to let us in?" Brooklyn is wearing a big smile like she is about to stay at a resort.

"Uh yeah come on in." It is obvious that the door must have woken up Stanton and he is still a little out of it.

"The last time we saw you, you were much more put together. But this whole messy look is working for me." With that Brooklyn winks at him and I can tell that Stanton is shocked while being a little embarrassed. Deciding to save my brother I step around the corner with Miles. "Hey guys! You made it!" I rush over to them and am enveloped in a group hug. Miles giggles as we are all squeezing around him.

"Before y'all get into trouble, I am going to head out." Stanton reaches for Miles and Miles practically leaps out of my hands to get to his dad.

"Sorry I wasn't here when you got here. I hope you were able to get some sleep though." I give Stanton a quick hug as he heads to the front door.

"Miles was enjoying that box again so I sat on the couch to wait for you and don't even remember falling asleep." Stanton grabs the diaper bag by the door and fishes his keys out of the front pocket.

The girls have wandered into the living room so I turn to Stanton, "my offer still stands Stanton. I am willing to take Miles whenever you need. Maybe before I head back for the new school year I can take him for a night or two so you can get a full night of sleep. How about you drop him off next Friday evening and I will keep him until Sunday. Gives you some time to recharge. You know self-care and all that stuff you constantly tell us about."

Rolling his eyes at me for throwing his therapy talk back at him, he still reluctantly agrees. "Okay fine, only because you keep bugging me about it. Next Friday it is. Maybe I will see if dad wants to catch a baseball game together."

"You know he would love that. Love you Stants."

"Love you too Sage. Thank you." He jogs to his car. I glance over at Lucas's house and notice his patrol car is still gone and the lights in his house are off. Must be a crazy weekend after all for him.

Once the girls get settled into their rooms we decide to make a bunch of appetizers to eat while we watch some movies. All three of us are in the kitchen making various snacks. I am at my air fryer making some mozzarella sticks, Brooklyn is making some queso dip on the stove, and Gracie is putting together a charcuterie board with meats, cheese, fruits, and veggies. Brooklyn goes over to the sink to wash her hands and notices the whiteboard next to the sink. "Hey Sage, why do you have a whiteboard chilling over here?"

Unsure on how much I am wanting to tell them about Lucas since it is still new and honestly don't even know how to explain our relationship at this point. "Oh it's just for some notes." They don't think much about it as we continue working on our food.

Once the food is all ready to go, we place it on the coffee table. I go back to the kitchen to get down some cups for some drinks but notice motion in Lucas's window as I am passing by. I stop at the sink and see him writing out a note.

*Saw a car in your driveway when I got home. Hope you have a fun night :)*

The girls notice I am standing there smiling at the window when they come back to check on me. "What are you over here smiling at?" Gracie races over to the window. When she realizes that there is another person across the way looking our way you can see her start to blush and give a small wave. This makes Brooklyn run over to see what is going on. "Hot damn. That guy is your neighbor?! Why didn't you tell us you are living next to a hot cop? Please tell me he is single." Brooklyn gives Lucas a wave. My stomach drops when I see him smiling at her. Almost at the same time they notice the whiteboard in his hand. "Oh so this is what you were talking about when you said it was for some notes. You have some explaining to do missy." Her and Gracie grab their cups and head towards the living room.

I snag my whiteboard and write out a message to Lucas.

*Now I have to go explain to my best friends*

*why I didn't tell them that I currently live next to a hot cop. Pray for me.*

I hold up my whiteboard and the smile I get in return steals my breath away. I give Lucas a small wave before grabbing my drink and heading into the living room. "Okay guys, which movie should we start with tonight?"

"No way. There is absolutely no way we are watching a movie right now. Now spill." Brooklyn does not mess around when she is wanting information. It is the lawyer in her so I know there is no choice but to fill them in on Lucas.

"Do you guys remember Stanton's best friend Lucas? He came to visit Knoxville once with Stanton."

"Yeah wasn't that the guy that you couldn't stand. You guys grew up together but you two bickered like crazy that weekend like you couldn't stand being in the same room together." You can tell that Gracie's wheels are turning on why I would be bringing him up.

"Well the guy you just waved to was Lucas....." Brooklyn and Gracie both look at me with their jaw dropped. They look back towards the window and then back at me.

"Wait, the guy that you grew up competing with, the one that was like your arch enemy in high school is now the hot cop next door?"

"The same hot cop that you have a whiteboard

next to your kitchen window so you can write notes to each other?" Brooklyn is beaming at this point. She loves a good love story. But I am going to have to break it to her that Lucas and I aren't like that.

"Yep. That's the one and only. I still can't stand him most of the time but after he moved next door we have seen each other more." Heat rises to my cheeks at what the girls could be implying.

"What do you mean you have been seeing each other more?" Gracie looks tentative in the question as if she knows I am purposely not saying something.

"Uh well one night he came over to help me put together furniture after he saw me lying on the floor giving up, then he came over because I tried to give him that basket Matt sent me," the girls roll their eyes at that. I sent them a picture of the basket and note before I thought I was super sneaky in leaving it on Lucas's doorstep, "then last night he came over to help me put together the beds in the guest room."

"Okay I am going to need some processing time for this one." Brooklyn lets out a dramatic sigh. "What does this mean? Do you like him? Are you guys friends now? I mean the whiteboard messages may be the cutest thing I have ever seen but with your history together it seems complicated."

"Yeah, that's exactly where I am at. Complicated." I give them a small smile. These girls went through my healing process with me after Matt so they know that I am hesitant to let any men into my life besides my dad and Stanton. "I think we are becoming friends. I mean we still bicker and he still teases me every chance he gets, but he also has really sweet moments."

"What kind of sweet moments?"

"Yeah Sage because if any man is mean to you or hurts you, they will have us to deal with. And since I am a lawyer I know ways to do it without getting caught." I laugh at that because Brooklyn is truly brilliant and would do anything for someone that she loves.

"Well…" unsure if I should share the moment we had last night but decide to continue, "last night when we were putting together the bed I told him about what happened with Matt. Instead of making me feel smaller with pity, he was very sweet. He told me that I am a diamond and Matt was only tarnishing it and that I need to find someone that lets me shine. I need to make sure to not settle for anything less than what my parents have or the love I see in the movies."

Now these girls are jaws are fully dropped. They look at each other having a conversation with their eyes that I don't understand then turn back to me.

Gracie grabs a mozzarella stick, dips in in marinara sauce and says "Wow Sage, that is very poetic. I mean he isn't wrong."

"Damn straight he isn't wrong. That is exactly the love you deserve!" Wanting to shift the conversation before I have to explain how what he said made me tear up and he gently wiped a tear off my cheek I ask them about movies again. "Alright now that we got past that, what movie are we watching?"

"Wait!" Gracie looks around the room. "Why do you have a bunch of dog stuff. I noticed it earlier but as far as we know, you didn't get a dog."

"Oh! Lucas has a husky named Aspen. She is the cutest thing. When he comes over, he always brings her so I wanted to get her some stuff to make her feel more comfortable." The girls look at each other again and give each other a look and a smile and nod as if saying they are satisfied with the information given. "Let's watch Crazy Rich Asians. I'm feeling a boujee kind of love tonight."

Laughing at Brooklyn because whoever she ends up with better live up to all her expectations, I turn on the movie and we dive into the world of romantic comedies for the night.

The weekend flew by with the girls. After Friday night we didn't have any more Lucas sightings. On the couple times we left the house

I noticed that his patrol car was nowhere to be seen and his lights were off. I was a little disappointed that he never texted me to ask if I would take Aspen for him. But since he didn't ask, he must have come home each night and I just didn't ever see him. Now it is Sunday and the girls are getting the car packed up to head back to Knoxville. "You guys need to come back soon. It was so good to have you here. It felt just like old times when we lived together in college." I smile as I think about those years and all the memories we made.

They must be doing the same because they both have a similar smile. "We will Sage. Pennystone is a dream. It is so peaceful."

"You know there is always a home for you if you decide to make the move here Gracie." She gives a small nod. "And you Brooklyn. I would love both of you closer."

"If we keep having amazing weekends like this it may be hard to say no." We exchange hugs and right as they are about to leave Lucas pulls into his driveway. He gives us a wave and pulls into his garage. Brooklyn leans over. "Do you think he will come say hello?!"

"Uh, I don't know... he probably had a long weekend and wants to relax on his Sunday." Lucas's garage door slowly closes and I ignore the disappointment I feel at the sight. The girls are about to get in the car when Lucas's front door opens. Aspen comes sprinting towards us.

I crouch down in hopes to slow her down a bit before she gets excited over some new friends. She immediately comes to me and gives me all the kisses. Laughing I turn to the girls and introduce Aspen to the girls, "This is Aspen. Lucas's dog."

"Oh my goodness! She is beautiful."

At this point Lucas makes it over to us. "Sorry guys. I saw you standing out here and assumed that Aspen would want to see Sage since she hasn't gotten to all weekend. I didn't expect her to bolt like that." Lucas runs a hand through his hair showing he is a little nervous as he eyes my friends. "Even though we met previously and through the window the other night, it is nice to see you ladies again. It's Gracie and Brooklyn right?"

Brooklyn looks at him and then me and then back to him. She then gives him a big smile. "Yep! That's us." Gracie is still too preoccupied with petting Aspen to acknowledge Lucas. "Look at those blue eyes. I don't know if I have ever seen more beautiful eyes." Lucas looks at me and then Aspen and I hear him mutter quietly, "I have."

Before I can think more about that, Gracie pops up. "Hey Lucas, it is good to see you. Thanks for checking in on our girl and making sure she had some help with her furniture. We know how she gets when they don't go the way she wants." She gives me a wink at that and I know for a fact I am blushing.

"Nah, Sage would have been fine without me. She was just lying on the floor to take a break that night." Lucas looks at me with a smirk to which I naturally roll my eyes. Watching the interaction, Brooklyn and Gracie look at each other and smile. "Well make sure you keep an eye on our girl. We aren't afraid of getting our hands dirty if she ends up hurt again." Gracie cringes and whispers quietly, "Brooklyn! You can't threaten a cop."

"Well I sure hope those hands got dirty with Matt. And if not, contact me and we will set something up." Everyone laughs but Lucas, he looks at them very seriously.

"Alright y'all should get on the road before traffic picks up. Love you guys. Thanks for coming to see me!" We exchange another round of hugs and Lucas lets them know to avoid Main Street due to an accident. They slowly pull out of my driveway and we stand there waving them goodbye.

Lucas then turns to me and gives a small smile. "I know you had a busy weekend with the girls, but is there any way you planned on cooking dinner tonight? I am getting real sick of frozen meals and peanut butter and jelly sandwiches at the station." It takes all of me to not show my excitement. "I actually was planning on making dinner and it sure does make a lot. Should be enough to feed you."

"Oh thank goodness. You are a saint"

"Did Lucas Walker just call me a saint?! Someone write the date down." Lucas smirks and turns towards my house calling for Aspen to follow. "Make me a home cooked meal and I will call you anything you want." And dang it, does that make my mind go to places it shouldn't.

# CHAPTER 12
# - LUCAS

I do my best to hide my smile as I walk towards Sage's front door. The blush across Sage's cheeks was perfect. Aspen follows after me but then cuts towards the backyard. "I don't think Aspen knows where your front door is." I chuckle as I look back at Sage.

She catches up to me, "oh that's right she has only gone through my back door. Should we tell her to come or let her go around back." Smiling down at Sage, "I bet if we go through, she will be sitting at the back door. Maybe I should walk around back too. Are you sure you want me to come through the front door?"

"Oo maybe you should go around back before anyone sees you going through the front. We don't want your bachelor status to be ruined like that." Sage smirks up at me. The infamous bachelor status that I can't stand. What everyone doesn't realize is that I would love to find my person. I grew up watching Mr. and Mrs.

Calloway sneak away for a slow dance in the kitchen or pass secret glances at each other as if they were the only people in the room. I want that type of love. I want a best friend, a partner, and a soulmate. But in the meantime, I am doing my best to become worthy of that love.

"Come on Blue, live on the wild side. Let those ladies have another person to gossip about." She gives me a look that looks like uncertainty as we get to the front door. "Hey if you really don't want me to go through the front, I can slip around back."

She seems shocked at first, "No it's okay, don't be ridiculous you can come through the front door."

I am equally as shocked as she is when I put my hand on her lower back to guide her into the house. As we continue walking through the house we see Aspen is in fact sitting at the back waiting at the door. Sage runs over to the back door and lets Aspen in. Aspen quickly stops at the door which confuses me because she always, and I mean always, sprints to the couch and snuggles in. She stops in front of what looks like dog bowls and looks up at me.

Confused, I look over to Sage who also noticed the immediate stop from Aspen. "Uh Sage, why are there dog bowls on your floor?" She looks a little nervous, "Well I was just thinking about the other night where you had to take Aspen home because she didn't have food and water over here. Then I was thinking about how if you ever needed me to watch Aspen for you, you would have to bring all your supplies over and how if you were in a hurry you could forget something."

She takes a breath before continuing so I slip in. "I mean you could just have a key to my house and then that's not an issue." As if she didn't hear me she continues, "and then I was at the pet store and saw the bowls first and then figured that if she had food over here I should get her treats because she is a great dog and deserves treats. And then I obviously needed a jar for the treats. To get the jar I passed by the toy aisle and come on, you can't go by the toy aisle without getting her a toy." She takes another breath and then finally realizes what I said. "Wait. Did you just say I could have a key to your house?" She looks at me like I grew two heads.

I nod with a smile, "Yes. If you are planning on me watching Aspen, I should give you a key just in case you need anything." I can feel my smile growing as I can see the shock settle on Sage's face. "So when you watch her I will make sure you get a key. But you didn't need to buy all this for Aspen." Aspen gives up on the bowl but spots the basket of new dog toys and takes off to sniff them out before tearing into them.

"But look at how happy Aspen is. I wanted her to feel comfortable here." This girl. Her heart is too big. "Sage, Aspen loves your house. You didn't need anything to make her love it here. She loves it here because you are here." Sage looks at Aspen and back at me. It is clear that she is deciding how to respond to that.

"Well now she will love my house even more. Maybe if she is lucky she can stay forever." For some reason I am not jealous of that statement. Aspen would be one lucky dog to get this kind of love forever. Sage heads off to the kitchen and I follow after her.

"Can I help you with anything?"Sage scans the kitchen as if thinking of a job for me. "Or I can just stay back and let you do your thing."

"No, I will let you help."

"You're just trying to think of something I can do without messing it up aren't you?" I laugh as she heads over to the refrigerator and pulls out some butter.

"I mean can you blame me? You tell me you live off of frozen meals most nights." Okay, so she may have a point there. "But tonight you are going to enter the world of home cooking... Maybe starting small".

I laugh again as I round the kitchen island to stand next to her. " Okay boss, put me to work." She heads to the pantry and grabs a loaf of french bread. "Alright go ahead and cut the bread in half down the middle and put butter on both sides. Then you are going to sprinkle on some garlic seasoning and parsley before we throw it in the oven to toast."

I roll up the sleeves of my uniform. "Sounds simple enough." I take the bread as she hands it over and get to work.

As I am focusing on the bread, Sage flies around the kitchen making some type of pasta. Whatever she is making, it smells amazing like always. She glances over to me, I'm sure to make sure I am not messing up, and I watch as her eyes track my hands as I am sprinkling on the seasonings. I look up to her in question about if it is good. She blushes a little then gives me a smile and spins around to continue working on the pasta. I take that as a yes and slide the bread into the oven.

Before I know it the dinner is ready and somehow Sage finishes at the same time as I pull out the bread out of the oven. Maybe I do need some training in the kitchen. Tonight we choose to eat dinner inside since it began raining while we were cooking. Aspen won't mind though with all the new toys. I don't think we could pull her away from those toys even if we tried. "We haven't had the chance to sit at your table. You picked out a really good one Sage." She looks at the table with a smile on her face.

"I wanted something timeless. Something with enough seats for when my family or friends come over and one day big enough for my own family." An image pops in my head of Sage around this table with a crew of little kids running around. The question is am I in this picture? I shake my head at the ridiculous thought. "Okay so tell me about your weekend with Gracie and Brooklyn."

She smiles and you can tell she enjoyed her weekend with her friends. "It was great to see them. We used to live together in college so it felt like old times. We watched movies each night and were able to catch up. It has been a while since we have been able to have a girls weekend. I am really grateful that they were able to drive down and stay here." It is obvious that Sage loves her friends and I am grateful she has them. Sage deserves people that will have her back in good times and bad.

"They seemed really great. Obviously I met them back in the college days but I am glad to see that you guys are still close."

"Yeah they are great. I am lucky" Sage's smile is bright tonight and I am glad to be on the receiving end.

"And what did you tell them about the hot cop next door?" I make sure to emphasis the word hot to make sure she knows I caught that in her text.

Her cheeks turn a little pink. "Well they didn't recognize you in the window but then I explained who you were. They remembered when you came with Stanton to visit me in Knoxville. Safe to say they were quite shocked when I told them that we have been spending time together and not plotting each other's murders."

"I'm still not so sure that you aren't. I could

wake up tomorrow in need of poison control." She rolls her eyes as I smirk.

"How was your weekend? I only saw you once on Friday night. Was it as crazy busy as you thought it would be?" Sighing I think back on my weekend, "Honestly it was. I think I wrote over ten speeding tickets on Friday, mostly teenagers racing in front of the high school. We then had to go to the county courthouse to file a statement on a case we closed last month. That is probably why you didn't see me all day yesterday. Since James recently moved here, we decided to stop at The Diner on the way back for dinner and of course Susie wanted to get to know him so we ended up staying later than we expected. I am sure you guys were already watching Crazy Stupid Love by the time I finally got home." Her smile tells me that I was correct. In that moment I can't take my eyes off her.

Tonight she is wearing some joggers with a Pennystone elementary school tshirt and her hair is in a bun on the top of her head with some strands sticking out as if they sprung free as the day went on. My mind can't understand how she can look stunning no matter what she wears or does with her hair. I see that we both have finished our meal. "As always this meal was delicious Sage."

"The bread may have been my favorite part." She smirks at me as she stands up to take the dishes to the kitchen. I jump up and take the dishes off of her hands and take them to the sink. This has become my typical job on the nights I eat over here. As I head to the sink, I hear Sage come in to put away the leftover food. If I am lucky, she will give me some for lunch tomorrow. "Lucas, I hope you know that I don't expect you to do my dishes."

"My mama taught me that when a pretty woman cooks for you, you make sure to clean up for her." I glance back at Sage to see her smiling down at the tupperware. I turn back to the sink with a smile of my own and finish up the dishes.

"Wait so you're telling me that after a long day of work you heat up a frozen meal and then turn on a romcom to unwind from the day?" Sage can't help but giggle at that thought. "Okay hold up. This is coming from the girl that can quote any romcom out there." I can't help but smile at her from across the couch. We had just settled in on her couch with Aspen lounging between us. I think both of us were shocked when Sage asked if I wanted to stay and watch a movie after dinner. We were scrolling through Netflix when my secret came out.

"Well yeah… but I am a girl. That is a very normal thing for us. But you?" She waves her hand up and down my body before busting out laughing again. "This is too good. Wait until the ladies of Pennystone find out what their yummy bachelor does in his spare time."

I look down at Aspen and then back at the screen while she continues scrolling through titles. "Okay laugh it up. But growing up I would see you and your dad watching these together all the time and he always looked at you with so much joy during the movies. When I went away for college and was on my own for the first time, especially when Stanton was so focused on Jessica, I would get stressed and lonely. These movies reminded me of some of the good times in the Calloway house."

Sage stops scrolling and glances at me with a look of slight shock. She quickly recovers, "Alright Lucas I guess your secret is safe with me. But only if you tell me which one is your favorite."

No pressure but I feel like there is some weight behind my answer on this one. Remembering which one I saw Sage and her dad watch the most I give her my answer. "Easy answer. Definitely How to Lose a Guy in 10 Days. The banter between Andie and Ben is just too perfect." My lips tip up as I see Sage's eye brighten.

"That movie is top tier. No questions asked." She turns back to the screen but not before giving a smile. "Alright, what should we watch tonight?" Sage continues scrolling until I see one that stands out. "Oo do that one, 17 again. Another classic."

"I love this one! Once you get past the fact that he hits on the mom when he is 17, it is so sweet. The letter in the courtroom makes me tear up every time." She fires up the movies and we settle in. As the movie plays, I can't help but think back to when we were 17. How much would our lives be different if we were willing to set aside our competitiveness and choose to be friends back then? Have I missed out on the most amazing girl I have ever met for the last ten years?

The movie ends in a blink of an eye as I stay lost in thought. When I look over, I realize that Sage has fallen asleep with Aspen curled up next to her. She has had a busy weekend and must be exhausted. I stay where I am for a minute watching Sage's chest rise and fall in a steady rhythm while trying to decide if I should wake her up or carry her upstairs to her room.

Since we worked in the two guest rooms, I have a good idea which one will be the master bedroom. I decide that I really don't want to wake her up but I don't want to leave her on the couch all night so that leaves me with making sure she makes it to her bed.

Hoping that she is still as hard of a sleeper as she was when we were kids I walk over to the other end of the couch and scoop her into my arms. She stirs for a moment before settling into my chest with a sigh. I stay still for a moment to make sure she stays asleep. I don't really want to know what her reaction would be if she wakes up in my arms.

Aspen hops down from the couch and trails after us as we make our way upstairs. Lucky for me, her bedroom door is the only one that is open so it is an easy find. Also thankfully she is in sweats and a tshirt so I don't need to worry about her clothes. I place her head on her pillow before putting the rest of her body down, throwing on the blanket at the bottom of her bed, then sneak back out into the hall in case she wakes up.

Once Aspen and I make it back down the stairs I let out a big sigh. "I think we are in the clear, Aspen. Now it's time to head home." Aspen cocks her head at me and glances back up the stairs. For a minute I am worried that she will bolt back upstairs and into the bed with Sage but she trails after me into the kitchen. I grab the tupperware from the refrigerator of the food that Sage told me was for my lunch tomorrow and write a quick note on her whiteboard by the sink.

"Alright Aspen I know it is against all your beliefs but we are going to have to go out the front door so that we make sure Sage's doors are locked up. We gotta make sure our girl is kept safe."

I pull the front door open and Aspen comes up very unsure of this new route. I smile down at her. "Yeah I know girl. The back door is our door but this is better tonight." I spin the lock from the inside and shut the door only leaving once I know it is locked. I head back towards my house hoping that the doorbell notification doesn't wake up Sage and catch myself smiling. Tonight was another great night. A really great night.

# CHAPTER 13
# - SAGE

Waking up the next morning, I blink away the blurriness of the morning and try to piece together how I got into my bed. The last thing I remember is that Lucas and I were watching a movie on the couch when I started to get a little sleepy. I glanced over at Lucas but he looked super zoned in on the movie and I didn't want to have to make him leave. I thought I only rested my eyes for a brief second.

I sit up and try to remember if he woke me up and I wandered to my room after he left. Looking down I realize that I am wearing the same clothes as yesterday and I am not even under my covers. I just have a blanket on top of me that is usually at the bottom of my bed or in the basket in the corner. Lucas must have carried me to bed.

I fling back onto my pillow with an arm over my eyes. There's no way I fell asleep so hard that Lucas scooped me up and carried me to bed. I look over at my nightstand and see that my phone is on the charger. He even went as far as making sure my phone was charging for me before sneaking out. I grab it from the nightstand and see I have some missed texts from the girls.

Brooklyn: we made it back! Thanks again for the weekend away.
Gracie: I made it to my apartment too, Brooklyn. All safe and sound.
Brooklyn: um Sage? You alive over there?
Gracie: I bet she is busy spending the evening with her hot cop.
Brooklyn: Sage Calloway if you don't answer your phone in the next ten minutes you will have lots of explaining to do in the morning!

(2 hours later)

Gracie: Hope your night was amazing Sage. We need details in the morning!

Oh goodness. I have no doubt that they are thinking that I had myself a great night with Lucas. Well I did have a great night, one of the best. But not in the way they are probably implying. Sighing, I decide to FaceTime them.

"She's alive!" Brooklyns face pops up and I can see that she is getting ready for work. "Hold up are you still in bed? Please tell me that you aren't about to show us a naked Lucas." Gracie is at her table eating a bowl of cereal.

Blushing I shake my head but before I can

respond Brooklyn jumps in. "I mean, did you see that man?! I wouldn't mind just a little sneak peek to know what you're working with Sage." Both her and Gracie break out into giggles.

"Alright slow your roll girls. I had Lucas over for dinner and we ended up watching a movie. Apparently I fell asleep on the couch and woke up this morning on my bed with a blanket." I jump up from my bed to show them that I am in the same outfit as yesterday then make my way downstairs to grab some water.

"Wait, that is a lot to process." Brooklyn stops working in her hair and turns to the camera. "Lucas stayed over after we left."

"Yep"

"Then you guys had dinner together."

"Yep. He helped me make it too."

"Okay you LET him help you make dinner. Then after eating dinner together you ended up asking him to stay and watch a movie with you?"

"Still correct" Gracie is smiling at the camera at Brooklyn's dramatic run down.

"You ended up falling asleep. Lucas then scooped you up and carried you to bed without you waking up before he went home."

"Yep, that is exactly what happened. Thanks for the play by play." I smirk at her as she rolls her eyes.

"Is there anything else that is important to note?"

"Uh I found out that he watches romcoms to

unwind and his favorite is How to Lose a Guy in 10 Days." I chuckle at the memory of him telling me. Gracie and Brooklyn both stare at me.

"What?"

"Is he real?"

"Yes he is very annoyingly real" I roll my eyes at them. I stop in the living room before heading to the kitchen and notice that my pillows are placed back on the couch where they should be and all of Aspen's toys are picked up. Sighing, I look back at the girls.

"Sage if you don't jump on that, I will" I know Brooklyn is just teasing me but it still causes my stomach to drop at the thought.

"Alright Brooklyn, let's give Sage some more time to process her feelings." My jaw drops at the two of them.

"Oh shoot I gotta run!"

"Me too. Sorry Sage. If I don't leave now I'm gonna be late."

"No worries guys! Go be amazing. We will talk soon." We say our goodbyes and I head to the kitchen for that water. I stop short when I notice my whiteboard standing by the kitchen sink with a new message written on it.

*Good Morning Blue, thanks for another great night. Remind me to only watch movies with you when I know you can make it to the end. Although you sleeping was pretty adorable. I missed seeing your reaction when Mike poured out his heart in the courtroom. I expect a rewatch. Enjoy your Monday. PS I cleaned everything up for you and ordered breakfast which should be delivered before you start your day.*

The doorbell rings and I can't help the huge smile on my face as I open the door and accept the food that Lucas ordered for me. I smile as I bring it back to the kitchen walking to the refrigerator to get a drink of water. Glancing at the clock I realize that since I fell asleep on the couch I didn't get to set an alarm. Thinking about what to do with my day, I decide to run some errands. I have some walls I want to paint before my weekend with Miles.

The week flies by. I only see Lucas one night where we shared a quick whiteboard exchange before he had to run back out. He asked me if I could watch Aspen for him overnight since he wasn't sure how long he would be out. It is the last week of summer and from what I have heard around town, this group of high schoolers are a wild bunch. I was so excited to have Aspen since she is the best dog. I may have let her sleep in my bed with me (which I don't tell Lucas about). He was so busy it was a quick drop off and pick up.

It is now Friday evening and I am checking the house to make sure that everything is set for

Miles to stay with me. I have a pack and play in the guest room closest to mine. I saved some large boxes for us to sit in and play plus I have the kids profile on Netflix ready to go. I am excited for the weekend with Miles, I love that little guy. I am also glad for Stanton to get time away from being a single dad for a little bit. Hearing the doorbell, I run downstairs and open the door to a smiling Miles and Stanton looking rather anxious.

"Hey Stants. And here is my favorite little man. Come on hand him over, I get him this weekend all to myself." Stanton lets me snag Miles from his arms as he walks into my house with a bag for Miles.

"Are you sure you wanna do this Sage? It's okay if you change your mind and don't want to keep him as long." You can tell Stanton is going to need a little push here.

"Stanton, I know you haven't left Miles for this long before. But I really do think you need to take some time to relax and reset. Please don't make me pull your therapy stuff out again." Stanton rolls his eyes at me but I can tell he is trying to fight a smile. "Okay but will you promise me that if it becomes too much that you will call?" Yeah sure. But we both know it is going to be fine.

"Yeah I promise I will call if I get overwhelmed. But Stanton come on. I have been babysitting since I was 14 and make a living off of taking care of small children. I know you are worried about

Miles and you are an amazing dad for that, but seriously I got this." Stanton seems to ease a bit. He shows me where he packed the formula in the diaper bag and the bag of baby food he brought with him along with his diapers and wipes. He reminds me about Miles' night routine and about how much Miles loves his baths.

"I got this Stanton. Now go out, get some sleep, and enjoy your time off." I smile as he hesitantly walks to the door. "Alright buddy" He grabs Miles and gives him a tight hug. "I will be back on Sunday. I love you so so so much."

He hands Miles back over to me and gives me a hug. "Thank you for doing this Sage. I appreciate you and Miles is lucky to have you as an aunt."

"Love you too Stants. This weekend will be great for me too. The best way to end off my summer." Stanton slowly walks to his car and before he can decide to come back I spin around and walk into my house. "Alright little man, this is going to be the best weekend."

Miles and I are sitting in a large box with toys when I hear a bark at the back door. My heart leaps each time I hear that bark. Seeing that Miles is still content in the box, I step out and head towards the sliding glass back door. Opening the back door I make sure to say hello to Aspen first then look up and notice Lucas is looking down at us with a smile.

My gut drops a little when I see him standing there in his cop uniform with his hands in his pockets. Of course his sleeves are rolled up to show a little bit of his forearms. Man, when does this man find time to exercise to maintain his body? In that moment I wonder why he never changes out of his uniform before coming over. Shaking my head I stand up, "Hey Lucas, come on in I have Miles here with me and need to make sure he is still in his box with his toys." Lucas tilts his head at me with a look of amusement on his face. Him and Aspen slip inside after me as I walk to the living room and see Miles still happily playing in his box.

When Miles sees me he gives me a big smile. Teething was rough but he now has two teeth on the bottom poking out. I didn't think this kid could get any cuter and then he got teeth. My goodness. When he notices Lucas come up and stand next to me he lets out a little squeal while lifting his hands up to him. "Well apparently Miles is very excited to see his Uncle Lucas." Lucas smiles and grabs Miles from the box. Miles lays his head on his shoulder for a solid minute before perking back up and looking over at me.

"Isn't he the cutest thing to ever be born?" Miles has yet to notice Aspen but Aspen has definitely noticed Miles. She lets out a little bark and that grabs Miles' attention. Miles tries to squirm out of Lucas's hands until he finally lets him down.

"Is Aspen good with him?" I ask even though I am sure that Stanton has been to Lucas's house before. "Yep, she is great with him. Miles loves to crawl around after her. Just wait until Miles finds Aspen's toys. They will probably wear each other out by the end of the night." We both smile at Miles as Aspen lays down next to him to let him pet her. Well more like Miles is trying to crawl over her. Aspen hops up and walks away with Miles trailing after her.

"So… you're on baby duty tonight I see. Where is Stanton at?"

"He has the weekend off from being super dad. I convinced him that he needed some dedicated time for himself and to get some sleep after he fell asleep on my couch last week." I glance over to Lucas as he is looking after Aspen and Miles with a serious look on his face.

"I've been worried about him. He is working himself to his bones with the practice and still managing to be an amazing dad to Miles. I wish he could see what we all see. If I could convince him to let me take Miles so that he could have a break I would." Lucas then looks over at me, "I am really glad you got him to do it Sage. You are a great sister and aunt."

Deflecting from his compliment, "I am the lucky one to get Miles for the weekend. Anyways, have you eaten dinner yet? I was just about to throw it together."

"Come on Blue, you have to know that answer by now." I laugh while walking towards the kitchen, "You're right of course you haven't eaten, that's why you are here." Lucas's smile drops a little and I am not too sure on why.

"Uh well tonight is going to be fairly simple. I wanted to keep it simple since I have Miles. I am thinking some grilled turkey sandwiches with some roasted potatoes. Does that sound okay?" I glance over to Lucas from the refrigerator and it seems like he has shaken off whatever upset him.

"I don't see how that is simple but it sounds delicious. What do you need me to do tonight?" Thinking about my options, "are you okay with feeding Miles for me so I can focus on throwing this together? Stanton brought some baby food with him and it may be easiest to feed him before we eat so he doesn't get too fussy." I can spot Miles still in the living room now checking out Aspen's toys.

"I can most definitely do that. Do you happen to have a high chair? Or did Stanton bring the one that connects to the table?" Lucas looks towards the kitchen table. "Ah, I can see the portable one that Stanton must have brought. I can go feed the little man." Lucas takes off towards the living room to snag Miles and put him in his chair. I have to remind myself to focus on dinner and not staring at the way Miles keeps giggling as Lucas makes funny faces at him while he is eating.

Once I finish up dinner we quickly eat while Miles and Aspen are crawling at our feet under the table. As always, Lucas doesn't let me do any of the dishes. And before we know it, it's time for Miles' bath and bedtime routine. We go upstairs to the guest bathroom next to the room that Miles will be in and get him in the bath. "Stanton told me that Miles' bath helps him wind down. But honestly he seems equally playful right now." Miles is in the bath splashing water with his arms and squealing.

Lucas is leaning in the doorway as I am kneeling at the bathtub, getting pretty wet from Miles splashing around. "Maybe this is the way he gets his last bit of energy out." I look back at Miles and see him now crawling around in the water. He truly loves his bath and I can see why Stanton told me to make sure it is part of his bedtime routine. I bet Stanton loves this time of the night to see his little boy so happy.

Once we decide Miles has become enough of a little raisin, I hand him over to Lucas who is holding the towel for him. Lucas walks over to the bedroom where Miles' pajamas are laid out and gets him dressed. We head back down stairs to finish off Miles' night with a bottle and throw on a movie for him. "Well Blue, we probably will have to choose a kids movie tonight. You think you can manage to stay awake?" Lucas smiles at me as I grab the bottle and head towards the couch with Miles in my arms.

"Ha. Ha. Very funny Lucas. Yes, I should be just fine tonight." When we get to the couch we sit down and Lucas grabs the remote to turn on Encanto, Stanton said it was Miles' favorite right now. It's a good one so I settle into the couch and feed Miles his bottle. After Miles drinks his bottle and has a good burp, he reaches out to Lucas. "I think someone wants you Lucas. You ready for some baby snuggles?"

"I will never say no to some snuggles." He reaches out for Miles and I pass him along. I watch them for a moment as Miles get comfortable settling into Lucas's chest. You have to be kidding. It is not fair for him to be holding the cutest baby in the world while still in that cop uniform.

By the time the movie is halfway through I look over and notice that not only is Miles asleep, so is Lucas. Wanting to make sure Miles gets to sleep in his portable crib, I carefully slip him from Lucas's arms and carry him to the guest bedroom. With a kiss on his forehead, I place him in the crib. He is out like a light.

When I get back downstairs, Lucas has shifted on the couch so that he is completely laying down now. I guess he must have been exhausted. Aspen is settled in her dog bed next to the couch and also asleep. My brain knows I should wake them up but my heart wants them to stay so I choose to be selfish and turn off the TV, throwing a blanket on Lucas before sneaking upstairs to get ready for bed. Something about the fact that I have Miles across the hall, Aspen downstairs, and Lucas sleeping on my couch makes me feel more safe and at home.

# CHAPTER 14
# - LUCAS

I wake up as the sun is rising through Sage's front window. I look over from where I am on the couch to see Aspen asleep on her dog bed, sprawled out on her back. Looks like I'm not the only one that slept good last night. I stand up, fold the blanket, and head to the kitchen. The house is quiet so I'm assuming that Sage and Miles are still asleep upstairs. Miles is a kid that wakes as soon as the sun does so I'm sure they will be up soon. Staying as quiet as possible to not wake them in case Miles chooses to let Sage sleep in, I start making some breakfast. Lucky for me, Sage's kitchen is organized perfectly so it doesn't take long to find what I am looking for.

I am in the middle of flipping pancakes when I hear Sage's soft footsteps come down the stairs.  As she comes around the corner the spatula in my hand stalls. Sage is wearing a little blue pajama set that perfectly matches her very sleepy eyes. It looks like she threw her hair into a bun when she woke up. She looks completely adorable and that's not even with the help of Miles smiling away in her arms. "Good morning Blue. Thanks for letting me crash here last night."

She smiles tentatively as she comes into the kitchen. "And here you were teasing me that I couldn't make it through the movie the other night." A look of nervousness passes through her face. "Sorry I didn't wake you to let you go home. You seemed pretty tired and I didn't want to wake you up, hopefully you slept okay on the couch"

I slept harder last night than I have in months, even while wearing my uniform. I don't know if it was the fact that Sage's couch is surprisingly comfortable or if it was because I fell asleep with Miles in my arms. Whatever the reason, I slept amazing. "I actually slept really really well." Aspen trots in at this point and looks up to Sage looking for love. "Aspen was sprawled across that bed you got her when I woke up. Looks like she liked sleeping here too." I return my focus back to the pancakes before I embarrass myself by burning them. "I hope you don't mind but I slightly raided your kitchen. You are always making me meals, I figured it was my time to cook for you."

"Pancakes? I thought you were a newbie in the kitchen." Sage puts Miles in his seat and comes back to the kitchen to grab his breakfast.

"Pancakes are one of the things that my mama made sure I knew how to do. Before I left for college she told me that I needed to at least be able to make simple things so she could know I wasn't starving. Plus she told me that when a pretty lady is over for breakfast, I need to make sure to serve her something more than a bowl of cereal." I glance over to see Sage smiling and I don't blame her, my mama has a heart of gold.

"Well I'll have to thank your mama the next time I see her." Sage has made it back to Miles and he is gulping down his food. If he is anything like Stanton, Stanton is going to have to make sure to always have his house stocked with food. A second later we hear the doorbell ring. It is apparent that Sage isn't expecting anyone. "Are you planning on someone coming over?" She glances up at me from where she is finishing up with Miles and shakes her head.

"Check your camera real quick and I can go get it." She better be checking her cameras even when I'm not here, especially since her ex knows where she lives. She smiles and nods at me, "you can go get it. Or I can just wash my hands real quick and grab it."

"No, I got it." The pancakes are now done so I jog off towards the front door. It isn't until I'm there that I realize she didn't tell me who is at the door. I open the door and find Mrs. Calloway on the other side with a look of surprise. Not an angry shock but definitely surprised. That's fair.

I am opening at her daughter's door in the same clothes that I wore yesterday. "Oh hi Lucas. Am I at the wrong house?" She chuckles as she looks over to my house next door.

"No ma'am you are in the right place. Come on in. Sage is in the kitchen feeding Miles." Mrs. Calloway heads to the kitchen with a smile on her face. Miles is about to get smothered with some kisses in 3... 2... 1...

"There's the beautiful boy! Grandma is so excited to see you!" There it is. I catch up to her as she is pulling Miles out of the chair. Miles is in a fit of giggles as Mrs. Calloway is giving him lots of kisses and tickling his tummy.

Sage is at the refrigerator pulling out some orange juice and grabbing the syrup from the pantry. "Hey mom. I didn't know you were planning on stopping by." Mrs. Calloway looks a little guilty. "Stanton and your dad are headed to the city for a baseball game. I was feeling a little lonely and left out so I decided to come here and see two of my favorite people." With that she looks over at me, "oh sorry Lucas I meant three."

She gives me a big smile. "I didn't know that Lucas was going to be here with you two this morning. Sorry if I was interrupting your breakfast plans." I glance over at Sage and see her cheeks starting to turn pink. "You're not interrupting mom. Lucas was just making us some pancakes. Did you eat or would you like some?"

Mrs. Calloway turns to me as her eyes brighten. "That was very kind of you Lucas." She turns back to Sage, "but I ate before coming here. I'll take Miles into the living room to play while you guys eat." She snags Miles out of his chair and bolts out of the room.

"Well Lucas, you may have just made my mom think you spent the night here." I shrug, "I mean I did spend the night here." Sage rolls her eyes, "I mean like *spent* the night here..."

"You didn't say anything Blue. Maybe you want people to imply that." I smirk at her as her cheeks pinken more. "In your dreams Lucas." I laugh as she hands me a plate. "Let's dive in." She starts dishing up her plate before she stops. "Wait, should I be worried that this is edible. I mean it would be pretty easy to poison me with this...."

I roll my eyes as she uses one of my own tactics against me. "I promise no poisoning happened this morning. Mama Walker never taught me that skill." I smile as she continues dishing up. We eat breakfast quickly and clean up. Sage rolled her eyes when I told her that I was still doing the dishes even though I cooked. Once the kitchen is all tidy again, we join Mrs. Calloway in the living room.

"So what are your plans today with Miles? Lucas, are you working or are you spending the day here?" I see Sage not so subtly glance my way before returning her focus back to Miles who is on her lap with a board book. "Lucky for me, I don't have work today but I am going to get out of your hands. I told my mama I would come by today since I haven't had the chance recently being so busy at work." I swear I see a slight look of disappointment from Sage.

"Oh dang. I was hoping you could come with us to the aquarium. Sage I wanna take you and Miles if you are free." I remember the earlier mention of Stanton and Mr. Calloway being gone for the day. Sounds like Mrs. Calloway really was feeling left out.

"Yeah mom that sounds great! It's almost time for Miles' morning nap but we can head over there after. Maybe stop in at The Diner for lunch before we head to the aquarium?"

"That would be perfect. A day spent with two of my favorite people is just what I need." Sage looks up at me as if to ask if I'm sure I can't come.

"Well ladies I should probably head out. I want to make sure I pick up some lunch on the way to my mamas house." I see Mrs. Calloway mouth to Sage 'go walk him to the door'. She rolls her eyes but stands up and hands Miles to her mama. She heads towards the back door and I motion to Aspen to follow. "Thank you for breakfast Lucas. And for your help with Miles" Sage seems timid but I'm sure it's because we can both see her mama watching us.

"You wouldn't have needed my help but thank you for letting me be part of your night. Have a fun day with your mama and Miles."

"Say hi to Mama Walker for me." She smiles up at me and I don't know how my knees don't give out. I blame it on the blue pajama set that Sage is still in.

"Will do. See ya!" And with that I walk across my yard with Aspen in need of a shower and to get out of my uniform that I have been wearing since yesterday.

Since it is Saturday and I don't know my mamas plan for the weekend I call her before I head out the door. She tells me that I am always welcome in her home and she doesn't have any plans for today. I stop by her favorite deli, Persnickitys, to pick up sandwiches and a Ceasar salad for lunch. Thankfully my mom lives just down the road so I don't hit any of the last weekend of summer traffic. Because I know my mama would beat my butt if I knocked, I walk on in when I get there. I stride into the living room where I find her reading a book. "Hey mama" I walk over and kiss her cheek.

"There's my most favorite son." She gets up and heads to the table after seeing that I brought lunch with me. I don't even try to remind her that I'm her only son. She knows, she still tells me each time that I'm her favorite. She grabs a pitcher of lemonade and some cups before we sit down. "I brought sandwiches and salad from

Persnickitys".

"Ah see, this is why you are my favorite." She gives me a big smile before we dig into our lunch. "So not that I am complaining because you need your own life, but you haven't been around much. Has work been busy?" She looks at me with concern.

"Yeah the end of the summer always brings in a new wave of activity. Sorry I haven't been coming over for dinner as much lately." She looks at me very serious, "Lucas you know I love your company whenever I can get it but it is never expected. You are a young man in his late twenties. I would be more concerned if you were hanging out with me every night."
I give her a boyish smile, "you know you are my favorite person to hang out with."

"Yes I know. But son you need to find a new favorite person one day or it's gonna start being weird." Her smirk tells me that she is joking so I roll my eyes at her. "I'm also worried that you have not been eating normal food if you have been on your own lately." I used to come to my mama's house often to get a home cooked meal after a long day at work.

"Well… I haven't really been eating at home." My mom looks a mix of confused and shocked. "Lucas Allen Walker, what does that mean? Have you been eating at the station?"

"Not exactly. I moved into my new house this month and I don't know if you noticed when you stopped by but the white and blue two story house next to mine is Sage's new home." She processing that for a second, "Wait, Sage Calloway?"

"The one and only." I can't help when a small smile starts to spread on my face. "What is that face for? Are you guys friends now? Wait, that is where you are eating dinners? My son better start filling me in on one of the biggest bomb drops." She folds her arms as she waits for me to fill her in.

"Yes ma'am." I laugh and she waves me to continue. "When I was moving in Aspen took off to the neighbors yard. When I followed her around back I found her there with Sage. I don't know how it happened but we ended up buying houses next to each other. I noticed that she was putting together some furniture one night and offered to help. She made dinner that night and then it just started happening more often." I can tell that she isn't satisfied with my vagueness.

"Are you being kind to Sage?" I roll my eyes at my mama, "Yes ma'am."

"Don't you roll your eyes at me. You love teasing that poor girl. You are doing the dishes right?"

"Yes ma'am, I wouldn't let her do the dishes after cooking for me." Mama stands up to clean up lunch but I jump up and take it from her. "Good good. So does this mean you two are friends again?"

"Uh, I'm not sure. I mean I still push her buttons and she still acts annoyed with me most of the time. But she is also extremely caring and smart. I look forward to the nights where I know I can pop over." My mama gives me a smile as we head into the living room. Knowing this conversation is probably not over I sit down on the couch.

"I mean I am not totally surprised. You and Sage were best friends at one point."

Confused now, "Uh no... I have always been best friends with Stanton and sure while we were little Sage would play with us until she went off on her own."

"Oh no sweetie, when we first moved here you and Sage were almost inseparable. Sure, Stanton was there too but you and Sage were like partners in crime. I was shocked when the dynamic shifted between the three of you." I think back through my memories of when the Calloways entered my life but I always assumed it was me and Stanton with Sage trailing after. Noticing my shock my mama continues, "No matter what has happened in the past, I am really glad that you two are friends again and that Sage is making sure my son is being fed." That thought has me smiling. I spend the rest of the afternoon with my mama as she tells me all about the books she has read lately and the drama at book club.

◆ ◆ ◆

Once I leave my mama's house I head over to meet Stanton at his house. It's going to be weird to not have Miles there with us, he's my little buddy. I wonder how Sage's day has been with her mama and Miles at the aquarium. I pull in front of Stanton's house and notice his car is in the driveway so I hop out and head to the front door. Stanton opens the door after I ring the bell and the first thing I notice is that he looks like he finally got a good night of sleep. "Hey man. How's it going?" Stanton leads me through his house to his loft which he has converted into a theater room.

"Good, I just left my mama's house."

"How is Mama Walker doing? She still going to book club?" I smile because we both know she only goes to watch all the drama that exists between the ladies of Pennystone.

"Yep, still going to bookclub." I chuckle. "I guess the newest drama involved Marybeth's grandson dating Susanna's granddaughter but then they decided to break up and now Marybeth's grandson is trying to date Susanna's granddaughter's best friend. Honestly I could barely follow what my mama was telling me."

Stanton laughs, "the joys of small town living right there. I'm just glad that we aren't the talk of the town anymore. Leave it to the grandkids." He takes a seat and grabs the remote turning on the projector. "Alright what are you up for tonight? Are we thinking action, suspense, or drama?" I will never tell Sage but Stanton also loves a good romance movie. Stanton knows them all after having to watch them with Sage and his dad but still loves a good happy ending. Well at least he did until Jessica.

"It's your night off so you choose." I smile as he starts to scroll with a very serious face.

"Alright let's start with action and see where it takes us. Have you heard of the movie about the F1 racing?" I shake my head. "John told me it was really good. You good with that?"

"Sounds great to me."

We take a break after the movie ends, turns out it was actually really great, and head downstairs in search for some ice cream. "So... how's being neighbors with Sage?" You can tell he is hesitant and unsure of how much to ask. I am equally hesitant on how much to share. Does he really need to know that his best friend has been hanging out with his sister every chance he gets?

"It's been good. We are both busy so we don't see each other much. She let me help her put together some of her furniture and I popped over last night when she had Miles." At the mention of Miles you can tell Stanton misses his little boy and I can't blame him. "He did really great by the way. He is a very happy kid. You may not think so but you are doing a great job as a dad."

"He's my world." Stanton turns to grab the bowls and we start scooping. "Thank you for helping Sage with her furniture. I told her to let me know when it was delivered so I could help but we all know how stubborn and independent she gets."

I laugh as I remember the night I found her lying on the floor looking at the ceiling. "Yeah I think when I offered she must have been desperate." Stanton glances over at me. "And y'all didn't kill each other while putting together furniture?"

"Surprisingly no, she just needed an extra hand. We got it all put together in no time." We grab our bowls and head back upstairs. We watch two more movies and by the time we are done it's later than we expected so Stanton offers me to stay in his guest room. I ignore the disappointment I am feeling that I didn't get to see Sage and Miles again tonight as I climb into the bed.

# CHAPTER 15
# - SAGE

Saturday with my mom and Miles at the aquarium was a lot of fun. We took tons of pictures for Stanton so that he wouldn't feel too left out. I was also able to clarify why Lucas was in my house to my mom. It seemed like she didn't fully believe me when I told her that Lucas and I are just friends. Saying that was weird. We are friends now right?

By the time we got back to my house, had dinner, and did the bedtime routine Miles was out for the night. I was a little disappointed to see that Lucas's house was still dark when I peeked through the blinds before heading to bed myself. Maybe he had plans after seeing his mom. Maybe he had a date. Oo that thought doesn't sit well with me.

It is now Sunday evening and Stanton already rushed over here this morning to get Miles. He was very appreciative of his time off but you could tell he was dying to get Miles back. I have never seen that little boy so excited as he was when he saw his dad at the front door. It honestly made me tear up a bit which of course Stanton teased me about before giving me a big hug and headed back home.

Now? I am sitting in my kitchen making a meal plan for the next week. I return to work tomorrow and while the students don't start until Wednesday, my normal schedule is about to begin again. I am still deciding between stuffed mini bell peppers and pesto chicken sandwiches when I receive a text.

Lucas: Look up.

I look up and out the window to see Lucas standing at his kitchen sink with his whiteboard and a grin. Looks like he is in casual clothes today so he must not have gotten called in.

*You off of baby duty? Sad that I didn't get to say goodbye to Miles before he went back home*

I smile as I grab my whiteboard from next to my sink and write out a response.

*Lucky for you, Miles' dad is your best friend. I am sure you will see him soon*

He tips his head to the side before looking down at his whiteboard. Then he quickly puts it back up to the window.

*Nope not the same. Plus I missed bedtime routine, Miles is the best sleeping buddy*

Smiling because I also missed having his help during the bedtime routine last night I write out a message. I am a little nervous on his response to this one.

*Any dinner plans? We owe each other a movie where neither of us falls asleep.*

Lucas looks at my whiteboard and then looks at what I assume is the clock with a frown before he disappears out of sight. Maybe he has to go to work and that's why he looked at the clock with a frown. He doesn't reappear so I go back to finishing up my menu for the week. Less than two minutes go by when I hear a bark at my back door. Smiling and shaking my head I head to the back door and open it for Lucas and Aspen.

Is there anything Lucas wears that doesn't make him attractive? He is wearing a black henley with some dark jeans. His hair doesn't have as much gel in it as he normally does when he is in uniform but it still looks like he styled it after a shower. And my goodness, he smells heavenly. With the setting sun his green eyes draw you in. To avoid his stare I focus on Aspen. "Fancy meeting you two here." I bend down to greet Aspen before popping back up.

"Don't act so surprised." Lucas laughs. "You're the one that invited us over. Does your offer still stand on dinner?"

"The offer definitely still stands." I try not to show that I am concerned about the fact that he didn't look too happy when I offered. Is he over here just because he is a nice guy and didn't want to reject my offer? Lucas must see my emotions play out on my face, "Hey Blue where did you go just now? Your face just did the same thing it does during the sad part of a movie."

"Oh uh… It is silly but when I asked you if you wanted to come over, you looked away and looked upset. I just hope you know that you don't have to come over if you wanted to stay home or if you have plans. I know you are probably just being a nice guy and didn't want to hurt my feelings. But honestly it's okay if you had other plans and can't do dinner tonight. Totally fine." I ramble and sound anything but fine.

Now I am even more embarrassed and decide it is best to walk to the kitchen. Either way I will have to make dinner right? Either for myself or for both of us. "Okay hold up. First off, thank you for acknowledging that I am a nice guy." Lucas smirks at me and I roll my eyes. I also feel myself starting to smile. "Secondly, you're not wrong." My stomach drops and so does the smile that I was beginning to have. "I did frown when I saw your message but not because I didn't want to come over for dinner and a movie but because I know that you start work tomorrow and I am worried that if we try to squeeze in a movie that you will stay up too late and be tired for work."

"Oh." the smile is coming back.

"Yeah. So here is what we are going to do. We are going to make something delicious and maybe eat out back tonight because it was nice when I was walking over. You are going to tell me all about the aquarium and show me the pictures I have no doubt that you took. Then after we clean up I am going to get out of your hair and you are going to go to bed early to make sure you get the sleep you need for tomorrow." Wow this man really has the whole evening planned out.

"Okay I only have one question." Lucas looks at me like I am exhausting him, "Okay Blue what is your question?"

"Are you also going to tell me what pajamas to wear?" I smirk at him and he rolls his eyes. "I most definitely can if you need me to. But I will probably just put you in the adorable blue pajama set you wore the other night that matches your eyes."

I can feel myself starting to blush. "Okay bossy. But you are helping with dinner tonight and something more difficult than the bread." Looks like Aspen, who was sitting next to Lucas during that exchange, realizes that she could be playing with her toys instead and takes off towards the living room.

"Whatever you need, chef. What's on the menu tonight?" Lucas walks around the corner and sees the menu I was making for the upcoming week. "Sage. If you put your menu out like this just be ready to have me at your door each night."

Laughing I move the menu I was working on to another section of the countertop away from where we will be making food. "Tonight we will be making some orange chicken with rice and roasted veggies. Something simple but yummy."

"You never cease to amaze me in the kitchen." Though a little hesitant he asks, "What can I do?"

"Okay this meal is an easy one and I am going to put you in charge of the rice. In the pantry you will see the box of rice, it is hard to miss and you will just follow the instructions on the package."

"Blue, I am not that naive in the kitchen. I know how to cook a pot of rice." Lucas heads towards the pantry to grab the rice.

"Well excuse me. Before now all I knew you could cook were pancakes." I work around Lucas grabbing the items for the chicken and veggies.

"Well you can add rice to the list." Lucas smirks as he goes to the sink to get water for the rice. "So tell me about the aquarium. I know you have been there before since we went on a class field trip in 5th grade to it. Do you remember that one? You wore a pink romper with daisies all over it because you said the fish love bright colors and flowers. Has it changed since then?" I continue working and tell Lucas about the aquarium as we both do our separate tasks. "The aquarium was a lot of fun. It has actually changed quite a bit since we went when we were kids. They remodeled the stingray zone but obviously Miles was a little too young to participate in it. Then they added in a mosaic exhibit where there are some digital interactives and hands-on activities. Miles loved seeing all of the sea creatures. I honestly thought he was going to lose interest but the whole time he seemed like he was in heaven."

I am running around the kitchen as Lucas is standing by his pot waiting for the rice to absorb the water. "I was disappointed when I had to turn down your mama's offer for me to join. It would have been fun to see Miles' reaction to everything."

"You went and saw your mom right?" I look over my shoulder to Lucas smiling. "Yeah it was good to catch up with her. I used to go over more for dinner before I moved. With work being crazy I haven't been able to see her much." I feel like the worst person in the world because now he is spending time with me for dinners. Lucas must notice the guilt I am going through because he adds "I told her I have been coming over here for dinner and she was more than happy. She told me that it is weird for me to hang out with her all the time." I smile because it sounds like something his mom would say.

"I hate to break it to her but you are already weird." Lucas chuckles and shakes his head. "Well I hope you know that you never *have* to come here for dinner. If you have plans with her" I gulp "or anyone else, you can just let me know that you are busy if I invite you over for dinner on those nights." I remain focused on the food so I don't see his reaction.

"Same goes for you. If we pop over and you hear Aspen barking out back but you are busy, you can just shoo us away."

I spin towards Lucas and smirk. "I would never shoo Aspen away."

"Never Aspen right? But me?"

"Oh most definitely." I try my hardest to not sound too interested in my next question. "After you saw your mom what did you do? I noticed you were still gone when I went to bed."

Oh brother. I now realize that it sounds like I was waiting for him to get back home and watching his house like a creeper.

Lucas laughs a little and smirks. "Were you watching for me Blue?" I roll my eyes and he continues "you didn't need to worry though, I went over to Stanton's after seeing my mom and we ended up staying up too late watching movies so he let me crash in his guest room." I should have known that with his day off Stanton would want to hang out with Lucas. It all makes perfect sense now and I feel a little silly.

"I bet Stanton needed that. I am glad you guys got some time together while he was enjoying his weekend." Stanton and Lucas used to be glued to each other's hip growing up. I know that having Miles changed that for Stanton and I would assume their relationship has shifted slightly. We both go back to finishing up our tasks for dinner. We get ourselves plates and dish up before heading out back. Lucas was right, it feels great out here. The perfect weather to indicate the end of summer.

Once we are settled in a new conversation begins. "So the other night you mentioned that you were envious of Stanton when Miles was born. Do you want to be a dad one day?" You can tell that Lucas is conflicted on what to say next and I can't figure out why. "Uh yeah. I would like to be a dad one day. I hope to be at a point where I am confident that I could be a great one but yeah I would like to experience it one day."

I become more confused by his response. He is great with Miles and I have never seen him have such low confidence in his abilities. "You are a really great uncle to Miles so I have no doubt that you would be just as good with kids of your own one day." I can see that he remains unsure so I continue "I mean no one truly knows how to be a parent until they are a parent."

"Yeah some people just have a better foundation." I tip my head to the side, continuing to be confused. Lucas is one of the best men that I know. He is amazing with Miles and has many traits that would make him a great dad. Before I can get clarification Lucas spins the conversation back on me, "Back when we were younger all you could talk about was being a mom. Is that still something that you want for yourself?"

I smile as I think about my future with my own kiddos running around. I look off into the trees. "Yeah I still really want that. I love being an aunt to Miles more than I thought was possible and I love being surrounded by little people each day at the school. But I desperately want the experience of being a mom one day."

I look over at Lucas and see that he is staring at me, lost in thought. The tension breaks as Aspen lets out a bark as the stick she is playing with springs free. Shaking off the conversation, we head to a safer territory where Lucas tells me all about the most recent police events from around town. I learn that the high school is the hub for all high schooler meetups, that James recently got himself a german shepard and is considering training it as a K9 police dog, Lucas apparently hates when people at the station forget to take home their old food making the refrigerator overfilled, and that he is looking forward to the new school year in hopes that the summertime craziness dies down.

As the sun sets completely, we head back inside with our empty plates. Lucas heads to the sink and I make up a to go container for him and myself so that we both have lunch tomorrow. Once the kitchen is all cleaned up I walk him and Aspen towards the back door. "Thanks for spending your evening with me again."

"Sorry that we have to take a raincheck on the movie. One of these weekends, it will happen I am sure." Lucas looks down at me with a look that I have never seen from him. Unsure of what to do next I use my best coping mechanism, sass and humor. "Well I better go upstairs and get into my jammies before Mr. Bossy comes back out."

Lucas chuckles but nods "Yep, you need to get a good nights sleep before your first day back tomorrow." With that he opens his arms and leans in for a hug. I shock myself as I hug him back with my arms around his waist as his arms come around my shoulders. "Good luck tomorrow Sage. I can't wait to hear about how the first day goes." Lucas breaks the hug and steps back motioning to Aspen to follow.

"Goodnight Lucas, have a great Monday." I smile as Lucas spins around and walks through the yard to his house. Once he gets to his door I shake my head and head inside with a smile still on my face. Yep, Lucas and I are definitely friends.

# CHAPTER 16
## - SAGE

I wake up extra early the next morning to make sure I have everything I need for work and take my time getting ready. Today is a big day. It marks another new chapter. Even though students don't come back for two more days I know today is going to be extra busy with everyone prepping. Plus I have a meeting with the teachers I will be overseeing where they will find out that I will be head teacher this year. I am a little nervous how they will take it since I am still considered one of the youngest ones.

I head downstairs to eat a quick breakfast before I need to finish getting ready and be out the door. As I head into the kitchen I notice a light on in Lucas's kitchen. The light above his sink is on and shining down on his whiteboard.

*Happy First Day back at work. The teachers are going to love you. Go show them how amazing you are.*

My heart swells as I think about how we said goodbye last night. It feels like Lucas and I crossed into a new territory. Looking over at the clock I realize that I will need to hurry if I want to beat the morning rush of traffic. I scarf down a bowl of cereal then run up stairs to brush my teeth and grab my shoes. I'm out the door 5 minutes before I wanted to be and call that a win.

Once I get to the school, I hurry and park heading inside. My nerves about that meeting are now catching up to me and I still have a couple of hours before it. "Good Morning Ms. Calloway. Welcome back!" I look over to see Mrs. Brown smiling back at me and give her a big smile back.

"It's great to see you again Mrs. Brown. Did you enjoy the rest of your summer? Did Gabby have any more dance showcases?" Mrs. Brown beams at my question. "That little girl is so talented. She had another one last weekend. Here let me show you the newest video." She pulls out her phone and we take a couple of minutes to watch her granddaughter. She really does have a talent for dance. "She's amazing Mrs. Brown. I hope she continues to follow that dream."

"Oh I have no doubt she will. She begs her mama to put her in more and more classes because she can't get enough."

"It's definitely paying off for her." I smile at the thought of such a determined little girl. "Well I better head to the classroom and start getting things ready before that meeting today."

"Oh goodness, I am always holding you up from your job. Head on back Sage, I'll buzz you in."

"I love talking with you and make sure to keep me updated on Gabby." She nods and gives me a big smile before I push through the doors to the hallway. There are many doors propped opened as teachers are busy working away getting ready for the students to return. I pop my head into Julie's class to say hello before heading to my own. Now I am feeling really grateful that I came over this summer so I wouldn't be too stressed today. Stepping into my room I decide it was best that we didn't move the desks.

"Sage, you did amazing. Everyone is really excited for you to be heading the K through 3rd grades this year." Julie came up to me right after the meeting. We are walking back to my classroom now to eat some lunch together.

"But I'm a little irked that you didn't tell me sooner and I had to find out when everyone else did." We reach my classroom door and find Michael leaning against the doorframe waiting for us. "Find out what?"

"Our little Sage here is growing up. She is now the head teacher over kindergarten through third grade." I roll my eyes at her considering I'm two years older than her.

"That's amazing Sage. You are an incredible teacher so I'm not shocked." Michael smiles over at me with such admiration that I quickly look away feeling the heat of his stare. I'm not one to take praise without feeling embarrassed. "And she killed it in that meeting. I know all of us teachers were really excited at your ideas and I love that you show that you are here to help us, not judge us."

"Sage would never judge someone. She's way too kind." We step into my classroom and pick out a group of tiny desks. I swing by my desk and pick up my leftovers and heat them up in my microwave. While I'm waiting for my food to be done I think back to what Lucas mentioned about Michael in high school. My food beeps and I go sit down with my friends. "Anyways…" I say with an awkward laugh. "You guys ready for the kids to come back?"

"Yep! My classroom is" *chefs kiss* "perfect. Plus I know that most of my students were in your class last year so they are probably little angels." I am equally as happy as Julie that my little ones from last year are headed to her. It's always comforting when you know they are moving on to good one.

Michael nods, "The library is all ready to go. I ended up reorganizing the mystery section since the last time we talked but now I am feeling really good about it. I also set up a little reading corner." Michael glances at the corner of my classroom, "kind of like the one you have but think bigger and tree house vibes."

"We should have had lunch in there today. It sounds amazing Michael." Michael's cheeks start to get a little pink at the praise so he shifts the conversation. "How's the new house Sage?"

"It's really great and I love it. It was nice to move during the summer so I could take my time setting everything up before worrying about work." I then turn to Julie. "Were you ever able to find a roommate over the summer for your apartment?"

Julie shrugs. "Nah, I decided I like living alone and not worrying about someone judging me when I walk around in my underwear." Michael and I both laugh at that. To have the confidence and personality of Julie. We are just about done eating. "What are your guys plans for the rest of today?"

"I need to make copies for the first week. I forgot how much work the getting to know you week is. I have been collecting magazines all summer for first day collages." See what I mean, Julie is a good one.

"I might just see if Mr. Hanson needs some help." Mr. Hanson is the oldest teacher we have. Michael is sweet for always checking in with him. "What about you Sage?"

"I need to pop over to some teachers and formally introduce myself. Should be a busy afternoon." I start feeling nerves again as I think about those conversation. Julie pops up from her seat. "We will get out of your hair then. You're amazing Sage, teachers are going to love you."

Michael slowly gets up as if he is hesitant to leave. I smile at both of them, "Good luck with Mr. Hanson. I'll see you guys around and if not tomorrow."

I spend the afternoon popping into classrooms and making sure teachers are feeling ready for their new students. Some of them ask me for my opinion which I happily give. I walk out the door that afternoon feeling pleased and excited for the new year.

I pull into my garage and feel pretty exhausted. I am so grateful that I had everything for my students ready before today. I spent all day hopping around to other teachers to see if I could do any last minute things for them. Everyone accepted me so warmly and now I am even more excited for the new position.

I am planning on going straight up stairs, putting on some joggers and one of my old oversized tshirts. Stopping in the kitchen to drop off my dishes from lunch I notice Lucas racing around his kitchen. He is in his uniform and looking like he is about to head to the station. He notices me and stops in his tracks. He gives me a small smile and then holds up a finger. I rinse out my dishes and place them in the dishwasher as I wait for him. He holds up his whiteboard with a sad look on his face.

*Wanted to hear all about your first day. Got called into the station. Gonna miss dinner :(*

I look down before he can see my disappointment and grab my whiteboard.

*It's all good. Today was great! I'll tell you about it next time. Go save lives*

Lucas looks at my board and then at me and gives me a small smile with a look of regret. Then he disappears out of sight. I let out a big sigh and head upstairs to get in my comfy clothes.

Turns out comfy clothes also meant lying on my bed staring up at the ceiling thinking about my day. I start to think about the things I need to get done tomorrow before the kids come back on Wednesday. Grabbing my phone I decide to write out a list so I don't forget and see some texts I must have missed.

Gracie: happy first day back Sage! I bet you were

as amazing as ever.

Brooklyn: yay new school year! Time to show these kids how to use their brains!

I have the greatest best friends. I smile as I send them a thank you and a quick run down of my day. I go to my notes app to make my list. As I am about to finish I get another text.

Lucas: ugh, you were supposed to make pesto chicken sandwiches tonight weren't you?

Me: yep! With some green beans and potato salad.

Lucas: don't do this to me Blue.

Me: sorry Lucas, looks like you are missing out.

I wait two minutes for a response but nothing comes so I head to the kitchen to start preparing dinner. He must be busy on patrol. I decide to put on some music while I cook and eat. It seems weird tonight to be on my own. Too quiet and as I look around my house at the dog bowls by my back door, and Aspen's toys and bed by the couch I realize why I'm feeling pretty lonely. After dinner I throw together a take out container with some of the leftovers and decide to go over to Lucas's and put it in his refrigerator. He gave me a key when I watched Aspen and I know how bummed he was tonight about missing dinner. I'm going to go through the back door since last time he caught me with his camera.

Once I get to the back door I peek in first and see Aspen lying on the couch. She notices me standing at the back door and pops her head up. By the time I am through the door Aspen can barely contain her excitement. I make sure to place the food down on the counter before giving her some love. She is probably confused on why I am here.

I turn on a light in the kitchen and slide the food into Lucas's refrigerator. Once I know it's set, I spin around and take a look at Lucas's house. I have never been inside before and a part of me feels bad for creeping over here uninvited. But then I say to hell with that thought and look around.

Lucas's living room and kitchen are very clean with nothing out of place. I should probably leave now. I came in and dropped off the food, looked around and now I should leave before I invade more of his privacy. But I can't help myself as I stroll down the hallway and peek into the rooms.

His house is smaller than mine with only 3 bedrooms and 2 bathrooms. The first bedroom must be a guest room because it only has a bed in it. Next to that there is what I'm assuming is an office of some type. There is only a single desk and chair. Neither room has any pictures on the walls or any type of decor. That makes me a little sad. I know the last door must be his bedroom. Do I look inside that one?

Ugh. I'm a terrible person. I continue down the hall and walk in. This room is again very minimal. Maybe he just doesn't like to decorate? He has a king size bed centered on a wall between two windows and two matching nightstands. Across from the bed is a matching dresser with a tv on top. Simple but at the same time it fits Lucas.

I refuse to let myself look in his bathroom. That seems like it would be going WAY past the line. I turn to see Aspen sitting at the door of the bedroom staring at me. "Yeah yeah Aspen I know I took a little peek. Don't tell your dad." I pet Aspens head as I head back to the back door. Aspen trails after me and looks very sad when I slide the door shut as I step outside and she remains inside.

Because I am a sucker I open the door back up and let Aspen out for one more bathroom break. Once she has done her business she happily comes back inside and leaps up on the couch. I close the door and lock up before heading back home. I need to get my things together for tomorrow and head to bed. It'll be another busy day of preparing and helping other teachers.

I fall asleep as soon as I hit the pillow without the opportunity to overthink the fact that I just looked around Lucas's entire house like a creep.

# CHAPTER 17
# - LUCAS

I put my phone down with a sigh as James hops back into the car. We are at the gas station filling up before we go out to our designated area to patrol. "Everything okay?" James looks over to me with wariness.

"Yep. Just didn't expect to be on duty tonight." I turn the engine back on and let the engine warm up. It's been raining since this afternoon so luckily we aren't sweating waiting for the AC to kick on. Plus when the sun set an hour ago the temperatures dropped significantly.

"Yeah I know what you mean. It sucks that Officer Johnson got food poisoning and called out tonight. Were you planning on going to dinner over at your mom's house?" James crack open a coca-cola as I pull out of the gas station.

"Uh not exactly. I was hoping to have dinner at Sage's house tonight and see how her first day back at work went." I glance over at James to find him staring at me. I shrug as if I didn't just drop a bomb on him, "but it is what it is you know?"

"Wait wait wait. Did you just say you were planning on having dinner at Sage's house? The same Sage that called you the yummiest bachelor in Pennystone and was complaining to her mom about you? That Sage?" James looks fully shocked by this point. I smile as I think about how far we have come since the 4th of July. "Yep, that's the one and only. Turns out she bought the house next door to mine and now we have become friends."

"Bro, this all has been happening for the past month and you didn't think to fill me in?" I shrug, "I mean it kind of just happened and I am still trying to figure out what it all means. I mean I think we are friends now. But it is still kind of new for us." What I don't tell him is that I haven't told him or anyone much about Sage because I want to keep her to myself.

"Wow. I mean I'm not entirely surprised but y'all were acting like you couldn't stand to even be near each other." James shakes his head and he finally looks towards the road.

"I can hardly believe it too. But Sage has such a great heart. When she talks about her students and especially Miles, you can tell she has such a passion." I continue driving until we find a place to park near the high school. "She is also an amazing cook." James smiles and shakes his head, "Ah, so you aren't living off of frozen meals or your mom's cooking anymore?"

I laugh "I mean there are still some nights where our timelines don't cross but I have been eating really well lately. Plus Aspen loves it over at her house. She may like Sage better than me now."

"Well I mean anyone would probably like Sage better than you." I roll my eyes and he continues, "I am glad you two live next door to each other. It probably feels less lonely when you have a friend that you can pop in on and steal their food." I notice that James gets a distant look in his eyes. "How are you liking your new place? How is the K9 training going?" James recently moved into a house close to the station in a neighborhood where the houses were built back in the 1960s. He has been remodeling and updating his home. He says staying busy helps. He also got himself a German Shepard and has been taking him to K9 training to become registered to take with us on patrol.

James smiles, "The house is good. It is a lot of work to renovate and restore a historical house but it keeps my mind from drifting." I am sure James has some trauma from his deployments, another reason he bought a dog. "I have completed both bathrooms so far which seemed like a disaster in the beginning but turned out good. I need to tackle the kitchen but since we have been so busy I am worried I won't have enough time to do it in one stent and haven't decided on if I want to live without a kitchen yet." I nod as I try to imagine life without the kitchen which causes me to smile because I could probably live without mine since I am constantly using Sage's.

"The K9 training is going well. Trigger seems to be enjoying it and learning really fast. I am hoping that he passes all his requirements within the next couple of weeks so that we can have him with us full time." We radar a car going 11 over the speed limit. Not worth our time. "I am really glad you convinced me to get him. He has helped me quite a bit with my anxiety."

James opened up to me one day about having flashbacks at night from his time in Afghanistan. He told me that he would feel wound up the next morning and couldn't shake his anxiety. I told him that he needed to go meet with Stanton about his PTSD but also that a dog could help him feel less alone when he is struggling and be a constant in his life. I explained that when I got Aspen she helped me with my own struggles. James ended up researching quite a bit before getting Trigger to make sure that we could get him K9 certified to keep him with us at all times but since he has gotten him, James seems to be sleeping better.

"I am really excited to have Trigger with us all the time. He is a super intelligent dog. He is going to be a huge asset but it will also be nice to have a buddy along for the ride." This thought makes me miss Aspen. I hope she is doing okay at home right now. I should have asked Sage to take her tonight but I didn't want to add to her stress.

Before I get the chance to change my mind and text Sage about Aspen, our radio goes off. "We have a 10-50F on County Road 45, mile marker 231. Again we have a 10-50F on County Road 45, mile marker 231. Officers Sandoval and Darrell are already at the scene, requesting backup." 10-50F? A car crash resulting in a fatality. James grabs the radio from the dash, "Officers Walker and Miller are enroute." I flip on the lights and siren and head towards County Road 45.

We arrive to the scene right as the ambulances are starting to load up. Lucky for everyone the rain has finally stopped. We step out of the patrol car and make our way to Officer Darrell who is next to a Honda SUV that is completely crunched. "What do we have tonight?"

Officer Darrell nods to us before continuing, "The accident happened as the driver, Mr. Brandon Reynolds hit a patch of water causing the car to hydroplane. Mr. Reynolds lost control of the car which sent the car sliding to the ditch. It would have been a straight shot except they were going the speed limit of 55 miles per hour and hit a divot in the road causing the car to flip twice before landing on its side in the ditch."

James looks at the car with concern, "How

many people were in the vehicle?" We both know that he is also asking the status of each passenger. "There were three people in the vehicle at the time of the crash. Mr. Reynolds's wife, Lauren, was in the passenger seat and their daughter was in the back seat, thankfully in her carseat. Mrs. Reynolds was dead when we arrived. It looked like she may have been turning in her seat to check on her daughter when the crash occurred. Mr. Reynolds is currently being loaded into ambulance one, the paramedics believe he may have cracked ribs and has internal bleeding so they are rushing to get him to Northern Georgia Medical Center Lumpkin"

My gut sinks. That is at least a 45 minute drive even with sirens. Pennystone has a hospital but it is not equipped for high level trauma. "The daughter is being loaded into ambulance two to follow after them. She may have a slight concussion and will need stitches on her arm due a cut from when the window shattered but she appears to be okay." Thank goodness for that. Now we pray that her only remaining parent survives the night. Swallowing the lump on my throat, "Is the coroner already on the way for Mrs. Reynolds?"

"Yes, he should be here in the next 10 minutes." Officer Darrell looks towards the car with grief in his eyes. I get it. It never gets easier. "Alright, where is Officer Sandoval now?"

Officer Darrell tips his head towards the

ambulance. "The little girl is pretty scared. She knows her mom is already dead and is worried about her dad. She was really upset that she couldn't go in the same ambulance as her dad. Officer Sandoval was able to talk to her and calm her down but now the little girl refuses to let her leave her side." Thank goodness for the heart of Officer Sandoval, she always connects with the kids the best.

I can see the little girl is sitting up which is a good sign but you can tell she is shocked as she looks towards Officer Sandoval each time the paramedics ask her a question. "It looks like they are about to roll out. You go ahead and join your partner in the ambulance with the little girl. Since we are dealing with a minor, we will need someone with her at all times until we know more about her dad and extended family. I am assuming the little girl will want that someone to be Officer Sandoval."

Officer Darrell nods, "You got it, I will head over there now and let them know we are good to go. Are you two good finishing everything up here?" James looks from what is left of the car and back to us, "Yep. We have it handled just go make sure that little girl is okay. No one deserves to watch as they lose their mom. Let's start praying that the dad makes it."

Officer Darrell gives a quick and grim nod before heading off to the ambulance to fill his partner in. Within minutes they pull off onto the road to catch up to the other ambulance.

James and I stay at the scene for the next couple of hours while the coroner collects Mrs. Reynolds, we fill out the necessary paperwork, watch as the tow truck hauls off the car to the dumpster, and make sure to clean up any leftover glass and other pieces of the car. We don't say anything other than what is necessary as there is a feeling of grief settled over the area. Once the scene looks like nothing happened besides the two skid marks on the road, we head back to the station.

Back at the station I beeline it to our chief's office. I give a knock at her open door and she looks up, "Hey Lucas, come on in." Chief Harrington is on a first name basis with everyone. She says it contributes to the culture she is building here at the station. She wants us to know that we can always come to her and that the station is a safe space for anyone. But you get her in the field and she becomes the most serious and by the book detective I have ever seen.

"Hey Chief, sorry to bother you so late" By the time we got back to the station it was close to 10pm. "I am surprised you aren't at home with the family." Chief Harrington's husband must be home with their 3 little kids.

"I am getting close to leaving. My husband

may kill me but I was closing up a case and wanted to get all the paperwork in so that I can take the kids shopping tomorrow before they go back to school." She smiles as she thinks about her two sons and daughter. Her sons are in 5th and 3rd grade with her daughter starting kindergarten this year. If she is lucky she will have Sage as a teacher.

"I don't want to hold you here too long. I just had a quick question. Have you heard the status of Mr. Reynolds and his daughter?" She gives me a sad smile, "I heard about the accident. It sounds like it was awful. I'm sorry Lucas but I haven't heard an update. But sometimes no update is a good update. I am sure Officer Sandoval and Officer Darrell will provide one as soon as they know anything." She looks over at me and sees James leaning in the doorway.

"You two should go home and get some sleep. I will make sure if I hear anything you are the first ones I contact." I stand as she does, "Yes ma'am. Thank you and enjoy the rest of your night and shopping with the kids."

James and I walk out to our cars in silence. Something about this one is hitting differently. Maybe its the risk that the little girl may lose both parents tonight. We say our goodbyes and head home. When I pull into the house I know that I need to get upstairs to change and shower. Aspen greets me at the front door and I am shocked when she doesn't act like she needs to go out to go to the bathroom. Too tired to try to convince her I let her follow me through the house.

Before I make it to the hallway towards my room my stomach tells me that I need to stop at the kitchen first. James and I didn't get a chance to eat tonight after being called to the accident. Pulling open the refrigerator to see my options, I see one of Sage's tupperwares with a note on it.

*Hope the yummiest bachelor in Pennystone saved some lives tonight. I know how much you were wanting to try this meal and while it is better fresh, you'll just have to reheat it and enjoy.*

I smile as I remove the note and see a pesto chicken sandwich, a side of green beans, and a side of potato salad in the container. At that moment my stomach lets out a large growl signaling that it is very satisfied with our dinner option tonight. I eat one of the best sandwiches of my life and then head to my bedroom. While getting ready for bed, I try not to think about the life I couldn't save tonight and pray that it was only one.

# CHAPTER 18
# - SAGE

I wake up excited for another day at work. I am really enjoying being the department head and building relationships with the other teachers. Right when I am about to leave my house I realize that I haven't checked the mail in a while so I walk out to my front yard and snag it before heading back inside. Most of it is ads that I am sure all the new homeowners are getting but I do notice one addressed to me without a return address. Inside is a card all about new beginnings and finding the rainbow after the storm. That isn't what sticks out to me, it's the handwritten message inside.

GOOD LUCK ON THE NEW SCHOOL YEAR. I
HAVE NO DOUBT THE STUDENTS WILL LOVE
YOU. IT IS IMPOSSIBLE NOT TO LOVE YOU. -M

I roll my eyes and throw it down on the entry table. I don't have time for Matt this morning. I need to get to work and do the job that I love. It's not my fault he realized what he had after he lost it. I shove the card out of my mind, grab my keys, and head to the school.

My day goes exactly how I expected it to. I spent about 30 minutes in my room double checking my lessons for the next day before I went off to talk to the other teachers and make sure they have everything they need. Everyone seems ready and excited for tomorrow. The beginning of the year brings such an exciting vibe to the school.

For lunch today the administration team provided us with sub sandwiches and chips. Fact of the day, teachers love free food. Julie, Michael, and I decided to eat our lunch in the library so we could check out the "treehouse" reading corner. It turned out great and Michael is really excited for the kids to see it. I am now just about to finish labeling the backpack cubbies with my new students name when Julie pops into my classroom. "Hey, have you checked your email lately?" Julie looks concerned and anxious and my guard immediately goes up.

"I haven't in a while, why? Is something wrong?" Julie stops chewing on her thumb nail and drops her hand. "I am not sure. We both got an email from Mrs. Applewood that she wants us both to come by her office when we get a minute." My mind starts racing on reasons why she would want to talk to the two of us. "Hmm that is a little weird. Do you want to head there now?"

"Yeah let's get it over with. I just keep thinking that it has to be about me and since you're now my department head she needs you in there while she yells at me." We leave my classroom and make our way to the front of the school.

"Come on Julie, she is definitely not going to yell at you. You are one of the best teachers here. There is a reason I requested my students from last year to transition up to you." That finally has Julie cracking a smile and you can see her relax a tiny bit. When we get to Mrs. Applewood's office, her door is open so I poke my head in. "Hey Mrs. Applewood?"

"Oh hey Sage, you must have gotten my email. Did you bring Julie with you?"

"Here." Julie steps up next to me and raises her hand. Poor girl really must be nervous and the next thing Mrs. Applewood says doesn't help. "Can you two come in and shut the door?" We both step in and I shut the door before we take a seat in the two chairs opposite of Mrs. Applewood's desk. She becomes very serious and her face shifts to one of deep sadness. "I received some news about one of our students this morning. Sage, do you remember Parker Reynolds from your class last year?"

"Yes ma'am. She was one of my top students and cute as a button." She really was one of the best and was an incredible reader at such a young age. "Is she okay?"

"Well there was a car accident." My stomach drops and my mind goes to the worst case scenario. "She was in the car with her parents when the car hydroplaned from water on the road causing the crash. Her mother died on impact and her father ended up dying at the hospital the next day. Parker survived the crash with a mild concussion and stitches in her arm from the glass. Thankfully she was in her carseat." Mrs. Applewood pauses allowing us both to process what we were just told. Julie remains quiet and you can see the shock on her face. Poor Parker. She must feel so alone right now. With that thought in mind, I ask my first of many questions. "Where is Parker now?"

"She is staying with Mrs. Adams and her family right now. She has a daughter, Lola, who is a good friend to Parker and they offered to take her in for a couple of days." I also had Lola in my class last year and I am not surprised that is where she is staying. For now at least.

"What will happen to Parker? Does she have any family like grandparents or aunts and uncles that will take her?" Mrs. Applewood looks down for a second then back up with grief on her face. "Parker doesn't have any living grandparents or extended family. The only person they connected so far was a distant uncle on her mother's side but they haven't been able to reach him yet. Since there is no family that is stepping in, Parker will more than likely end up in the foster system."

I am at a loss for words at this point. Not only did this little girl see her mom die, she then had to witness her dad dying at the hospital. Now she is staying at a friend's house probably scared and alone with no family to come take care of her. Mrs. Applewood turns to Julie at this point seeing that I am shocked and out of questions. "Julie, I called you in here as well because Parker is going to be in your class this year. There is a chance that when she is placed in foster care that she could end up being relocated somewhere else. I would like you to keep an eye on her and make sure to keep her school counselor updated."

Oh goodness, now there is a chance she has to leave all her friends to go live with strangers? "Yes of course Mrs. Applewood. I will make sure to keep my eye on Parker. My heart breaks for her." Julie looks like she is almost about to be in tears and if she starts, there is no way I hold it together.

"Thank you. I know between the both of you, she will be taken care of here at school. Then we just have to wait to see what happens and do our best to help her transition to wherever she goes." I am still in shock as Julie and I both stand up and say our goodbyes to Mrs. Applewood. I make sure that everything is set for tomorrow morning and head to my car to go home for the day. My day started out so smooth and now I feel like I am in a fog.

◆ ◆ ◆

I remain in a fog the rest of the afternoon. When I got home I went upstairs and put on comfy clothes and tried to watch one of my favorite movies to distract myself but my mind kept wandering to Parker's situation.

It's not fair. She shouldn't have to be forced to move away. She already lost her parents, she shouldn't have to lose everything she knows. Her parents were really great ones too. They always came to all the events and were the first ones to arrive on parent teacher conference nights. You could tell they loved Parker with all that they had. It's not fair that she lost that type of love at such a young age.

I walk over to the kitchen sink to wash my hands so that I can prepare dinner. I am not really in the mood but know I need to eat something. Tomorrow is still a big day. I look up to see Lucas across the way looking concerned. He holds up his whiteboard.

*You okay Blue? You look upset.*

I try to smile because it is sweet that he is concerned but it probably isn't even noticeable. I write him back.

*Long day with a lot on my mind. Feels like I am in a fog. Not sure if I will be great company but I was just about to make some dinner.*

Lucas looks at the board, reads it, then looks back to me. My emotions must be all over my face because he shakes his head and holds up a finger before disappearing from my view.

Less than five minutes later I hear a knock on the back door. I make my way over and feel myself smiling slightly as I see Lucas and Aspen. Lucas is casual again tonight with some sweatpants and a tshirt. You know the type of sweatpants that sit low on the hips and you just know that if he reaches up to grab something, you'll get a peek of some abs. Hmm, maybe we need to use the cups from the top shelf tonight.

Opening the door I make sure to greet Aspen before she takes off to my couch. Apparently she just wants to snuggle on the couch tonight. Me too girl, me too. I glance back at Lucas right before he suffocates me with a hug. I let myself take a deep breath and wrap my arms around him.

When we separate he looks down at me. "When you held up your last message it looked like you needed a hug. I came as quickly as I could but Aspen was asleep and couldn't figure out my urgency." I would normally tease him about him being impatient but I don't feel like it tonight.

Tonight things are too heavy. "Thanks Lucas, I did need a hug and maybe some Aspen snuggles in a little bit." We step inside and I head towards the kitchen.

"Alright so tonight the plan was blackened salmon with some green beans and rice. Does that sound okay?" I turn back to look at Lucas for his answer and find him shaking his head.

"Not tonight Blue." I let out a big sigh, today is hard. "Alright, uh let's see what else I had planned for this week." I head over to the refrigerator to look at the menu I have written on the side but Lucas stops me before I get there by grabbing my wrist and spinning me to him. "No Sage. I meant you aren't cooking tonight. You had a long day and look exhausted. I ordered pizza before coming over and it should be here in about 15 minutes."

I feel such a relief at the thought of not having to cook that I could cry. Plus pizza is my favorite. "You keep treating me this way and I may just keep you around." He rolls his eyes and that finally gets a smile out of me. "Alright while we wait for the pizza, you are going to go into the living room and snuggle Aspen while you finish that movie you apparently paused earlier. I am going to get a salad and drinks ready for us." Lucas looks like he will throw me on the couch himself if I argue with him right now.

"Mr. Bossy is back tonight I see." But I still do what he says and walk over to join Aspen on the couch. Aspen and I are enjoying the movie when the doorbell rings about 10 minutes later.

"Don't get up! I got it!" I hear Lucas yell from the kitchen before he jogs over to the door. He happily takes the two pizzas and I am assuming a box of breadsticks from the delivery guy before giving him some cash as a tip and saying thank you. He shuts the door and turns towards me but in the process he notices something on my entry table. "What the hell is this?"

Oh brother. Here we go. I forgot about that dang card from Matt that I opened this morning. "Oh that. I checked the mail this morning before work and saw that. I was running out the door so I didn't have time to burn it." I hop up from the couch and head to the kitchen. The pizza smells amazing and it is from my favorite restaurant.

"Blue. Is this the only thing you have gotten since the basket?" Lucas follows me into the kitchen where he puts the pizzas on the counter before turning to me and crossing his arms.

"Yes Lucas. I was honestly surprised when I got that card. But we already knew he knew my address so it can't be that shocking." I walk over to the cabinet and grab each of us a plate.

"I don't like that he continues to do this." You can see the fire in Lucas's eyes at this point. I start dishing up. Honestly this conversation is not going to ruin my time with this pizza. "Yeah but what can we do, you know? He is just obviously still upset because he missed an opportunity of a lifetime."

"Damn straight he did Blue." Lucas grabs a plate to dish up and I sigh in relief that this isn't going to become a bigger thing than it needs to be. "But if he continues to do this type of stuff I can help you file a restraining order." Hmm, that's not a terrible idea but seems like a lot of unnecessary work. "I promise I will keep it in mind. At some point he will get bored and forget about me."

I spin towards the table and I swear I hear him say "there's no forgetting you Blue." but it was too quiet that I am not sure.

Once we are sitting and diving into the pizza Lucas speaks up again. "Okay so tell me about being back at school and why you look like you are carrying the weight of the world on your shoulders tonight."

Sighing I start with the positives, "Being back has been really good. At the end of last year I was asked to become the department head over kindergarten through third grade. This means that I oversee the teachers in that section and make sure they have all the support they need. I am pretty much their go to person if they need anything. And turns out I love it. I have been able to connect with so many teachers and they are really taking what I am offering in stride."

Lucas smiles at me "that's really great Sage. I am not shocked you are killing it as you do with everything." I shake my head but continue "I really hope it continues to go as great as it has so far." Lucas is listening so intently that I hesitate before continuing, "Today Mrs. Applewood pulled me and my friend Julie into her office. One of my students from last year, and now Julie's current student this year is in the foster care system and we found out that she may have to move away since the state is in charge of her placement. She would have to leave all her friends behind. It just doesn't seem fair for this little girl. She was one of my best students and is so bright. One of the happiest kids too and I fear that she is going to lose that sparkle."

You can tell that Lucas is processing and going through all the potential ways to fix it. Lucas is a major fixer if you didn't notice by now. Before he can give out ideas I tell him mine. "I think I might want to foster her." Lucas's jaw drops and it is obvious that he did not think of that solution. "You want to foster the little girl?"

I nod with a smile, "Yeah I think I do. I know it probably sounds crazy and I don't even know how that would work since I am not registered right now to be a foster parent. But if I could, that would mean she wouldn't have to leave the town she was born in and all her friends." I pause for a second. "Do you think that is a crazy idea? I have been thinking about it all afternoon but I'm not sure if I am being crazy."

Lucas rubs a hand down his jaw. It is

obvious that he didn't shave this morning and is sporting a very handsome five o'clock shadow look tonight. It distracts me momentarily until his response brings me back. "It does sound a little crazy, Sage. But it also sounds like you truly care about this little girl and she would be lucky to have you in her life." He smiles at me before continuing, "but I would really think about it before you offer anything. This is a life changing decision for both you and her."

Nodding, I know he is right. This would change everything. We clean up dinner and Lucas watches the end of the movie with me. It is one he said he has already seen so he didn't mind not starting over. As we finish the movie Lucas must have noticed me yawning away. "Alright Blue, time for me to get out of your hair so you can get some sleep. You have a big day tomorrow with the kids coming back." I nod in agreement and the three of us walk to the backdoor.

"Thank you for getting me pizza tonight Lucas and for being here." I look up at him as he looks down. "You're welcome. I hope you know just how amazing you are. The fact that you are even considering taking in that little girl shows how much of a heart of gold you have." Unsure how to take that compliment I feel myself blush and look away.

Lucas pulls me into a hug that I melt into. He breaks away too soon. "Goodnight. Tomorrow is going to be amazing. Tomorrow you get to change lives." With that he calls for Aspen and strides across his yard. He looks back over his shoulder when he gets to his back door and gives a wave m. I wave back and step inside.

As I am getting ready for bed I think over the possibility of taking in Parker. I know I shouldn't jump the gun but I am now thinking about which bedroom I think she would like better and all the things I would need to buy to make it perfect. Lucas was right, tomorrow I am going to change lives, including my own.

# CHAPTER 19
## - SAGE

The next day goes by in a blink of an eye. The first day is always an adventure in kindergarten. I only had 3 students this year cry when their moms dropped them off, so that was an improvement from last year. I have a great bunch this year including Chief Harrington's daughter Jasmine who is such a little spitfire and will be running this class by the end of the year and Susie Myers's granddaughter Anne who loves to read any chance she gets.

I feel like I haven't stopped running around all day. At lunch I ate as fast as I could then stopped by some of my teachers rooms to check in. They all seemed like they were really enjoying their day and their new classes. We have about 20 minutes left with the students and we are currently outside for recess before we go back inside to get their backpacks for pickup. I'm standing next to Julie as we watch the kids play. "How has Parker been today?" Julie glances over at me and then back at the playground.

"She is such a sweet kid. I almost wanted to cry when I saw her see all the other moms drop off their kids. You could tell she was sad but she lifted her chin, found her backpack cubby, and went straight to the morning mat to sit with Lola." Julie shakes her head. "I wish it was different for her but she is resilient." We both smile as we see Parker, Lola, and Amanda race by towards the swings giggling. I pull out my phone and decide to pull the trigger and send the email I have been thinking about all day to Mrs. Applewood to see if she can meet with me after school today.

With the Georgia clouds rolling in we usher our students back inside. Once inside, all the kids grab their backpacks and line up by the door to walk to the buses or pickup line. Once everyone is ready to go, I get a notification on my phone from my email. Mrs. Applewood is free after school. I take a deep breath and remind myself to focus on making sure these kids get home safely before worrying about how that meeting will go.

As soon as all of my students were either on a bus or in their parent's car safely, I head to Mrs. Applewood's office. I knock on the door and hear "come on in". Stepping inside, I close the door behind me and take a seat. She looks at me with a nervous look. "Please tell me that you aren't here to tell me that you won't head your department. You are doing amazing and the teachers have spoken so highly of you."

I smile at the praise, "oh no that's not why I am here. I love the position." She nods her head with a smile. "Thank goodness. What can I do for you then Sage?" I pause and hesitate before continuing. Am I really about to do this?"I was wondering if I could talk to you and Parker's social worker about me becoming her foster parent."

Mrs. Applewood takes a minute to process then a big smile grows. "I believe her social worker is actually here today. Let me see if we can get him in here." She then calls her secretary and finds out that the social worker is still here and calls him in to join us. When the social worker comes in, I stand up to shake his hand. "Hello, I'm Sage Calloway. It's nice to meet you."

He seems a little surprised and confused but shakes my hand regardless. "Hello I am Mitchell Stevens. I'm assuming you know that I am Parker's social worker since you called me in here." With that he turns to Mrs. Applewood, "it's great to see you again ma'am."

"Thank you for coming down, Mitchell. Let's sit." We both sit in the seats opposite of her desk. And Mrs. Applewood turns to me urging me to start the conversation. I turn to Mitchell and explain. "Okay so I was Parker's kindergarten teacher last year. I knew Mr. and Mrs. Reynolds and am devastated for Parker. From what I know, she doesn't have any extended family that has stepped up to take her in and she may end up in the foster system."

"That's correct. Unfortunately this happens more often than people think." You can tell that Mitchell hates that part of his job. I take a deep breath before continuing, "well I am worried that if that happens she will be taken away from the town she knows and the friends and people she knows here. She already lost so much." Mitchell nods but looks confused so I continue. "I was hoping you could tell me if it would be possible for me to foster her and if so, how we start that process."

It seems like Mitchell has finally connected the dots on why I asked to speak to him. He looks to Mrs. Applewood to confirm that it's real, who smiles and nods. He then turns back to me with a smile.

"Alright so I'm assuming you are not currently approved to be a foster parent." I shake my head. "No sir."

"That's okay. What I am thinking we do is I can take your information and have you complete an application for temporary status. This will give you the ability to receive approval to take care of Parker while you are working through the process of getting fully approved."

I am taking it all in as he continues, "Since

you are employed by the state already for the school, they already have the background check and the fingerprint clearance which will make gaining temporary clearance easier and quicker. Then to obtain full approval you would need to complete an orientation, complete the IMPACT Family Centered Practice training, and complete a home visit. After those are all completed, you will transition from a temporary foster parent to a permanent foster parent with the ability to adopt."

Wow this is really happening. Mitchell must see the emotions hit my face as he takes in a breath. "Sage, this is a lot to process and can be a huge commitment. You can take some time to think about it if you need to. No one will judge you if you decide it is too much." The thing is, it all makes perfect sense and with each step he told me, I was thinking about how this could really happen.

"I have thought about it. I know this may seem rash or impulsive but I really do feel like I need to do this for Parker." He smiles at me and I glance over to Mrs. Applewood who has a very proud look on her face. I turn back to Mitchell. "Okay so let's say we do the application today. How quickly would it go through before I would know if I am approved for that temporary status?"

"It really just depends. Unfortunately I can't give a definite timeline since we are working with the government and you know how that is." I do, it took me eight weeks for my teaching certificate to be mailed to me back when I graduated. "But since Parker is in what we consider emergency placement, I may be able to push things along quicker. And again since you already have the majority of the information filed with the state already, there is a chance it goes very quickly. Best case scenario, you are looking at taking Parker home on Friday after school." This Friday? That is two days from now. Wow I am going to need to go shopping asap if I want her room ready by then.

"I do have one more question. Once we get the approval, could we talk with Parker to see if she wants to come stay with me? I don't want to make that decision for her." Mitchell smiles, "Yes we can talk to Parker about her options, you being one of them, and make sure she feels comfortable. I am assuming that if you had her as a student that you two already have a good relationship so I don't see it going poorly."

I want to make sure Parker has a say in where she ends up going. While I don't think she will want to leave Pennystone, she also deserves the right to choose where she is most comfortable. I just hope that it's with me. "Alright that sounds like a plan. Parker shouldn't have to live in limbo. Do you have the application with you by chance? Can we start it right now?"

For the next hour, Mitchell and I work on the application and get everything sent over to the state. He promises he will be in contact with me as soon as he hears anything. I head to my classroom to grab my bag and then I am out the door. As I get in my car and drive home I think about all the things I need to do before Parker comes. I am really doing this.

I don't get home until close to 5pm after spending the afternoon at the school filling out the application. I am pulling up to the house right when Lucas is shutting his garage door. I get giddy as I think about telling him about what just happened. Once I am parked in my garage, I quickly run inside and go straight to the kitchen window. Happily surprised to find Lucas already standing there, I write out a message on my whiteboard.

*I have BIG news. Come over?*

He smiles and nods his head. I quickly run upstairs to change into some comfier clothes and use the bathroom real quick. Once I come back down, I head to the back door and see Lucas out back playing fetch with Aspen and a stick she found. Lucas must have also taken a minute to change clothes as he is no longer in his uniform but some basketball shorts and a tshirt with the logo of his favorite football team. He turns when he hears the door open. His eyes meet mine and he smiles. "Hey Blue. What's the big news?"

"I applied to foster that little girl today." I see as his eyes widen.

"You decided to move forward with it." He throws the stick for Aspen who takes off running after it. "That's amazing Sage. You are going to bless that little girl's life more than you can even understand." My knees get a little wobbly as I take in his smile.

"Well once I get the green light, we are going to ask her if she wants to come live here. I don't want to take away her right to choose anymore than it already is. But yeah, I'm really doing it." I smile back at him and Aspen finally loses interest in her stick and notices me. "Hey beautiful girl. How about we go inside and get you some water. It's pretty sticky out here and some rain clouds are starting to roll in." I give Aspen a good petting before stepping inside with Lucas following close behind me.

I go to pick up Aspens water bowl but Lucas grabs it first. I follow him into the kitchen as he fills it up and puts it back down for Aspen. "So what is the process now? I'm assuming you can't just tell someone you want a kid and you get the kid. We have social workers come to the station at times but I have never asked about what it takes to be a foster parent."

Lucas sits down on a barstool at the island while I head to the refrigerator to pull out supplies for dinner. I fill him in on what I was told by the social worker this afternoon while I make dinner. "Wow, so since you already have your background check and fingerprints in the system with the state, he thinks it could be processed quickly?" We head to the kitchen table to eat and Aspen follows, laying at our feet.

"Yeah isn't that crazy? He told me that best case scenario I could be bringing her home on Friday with me." I smile as I think about how amazing that would be. Parker deserves a home where she knows she is going to stay for a while.

"Yeah, definitely crazy. Do you have a room ready for her just in case it does happen that fast?" Lucas is diving into the ham and cheese pinwheels with a veggie medley. I keep that noted for future meals. "I am thinking I will put her in the guest room closest to me. The same one that we put Miles in. I just need to go to the store and get a cute bedspread and matching pillows. I don't want to decorate it until she is here so she can choose for herself what it looks like but I want to make sure it's enough so that she knows I'm excited." I am lost in thought for a minute thinking about how I will definitely let her paint if she wants, put things on the wall, and may even convince Lucas to build us a small fort in the corner as a reading nook.

Lucas pulls me back into the conversation, "Are you free tomorrow after school? We could go and look for that stuff and maybe get ideas on

what else she could do so she has some options."
My heart. I love that he wants to be part of
this and make Parker feel welcomed here."I was
actually thinking the same thing. Especially if
she comes on Friday, I need to have everything
ready to go. Are you off tomorrow?"

"I have to work the morning shift so I should
be home by 3pm. I know you typically get
home around 3:30pm so I'll make sure to be
ready to go for whenever you want to head
out." Lucas finishes his plate and then goes back
for seconds. Alright this meal is definitely a
keeper. "You sound a little creepy knowing my
entire schedule." I say loudly as he goes into the
kitchen. He comes back a minute later and rolls
his eyes at me.

"Sage, you literally leave for work and get
home at the same time every single day." I try
to hide my smile, "yeah sure that's what it is." I
swear I see a little pink spreading to his cheeks
but save him when I redirect the conversation.
"How was your day? Has it slowed down with
school back in?"

We talk about my life a lot and I have noticed
that Lucas doesn't bring up his much unless I
ask. The thing is I find myself desperate for more.
I want to know about his life and how he has
become the man that he is. "It definitely has
slowed down since summer ended. Which is nice
because if we are slow we can go over and work
with James's dog, Trigger, with his K9 training.

He should be certified within the next few weeks then we will have him wherever we go." Lucas grabs our empty plates and heads to the kitchen. I follow behind him.

"How long have you and James been partners?" I begin to pack up leftovers for both of us to have lunch tomorrow while Lucas does the dishes, like usual. "James moved to Pennystone a little over a year ago. When he joined our force my previous partner had left to stay home with her kids so it was an easy spot to fill. I am pretty lucky that the timing worked out. I would trust him with my life." My stomach drops at the thought of the possible danger that James and Lucas could be involved in. I know it is part of the job but that doesn't make it easier for the people they leave at home.

"I'm glad you have James. He seems like a really great guy." I paused and then continue. "He has to be pretty amazing to put up with you all day every day."

Lucas whips his head around from the sink to glare at me. I laugh as I walk to the fridge. "You wound me." He dramatically puts his hand over his heart. I roll my eyes and he laughs as he finishes up the dishes.

We head to the living room and sit on the couch next to Aspen. "So when we were growing up you always said you wanted to make it to the NFL, did that change once your dad died?" I can feel Lucas tense up and I glance down at my lap not knowing if I said something that upset him. Maybe bringing up his old dreams was a bad idea.

Lucas finally answers after a minute, not looking directly at me. "Growing up I loved football but when I was preparing for college, I realized the joy I had for playing was gone so my mindset for my future changed." He pauses and looks like he is contemplating how much more he wants to tell me. "I became a cop because I was tired of seeing injustice happen. I thought that if I could even help one person, it would be worth it." I can tell that he is holding back but I choose not to push too hard. "Do you feel like you have been able to do that? Help at least one person." I continue to be timid as I can tell he is slightly uncomfortable.

"I like to think I have but it's also hard when there are people I am not able to help or save." Lucas looks up at me now and I can see the emotion and pain in his eyes. "You are a great cop Lucas. I know the citizens of Pennystone really appreciate your service."

Lucas gives me a small hesitant smile. "Thanks Blue." Not sure how to handle this side of Lucas, I chicken out and shift the conversation. "Okay so how long are you hanging out tonight? I am planning on watching a girlie show so if you choose to stay, just warning you may hate it."

Lucas laughs and reminds me of his guilty pleasure. "Sage, you remember that I watch romcoms in my free time right?" I laughed, "Alright fair. Looks like you are watching The Bachelorette with me tonight." I turn on the TV to load it up.

"Wait, is this the hometown episode or is there one more episode before then?" My jaw drops as I look over at Lucas. He starts laughing. "I may have watched a season or two with my mama. She also loves this show. I mean it's not terrible but the people never stay together which is always disappointing after all that time invested." I smile as I press play. "That's fair but it still sucks me in every season."

Lucas jumps up off the couch and heads towards the hallway by the kitchen. "I am going to go to the bathroom real quick before we start, but go ahead and start it without me." I pause the episode until I can hear him coming back so he doesn't miss anything. When he gets back he sits right next to me. Typically when we sit on my sectional, we have quite a bit of space between us but for some reason when he came back he chose to sit directly next to me. I can feel the heat from his body and feel my heartbeat rise.

To distract myself I decide to update Lucas on the season, "Okay so this season Katherine is down to her final 6 guys. So it is the week before hometowns. Now I feel like Johnny and Aydan are obvious front runners and could be the final two honestly. Then you have Fredrick who I think she will friendzone this episode for sure.

He is just not at the same level as the other guys."

Lucas looks at me amused and we continue watching the episode. By the end you can tell we are both tired and need to head to bed soon. About half way through the episode my head ended up dropping to rest on his shoulder and he never said anything about it or shook me off so that is where it stayed.

"See I knew it! Poor Fredrick got his heart broken. She was not going to get there with him." I look up at Lucas and he looks down at me still on his shoulder. At this moment I realize how close our faces are. I sit up quickly and hope that it wasn't too awkward. I get a big yawn that makes my eyes water.

"Alright Blue, I think that is my sign to head home." He gives me a small smile before standing up and going over to wake up Aspen from her dog bed. I walk the two of them to the back door. "Are you sure you are good for tomorrow afternoon to help me shop? If you have plans or have something else to do, it's okay."

Lucas shakes his head, "Nope I only have one plan and fortunately for you, it involves you."

"Fortunately or unfortunately?" I smirk.

"We were about to end on such a good note Blue. Better luck next time I guess." I roll my eyes and laugh.

"Goodnight Lucas. I will see you tomorrow afternoon." He gives me a hug, which apparently is a normal thing for us now, and my heart rate spikes again. Lucas heads across the yard with Aspen and slips inside his house. I head inside mine and fall asleep as soon as my head hits the pillow. This upcoming weekend could change everything.

# CHAPTER 20
## - LUCAS

The next morning I wake up ready to get through my shift and get back home for shopping this afternoon. The fact that Sage is so willing to take in a little girl and be a place of safety and love reminds me how amazing she is. I don't know if I deserve her goodness in my life but I refuse to take it for granted.

I pull out of my garage before the sun is rising and head to the station. As I am walking through the door I stop to say hello to our receptionist Billy. "Good morning Billy. Do you know if Chief Harrington is here today?" I wanted to ask her an update on the father of the car crash yesterday but she took the day off to be there for her kids first day of school.

"Hey Lucas. Yeah she's supposed to have a meeting today at 10 so I'm sure she will be in before then." I tap on the desk with my knuckles. "Awesome thanks man!" "Anytime. Have a good one." With that he buzzes me through to the bullpen. As I am headed to my desk, I notice James is already here and talking to some other officers about Trigger.

"I'm waiting on the green light to start bringing him on patrol with us. He's doing really great in his training sessions and they say they will certify him soon."

"It's going to be great to have a K-9 unit with us. Get ready because y'all will be getting called to a lot more stops." I am excited for Trigger to join us and especially for James to have him with him all the time, but now I am a little worried that we are going to become more and more busy. Sage is about to become a single parent, what if she needs me around to help?

James notices that I have made it back to our desks and gives me a head nod before continuing. "We will just have to wait and see. But he should be joining the force within the next couple of weeks. I'll keep you guys posted." With that he leaves them and walks over to me.

"Good morning James. Heard you talking about Trigger. Other officers are really excited to have him join us. It's like we are getting a station mascot." I laugh as I imagine all the attention Trigger is going to get when he joins us. He is going to be in heaven. James must be thinking the same thing because he also chuckles, "hopefully we will be out on patrol often so he doesn't get too spoiled here. He's not going to want to come home each day."

I smile at the thought and turn to my computer. "Alright do you want ticket duty or report duty?" Each month we have to go through all of the speeding tickets we gave to make sure they were resolved by the person that received it. If not they will receive a nice little reminder in the mail about it. We also have to go through all the other reports that we made in the past month and double check them before we turn them in to the chief. "Oo that is a hard one Walker." He goes to his desk that is across from mine. "I'm gonna take the speeding tickets this month. You are better at the fine details for the other reports."

"Done deal. Let's get this done quickly so we can hit the road." James and I work in silence for the next couple of hours. Right when we are finishing up and thinking of going out on patrol, I notice that Chief Harrington is in her office. Needing to drop off my reports anyways I get James's attention and nod my head towards her office. "I am going to drop these off before we leave. I also wanna see if she has an update on Mr. Reynolds." James nods and stands to come with me. He has also been wondering about if the dad from the car accident made it. Gosh we hope so if not I'm not sure what will happen to that little girl.

When we get to her office we knock on the opened door. "Come on in, guys." Chief Harrington is sitting behind her desk so we come in and sit in the chairs opposite. "I just wanted to drop off these reports. They have been double checked and completed." I hand over my stack to her.

"Awesome. Gotta love that time of the month. My old partner and I used to divide and conquer and tackle them together." I smile as I realize that is exactly what James and I do.

"Not to bug you first thing in the morning ma'am, but we also were wondering if you received an update on Mr. Reynolds." Chief Harrington face drops. "Yes, I was going to come find you two and officer Sandoval and Officer Darrell this morning to update you all. Mr. Reynolds ended up having too much internal bleeding and passed away the following morning." I wasn't kidding when I told Sage that it is hard when there are lives that can't be saved. James must be feeling the same way by the look on his face. "What about the little girl?"

Chief Harrington's face gets even more grim. "She is okay. She ended up having a mild concussion and received some stitches in her arm from the cuts from the glass." "And what will happen to her now that she lost both parents?" She visibly grimaces. This can't be a good sign. "They are working on contacting extended family. Her parents were only children and their parents have previously passed away. So they have reached out to extended family members to see if they are willing to take guardianship over her. That's the last update I received on Tuesday." I nod my head and James and I stand up. I am fully shocked so James says our goodbye for us. "Thank you for the update Chief. Hopefully they find a family member to take her in."

"I hope so too. Be safe out there officers." With that we head out of the station and jump into James's patrol car.

We ride in silence for a few minutes before James breaks the silence. "I hope they find someone good for that little girl."

I stare out my window and respond, "it's not fair when good parents die and leave kids behind when there are so many bad parents out there hurting their children." I'm sure he can sense the tension coming off of me, he glances my way before turning back to the road. "You wanna talk about it?"

"No, I'm just really sad for that little girl."

"Walker, you know you can talk to me. I know how it gets when you get triggered by something. In my experience it is a quick fall to a dark hole."

I shake my head. "No it's okay. If I let him overpower my emotions, I let him win. I promise I'm okay." I look over and see the tension in James's jaw. "But thanks man. I promise I will talk about it if I feel it weighing me down."

"Alright, that's fair. Just know I am here for you man." We continue through our shift and one of the things that gets me through the day is knowing that I am going to see Sage this afternoon.

I pull into my garage a little after 3pm, take Aspen out back, then head upstairs to change out of my uniform. I still have maybe 10 minutes before Sage gets home so I head to my kitchen, grab an apple and hop up to sit on my counter across from the window to wait. Aspen comes over and tips her head to the side confused at what I am doing before she prances away.

Almost exactly 10 minutes later I see Sage walk into her kitchen. She puts her bag on one of the barstools and looks up to the window. The smile she gets when she sees me waiting to her would bring me to my knees if I wasn't already sitting. Man, she's beautiful. Today is one of the first time I have seen her in her professional attire. She is wearing a cute blue sundress with white vans. Her hair is half up on her head and half down with her long blonde hair curled. You can tell that her hair probably started in a neat bun but as the day went on it became looser and messy. It makes her look even more adorable.

She walks over to her window and I can tell she is writing out a message for me.

I hop down from the counter and get closer to the window while she writes. She is smirking as she puts it up so I know it's gonna be good.

*I should've taken a picture. The yummiest bachelor in Pennystone was sitting around waiting for me.*

I laugh and grab my whiteboard that is on a stand next to my sink. One of my best investments was buying this whiteboard.

*Little do you know I actually sit there all the time. It's my favorite spot in my house*

I see her roll her eyes before she wipes her whiteboard and writes again.

*Whatever you say Lucas. You ready to go?*

I nod my head and walk to the front door. It bums me out that I need to go out the front door but I need to lock the house before we leave. I'm considering going to Sage's back door but I don't know if that would be awkward. I like that Aspen and I always go through the back door. It feels like it's our own special entrance. I try to not let the ick settle in as I knock on Sage's front door.

Before she comes to answer I also turn to her camera and give it a wave and funny face just for the heck of it. She opens the door right when I am making a funny face at the camera.

She laughs, "you're such a dork." She steps aside and I walk in. "Alright, are you ready to go? You know where you want to go today?" I follow her into the kitchen where she grabs her bag.

"Yep! We can head out this door to the garage." She starts heading towards her garage but stop when she hears me say, "uh no Blue."

Spinning around you can tell that she is confused, "are you not ready to go? Do you need to use the bathroom before we hit the road?" I smile and shake my head, "no I don't need to use the bathroom but thanks for checking" this makes pink stain her cheeks, "we are taking my car. So we need to go out the front door."

She doesn't follow me as I walk to the front door so I turn back around to her. "Come on Blue, I know you want to ride in my patrol car."

"Well I mean yes I do because who doesn't, but we can take my car since we are going shopping for me." I shake my head at that thought. "Nope I am the one who asked you to come so I will be driving." She just stares at me. "Don't make me pick you up and carry you to my car Sage. I will make you sit in the back if you keep being stubborn."

She smirks at me, "are you going to handcuff me too?" Yep, my mind definitely went where it shouldn't go and she must see it on my face because now her cheeks are turning a bright pink. Before I can say anything snarky back at her, she races to the front door and calls back "Come on Lucas you're burning daylight standing there daydreaming." She winks and steps outside.

My feet finally listen to my brain and I head to the front door. We lock up her house and walk over to mine where I have the garage door open. She goes around to the passenger side and I follow closely behind. She notices and glances back at me, "You going to let me drive Officer Walker?" She is going to need to calm down or else the evidence of how it's making me feel is going to become very obvious. "No ma'am, I would prefer to live today." She rolls her eyes. "I am over here to get your door." With that I lean around her and open the passenger door for her before she climbs in.

"That is very gentlemanly of you sir." She smirks at me and I roll my eyes. "This should be your expectation Blue. It has nothing to do with manners and everything to do with respect." You can tell that she is a little shocked. "Plus what would the ladies of Pennystone think of me if I didn't open your door. I have an image to keep." She rolls her eyes again but I can still see the small smile spreading across her face as I shut the door. I round the car and slide into the drivers seat. I turn to Sage, "Where to first?"

◆ ◆ ◆

We have gone to three different stores and Sage finally picked out a comforter and matching pillow set at our last one. You can tell that she is nervous and wants things to be perfect. I don't think she realizes how lucky the little girl will feel just by having Sage take her in but I can understand why Sage is nervous, it is a lot to take on.

As we were shopping, Sage told me her ideas on painting the room and a possible reading corner. Apparently she thinks that I can build a reading nook/fort. I better start watching some YouTube videos on how to do that.

We are now headed back to the car after finishing at the last store. I open the back door to put in the bags of supplies. Then I race over to Sage's door to open it for her. Surprisingly, she has waited for me to open it at each store and hasn't fought me on it. I am glad she understands that I will be upset if she doesn't let me do this. Once we are both seated, I turn to Sage. "Okay so we have two options." She looks over at me confused. "We can either go out somewhere for dinner or we could pick something up and take it back to your house."

She smiles over at me, "Let's grab something and head back to my house. I know you worked all day so Aspen probably wants some time and attention." I smile and pull out of the parking lot. "I am thinking sushi from Lin's. Are you okay with that? Do you still like the California roll the best?" I look over at her and she is looking at me a little shocked. Yep, I know her favorite sushi but only because that was the meal her mom and dad would get when she was extra stressed with school. She seemed stressed when we were looking around the stores, so sushi is needed.

She finally processes and gives me a smile, "Yeah that sounds perfect. And yes, the California roll is still my favorite but you can get us whatever you want. The best part of sushi is trying all the flavors of the different rolls." As we drive towards Lins, I call ahead and place the order. It may have been a little too much food but Sage can eat the leftovers for lunch tomorrow.

"Wow, are we inviting more people over tonight Lucas?" I roll my eyes and she laughs. "That is quite a lot of sushi."

"You made a good point about trying different rolls. I may have gotten carried away but now you will have lunch tomorrow." We are pulling up to Lins and I hop out of the car and tell Sage to go ahead and stay inside the car while I grab it. Thankfully, they were almost done so I only have to wait about 5 minutes.

When I get to the car, Sage is just finishing up a conversation on the phone, "I will update you this weekend, I gotta go... Yes Brooklyn, I am with Lucas." She pauses as I slide into the driver's seat and hand her the bag of food. "Okay I will tell him you said hello. Love you bye." She laughs as she hangs up.

"Brooklyn said and I quote 'make sure to tell your hot cop friend hello for me', she's so ridiculous." She is shaking her head with a smile as she looks down at the phone. "Come on Blue, it's okay if you admit that I am your friend." I glance over at her as I drive. "Lucas you have carried me to bed, slept on my couch, and you eat dinner with me almost every night. We are definitely friends at this point."

I don't know what is wrong with me but my heart swells at that and I look over to her with a big smile before turning back to the road. It has been 20 years since Sage and I were friends and now that feels like wasted time.

# CHAPTER 21
# - SAGE

Last night was really great. After Lucas and I got back to my house, he brought Aspen over and we ate our sushi while watching the Thursday Night Football game. Lucas was telling me all about his fantasy football league that the station has. Apparently it is a big deal and he is hoping to win the championship this year after getting 3rd place last year. The night ended when Lucas saw me yawning away and told me he was going to finish the game at home so I could get some sleep.

When he was leaving out the back door, he gave me a hug and told me that no matter what happens with the little girl, he thinks I am pretty amazing for being willing to take her in. I was surprised when I felt sad when he broke the hug and walked back to his house. I shake my head from daydreaming about last night. My students are currently at art class so I have about 20 minutes before they get back. I am walking down the hallway to check on Ms. Culhane, another one of the teachers that I am over when Mrs. Applewood sees me and stops me in the hall. "Hey Sage, any update from Mitchell on the fostering application?"

I sigh, "not yet. He said best case scenario would be today but I haven't heard anything yet." She nods, "Okay well I believe he is planning on coming by today so maybe he will come with some news."

Feeling my anxiety start to rise I nod. "Okay great. Hopefully we get news soon. I am going to head over to Ms. Culhane's room now and check in on her while my kiddos are in art." She smiles, "don't let me keep you trapped here in the hallway. Tell her that I said hello."

"Will do, thank you ma'am. I will let you know if I hear anything from Mitchell." She smiles and nods before walking towards the front office. I continue down the hallway and check in with Ms. Culhane who is amazing and having a great start to the year. She didn't need anything from me but it was great to catch up with her.

As I walk back to the art room to go get my kids, I can't help but get in my head about Parker's situation. What if someone else snags her? My heart is heavy at that thought so I try to brush it off and continue through the day.

◆ ◆ ◆

The best part of Fridays is that the day ends a little earlier than normal. We send our kids off about 30 minutes earlier so that we can all get a jumpstart on the weekend. As I am walking back to my classroom after making sure my kids get picked up and on buses, I get an email notification on my phone. It is an email from Mrs. Applewood asking me to meet with Mitchell in her office. I change direction and head directly there with my heart pounding. As I walk into her office I can see that Mitchell is already there sitting across from Mrs. Applewood. I knock lightly and they both stand up. Mitchell extends his hand as I come into the room, "Sage it is so great to see you again."

"You as well Mitchell. I am hoping you come with some good news." We all sit down and Mrs. Applewood has a bright smile.

"I do have some news Sage. Your application did what I expected and went through the system quickly. As of today, you are officially on temporary status to foster."

"Oh wow. That's amazing!" I can't help but smile. "What happens next?" Mitchell returns the smile before continuing. "Okay so next would be having that conversation with Parker and then from there you could take her home. I had her teacher keep her here after school so we could all meet." With that Mrs. Applewood calls down to Julie's classroom to have her walk down Parker.

As soon as Parker walks in the room I am worried my heart is going to burst from being so anxious. I really want her to feel safe and comfortable with me. "Hey Parker. How are you doing today?" Parker looks over to me and smiles, "Hey Ms. Sage" I don't try to get a bunch of 6 year old kindergarten kids to say my last name so all the students just call me Ms. Sage. "I am doing good. How are you?"

I smile at her manners, "I am good Parker, thank you for asking. We wanted to talk with you for a little bit. Do you want to climb into this chair next to me?" Parker looks at the chair next to me and walks over to sit down. Then she looks to Mitchell. "Hello Mr. Stevens. It is nice to see you again."

Mitchell gives Parker a smile. She really is such a good kid. "Hey Parker. Remember when we talked about how you would one day need to leave Lola's house and live with someone that is going to take care of you?" Parker looks sad for a moment but nods and answers, "Yes".

"Well it turns out that Ms. Sage would like to be your foster parent. This means that you would live with her and she would take care of you. Does that sound like something you would like?" Parker looks at him and then looks at me and I swear they may need to call an ambulance. My heart is beating so fast and my hands are so sweaty. "Wait, I can go live with Ms. Sage?" Parker finally begins to smile again.

I choose to step in now. "Yeah Parker, you can come live with me. But only if you want to. I have a bedroom all ready to go with lots of books that we can read. I was thinking tonight we could have pizza and watch movies on my couch if you want." It may sound like I am bribing her but those were truly my plans if she were to come home with me. She looks at me and then at Mitchell and back at me before she nods excitedly, "I want to live with Ms. Sage."

I blow out the breath that I didn't realize I was holding. Mrs. Applewood is sitting behind her desk with a smile and eyes that are glossy. Julie is still in the doorway with a smile. Mitchell turns back to Parker, "That sounds like the perfect plan to me. I just need Ms. Sage to sign some papers for me and then you two can leave. Do you want to color for a little bit while you wait?" Parker nods and goes over to the table that is in the back corner of Mrs. Applewood's office. The table already has coloring pages and markers and crayons for when kids are in here.

I whisper to Mitchell, "Did that really just happen?" He smiles and nods, "Yep. That was one of the coolest moments I have had with a client and a foster parent. Let's get these papers signed so you can get home and enjoy the weekend." We take the next ten minutes to sign papers that give me guardianship over Parker. After we complete those, I am walking out the door of the school holding Parker's hand and feeling overwhelmingly excited. Luckily, Lucas reminded me to buy her a carseat yesterday while we were shopping. We get to the car and I get Parker buckled and we head home for the first time as a little family. Before I take off I send Lucas a quick text.

Me: We will have another person at dinner tonight. I got Parker today!

We stopped by the Adams's home to pick up some of the things that Parker had while staying with them. I heard Parker tell Lola "I get to go live with Ms. Sage and I am so excited!" which made my heart so happy. We step inside my house and I can see her eyes get big.

"I just moved into this house. Do you want to go see your room? I was thinking you could help me decide what color to paint it and what we can put on the walls." She nods her head excitedly and follows me upstairs. When we get to her room I let her step in first.

"This is my room?" She turns back to look at me. "Yep. Unless you don't like this one, there are other rooms you can pick but this one is the one closest to my room." She smiles and looks around the room again. "It's perfect." I feel relieved that she is okay with it.

"I remembered that your favorite color is

yellow so I got you a new comforter for your bed. If you have one from your house, we can switch it though." Parker looks a little sad for a moment as she thinks about her old house. "No it's okay I like this one. This bed is much bigger than my last one. It's huge!" I laugh as she sits on it and I go sit down next to her.

"Parker I am really sorry that you lost your parents in that car accident. They loved you very much." I look down at her and she is looking down at the floor. This may not be the best time to have this conversation but she needs to know she is okay to feel all her feelings here.

"Yeah I love them a lot and miss them. Officer Sandoval told me that they were needed in heaven. They were such good people that God needs them to help him be angels. Now they watch over me."

I can feel the tears well up in my eyes as she speaks. "You're right Parker. You will always have your parents with you no matter where you go. I want you to know you can talk about them any time you want. You are safe here with me and I will make sure to keep you safe. I promise." Parker looks up to me and smiles, "I know Ms. Sage. Thank you for letting me live here."

My heart. "Of course Parker." Trying to shake off the tears I remember what I promised we would do tonight. "How about we go downstairs and order some pizza then we can watch a movie. Does that sound good to you?"

"Yes! Let's do it." Parker jumps up from the bed and heads out the door. Laughing, I follow after her. When we reach the bottom of the stairs I hear Aspen barking out back. I smile and head to the back door. Parker stops and looks up to me, "Do you have a dog?!" You can tell she is so excited at the possibility.

"Not exactly." I smile down at her. "Aspen belongs to my friend Lucas who lives next door. They come over for dinner sometimes so that's why I have dog stuff here." Parker looks back to the door. "That's awesome. Does that mean I can play with her?" I smile as I imagine Parker and Aspen together. "Yeah I am sure Lucas will love it if you play with her. Aspen is super nice."

We reach the back door and see Lucas smiling at the both of us and Aspen's tailing wagging a million miles an hour. As I go to open the door I see Lucas's smile drop a little as he looks fully shocked. I'm just not sure by what. "Hey Lucas, this is Parker Reynolds. Parker, this is Lucas and his dog Aspen." Aspen gets super excited when hearing her name and comes up to us pushing her head against my hand for me to pet her. Parker follows my lead and gives her some love too. You would assume Parker and Aspen were long lost friends with how excited they both are.

Parker then looks up to Lucas. "Mr. Lucas, can I play with your dog in the yard?" He blinks a few times and seems to shake himself out of his shock. "Yeah Parker go ahead. Aspen loves to play fetch if you can find a good stick."

"Come on Aspen, let's go find a stick!" Parker takes off running and Aspen happily trails behind. "One of the good things about me taking Parker may be a friend for Aspen" I smile at Lucas and he is staring at Aspen and Parker playing in the yard with a concerned look. "I am sure they will be okay together…"

Lucas finally looks at me and must see the confusion and concern on my face. "I was there Blue." He pauses and I have no idea what he is talking about until he continues. "Do you remember that night that I was called into work and I was sad to be missing the pesto chicken sandwiches with you?" I do remember that night. It was the night I snuck over to his house to drop some off for him and creep around his house. I nod yes to Lucas and he continues.

"That night we got a call about a bad car accident" it is that moment when I realize what he meant. He was at the accident that took Parker's parents lives. "I saw the aftermath of the accident. We weren't the first ones on the scene and by the time we got there we discovered that Mrs. Reynolds had already passed away. Mr. Reynolds and Parker were getting loaded into ambulances. I barely saw Parker, only briefly as she was in the ambulance with another officer."

I look out to where Parker and Aspen are running around with Parker giggling as she continues to throw a stick for Aspen. "I don't even know what to say." I am truly speechless. "It is a miracle that Parker survived that crash and to only walk away with a mild concussion and stitches is unheard of. She could have died, Blue. I came home that night to the note in my refrigerator from you. I hate that I wasn't able to save any lives that night."

From what he told me and what I know of the accident, Lucas couldn't have done anything to save Parker's parents that night. He is still watching Parker and Aspen as I walk over and taking his hand and interlace my fingers with his. He looks down at me and I give him a small smile and gently squeeze his hand. He gives me a small smile back and then looks back to the yard. "I don't know how I didn't connect the dots before that Parker was the little girl you were going to take in." We both fall into silence as we watch Aspen and Parker play.

After about ten minutes of playing, Parker runs over to us all sweating and her face all red but she seems really happy. I smile at Parker and she smiles back. "Looks like the two of you need some water. Let's head inside." I let go of Lucas's hand and slide the door open. We all step inside and I head to the kitchen to get Parker a water bottle from the refrigerator and Lucas grabs Aspen's water bowl.

I hand over the water bottle to Parker. "We need to get some dinner in our tummies. Lucas, we were planning on doing pizza. Are you free tonight to stay and hang out with us?" Lucas seems to be out of his little funk now. He looks at the two of us and smiles. "Yep, before I came over I placed an order for pizza. It should be here any minute."

I don't know how he read my mind about needing pizza tonight. As if scheduled, the doorbell rings. "That must be the pizza, I will be right back." He heads to the front door and I turn to Parker. "What kind of pizza do you like, Parker?" I should have asked earlier. She smiles, "I like cheese and pepperoni." I shake my head as Lucas comes around the corner with four boxes of pizza. Parker's eyes get really big when she sees Lucas with the pizza. "Wow, that is a lot of pizza."

"I didn't know what kind you liked Parker so I got a lot of them so we can try them all." Parker is beaming at Lucas like he hung the moon. Me too Parker, me too.

"Alright so let's see what we have". Lucas flips open a lid. "We have one with sausage, ham, and pepperoni. How does that sound Parker?" She looks at him timidly and shakes her head no. "That's alright. What's next?" He opens the next box of pizza. "Veggie pizza." Parker again shakes her head with a disgusted face. Lucas leans in and whispers "maybe we can feed that one to Aspen." Parker giggles and covers her mouth with her hand. "You can't feed pizza to dogs Mr. Lucas."

I smile and turn to him, "Yeah Lucas, maybe

you should eat that one. You're a growing boy, you need the veggies." He whips his head to me and shakes his head no. Aspen, who is sitting at his feet, barks. "Looks like Aspen wants it" looking down at Aspen and then he looks back at Parker and winks. Parker giggles again with her hand over her mouth shaking her head.

"Next one up is cheese pizza and then we have pepperoni. What are you thinking Parker?" Parker looks to be thinking for a second. "Can I please have cheese and pepperoni Mr. Lucas?" Lucas smiles and nods "one slice of cheese and one slice of pepperoni coming right up. And what about for you Ms. Sage?" I roll my eyes at him being dramatic. "I will take one pepperoni and one veggie please."

He fills my plate and then walks both of our plates over to the table. He sets them down on the table before he heads back to the kitchen to dish himself. Parker walks over to her chair and sits down. "Do you want anything to drink Parker?" She looks at her water bottle that is still half full. "No, I still have my water." I nod and smile then head back to the kitchen to get myself a water. When I go to grab a water bottle, I feel Lucas behind me before I hear him whisper in my ear, "You are doing really great Sage. You can tell she adores you already."

I grab my water bottle and slowly spin around. Lucas makes no effort to back up to give me space. Did someone turn off the AC in here because it is feeling rather warm all of a sudden? "Thank you Lucas. I think Aspen and pizza won her over for the first night here." He smiles and backs away to head to the table with Parker. We eat more pizza than we should while Parker tells us all about what she likes to do which includes gymnastics, reading, and drawing. Lucas keeps the conversation going and looks genuinely interested in everything Parker says. Parker can see it too which helps her open up.

Once our bellies are as full as they can get, we head to the living room and spend the rest of the night watching Frozen 2. I swear I see Lucas tear up a little bit when Olaf leaves Anna alone in the cave but I don't say anything. I'll save that for another time. By the end of the movie Parker is almost asleep so I take her upstairs and we get her in her pajamas and in bed.

As I am walking out of her room I stop when she says "thank you Ms. Sage. I love it here." I turn back to Parker and smile, "I love having you here Parker. I will see you in the morning, okay?" She nods and snuggles into her "huge bed". I turn off the light and close the door. I make my way back downstairs to turn off the lights and lock up when I notice that Lucas is still here. He is in the kitchen bagging up the leftover pizza to put in my refrigerator.

"You better be taking some of that to your house. We will never be able to finish all that pizza." He smiles as we looks at all the leftover pizza. "Okay fine but don't expect me to take the veggie pizza."

"I would never." I laugh. "Honestly I am shocked you got that one. I don't know any little kid that likes veggie pizza." He gets a little bit of pink in his cheeks, "Yeah I know. I was just worried that maybe she came from a home that was super into healthy foods. I wanted to make sure she had all the options." He finishes putting half the pizza in my refrigerator.

"Thank you for getting the pizza tonight. I don't know how you knew that was my plan but I really appreciate it. I feel a little in over my head when it comes to this whole parenting thing. I just don't want to mess anything up." I am looking at the counter not wanting him to see my vulnerability. Lucas lifts my chin with his hand so I am looking at him, "Parker is extremely lucky to have you. You aren't messing anything up and you aren't going to. You are going to show that little girl so much love that she won't know what to do with it. You are amazing Sage, don't overthink it."

I am a little shocked momentarily. "Thank you Lucas. I think she may adore you more than me after tonight. You two really hit it off." He smiles and looks over to Aspen, "I have a secret weapon with Aspen." he looks back at me, "But seriously, Parker is awesome. I am really glad you took her in." He heads to the back door and Aspen hops off the couch and comes with him. "What are your plans tomorrow with Parker?"

"In the morning she has gymnastic practice so we will be there for about an hour or so. Then I need to tell my family that I took her in. It has been a little crazy so I haven't been able to. So I will probably go over there for dinner and let her meet all of them." I get a little nervous about that because this all happened so fast and I am not sure how they are going to respond.

Lucas must sense my anxiety. "Hey, they are going to love Parker. They may be a little shocked that they have another grandkid all of the sudden but you know your parents will be so excited to have another kid to spoil. Once they hear Parker's story, they would be mad at you if you didn't take her in."

He's right, this is just the thing my parents and even Stanton would easily do if they were in my shoes. Not wanting to face that dinner alone I ask Lucas what his plans are and if he happens to be free tomorrow. "Is there anyway you want to come to that dinner with me in case they freak out?"

Lucas looks at me with a sad expression, "I'm sorry Blue but I have to do the afternoon shift tomorrow. I won't be able to come and I really wish I could."

"It's okay, I completely understand." I hope I am not sounding as disappointed as I feel. "It is going to be great though Sage. They love you and they will love her just as much." With that

Lucas wraps me in a hug. I take a deep breath as I feel my stress loosening as I inhale his scent. He always smells earthy and warm like sandalwood mixed with vanilla. I nod and take a step back, "Thanks Lucas and thank you for tonight. I am really glad I didn't have to do that first night alone."

"You will never be alone now." I know he means because I have Parker but it also feels like more. "Goodnight Sage and good luck with dinner tomorrow."

"Goodnight Lucas. Stay safe tomorrow." Lucas motions for Aspen to come and they walk across their yard. He waves to me before I head inside, locking up.

# CHAPTER 22
# - SAGE

Turns out Saturday mornings with a 6 year old are very busy. I used to sleep in on Saturdays, be lazy all morning then clean my house and do laundry before sitting down to read a book for most of the day.

Now? Saturdays mean gymnastics, play dates, and errands together. But I have loved every second of it. Mitchell called this morning to check in and filled me in more on Parker's legal situations. Her parents had their house completely paid off and hefty life insurance policies. Parker is now the owner of a two story, five bedroom house in town and has a trust fund of 2 million dollars that she will be able to access when she is 18.

Mitchell told me that legally once I gain permanent foster status, I will be able to apply to the courts to pull out money from the trust each month to cover Parker's needs. I told him that wouldn't be necessary. I want that money to only go to Parker. She could go to any college with that and live any dream she wants with that kind of money. Her parents left it for her and that is who is going to choose what to do with it.

At some point we will need to go to her house and see if there is more of her stuff that she wants to bring to my house. But I am thinking of holding off on that until we are fully settled. Personally, I would want some time to adapt and heal before that. I plan to talk to Parker about it at some point.

We have finished up gymnastics which conveniently Lola is also in. After the class was over, Lola asked me if we could go to the park with her and her mom to play for a little bit. Ashley and I decided to stop and get some lunch for the girls before we head to the park. The girls ate their sandwiches from Persnicketys, a local deli and bakery in town, and ran off to the jungle gym. Ashley looks over at me and smiles. "It is really amazing that you chose to foster Parker Sage. She seems really happy."

I look back over to the jungle gym where Parker and Lola are going down the slide laughing. "I am really happy it worked out. It broke my heart to think that Parker could have been moved to another town to move in with strangers." I pause and turn back to Ashley. "I know that the new family could have been amazing, but Parker deserves to stay in the town she knows and loves."

Ashley nods, "I was talking with my husband about taking her in myself but with the new baby on the way, we weren't sure if it would make us good candidates." She smiles as she puts a hand over her tiny baby bump. "Congratulations by the way. I bet Lola is so excited to be a big sister." She smiles as she watches Lola playing. "She really is. She asks me everyday if I know if it will be a brother or a sister. It is hard to explain to an impatient 6 year old that it takes time to figure that one out."

I laugh as I know how Lola gets when she wants to figure something out. "Yeah I can imagine. She's a firecracker." Ashley laughs, "That she is. She will probably run a company one day with her determination and drive." We smile and watch the girls playing pirates on the jungle gym. Oh to be that little with no cares in the world.

Ashley turns back to me, "I bet your parents are so excited to have another kid around the house. Parker is probably great with little Miles." I grimace at that. "You have told them about Parker, right Sage?" Ashley and I were friends growing up, with her being a couple of years older than me but lived down the street. Her family and my family remained friends throughout the years so it is safe to say she knows them well.

"Uh, not yet..." She laughs and shakes her head. "It all happened so fast and I didn't want to tell them when I applied in case it didn't work out and they got their hopes up. Then all of the sudden I was taking Parker home yesterday. We have a family dinner planned for tonight where they will meet Parker." She smiles and is still shaking her head, "so you are just going to show up and tell them that you are now fostering a little girl?" I can feel my nerves start rising about the dinner. Man, I wish Lucas was going to be there. "Pretty much." I give an awkward laugh. "They are going to be pretty shocked but they will fall in love with Parker instantly."

"I don't doubt that. Your family was always taking in kids that needed a home." I smile, my parents really are great ones. "Kind of like Lucas." That has me whipping my head to her in confusion.

Before I can ask her what she meant, the girls come running up. "Can we have a drink mom?" Lola is already digging in her moms bag looking for her water bottle. Ashley laughs, "yeah babe. But we need to head home soon. Your dad was supposed to mow the lawn while we were gone and then take us to the movies."

"Yes! I love the movie theater. Can we take Parker??" Lola looks up to her mom with puppy dog eyes and I can tell she knows how to get what she wants. "No sweetie, not this time. Ms. Sage and Parker have plans already. Maybe next time." Lola accepts that answer and we all pack up and head to the cars.

"Good luck tonight Sage. You are doing amazing with Parker." Ashley smiles as she turns to head towards her car with Lola in hand. "Thank you! We will have to get together again soon. See you two Monday at school." Lola and Parker wave goodbye to each other and we climb into my car. Parker buckles herself in and we head home to get ready for dinner.

As we are driving to my parent's house I tell Parker about my family. "My mom and dad's names are Sandy and Shawn. They are super nice and you will love them." I look in the rearview mirror and see Parker nodding. She looks nervous about tonight. "Then I have a twin brother named Stanton."

"You have a twin? That's so cool! Are you best friends?" I smile as I think of my relationship with Stanton. "Yeah we are definitely best friends. He has a little boy named Miles. Miles is almost 1 now so he is still small."

Parker seems to perk up with knowing there will be another kid there. We pull into my parents driveway and I open the back door for her. I don't warn her that my family has no idea that she is with me and I hope that they roll with it without making Parker feel uncomfortable.

Knowing my family, I shouldn't worry but I want to make sure Parker feels at home here.

If things continue as I hope, she could be with me until she graduates high school and goes off to college. That thought makes me excited and smile as I open the front door and usher Parker in. "Hey guys, I am home." I yell out towards the living room as Parker and I take off our shoes by the door. Parker then grabs my hand as we walk down the hall. My heart swells having her hand in mine. I squeeze hers gently as we get closer and she looks up at me with a small smile. I can definitely tell she's nervous.

My dad gets up from the couch and is shocked to see the two of us but shakes it off quickly. "Hey baby girl, it's been too long." He gives me a hug, all the while Parker still is gripping onto my hand. I nod my head as he hugs me. It really has been too long. I haven't been able to pop over recently with the new school year starting and then the craziness of getting Parker. We will have to plan a movie night soon.

"And who is this cute little lady?" He drops to one knee so that he is eye level with Parker and gives her a smile. "My name is Parker. I live with Ms. Sage now" She looks up to me with a hesitant smile. My dad's eyes go big and he looks up at me. "Yeah, where's mom and Stanton? I have some news."

He chuckles and stands back up. "Apparently you do. Let's head to the kitchen, I am pretty sure they are in there getting dinner ready." We follow my dad into the kitchen where my mom is racing around the kitchen, like always, getting dinner finished. Stanton is sitting at the table with Miles next to him in the high chair feeding him some baby food. He looks tired today. Hopefully everything is okay at the practice.

My mom stops when she sees us walk in and tips her head to the side when she sees Parker. "Hey guys, this is Parker Reynolds." My mom looks to my dad as I say her name. The town heard about their car accident and is putting together a funeral for Parker's parents. "I guess I will just rip off the bandaid with my news. I have registered to become a foster parent and am currently Parker's legal guardian."

My mom's eyes well up with tears but she doesn't let them fall. She comes around the counter slowly and squats in front of Parker. "Hi Parker, it's nice to meet you." She holds out her hand for a handshake. "My name is Sandy. I'm Sage's mom." Parker has to let go of my hand to shake my moms. But she smiles as she does it. "Hi Ms. Sandy." My mom beams at her. "That is Shawn, Sage's dad." She points out my dad and then to Stanton and Miles. "And that is Stanton, Sage's brother and his son Miles." Stanton gives her a wave and Miles babbles and giggles causing Parker to smile. "Hey Parker, do you wanna help me make some cookies for after we eat dinner?" My mom is the picture perfect grandma.

Parker looks up to me and I nod my head with a smile. She turns back to my mom, "Yes I would like that Ms. Sandy. Thank you". With that Parker follows my mom to the kitchen. My mom finds a step stool from the pantry so that Parker can see the counter and they start on the cookies. I guess she is going to leave dinner to cool while they bake. You can tell my mom is so excited to have another kid in the house. I walk over and sit at the table with Stanton and my dad follows and sits down next to me.

"Alright baby girl, you wanna explain how the last time we saw you you were preparing for a new school year and now you have a daughter?" I blush and smile at the title. I am not expecting Parker to view me as her mom because she already had an amazing one, but I can definitely see myself view her as my daughter. Stanton looks over with curiosity as well waiting for my answer.

"Well the day before the students came, Mrs. Applewood sat me and Julie down and told us about the accident the Reynolds got in. I was asking her what would happen to Parker and she told me that unless they could get extended family to be willing to take her in, she would end up in the foster care system. Since Pennystone is a small town without many foster options, Parker was more than likely looking at moving to another city to get placed." I look over to my dad and he is looking at Parker and my mom with sadness on his face. "It broke my heart that not only did Parker lose her parents, she was looking at losing everything she knows. After not being able to sleep because of it, the next day I sat down with Mrs. Applewood and her social worker and told them I wanted to apply to become a foster parent and take Parker if that was possible. By Friday afternoon, my application went through and Parker came home with me."

I can see they are both surprised. Stanton looks over from where Miles just finished his food, "So in less than a week you decided to foster and took Parker home?"

"Yep. It all happened so quickly. That's why you guys didn't hear about it. I didn't want to say anything after I put in the application because I was worried about getting my hopes up. And then she came home with me yesterday so I figured I would wait and tell you guys in person." My dad looks over to me with pride in his eyes. "So what happens next then?"

"Right now I am only on a temporary status until I complete some training and a home visit. After that point I will be considered a permanent foster parent. I plan to get that done as soon as possible to make sure Parker can stay with me." I look over at Parker and she is laughing as my mom is showing her how to grab a glob of cookie dough and roll in into a ball with her hands. When I look back and both my dad and Miles are staring at me.

"I know it is a big decision and a lot, but I just feel in my heart that Parker is supposed to be with me right now." I get teary eyed as I think of the impact Parker has already had on my life in the last 24 hours. "Oh baby girl, we are just shocked but so proud of you. You will fill that girl's life with so much love. You know we support you 100% and will love that girl as if she was our own." I wipe my cheeks as a couple tears have fallen.

"Thanks dad. She had amazing parents and it is unfair that she lost them. But that doesn't mean she can't have a full life with so much love." Stanton looks over at Parker and then back to me, "You are amazing Sage. Not many people would willingly take on single parenthood."

I smile at him and glance to Miles, "I learned from the best single parent I know, Stants."

"Hey, can you three set the table and then we can eat while the cookies are in the oven." My mom is just putting in a batch of cookies when Parker hops down from her stool and comes to me. "Ms. Sage, can I help too?" I smile, "of course Parker. How about you make sure each seat has a napkin?" She nods her head and I head to the pantry to get her some napkins. "Make sure you give one to Miles too. He loves to tear them to shreds." She giggles but nods and heads over to the table.

We set the table and start dishing up. I dish up a plate for Parker and then for myself. During dinner, my family takes the time to get to know Parker and what she likes. My mom brings over the cookies that her and Parker baked and some cups of milk. "And then last night I got to play with Mr. Lucas's dog Aspen who is so cute! Then we had pizza and watched Frozen 2. It was the best night."

Everyone looks over at me at the mention of Lucas spending the evening with us. My mom gives a knowing smile. "That does sound like a really fun night Parker." Saved by Miles, who starts getting fussy and rubbing at his eyes. Stanton pulls him out of his seat. "You all know what that means, it is time to get this little guy to bed."

"We should probably head home too Parker, we have had a busy day." Parker nods and stands up with me and Stanton. My parents walk us to the door and give each of us a quick hug, including Parker who has warmed up to them throughout the evening and gives them a squeeze back. When we step outside Stanton buckles Miles in while I open the back door for Parker to hop in.

Stanton turns to me and gives me a hug, "I am really proud of you Sis. You are amazing for taking Parker in."

"Thanks Stants. I really love having her." I smile as I glance back at my car and see Parker buckled up and ready to go. "Don't think you are off the hook about talking about Lucas hanging out at your house." He gives me a wink and heads to his driver door. "But I am really glad you guys are looking out for each other. Goodnight Sage." I am a little shocked that was his only reaction. "Goodnight Stanton, see you soon." With that I hop in the car and we drive home both singing to our favorite songs on the radio.

Once home, we go upstairs and both change into our pajamas and brush our teeth, before we head into Parker's room to tuck her in for the night. "Alright Parker, what book do you want to read tonight?" Parker looks to be thinking about it. "My mom was reading The Magic Treehouse books with me each night before I went to bed. We didn't get to finish before she died." Oh my heart. "Do you have those ones? Could we pick up where she left off?" She looks at me with so much hope in her eyes.

"I do have those ones. Let me go grab them from my office. I will be right back." I walk down the hall and grab all the ones I have, unsure of which one they were reading last. Parker points out the one they were in the middle of and tells me what she remembers from the story. We snuggle in together on her bed and I read her two chapters before it is obvious that she is getting very sleepy. I slip out from under the covers and walk towards the door. "Goodnight Parker."

I smile as she peeks up from the covers. "Goodnight Ms. Sage. Today was another really good day."

"I hope all your days are great ones, Parker." And with that, I turn off the lights and shut her door. She was right, today was a really good day but something or maybe someone felt missing.

# CHAPTER 23
# - LUCAS

This weekend at the station and on the road was surprisingly slow. Which is nice but also made the time go by so much slower and gave me too much time to think about how the dinner with Sage's family was going. I told myself I wouldn't text her this evening while she is at her parents house but I will check in tomorrow morning. James and I have tomorrow off so maybe I will sneak over to Sage's tomorrow and see if they have any plans for their Sunday. James catches me zoning out at my desk. "Hey man, everything okay?"

"Oh yeah. Everything is fine. Just was lost in thought there for a second." I can feel heat rising into my cheeks but James thankfully doesn't point it out. "I keep thinking about that little girl. I wonder if Chief Harrington got an update." I can see James swivel his head to look towards the Chief's office but her door is shut.

When he turns back to me I am smiling, "Why

are you over there smiling? Do you know what happened to the little girl." Pride fills my heart. "I actually do. Turns out the little girl, Parker, was in Sage's class last year. When the principal told Sage about what happened with the car accident, Sage reached out to her social worker and applied to become a foster parent. As of yesterday, Parker is now living with Sage."

James looks shocked. "Wow, that's amazing. Sage's heart is one of a kind for doing this for that little girl." He's right. She is one in a million.

"You should see the two of them together. You can tell that Parker adores Sage and Sage is doing everything in her power to make sure Parker lives a life surrounded by love. It is a really special relationship." I smile as I think about our pizza and movie night last night. James raises his eyebrows at me. "So you were at Sage's house again last night I take it?"

Well the heat that left my cheeks is now back. "Yep, I ordered them pizza for their first night together." James gives me a knowing look. "Sounds like you are there every night that you aren't here."

I look back to my computer and pretend I am working, "Yeah it does seem like it works out that way. Me and Sage are friends. It is nice when we don't have to eat dinner alone." James pauses as he lets me sit on that thought. "Plus you will need to try Sage's cooking one day and you will understand why I am constantly over there." As

I say it, I hate the thought. Dinners with Sage are my special thing. I am not sure if I am willing to share.

"Yeah sure, it's the cooking." I look up to see him smiling and I roll my eyes at him. Luckily he drops it as we dive into one of the cases we are working on.

By the time I get home that night, it is late and I assume that Parker and Sage are both asleep. I head to the back door to let Aspen out. When I step outside with her she takes off towards Sage's house. I jog after her and whisper yell for her to come back. "Aspen. I know you miss them, so do I but we will have to wait until the morning to see them." I continue jogging until I see Aspen sitting out back right next to Sage who is on her outdoor couch with a blanket.

"You planning on stopping by in the morning Lucas? You might wanna give me a warning." I laugh as I see her smirking.

"I did not expect you to be out here this late, but yes I am planning on coming over tomorrow to see you two. Do you have plans tomorrow?"

"I'm not sure what we will do tomorrow so no plans yet. I'm sure Parker would love to see you again", She smiles and then looks down at Aspen, "we missed you too tonight." I can't help but hope that she doesn't only mean that about

Aspen. I walk over and sit next to Sage on the couch and she puts some of her blanket in my lap. The fall chill is starting to finally settle in.

"How was dinner with your family? How did they take it?"

She sighs and smiles, "As you would expect. They love Parker and she loved being there with them. I am really glad they know now. They told me that they are proud of me and support me fully."

She is looking out at the stars when I respond.

"They should be proud, you are incredible, Sage. I am really glad that the dinner went well." She looks over at me before glancing back up to the stars, "we missed you there tonight. Parker was bragging about your pizza and movie night to my family." That fact does something to my heart.

"I missed you two too. I kept thinking about texting you for an update but didn't want to interrupt you with your family." She continues to stare out at the stars. It is obvious that she has been doing this for who knows how long.

"What's on your mind Blue? You look pretty deep in thought out here" She sighs and then looks at me. "What if I'm not enough for Parker?" I want to tell her that she is more than enough. She is the type of woman that all moms want for their sons and all kids want as a mom. Anyone would be lucky to have the love of Sage in their life. Realizing at this moment that she doesn't need me to convince her of that and tell her she's wrong for her thoughts, I sit in silence and listen.

"Parker already had an incredible mom and I would never want to replace her. I know I should honor their memories. What if Parker feels like I'm trying to replace them? What if she resents me for it?" Wishing I was Stanton right now with all his training for conversations like this, I do what I have experienced and try to validate her feelings.

"It is probably really hard to balance loving Parker as your own and making sure she knows that her parents still love her even though they are gone." I scoot closer to her and pull her into my side. Surprisingly she snuggles into me.

"I just want her to know that we all love her. She doesn't have to choose one or the other. She can accept all the love that is given." She pauses and looks out to the stars again. "But I would also really like to call her my daughter one day, and I'm afraid that makes me a terrible person." Okay I validated but now I'm going to need to stop her thought process. "I'm going to stop you right there." I grab her chin so she is looking at me. "You are the best person I know, Blue. You are not a terrible person for loving that little girl in there and wanting her to be part of your family. She is so lucky to have you in her life and throughout her life."

She lets out a small breath and it's at that moment that I realize how close our faces are. Man I really have an urge to cross a line right now and see what it's like to kiss Sage Calloway.

But realizing this is not the moment while she is being vulnerable I drop my hand off her chin. She keeps her head where it is and I don't move an inch. If she is wanting to initiate it, you better believe I will jump on that chance. Aspen, being the terrible wingwoman that she is, let's out a bark as she sees a firefly float by her head. Sage is the first to turn away and look to Aspen. She laughs a little as Aspen begins running after the firefly across the yard. "You don't realize how beautiful it is out here during this time of the year."

I don't take my eyes off of her when I respond, "yeah one of the most beautiful things I have seen." Sage glances back to me and sees that I am still looking at her. I see her begin to blush and realize that I should probably get Aspen back before she runs off into the trees.

Standing up I whistle for Aspen and she comes running back. I grimace as I look back at Sage's house. "Hopefully Parker is a hard sleeper and we didn't wake her up with all the barking and whistling." Sage stands and looks at the house, "from what I have seen so far, she seems like a hard sleeper."

"Noted." I mutter under my breath. "We should all probably head inside and get some sleep. I have big plans for the three of us tomorrow." Sage nods her head. "Thanks for listening tonight Lucas." She turns to Aspen and bends down to pet her, "and thank you for trying to keep me company".

"We will always be here for you Blue." Sage looks up at me and I can't help but smile. "Alright come on Aspen, let's let Sage get to bed." We walk across the yard and when we get to the back door I open it for Aspen and then turn to make sure Sage gets in and locks up.

I wake up the next morning right as the sun is rising, excited to spend the day with Sage and Parker. Lucky for me, they didn't have any plans. I jump out of bed and hop in the shower to get ready for the day. While in the shower I can't help but think of last night and how I was seconds away from kissing Sage. I wonder if her lips will taste like what she smells like, vanilla and citrus. Shaking my head as I step out of the shower, I finish getting ready and walk across the yard with Aspen.

Sage gave me a key when I gave her one of mine so I unlock the back door and step inside. I hear the tv going so I head to the living room. Aspen makes it before I do and jumps on the couch next to Parker. "Mr. Lucas, you're back!" She giggles as Aspen licks her cheek. "Hey Aspen." I smile at the two of them. They are already best buds. "Good morning Parker. Where's Ms. Sage at?" "Oh she's still sleeping. I didn't want to wake her so I came down here."

She looks a little nervous like she is unsure if she did something wrong.

"Good idea. Ms. Sage gets a little grouchy in the morning." I wink at her and she giggles. "I'm gonna go see if I can find her upstairs." She nods and turns her head back to the tv. Aspen calms down and lays down with her head in Parker's lap. I go upstairs, taking two at a time. Knowing which room is Sage's, I head straight there. I poke my head in first and see her curled up on her side surrounded by covers. I could easily slip in right behind her. Deciding that's not the best route, I sit on the edge of her bed. Her eyes flutter open feeling the pressure on the bed. "Good morning, Blue".

Her eyes get big and she sits up and the covers drop to her lap. Okay, I changed my mind. I think sleepy morning Sage may be my new favorite. She is in a matching violet sleep set and her long blonde hair is in a pony tail high on her head. Her cheeks are a little pink, probably from me waking her up and her face is free of any makeup. She's beautiful. "Uh, good morning? Is everything okay? Is Parker okay?" She reaches over and grabs her phone to check the time.

"Everything is okay. Parker is downstairs watching a show with Aspen." I smile as she visibly relaxes. "Okay that's good." She leans back on her pillows with a sigh. "I'm shocked I slept in. I am usually such an early riser. I must have been tired after the busy week." I grimace as I realize I could've let her sleep in more. "I wish I would've let you sleep longer." She shakes her head, "no I need to make sure Parker gets breakfast."

"Well that's good because I'm taking you ladies to breakfast before we go on our adventures. I'll go help Parker get ready. You take your time and meet us downstairs." Sage looks at me with her jaw open but I don't give her a chance to say anything as I jump off the bed and head back downstairs.

When I get downstairs, Aspen head pops up as I get to the living room causing Parker's head to turn to me. "Alright Parker we need to head upstairs and get you ready. We are going to go out for some breakfast and then some fun. Sound good?" She nods at me with a smile, turns off the tv and heads upstairs. I follow after her as she leads me to her bedroom. I notice that there is more stuff in here now and there is a stack of magic treehouse books on her nightstand. I walk over there and pick one up before turning back to Parker, "these used to be my favorite when I was growing up."

She looks over at me from her dresser where she was pulling out clothes and smiles. "My mom was reading those to me before bed each night before she died. Now Ms. Sage is going to read them to me." My heart aches for this little girl but at the same time I am impressed at how well she is taking the transition. Focusing back on our task of getting her ready, "alright Parker did you pick out some clothes for today?" She holds up a shirt and some shorts. "Yep!"

I smile at how excited she is. "Okay great. I'm going to go over to your bathroom so you can change. When you're done, go in there and we will brush your hair and teeth." She nods so I step into the hall and across to her bathroom. Luckily her toothbrush and toothpaste is in a holder on the counter and her hair brush was easy to find under the sink.

Within a minute Parker is skipping down the hall to the bathroom. "All dressed Mr. Lucas." I smile as she goes to the sink and grabs her toothbrush and toothpaste. Once her teeth have been brushed, she turns to me "can you braid my hair?" Parker has long curly brown hair and I feel out of my element. "Uh that might be more of a job for Ms. Sage." She looks sad at my response so I continue "but I promise I will learn and then next time I will definitely braid it." She likes that answer and gives me a nod and a smile. "Okay, you can just put it in a ponytail then."

Not having much experience with this, it takes me a second to figure out how to get her hair to stay but she remains patient with me. "Alright, I think it looks good." It looks like the pony tail that Sage had this morning. "We just need one more thing". I look at her confused so she continues, "we need a bow!" She runs out of the bathroom and into her room. She comes back with a bow that thankfully I just have to clip into her hair.

"Now it's perfect" she beams at me and her smile and joy remind me of Sage. These two are more similar than Sage realizes. "Alright let's head downstairs and check on Aspen while we wait for Ms. Sage." She nods her head and I follow her down the stairs. Parker runs over to where Aspen is sitting with her toys and starts to play with her. Now we just need one more cute girl to join us.

# CHAPTER 24
# - SAGE

Once Lucas leaves my room, I jump out of bed and head to my bathroom. Gosh I am glad I am in a cute set of pajamas and not in an old T-shirt and sweats. Oh no. I bet I had morning breath that whole time. I put my hand up to my mouth and breath out to check. Ugh, it's not great.

I jump in the shower to do a quick wash, not getting my hair wet. Once I am out of the shower, I grab my outfit for the day and start with my makeup. I can hear Lucas and Parker in her room probably picking out clothes. I send a quick text to my girls.

Me: I have HUGE news. We need to talk later today.

Gracie: Sage, you know you can't send a text like that and then expect us to wait all day to find out what it is.

Brooklyn: not cool Sage. Not cool.

Me: I know, I'm sorry. I'm headed out the door now but will call you later. Love you!

Brooklyn: You know we love you too! Better be good news later.

Gracie: talk to you later!

Smiling at what their response will probably be when they find out that I now have Parker. They will probably be here within the next weekend to meet her. I finish up my makeup as quickly as possible, with just a few swipes of mascara and a quick layer of foundation. I am brushing through my hair when I hear Lucas and Parker in the bathroom. She asks him to do braids with her hair and I am about to go save him when I hear him promise to learn how to for next time. Knowing Lucas, he will be practicing every chance he gets so that he doesn't disappoint her. He's a good one.

After brushing my hair I realize that my curls from yesterday have held up so I call it good with a quick spray of dry shampoo and head downstairs. By the time I reach the bottom of the staircase Lucas's eyes meet mine. I didn't get a good look at him earlier but now I take him in.

He is wearing a long sleeve black Henley that shows off his muscles just enough without being too obvious and some blue jeans. His hair is styled like it always is, with just enough gel to make me want to run my fingers through it to feel how soft it is. He looks shocked for a second so I look down at my outfit to make sure it doesn't have any stains or isn't too wrinkly. I am wearing leggings and an oversized sweater from college with my white vans. It all looks fine to me. I look back up and Lucas shakes his head and smiles, "You look beautiful, Sage."

I can feel myself blushing, "Thank you. You don't look too bad yourself." I smile at him and add with a wink, "but I think I like the uniform better." I turn to make sure Parker is ready to go. She is in a cute blue tshirt that makes her blue eyes pop, with some black shorts. Her hair is pulled into a ponytail, turns out Lucas can do that one well, and she has an adorable white bow in her hair. It looks like she is ready to go and is bouncing on her feet from her excitement. Lucas also looks like he is ready to get going as he stands up from the couch.

"Alright ladies, are you guys ready to go?" Parker nods her head and smiles. "Sage, are you okay if we leave Aspen here until we get back or do you want me to take her back to mine?"

I shake my head, "no that's okay. She's always welcome over here." Parker looks at Aspen and smiles, "that means I get to play with you later." I look to Lucas. "Are we taking my car since I have the car seat?" He shakes his head, "come on Blue, you know my answer is going to be no."

I laugh, "well I'll just go grab Parker's car seat then." He shakes his head again, "you don't need to do that. I picked one up at the store yesterday before my shift." Stunned, I watch the two of them head to the front door. Lucas glances back at me, "Come on Blue, you're burning daylight standing there daydreaming." I roll my eyes but smile as he throws my words back at me.

We step out of my house, I lock up, and we walk across the front yard to Lucas's house. He opens his garage with an app on his phone and Parker gasps loudly. We both look to her to make sure she is okay. "You have a police car?? Wait. Are you a policeman Mr. Lucas?" I smile at Parker's wonderment. I guess she hasn't had the chance to see him in uniform yet. He came over last night once she was already asleep. "Yep." He smiles down at her as he heads over to the SUV. Now it's my turn to be shocked. "Wait what happened to your patrol car?"

He opens the back door for Parker to crawl into the car seat installed in the back seat and shuts the door before going to the passenger door and opening it for me, "I asked Chief Harrington if I could switch it for this since I knew that I needed to have enough room for the car seat." He waits for me to climb in before shutting the door behind me and rounding the front to get into the driver's seat.

"You know you didn't have to do that." He looks over at me with a disappointed but also confused look so I continue "We could have just started to take my car. You could have even driven if that made you feel better." I don't want him to think that I meant he didn't need to because he wouldn't be with us.

He brightens back up and pulls out of his garage.

"I wanted to make sure that we both had the ability to drive Parker just in case." He looks back at Parker in the rear view mirror and winks at her. I can't see her without turning around but I know she is beaming and it has nothing to do with the police car and everything to do with Lucas.

Lucas brought us to The Diner for breakfast where Parker insisted that she needed to sit in the booth by herself which means Lucas and I are sitting across from her. I have been overheated this entire breakfast feeling Lucas's body heat next to mine. Of course Lucas doesn't seem to even notice considering he scooted in enough that there is only about an inch in between us. He's a large muscular guy, but he doesn't need to take the whole bench.

Parker is chatting away about the magic treehouse book that we are reading together and chowing down on her pancakes. "Mr. Lucas, what are we going to do after breakfast?" He looks up at Parker from his food and smiles. Parker may look at Lucas like he hung the moon, but the way Lucas looks at Parker does something to my insides. This girl is going to be surrounded by so much love.

"I was thinking about taking you girls to go mini golfing." Pennystone is a small town with not many options so I am not completely shocked by his answer. I remember going to mini golf with my family growing up. Lucas was typically there with Stanton. As you could probably imagine, we would get pretty competitive and my dad would have to remind us that we were only there for fun.

Parker gives him a sad smile, "My mom and dad loved mini golfing. That's where I had my last birthday party." I can feel a lump in my throat and my anxiety rising. Lucas must sense it because he reaches over and interlocks our fingers together. "Would it be okay with you if you show us how to play today, Parker?" She seems to shake off her sadness and digs back into her pancakes. "I can do that. My dad taught me all the tricks on how to get the ball in the hole in one shot."

"He sounds like he was really good at mini golf." Lucas looks at me and smiles and squeezes my hand before looking back at Parker. "Yeah he was the best! But I bet you will be good too Mr. Lucas. I'll teach you and Ms. Sage. My mom and dad would want you guys to have fun too."

I swear if one of them looks at me right now I may lose it. This little girl has a heart of gold and the world doesn't deserve her. Lucas keeps a hold of my hand the rest of the meal until it is time for us to leave, then reluctantly lets me go as we head back to the car.

We are headed to mini golf when Parker speaks up from the back. "Mr. Lucas, do you have Taylor Swift on your radio?" My kind of girl. Lucas looks over at me and smiles, "I actually do Parker. Sage, can put it on for us." He winks at me as he hands me the cord.

The rest of the drive is filled with Parker and I singing along and Lucas even joining in on a few which makes Parker giggle. When we get there Lucas opens my door first and then opens Parkers. "Mr. Lucas, you aren't a very good singer." I clap my hand over my mouth to keep from laughing out loud and Lucas sees my shoulders shaking. "I am definitely not as good as you and Sage. But did you know she loves to have dance parties at home?" Lucas gives me a smirk as Parker turns to me with an excited face, "can we do that together Ms. Sage?"

"Yes of course, we will even let Mr. Lucas join us with his terrible singing". I smirk right back at Lucas and he rolls his eyes. "Alright ladies let's go play some mini golf." Lucas leads us into the building, holding the door open for both of us and then puts his hand on my back as he trails in from behind. Is it just me or is it hot out here today?

Luckily it isn't too busy today. That is surprising because it is finally starting to cool off as we go into the fall season. We go through each hole and Parker gives us the tips that her dad taught her. Surprisingly, Lucas and I aren't being too competitive today and are excellent students for Parker's lessons. Maybe it is because Parker is smoking us and there is no way she isn't going to win.

We finish up our golf, and yes Parker won by a lot. She wasn't kidding about her dad teaching her. As we are heading out, Parker sees the arcade. She looks up to Lucas with her big blue eyes, "Mr. Lucas, could we go play some games before we leave?"He looks to me and I shrug and nod before he turns back to her, "let's do it!" She smiles and races off towards the arcade. She already has this man wrapped around her finger.

I stop Lucas before he heads inside. "Hey I need to make a phone call, are you okay if I step out while you guys play?"

"Yeah for sure, go ahead. We will just be in there whenever you finish up." He turns to follow after Parker and I step outside to a picnic table and have a seat. I'm not sure how long Lucas is planning on spending his day with us and if I don't make this phone call there may be wrath to pay. I dial both Gracie and Brooklyn and they both pick up at the same time.

"Sage Marie, you better tell us this news before I lose it." I roll my eyes at the typical dramatics of Brooklyn. "Did Lucas confess his love to you yet?" Wait what. I look around to make sure Lucas and

Parker are still inside. "Uh no, this is something else."

"Well get on with it, we are dying over here!"

I give them the run down of Parker's car accident and deciding to take her in. I tell them all about the first night with pizza and movies then meeting my family the next day. You can tell they are shocked. I check my phone to make sure I wasn't disconnected. "Y'all still with me?"

Gracie is the first to speak up. "Yep, still here just processing. Sage, this is amazing."

"So freaking amazing! You have always talked about wanting to be a mom. I mean at one point you and Matt were talking about rings and houses." I cringe as I think about that time period with Matt. Little did I know that while I was thinking of marriage, he was sneaking around with women to increase his career opportunities.

"You guys have to meet Parker! She is so amazing. She's super smart, loves to read, and is amazing in her gymnastics class. She is also so kind and polite."

"She sounds perfect Sage. We are really happy for you." I smile as I think about how my life got flipped upside down in the past week in the best way possible.

"And what is the news with Lucas?" I can just see Brooklyn raising her eyebrows up and down after that question. I see Lucas and Parker making their way towards me. Parker is carrying a stuffed elephant that I'm sure Lucas won for her. "Oh look at that, Lucas and Parker are coming back now. Gotta go!"

"Wait!! Tell us the details of you and your hot cop!!"

"Bye love you!" I laugh as I hang up. Parker is practically jogging as she gets to me. "Ms. Sage, look what Mr. Lucas won in the claw game." She hugs her stuffed elephant to her chest and my heart is about to burst. I look at Lucas who must be feeling the same way with the smile he has on his face. "That is super awesome Parker. Did you guys get to play all the games you wanted to?"

Parker smiles and nods, "yep! Mr. Lucas was trying to get you a stuffed animal too." She looks over to him with a smirk, "but he was only able to get my elephant. He tried like a hundred times." Lucas shakes his head with a smile. "That dang unicorn was blocking all the other ones and was too far in the corner for the machine to grab it."

"Well I am glad you at least got Parker the elephant. You two ready to go home?" Lucas looks to Parker who is nodding and back to me. "Absolutely." Then the cutest thing happens. Parker reaches up and holds Lucas's hand as we walk towards his car. You can see on his face how proud he is in that moment to be holding that little girl's hand. With one hand holding her elephant and the other holding Lucas's hand, she looks like she has had the best day. And it's not even lunch time yet.

# CHAPTER 25
# - LUCAS

"Alright, how about some sandwiches for lunch? I am pretty sure there are some chips in the pantry too?" We are back at Sage's house and Parker and I are sitting on the barstools while Sage is looking in the refrigerator. "That sounds perfect, Sage. Parker, what kind of sandwiches do you like?" I can't believe that there is so much to still learn about Parker even though it feels like she's been here forever. "I like turkey with cheese please." Sage nods her head and turns to me, "and you Lucas?"

"That works for me. Add mustard to mine please." Parker laughs next to me, "Ew mustard is gross." This gets Sage laughing as she heads to the pantry for the bread and chips. Shaking my head with a smile, I turn to Parker. "Do you wanna take Aspen outside with me? She probably needs to go to the bathroom and will want to run and play." Sage pops out of the pantry, "That's a great idea! I'll whip these together and then we can eat outside." Parker hops off the barstool and calls for Aspen, "Come on Aspen, lets go play!" She takes off to the backdoor with Aspen trailing behind her. I follow behind them and open the door so they can run out.

I take a seat on the couch out back and watch as Parker has Aspen doing laps around the yard chasing her. Less than five minutes later, Sage pops out balancing all three plates. I jump up, "Here let me help you." She gives me a small smile "thank you." I take all three plates and put them on the small table in front of the couch. "I am just going to get some water bottles for us." Before I can tell her I can do that for her, she is already slipping inside. I settle back on the couch and see that Aspen and Parker have found a stick and are playing catch now. "Do you think we should call Parker over to eat?" Sage stinks down on the couch next to me.

"Let's let them play for a little bit longer. It looks like rain clouds are starting to come in so we will have to spend the afternoon inside." We both look up at the sky and see that dark clouds are definitely coming in. "We huh? You don't have plans for your day off?" We both pick up our plates and start eating the best turkey sandwiches I have ever had. Sage must have toasted them with butter to make the cheese all melty. "The only plans I have are hanging out with my three girls." I can see a small smile spread as Sage continues eating.

The clouds are really starting to come in so Sage calls Parker over and she gobbles up her sandwich in record time. See, I am not the only one who thought the sandwiches were amazing. "Alright you three, let's head inside before the rain chases us in." I grab all the plates and the girls grab the water bottles. Parker gets Aspen's attention as she stands up and we all head inside. I head to the sink and look back over my shoulder as Sage and Parker "I've got these dishes. How about you ladies go pick out a movie?"

Parker nods her head at me and looks at Sage. Sage looks from me down at Parker and whispers something in her ear that makes Parker smile and take off jogging to the living room. "Thanks for doing the dishes Lucas." I place a plate in the dishwasher and glance back at Sage, "thank you for making us a delicious meal." She smiles before heading to the living room where I can hear Parker, "Aspen you gotta get up, we are making a fort!"

Sage does not mess around when it comes to movie forts. I should have anticipated that one. Growing up, Stanton, Sage, and I would help Mrs. Calloway make enormous forts in their living room and once their dad got home from work we would all crawl under and watch movies. If someone were to walk into Sage's living room, they wouldn't even be able to walk to the hallway, that is how big the girls made the fort. Luckily, they thought of everything and made a tunnel out of here to the hallway so that we could get to the bathroom.

Now we are laying on the ground watching CoCo with Parker and Aspen in the middle of me and Sage. I look over at Sage and notice that both her and Parker are asleep. Parker is laying on Sage's shoulder and Aspen is snuggled up in between them. I take out my phone and take a picture, sending it to Sage. She doesn't realize how great she is doing with Parker. You can tell that Parker loved Sage as a teacher, but now? There is a real bond between those two that will last forever.

I am caught staring as Sage blinks her eyes open as the final credits roll. She looks down to see Parker asleep and then looks up at me with a smile. "Hi" she mouths to me trying not to wake Parker and Aspen. I smile back at her. Man, this woman. Parker must hear the ending of the movie because she also stirs awake. Sage looks back down at Parker, "Hey Parker. It looks like we fell asleep during the movie." Parker looks over to the TV and realizes that it's over. "That's okay. I have seen that one before."

"I should probably go get started on dinner." Sage sits up and crawls out which stirs Aspen awake. She sits up with her tail wagging at

Parker.

"Parker, I am going to go help Sage make dinner. Do you want to stay here and play with Aspen or do you want to come help too?" Parker thinks about it for a second. "I am going to stay here with Aspen. We made sure her toys were in the fort too. "Sounds perfect. Aspen loves the orange ball the best." I smile at Parker and then crawl out of the fort and head to the kitchen.

Sage is pulling out a pan when I walk in. "Alright chef, what can I do to help?" She looks around for a moment, "I think it is time to increase your skills and see what your hands are good at. Can you dice up a cucumber, a tomato, and some red onion for me?" Smiling, I walk around the island to where the cutting board is, "I think I can manage. But Blue, there are a lot of things my hands are good at." I smirk as I can see a blush forming across her cheeks. She spins to the stove and begins cooking some chicken. I smile to myself and start chopping.

Once I finish dicing I ask her where she wants them, "You can put them in this bowl." I walk over to where she is at by the stove to add my chopped vegetables to the bowl she has out.
"How did my hands do?" She looks up to me at her side, looks down at the bowl, then back at me, "looks like you weren't lying about your skills. I'll keep that in mind." With that she gives me a little smirk and a wink before looking back at the chicken.

Two can play that game. I step behind her and feel her stiffen. "Blue, don't start something you can't finish." I whisper in her ear, keeping quiet. Sage spins around and I refuse to take a step back. She has to tip her head back to make eye contact with me. "We both know I hate not finishing something." I find myself fighting the urge to put our money where both our mouths are. But when I kiss Sage for the first time, I don't want to have to worry about it being interrupted by a hungry 6 year old.

As if to prove my point, Parker comes into the kitchen and hops onto a barstool. "It smells really good. What are you making?" She isn't even phased by how close Sage and I are standing but you can tell Sage definitely notices as she clears her throat and steps around me. I stay there staring at the stove, willing my heartrate to calm down. "They are chicken gyro bowls. I am not sure what you do and don't like but this meal you get to choose what you put in."

"What is a gi-ro?" I smile at Parker's innocence and her mispronunciation. "It is like greek style chicken. They eat it gyros in some places in Europe." Parker looks starstruck at Sage right now as she is explaining how it is usually eaten in a pita bread but tonight we are going to eat it with rice. I get it Parker, I am pretty enamored myself. "Alright I think everything is ready so let's dish up." She looks out the window at the rain, then back to us, "We are going to have to eat inside tonight."

Parker hops off the barstool and comes to grab a bowl. "That's okay. I like your kitchen table." I look over to Sage, "You should have seen it when Sage decided to skip a few steps." I smile as I think of my first night over here. "Ms. Sage, you obviously have to follow the instructions." I smile at Parker and nod, "Yeah Ms. Sage, obviously." Sage rolls her eyes at the two of us as we continue dishing up and sit down at the table.

"Oh we forgot drinks. What would you like Parker?" Sage goes to stand up. "I got it Blue. Parker, what do you want tonight?" Parker looks at Sage then back at me, "Can I get some lemonade Mr. Lucas?" This little girl is so polite. Her parents did a really great job raising her. I smile even though my heart is a little heavy in that moment, "One lemonade coming right up. What about you, Sage?"

"I will have the same, thank you." I speed off to the kitchen and grab three cups of lemonade and return back to the table. "Ms. Sage, why does Mr. Lucas call you Blue sometimes?" I glance up from my food. This is something that we have never talked about so I am curious on what she thinks is the answer.

"When Lucas and I were in the 7th grade, we were doing an art project." Parker is completely zoned in on Sage. So far she is going in the correct direction. "Well we had a kid in our class, Tommy, who was a little wild and thought it would be funny to flick blue paint at me."

Parker gasps, "did he get it all over your clothes?" Sage smiles at Parker's concern, "yep all over my clothes and face. Lucas and my brother thought it was super funny and ever since that day, he has called me Blue." I smile at the memory but Parker turns to me with a scowl, "It is not funny when people are mean Mr. Lucas." Sage covers her mouth to hide her smile.

"Parker, that story did happen. But don't worry at recess later I told Tommy I didn't want to be his friend if he was going to be mean to Sage." Sage's mouth drops open but I continue, "and Sage is kind of right with the story. But what she doesn't realize is that when the blue paint hit her face it made me realize that her blue eyes are the deepest blue I have ever seen. I call her Blue because that day I realized blue is my favorite color."

Sage looks completely shocked and you can see the wheels are turning in her head.

"Mr. Lucas, my eyes are also Blue!" Parker looks up to me and smiles. "I know. They are also my favorite color. You both have the best eyes in the whole world." Parker looks so proud, "don't forget Aspen has blue eyes too." I smile as I think of my three blue eyed girls. Sage doesn't comment on my story but falls into conversation with Parker about the upcoming fall break they have and what they want to do while they are off of school. Sounds like Gracie and Brooklyn are going to try to come down and meet Parker. Soon, we are all finished eating and I am in the kitchen doing dishes when I hear Sage tell Parker to head upstairs to take a shower, get in her pajamas, and brush her teeth before she goes up to read their book together.

Sage heads back into the kitchen and packs up the leftovers. "Did you really tell Tommy that you wouldn't be his friend anymore?" I shut the dishwasher and turn to sage, leaning my hip against the counter and crossing my arms. "I haven't spoken to him since that day." You can tell that she is in her head and doesn't know how to process. Tonight she learned that the nickname she thought was meant to tease her was really to describe my favorite part of her.

I push off the counter and stalk towards her. She finishes putting the lids on the tupperware and turns to me. I keep walking until my hands are on either side of her on the counter and she is looking up at me. "Tell me what's going through your head Blue." She looks towards the kitchen window where it is still raining and then back to me. Being this close I realize that her eyes are truly my favorite color. "I am thinking that the boy I thought as enemy number one has become my best friend."

Unable to resist myself any longer, I cup her face with my hand and bring my lips to hers. If I've shocked her she doesn't show it. It feels like I've waited my whole life for this moment and

I can't get enough. I tease her bottom lip with my tongue and she gladly opens up for me to get a full taste. Sage tastes just like I expected, like vanilla and citrus. She bites my bottom lip, getting a groan to come out of my throat. Needing more, I drop my hands to her waist and pull her flush against me before I cup her butt and lift her on the counter.

Sage spreads to her legs to let me in closer. She moans as she feels just how much this kiss is affecting me. Sage brings her hands up across my abs and to my chest before looping them behind my neck. I drop my mouth to her neck and find a spot where her neck meets her shoulder that must be a sensitive spot as she pulls slightly on my hair. Before we can continue, we hear Parker yell from upstairs "Ms. Sage, I am ready to read our book." We both stop our exploring and I put my forehead to hers. "You better not be regretting that because that was the best kiss I've ever had." She chuckles, "Should I go tell the ladies of Pennystone that their yummy bachelor just crowned his best kiss?" I lean back to look her fully in the eyes, "You can tell them anything you want Blue, as long as they know that I am no longer a bachelor." I can see the shock and I realize I may have jumped the gun a bit.

I step back and she jumps down from the counter, "I should probably go upstairs before Parker comes downstairs and I have to explain why you look so uncomfortable in those jeans."

She smirks at me but I don't miss how her eyes get bigger when she drops her eyes down my body and bites her bottom lip. "Blue, if you keep giving me that look, I will carry you up those stairs and apologize to Parker on the way to your room."

She rolls her eyes as she knows I wouldn't ever do anything to disappoint Parker. "You head upstairs. I am going to finish cleaning up and then I should probably take Aspen home for her dinner." She looks disappointed and that hurts. "Sage, if I could spend the night worshiping your gorgeous body I would. But you and Parker both have an early morning."

She reluctantly nods, "Okay okay. Will we see you tomorrow?" It's moments like these that I don't love the fluctuating schedule of being a police officer. "I work the evening shifts this week. So I won't be home until late each night." She could tell she is disappointed and hell so am I. "But can I come over on Saturday?" She smiles at me and my knees almost go out. "We would love that. Then we can ride over to Miles' birthday party together on Sunday."

"Ms. Sage, are you coming to read?"

"Yeah Parker, I am coming now!" She gives me a little smile. Knowing she needs to get upstairs I give her a quick but not too quick kiss. "Goodnight Blue. I will lock up on my way out." She slowly walks away and turns back before making it to the stairs, "Goodnight Lucas, thanks for the amazing day." With that she turns and heads upstairs.

I take a deep breath. Did that really just happen? I mean I have been wanting to do that for days now but even I am surprised by that kiss. Maybe this is what it is supposed to feel like when you find your person.

I finish up the dishes, put her leftovers in her fridge, whip down the counters before going into the living room and cleaning up the fort. As Aspen and I are headed to the back door I stop into the kitchen and write Sage a note before walking out the back door and locking up. Tonight I kissed my best friend and I have every intention of doing it again.

# CHAPTER 26
# - SAGE

I wake up the next morning with a smile on my face. Life is good. I've never would have guessed two months ago that I would be this happy. Now that I have Parker and Lucas in my life, I feel like everything leading up to this point has led me to them. I wasn't lying when I said that Lucas has become my best friend. Hopefully Stanton doesn't mind that I stole his best friend.

I cringe as I think of Stanton's response to what happened in the kitchen last night. The worst part of that earth shattering kiss? I'm not going to get a repeat of it for the rest of the week with our schedules conflicting.

Once I am ready for the day, I pop into Parker's room to wake her up and help her get dressed and her hair done for the day. She is excited and telling me about how Ms. Julie has a surprise for them today because they hit their reading goal for the month. I get her curly hair into a messy bun on the top of her head and she reminds me not to forget a bow. We head downstairs to eat breakfast before we need to be out the door for school. "Ms. Sage, it looks like someone wrote on your whiteboard." I look over from the pantry and smile as I recognize Lucas's handwriting.

> *Blue if you want to know how I feel about your eyes, listen to the first line in Tim McGraw by Taylor Swift. Counting down the seconds until I get to see you and Parker again.*

My heart is about to burst as I recall the song. "What does it say, Ms. Sage?"

"Oh Lucas just told me what his favorite Taylor Swift song is. He must have really liked singing with us in the car yesterday." She giggles as she remembers our little car concert. I will forever keep the memory of that day in my heart. "Can we listen to it on the way to school?" I grab two bowls and pour in some cereal. I typically make breakfast for us before we head to school but Parker knows on Mondays we keep it simple. "I love that idea Parker. Let's do it" she smiles as she digs into her cereal. We are out the door within the next ten minutes and as we listen to the song on repeat my heart swells more and more.

This week has gone by so fast, I'm grateful it's

already Thursday and there are only two more days before we get to see Lucas again. Turns out having a 6 year old keeps you very busy. Lucky for me Parker is a dream. She will hang out with me in my classroom after school while I get things ready for the next day and she will do her homework before we have to head home.

On days where she doesn't have homework or I have extra work to do, she will choose to sit in my reading corner or she will go down the hall and play with Amanda, another teacher's daughter who is in her class this year. Amanda loves to read as well and whenever they are playing in my room, I love it when I hear Parker tell Amanda about the magic treehouse book we are on.

While my students are in music class today I decide to pop over to the library and see if there are any more magic treehouse books that I can borrow. With how busy everything has been I haven't been able to pop in and see Michael or Julie much. I spot Michael behind the front desk and walk over to him. "Hey Michael, how's it going?"

He looks up from his desk and when he realizes it's me he smiles, "hey Sage, things are going great. How are you? I heard through the grapevine that you took in little Parker. That's really amazing." I feel a little guilty for not telling him myself, "yeah sorry you heard it through the grapevine and not from me, it's just been a little crazy."

He laughs, "yeah I bet. But hey you now get to have that family you have always dreamed about." Smiling as I think of my life with Parker, "yeah she's amazing. I'm really lucky honestly."

"I would argue that she is the lucky one." Still feeling a little uncomfortable when I get praised for taking in Parker, I pull the topic away from me. "She is actually one of the reasons I stopped by. Besides wanting to check in with you, I was wondering if you have any magic treehouse books. Parker and I have been reading them together and while I have some, I don't have them all."

Michael nods, "yep follow me". He comes out from behind his desk and I follow him towards his treehouse section of the library. Over the summer Michael decided to add a section to the library that looks like a treehouse fort. From what I have heard the kids love going in and reading feeling like they are in a special fort. "Michael I know I have told you before but this treehouse section is really really amazing."

Michael looks back over his shoulder and smiles, "thanks, the magic treehouse books actually were kind of my inspiration. Here we are. They should be right here on the second row... yep. Here they are. I'm pretty sure we have the complete set so you could borrow as many as you want."

"This is amazing Michael. Thank you! I'll snag maybe just one today but I'll be back for sure." I go ahead and grab one that I know for a fact I don't have and we head back to the front of the library to check it out. "I better head back to my classroom, my students will be back soon. It was really great to see you Michael. Let's figure out a day to eat lunch together with Julie."

He smiles at me. "I would love nothing else, Sage." I smile as I wave and head back to my classroom.

After school Parker and I run to the store to pick up a gift for Miles' party on Sunday. Who knew little errands would be so much more fun when you have a little buddy with you? Parker picked out a toy that comes with all types of sports items that I know Stanton is also going to love. Now we are back at home waiting for my dad to come over for a movie night with me and Parker. I get a call from an unknown number. Looking over at Parker who is coloring at the table, I decide to step out back and take it. It could be Mitchell with an update from the state.

"Hello this is Sage."

"Sage. Thank goodness you picked up. I wasn't sure if I was ever going to get you to talk to me." Ugh Matt. "Matt why are you calling me?"

"Babe, I messed up big time. I know that. You and I are meant to be together. Please tell me you will come back to Knoxville. I called your old school and they said they would love to have you back." I really did love that school. It was one of the best in all of Knoxville and I felt really proud when I got a job there right out of college. I shake my head, "I can't Matt. Please don't call me again. We both need to move on."

"Wait please don't hang up. Please tell me what I can do. I'll come to Pennystone and we can talk about it." I look back inside at Parker and my stomach sinks. "Matt please promise me you won't come here. I am fostering a little girl and nothing can mess up my chances to keep her. Matt I swear if you come here, I will never forgive you."

"You're fostering a little girl?"

"Yeah Matt. It fell into my lap and I am really really happy. We weren't good together and we both know it. It's time for both of us to find what makes us happy. Please don't call back."

With that I hang up the phone, shake my head and step back inside. I head to the kitchen and start making popcorn when the doorbell rings. "Do you want me to go get it Ms. Sage?"

Remembering what Lucas told me about checking the camera first, I pull open the app on my phone checking to make sure it's my dad then nod to Parker "yeah you can go open it. It's my dad." She smiles and hops down from the barstool racing towards the front door. I can hear when she opens the door. "I think I'm at the wrong house, this one has a cute little girl here, not my Sage." I hear her laugh before she says "Mr. Shawn, you know I live here now with Ms. Sage."

I hear the front door shut, he must have followed her in and then " oh that's right Parker. How could I forget?" She giggles as she leads him back to the kitchen. "Hey baby girl, how are you?" My dad comes around the island to give me a side hug as I continue pouring out the popcorn into bowls. "I'm doing great. Really great actually." I smile at him and I can tell he believes it with the smile I get back. "That's what I love to hear." He turns to Parker, "you are making my Sage very happy."

She smiles, "she makes me happy too. Her and Mr. Lucas are my best friends." Bless her heart, she may just make me cry tonight if she keeps it up. My dad though doesn't miss the mention of Lucas and gives me a look that tells me we will be talking about that later. My dad returns his attention back to Parker, "Okay Parker, now that the popcorn is ready to go, do you know what is the best thing to eat with popcorn?" She shakes her head no.

"Peanut m&ms." He gets nervous for a moment and turns to me, "Parker doesn't have a peanut allergy right?" I smile at his concern, "nope all good."

"Well great! I promise Parker it's SO good." We grab the bowls of popcorn and head to my living room. My dad notices the dog bed and the basket of dog toys. "Parker, did you bring a dog with you when you moved here?" She laughs like he said something silly, "No Mr. Shawn, that's for Aspen. She's Lucas's dog." Oh brother, that has my dad giving me another one of those looks. We will most definitely be talking later.

My dad lets Parker pick out our movie for the night and in that moment I realize that he has never picked a movie for himself, he always either let me pick or picked one that he knew I loved. I have the best dad in the world and I'm grateful that Parker now gets to feel his love. Parker and my dad share popcorn, in which Parker agrees the peanut m&ms make the popcorn better, and laugh together while watching A Bug's Life. Once the movie is over, I take Parker upstairs to help her get ready for bed and read a chapter of our book before she is down for the night. When I come back downstairs I find my dad in the kitchen washing the popcorn bowls.

"Hey dad, you didn't need to do those. I was planning on doing them when I came back down." He looks over at me and smiles, "I know baby girl but I wanted to. You should be very proud. That little girl admires you so much." I feel my eyes get a little misty "it helps she came to me pretty perfect. I will never regret taking her in." We head back to the living room and sit down. Before we have the conversation I know he is dying to have, he asks me about how the fostering process is going. "It's going well. I completed all my training and we did the home visit on Monday afternoon which Mitchell said was great. So now we just wait for everything to process." He nods, "that's great Sage. Do you think you would ever adopt Parker?" I have been thinking a lot about this ever since she came to live with me.

"I mean yeah I would love that. But I would never want Parker to feel pressure to do that. She had two amazing parents that loved her with everything they had. I hope she knows that I have no intention of taking their spot or trying to replace them. But if she ever came to me and asked me to be her parent, I would be the luckiest person."

"You're a really good mom Sage, with or without the adoption. I hope you know how proud your mom and I are of you." Here come the tears again. I nod as I try to blink them away. He gets serious again, "okay now onto Lucas. You have dog items over here and he is apparently Parker's best friend. What's going on there?"

I sigh as I think about where to begin. I can't help but smile as I think about how much things have changed since the last time I talked to my dad. "Well Lucas was coming over fairly often before I got Parker, to eat dinner with me. He helped me put together some furniture when I first moved in and discovered that he bought the house next door. After that he would pop by for dinner on nights he wasn't at the station. When I heard about Parker losing her parents I was talking it over with him and he encouraged me to foster her so she wouldn't have to leave Pennystone. He has been really supportive since I got Parker." I don't mention to my dad that he also kissed the living daylights out of me last night in my kitchen.

"Good. He is a good man Sage. I'm not shocked that you guys have finally reconnected." My dad must see the confusion on my face so he continues, "you and Lucas were two peas in a pod when they first moved to town. It wasn't until later that things shifted and he and Stanton became closer. We figured it was just the natural way of life sometimes with young boys and girls. But I am glad that you two have worked it out. He needs good people in his life." I'm not entirely shocked that we used to be best friends when it feels so effortless now. But I am confused about him needing good people. Isn't he surrounded by good people?

"Wait, what do you mean he needs good people? I know his dad died back before we started college but isn't him and his mom close and then obviously he has our family and the other officers?" My dad cringes knowing he may have said too much, "He does. But he also has a past that you may not be aware of." He can tell I'm about to say something and stops me. "It's not my place or anyone but his to tell you about it, Sage. When he is ready he will open up."

I nod my head and my dad stands up to head out. "I better get home to my wife. I love you baby girl and we love Parker. Your mom is so excited to see her again for the party." I smile as I go to hug my dad, "love you too Dad. Thanks for spending your evening with us."

We say our goodbyes as I walk my dad to the door and then make sure everything is locked up before I head back upstairs. As I am getting ready for bed and am lying in bed to try to get some sleep, I can't help it when my brain tries to figure out what scars Lucas must have and why he hasn't told me about them yet.

# CHAPTER 27
# - LUCAS

It is finally Friday which means I only need to get through today and tomorrow's shift before I get to spend the rest of the weekend with Sage and Parker. I woke up on Monday feeling on top of the world. I had the best weekend with Sage and Parker and let's be honest that kiss was a long time coming. "Walker, you good over there?" James looks over at me from across the desk with an amused look and I know I was spaced out.

"Yeah man. Just lost in my head for a second there." I shake my head and try to focus back on the case we are working on. Someone broke into the gas station in town. The problem is Mr. Johnson hasn't updated his camera since the 90s and it's close to impossible to get any details from the footage we have. "You must be thinking of a certain neighbor and her cute little girl." He smirks over at me.

"I can't even deny it man. Only two more days."

He gives me a little smile that almost looks sad, "I'm happy for you Lucas. Anyone that saw you and Sage together could see this coming from a mile away but now that she has Parker, you found yourself a little family." I can't help but feel grateful to have those two girls in my life. But what if I am not enough for them? What happens if history repeats itself and the cycle isn't broken with me? How can I move forward when there is a chance that I hurt them?

"I can tell by your face that your brain just went somewhere it shouldn't have gone. Don't let it Walker. You are a good man. You aren't like him." I hope that he is right. I don't get the chance to respond before I see my two favorite people walk through the precincts doors. Sage sees me and smiles, making her way over. Once Parker sees me, she jogs over causing Trigger to come out from under James's desk and stand on guard.

"Mr. Lucas, you have a dog here too?!"

James smiles at Parker as she stops but is bouncing on her feet excited to see Trigger. "You must be Parker. And this is Trigger, he is a police dog but is very nice and would love it if you wanted to pet him." Trigger completed all of his training and got certified as a K9 dog last week. It has been great to have him with us. She looks at me with so much excitement, "can I Mr. Lucas?" I laugh, "of course you can, Trigger is the best boy."

While Parker is petting Trigger with James, I

look over to Sage. Man she is beautiful. Today she is in light wash jeans that have some frayed holes at the knees and a Pennystone elementary shirt. You can tell that she must have done an art activity today because she still has some splatters of paint on her arms. What stops me in my tracks of checking her out is the concern on her face. "Not that I don't love seeing you two girls, but is everything okay?"

Parker pops up from petting Trigger, "yeah, Ms. Sage got a package at home today and then asked me if I wanted to come visit you to show you." You can see some redness start to make its way to Sage's cheek and my guard is officially up. "What package did you get?" I can tell that it came out a little gruff and harsh. Sage looks down to Parker and back up at me with wariness in her eyes. James, sensing the tension, turns to Parker. "Hey Parker do you remember Officer Sandoval? She was with you at the hospital after the accident." Parker looks over to him and smiles, "yeah she was super nice and really pretty."

"Well I bet she would love it if you go over to her desk and say hi."

Parker lights up and looks around spotting Officer Sandoval and Officer Darrell. "Okay! Ms. Sage can I go over and say hi?"

Sage looks down at Parker with a smile, "of course Parker, I'm gonna stay here and talk to Lucas and James really quick okay?"

"Okay!" And with that Parker bolts over to Officer Sandoval, who lights up when she sees Parker. "Okay Blue, I'm trying really hard not to freak out. What is in the package? Did Matt send it?" Sage takes a step forever and places the package on my desk, I open it up and see it is some toys, books, and clothes that I am assuming are for Parker.

"When Parker and I got home from school today it was by the front door. I made sure to check the cameras again but just like last time it was delivered by a delivery driver." James glances over at me and cocks on eyebrow. That is when I find the note and my blood starts to boil.

HAPPY THAT YOU HAVE STARTED THAT FAMILY
YOU HAVE ALWAYS WANTED. HOPEFULLY ONE
DAY WE CAN COMPLETE IT. -M

The fact that this guy thinks he will be a part of their family makes me want to laugh but at the same time makes me want to punch a wall at the fact that he ever got the chance to have Sage and screwed it up. Sage must notice the anger building in me. "I think I'm ready to file that restraining order now." I look up at her, "I wasn't worried about it when it was small stuff that felt like he was just trying to apologize. But now this with Parker? I'm ready." I try not to overthink the fact that she told me she would file the restraining order only if she felt like her safety was in jeopardy and now she feels that it is. Not only hers, but Parker's too.

"Absolutely. Let's get this filed as soon as possible and hopefully it will tell him that he needs to move on with his life." I stand to go grab the paperwork needed before James stops me. "Walker you know you can't be involved with this." I turn back to him with a glare, "like hell I can't. We need to make sure this loser stays away from Sage and Parker."

James takes a deep breath before continuing. "You know that's not what I meant. Sage absolutely needs to file the restraining order, especially if his actions have escalated. But you can't be the one to help her submit it. If something were to happen and it was taken to court, the restraining order could lack validity due to your..." he looks at the both of us, "relationship. Another officer is going to have to help her." I crossed my arms as James was talking. He is right and I know he is. Sage puts a hand on my arm. "He's right Lucas. You can't be involved. Can I work with Officer Sandoval on it?"

"Yeah let's go talk to her about it." We walk over to where Officer Sandoval is asking Parker all about her new school year. Parker notices us coming and perks up even more. "Hey Sage! This is Officer Sandoval. Shes SO nice." I'm really grateful that Parker has a positive connection to the night of the accident. I need to get Officer Sandoval something special as a thank you.

"Hey Officer Sandoval it's nice to see you again." Sage must see the confused look on my face. When have they met? I mean I guess it's a small town. "I met Officer Sandoval and Officer Darrell last winter when my car got a flat. I was in the process of popping it off to put on the spare when they pulled up and helped me."

First off, why couldn't I be the lucky one to find Sage in need? And second, I really need to get these officers something for being there for my girls. "Hey Sage, it's good to see you again. Hopefully no more tire issues." She laughs. "Miss Parker was just telling me how much she loves living at your house and that she has the best time when Lucas and Aspen come over." She gives me a questioning look which I return with a smile and a shrug.

Figuring Sage doesn't want to scare Parker about the package, James asks Parker if she wants to take Trigger outside. "Hey Parker, do you want to come with me to take Trigger outside. He probably needs to go to the bathroom and we have a really cool ramp that he likes to run on." She turns to Sage to make sure it's okay and Sage gives her a smile and a nod. "Yes Mr. James, I would like that." She smiles and bounces off with James, holding his hand. I do my best not to get jealous of her holding his hand. James better feel lucky.

"Officer Sandoval, Sage needs you to help her fill out a restraining order against her ex." Officer

Sandoval gets a concerned look and looks to Sage, "is everything okay? He's not harming you right?"

"Oh no, it's not like that. He just has sent me some letters and packages. I got a phone call from him earlier this week." I whip my head to her and she gives me a small apologetic smile. She should have told me about it but I trust her that she put him in his place. "We talked and I told him that it was time for both of us to move on. This last package was geared toward Parker and I just want it to stop before it scares or confuses her."

If it was up to me I would just drive to Knoxville and tell this guy myself to back off. Officer Sandoval must see my thoughts written on my face. "That's really smart Sage. This is a pretty simple process and he will get notified but this way you prevent any interactions that can lead to more serious matters." She says the last chunk looking my way and I roll my eyes. I just want to protect my girls, sue me.

Officer Sandoval and Sage spend the next twenty minutes filling out the restraining order, Sage giving as many details as possible to help solidify the case. Right when they are wrapping up, Chief Harrington walks over and notices the paperwork. "Officer Walker isn't giving you too much trouble Ms. Sage is he?" Word traveled through Pennystone quickly after our breakfast at the diner and mini golf. I am not even a little mad about it.Sage laughs, "nope he's a good one. My ex however, not so much."

Chief Harrington becomes more serious at that statement, "you let us know if he causing any more trouble and we will put a patrol out by your house if needed." Chief Harrington has her own past with a stalker during her early times at the station. Thankfully it never escalated from notes let on her car and a restraining order. But with her reaction, it is obvious she remembers the anxiety and fear that came with it. "Oh that's not necessary Chief Harrington. Lucky for me, I have this guy" she points her thumb at me, "right next door and popping by often. We are more than safe."

My pride swells as she just admitted that I make her feel safe. There's nothing I want to do more than to make sure her and Parker feel safe at home. Self doubt begins creeping in. Will she still feel safe once she knows all of me? My thoughts are broken as chief Harrington continues. "Well perfect. I didn't realize you are neighbors. Seems convenient." She turns to me and gives me a smile and a wink. "You know Sage, we are having a police banquet in a couple of weeks. You and Parker should come. I'm sure Officer Walker would love to show you off."

Sage blushes and turns to me with a smile before responding to Chief Harrington, "that sounds great. Will Jasmine also be there?" "Yep! She would love to see you. She tells me everyday that you are the bestest teacher in the whole world." Jasmine isn't wrong. Sage is truly the best.

Parker, James, and Trigger make it back inside. Sage sees Parker's red face and smiles before turning to all of us, "looks like it's time to head home. Thank you all for your help with this." Chief Harrington and Officer Sandoval both nod. Chief looks from me to Sage. "Make sure to let us know if anything else occurs. We protect the people of Pennystone and especially ones that care for one of our own."

"I promise I will. And I guess we will see you at the banquet."

"Here let me walk you guys out." I place my hand on Sage's back and I don't miss the little shiver she gets which makes me smile.

"Bye Mr. James and Trigger! Thank you for playing with me and showing me all your cool tricks." Trigger is laying at James's feet. He must have played hard to be this pooped. "Thank you Miss Parker for helping Trigger get his exercise. Sage, as always, it's been a pleasure. Please continue to feed our boy here." I smirk as Sage smiles and waves goodbye.

We make it out to the car and I first open Parker's door for her to climb in before opening up Sages. She stands outside the door as we say our goodbyes. "I just want you to know I had every intention of inviting you both to the banquet. I just hadn't seen you all week." Sage gives me a mischievous smile, "yeah sure, you wouldn't want to disrupt your bachelor title bringing the two of us." "Blue. I don't mind reminding you and honestly can tell all of Pennystone that I am no longer a bachelor." She seems surprised so I sneak in for a quick kiss to let her know that I am being very serious.

Okay, I meant for it to be quick but I may have gotten carried away but hey she didn't stop me. Parker chooses that moment to perk up from her car seat in the back. "Mr. Lucas, are you coming to eat dinner with us tonight? Can we see Aspen too?" I reluctantly step away from Sage and pop my head into the car, "sorry Parker I need to stay at work tonight." I can see her face drop a little which breaks my heart. "But hey can you do me a favor?" She perks up and nods excitedly. "Can you get Aspen from my house and play with her for a little bit before dinner?"

"Yeah I can do that! I love playing with Aspen. Can she stay for dinner too?" I glance over my head at Sage who is watching the interaction with a smile and she nods her head. I turn back to Parker. "Since Ms. Sage is the greatest, she said you guys can keep Aspen until I get home."

"Yes!" She pumps her first into the sky. I chuckle, "alright kiddo, be good for Sage tonight okay?" She cocks her head to the side, "I am always good for Ms. Sage. She's the best and I love her."

I slide out of the car and look at Sage who is looking shocked. She must have heard Parker. But honestly I don't know why she is shocked, everyone can tell that Parker thinks the world of her. "I'll sneak over and grab Aspen when I get home tonight. Don't worry about staying up though."

"Don't you work the morning shift tomorrow? How about I just keep her until you get off? Then you'll have to come see us for dinner." She winks at me as she says the last sentence. "Blue, you know I don't need any excuse. We both know I was going to be there whether Aspen was there or not." She smiles up at me. "But thank you for taking Aspen, she will love that."

I slide over to let Sage climb into the driver seat and shut her door. I wave to the two of them as they pull out of the parking lot. This is going to be a long 24 hours before I get to see my girls again.

# CHAPTER 28
# - SAGE

Parker woke up early this morning and she typically is great about letting me sleep in a little bit on Saturdays but this morning she came knocking on my door. She pokes her little head in the doorway. "Ms. Sage, is Mr. Lucas coming over today?" I pat my bed and she jogs in and jumps up. "Yep. He's supposed to be here for this afternoon for dinner."

"Yes!" Same girl, same. "I'm thinking we could go to the park after your gymnastics practice. How does that sound?" Parker nods excitedly, "yes please! I'll go get dressed now." Parker runs off to get ready. I roll out of bed and head to my bathroom to quickly get ready. I throw on a pair of leggings and on oversized sweater before putting my hair into a messy bun and put on a quick swipe of mascara. I keep it simple and lazy on Saturdays.

Once we are both ready and have eaten breakfast, we head out the door. I hope that staying busy makes the day go by fast.

I am watching Parker work on her back bend walkover when I get a phone call from Mitchell. "Hey Mitchell, happy Saturday. How are you?"

"I'm good, Sage. How are you and Parker doing?"

"We are doing great. We are at her gymnastic practice now. Parker is settling in really well and doing well in school." I don't know what he is looking for or if I am getting evaluated on this conversation and that makes me nervous.

"That is really great Sage. This call isn't a check in but I am glad to hear everything is going well." I let out a sigh. "I got some information from Parker's extended family today that you need to be aware of." Well there's the anxiety again. "Uh okay. Is everything okay?"

"Well it depends on how you view it and how it works out. So as you know, we reached out to Parker's extended family to see if any of them would like to volunteer for guardianship." Oh no. Does someone want to take Parker away? I want her to be where she will be happy and I know I am selfish for wanting to keep her for myself but I really don't want to lose her. "We finally heard back from someone. Parker's mom has an uncle that finally responded back to us. He is in the process of reviewing what would be entailed if he were to take Parker."

I don't even know what to say. My worse nightmare is coming true. I could lose Parker and it feels like I just got her. I can't help myself when I ask, "but why now? It's been weeks since her parents passed away." One thing I appreciate is that Mitchell always keep things honest. "Well Sage, honestly? We inform family members when there is a trust fund involved so that they know that they will be given access to help them provide appropriate needs to the child. This isn't the first time that someone has come out like this." He wants Parker to gain access to her trust fund? Ugh, I hate him.

"When this happened before did the people get the kids?" Please say no. Please say no. "More times than not, no. They see the chance for money yes but then they realize the work of raising a child and they back off." I let out the breath I was holding. So there is hope I can keep Parker.

Mitchell must hear, "Sage, we will do everything in our power to make sure Parker is in a safe and loving environment." "I know Mitchell. I probably sound super selfish because this uncle could be great and a connection to her mom. But I really love having her." I get teary eyed as I continue watching her and realize I could lose her.

"I know Sage and I know Parker loves it there with you. You aren't selfish for wanting to give her a positive future and a safe home. We will do what we can to make sure Parker's best interests are met. I'll keep you posted. Have a great rest of your Saturday."

"Thanks Mitchell you too." I hang up the phone and still feel the pit in my stomach. I know it will stay there until I hear that the uncle doesn't want to take Parker away from me.

Parker is playing on the jungle gym with other kids when I decide to call Brooklyn. I am not sure what will happen with the uncle but I wanted to get some legal advice on if there is anything I can do to prevent it. I have been doing my best not to show Parker that I am anxious but I need to talk it through with someone. I thought about calling Lucas but I don't want him to be stressed while at work, he has to have a good mindset to stay safe.

"Hey Sage. How is my small town bestie?"

"Well I'm kind of freaking out a little bit and need your advice." I start to pace as I talk to her. "It's a good thing that I love to give advice. What's going on? Is this about the hot cop? He better be treating you and your little girl well." Smiling, I think about how one day they will learn Lucas's name. "Lucas is great. Seriously no issues there."

"Alright that was vague and sounds like Gracie and I need an update. But we will get to that. What's going on then?"

"Well I got a call from Parker's social worker this morning that Parker has a great uncle that may want to take custody of her." My gut begins to turn again at the thought of her being taken away. "Isn't that a good thing Sage? I mean you knew they were reaching out to extended family."

"Ugh, this may make me sound like a terrible person but it is not a good thing because that means Parker may be taken away from me. Plus I am pretty confident that he only wants to take custody of Parker because she inherited a good chunk of money from her parents death and their house."

"Ah I see. He may be thinking he can dip into that trust fund each month to quote cover the expenses for having a child to take care of."

"Exactly! What if he is only going to take her away and swindle her out of her money? How do I stop this? Can I even do anything to prevent anything from happening? I don't want to lose her." I can feel my anxiety spiking. "Alright first off Sage, you need to calm down. I am sure you are away from Parker right now but you don't want to freak her out. I know she loves being with you so she would probably upset her if she knew she may be taken away." I take a deep breath trying to settle myself. "And while I wish I had some better news, unfortunately you have to leave it up to the state. There is a chance that they can deem the uncle as the best placement for Parker. But they could also agree to keep her with you."

"Yeah I figured it was a wait and see situation.

Her social worker said that many times the family members that are only interested in money back off once they realize the extent of what it takes to take in a child."

"Exactly. You will just have to wait and see Sage. But stop beating yourself up over wanting to keep her. You are amazing for that little girl." I sigh as I look back over to the jungle gym and see Parker laughing as she runs up the steps. "Parker has just made my life so much more full. I really love that little girl and I don't know what I would do if I lose her." I don't even want to consider it.

"You have yourself a little family Sage, it is not a bad thing to want to keep it. I am so happy for you. Gracie and I are trying to find the best time during your fall break to come down and visit so we can meet Parker."

"I would absolutely love that Brooklyn. Please let me know if you guys find a time to come and we will have everything ready for you. Thank you for taking the time to talk this over with me. What would I do without my amazing lawyer best friend?"

"Your amazing lawyer best friend is gonna have to run. You okay?"

"Yeah I'm okay. Thanks again Brooklyn. Love you!"

" Love you! Bye." Brooklyn didn't tell me anything that I didn't already know or assume but talking it over did help me. I head over to the playground to wrangle up Parker. I find her on the swings and when I tell her it's time to go, she skids to a stop and hops right off. We need to head home and start getting things ready for dinner. Our favorite person is coming over tonight.

"Ms. Sage, can I help you make dinner?" Parker is on a barstool across from me at the island. Tonight we are doing homemade pizza and it's a perfect meal for little hands to help. "Yep! I am just about to finish spreading out the dough then we can load it up." I grab the pan that now has the dough all ready to go and get all the toppings we need. "Okay Parker, I am going to pour on some sauce and I need you to take the spoon and make sure to spread it all over." Parker shakes her head with determination, "just like I'm painting a picture."

"Exactly!" I smile as I watch her spread out the sauce. She is determined to get every square inch covered. "Alright now we need cheese. You're going to take a handful of cheese, hold it above the pizza and sprinkle it all over." Parker immediately reaches for the bowl of shredded mozzarella cheese that I have and grabs as much as she can in her little hand before sprinkling it all over. Parker looks up at me after all the cheese is gone, "Just like that?"

"Yep! It's perfect. Now we just need some

pepperonis all over and then we can bake it."
We both spread out as many pepperonis over the
pizza as we can. Once it is done I pop it into
the oven and set the timer. "When is Mr. Lucas
coming over?"

As if on cue, we both hear a knock at the
back door. Parker's face lights up and she takes
off to the door. I laugh as I follow after her
with Aspen trailing behind. She has been waiting
for this all day. When I open up the blinds and
open the door heat immediately spreads through
my core. Lucas is standing there looking just
as excited as Parker with a big smile. He must
have changed out of uniform before coming over
because now he is in some black joggers and a
blink 182 concert tshirt. His hair isn't as styled
as usual meaning he has ran his hand through it
throughout the day. Man I so badly want to get
my hands into it right now. Lucas must see the
heat in my eyes as I check him out because he is
giving me one right back.

"Mr. Lucas! You're finally here!" He squats
down and she jumps into his arms for a hug.
I smile down at the two of them. "Hey Parker,
I missed you too. Did you have a good time at
gymnastics today?" The fact that he remembers
that he has gymnastics on Saturdays makes my
heart swell.

"Yeah it was fun! Then we went to the park! It
was awesome. I got SO high on the swings today."
Parker pops up and turns to me, "Ms. Sage can I

go play with Aspen before the pizza done?"

"That sounds like a perfect plan. I bet she would love to play fetch with her favorite stick." Parker nods and takes off running with Aspen trailing after her.

Before I can even realize what is happening, Lucas grips my face with his hands and kisses me. That heat in my core is definitely back and I try my best not to clench my thighs together. The kiss breaks way too quickly. "Well hello to you too." I chuckle as he lets out a deep breath.

He puts his forehead on my own. "This week has been too damn long and I couldn't wait any longer." He gives me another quick kiss before stepping back and to the side. I instantly miss the connection. "How are my girls doing today?" I look out to Aspen and Parker and remember the emotional rollercoaster that today brought for me. Lucas must see something pass through my face. He comes in close again and interlocks one of our hands together. "Blue, what happened? Did Matt reach out to you?"

I shake my head but keep watching Parker and Aspen. "No, nothing with Matt. I got a call from Parker's social worker today. Parker's mom has an uncle that returned their calls and is considering taking Parker in." I let out a deep breath and try to control my emotions but I can feel my eyes getting watery.

Lucas drops my hand, spins to stand directly in front of me, and grabs my face with both of his hands. "We will never let anyone take Parker away from us." I sigh and a tear rolls down my cheek. "It may not be up to us. If the state decides that it would be best for Parker to live with extended family, they could remove her from here and send her to the uncle." I can see anger rising in Lucas so I continue, "Mitchell said that most of the time family members come forward when they learn about the child gaining a trust fund but then back off when they really think about what it takes to take on a kid."

Lucas lets out a sigh but doesn't drop his hands. "Well then we hope that is what happens. And if it goes to court then we show them that Parker's best option is right here with us." I nod my head as Lucas wipes away the tear that fell on my cheek. "Blue, I hate seeing these tears. But I also understand how much love you have for that little girl. I will do everything in my power to make sure you both are kept together."

The timer on my phone goes off for the pizza and Lucas drops his hands from my face. "I better go pull that pizza out. Can you get those two to come inside?"

"Of course. I'll go carall them up." I laugh as I head inside. I am pulling out the pizza cutter when I hear them make their way inside. "Mr. Lucas I helped make the pizza. It's going to be SO good!"

"Are there any vegetables on it?"

"Oh no. Ms. Sage is the only one that likes

that pizza. She said that tonight we were going to have pizza that everyone likes." I turn to grab some plates out of the cabinet when they come in. I feel Lucas behind me a second later. "Here I got it babe." He reaches around me and gets the plates down for me.

I sit there stunned for a second at how much I liked that he just called me babe. We turn back around to see Parker looking at the pizza with wide eyes. "This looks SO good."

We both laugh and start dishing up. "You did a really good job on it Parker." She smiles brightly as she takes her plate to the table. We join her at the table and I don't miss when she sneaks a couple of pepperonis to Aspen. No wonder Aspen is obsessed with her. We spend the dinner listening to Lucas tell us about his week. Turns out Mr. Hanson and Mr. Tomlinson snuck out of the retirement home and decided to streak across the town. Parker is laughing so hard that she has tears coming out. "They were naked old men?! How did you catch them?" Lucas is also laughing as he tell her all about all the police officers surrounding them and throwing blankets on their naked bodies. We are all laughing and Parker tells him more about her gymnastics practice.

"Alright Parker girl, it's time to head upstairs for your shower." Parker nods and then heads over to put her plate in the sink before running upstairs. I stand to take the rest of the dishes.

Lucas snags them from my hand, as I expected him to but surprises me when he puts them back on the table.

"What are you.." I don't have the chance to finish the sentence before I find myself being gently pushed up against the wall and Lucas's mouth back on mine. He licks my bottom lip telling me he wants in which I gladly allow. One of Lucas's hands goes from my waist to my jaw as he tilts my head right where he wants me. The other hand now is snaking around my waist pulling me flush against him. I'm glad I'm not the only one feeling heat in my core as he pushes his lower half against mine. I let out a small moan which has him let out a growl before he breaks to trail kisses down my neck. "It's been painful sitting here staring at how beautiful you are without putting my hands on you." He makes his way back up to my mouth and I loop my hands around his neck and tug on his hair.

Lucas drops his hand from my face and joins it with his other where they drop to my thighs and he lifts me up to straddle him. Since I am still against the wall he pushes into me as he does. He's better be careful or the throbbing is going to become unbearable. I can't help the moan that comes out of my mouth, "Lucas". He breaks the kiss for a second. "Blue, you don't know how badly I want to hear my name on your lips as you come apart." Before I can respond, his lips are back on mine. This man knows how to work his tongue as he grips my thighs causing another moan to make its way out of my throat which encourages Lucas to push harder.

"Ms. Sage I'm done with my shower and I brushed my teeth. I'm ready to read!" Thank goodness Parker yelled that from upstairs and didn't come down. I really don't want to explain to her why we are both breathing heavily with swollen lips.

Lucas slowly puts me back on the floor. "I love that little girl but man her timing is killing me." I laugh and yell up to Parker, "I'll be right there Parker!"

"Can Mr. Lucas read to me tonight?" I turned to Lucas and he looks like he just won the lottery. He shakes his head excitedly. "Yeah! He's gonna come up!" I yell up towards the stairs and turn back to him, "looks like you won the heart of that little girl after all. You go ahead and go up, I'll get these dishes tonight."

Lucas looks down and then back up to me, "I'm gonna need a minute before I go up" I look down at his pants and laugh before getting the dishes and heading to the kitchen. A minute later I hear Lucas head upstairs to read to Parker. I hurry through the dishes so that I can go peek in on them before they finish.

When I get to Parker's room, I stop and lean on the doorway. Lucas and Parker are both fast asleep with the book on Lucas's chest. I walk over to the bed and carefully grab the book and place it on the nightstand. Parker is laying on Lucas's shoulder and I don't have the heart to wake either of them so I walk out the door turning the light off as I go and head to my room.

# CHAPTER 29
# - LUCAS

I wake up to a hand patting my cheek, "morning Sage". I am unwilling to open my eyes and thinking about how to convince her to stay in bed with me a little longer. "I'm not Ms. Sage." Parker giggles, "I'm Parker." I blink my eyes open to see Parker kneeling next to me on her bed smiling. Last thing I remember is the kids finding the pirates on the deserted island. We must have fallen asleep while reading.

"Good morning Parker. Looks like we fell asleep reading last night." I rub at my eyes and notice the sunlight shining in. I wonder what time it is. Is Sage awake?

"We had a sleepover! You're really big though and took up lots of the bed." I laugh and sit up. "Should we let Sage sleep in and go make some pancakes?" Parker jumps off the bed. "Yes!" She whisper yells and it's possibly the cutest thing. She heads out the hall and down the stairs.

I roll off of Parker's bed and am thankful she

ran out so quick. I don't know how to explain to a 6 year old why there is a bump in my sweatpants after thinking I was waking up next to Sage. I head downstairs and find Parker sitting by Aspen who is very excited that she slept over here apparently. "Hey Parker, do you wanna take Aspen outside so she can go to the bathroom and I'll get the stuff ready for the pancakes?" She nods her head and they take off to the back door. I wander into the kitchen and start getting all the supplies out. Parker and Aspen come back inside and Parker hops up on a barstool.

"Alright Parker, I'm going to need lots of help because you and Sage are so good at cooking." She nods her head. "Okay I'm going to measure the things out and then I need you to dump them into the bowl and stir it up really good. Sound good?" Parker smiles and shakes her head, "sounds perfect Mr. Lucas."

We are flipping the pancakes when Sage makes her way down. This damn woman is going to make me lose my mind. She is wearing the matching blue pajama set that she knows I love. I can't help my eyes wander down her legs and then back up her body. When I make it back to her face she is giving me a smirk. She knows exactly what she is doing wearing those pajamas and I can't say that I am mad about it. "Smells yummy down here. Whatcha making?" Sage walks up to the island and sits down next to Parker.

"Mr. Lucas wanted to make us pancakes and I helped!" My back is turned back to the stove to flip pancakes but I would bet money that Sage has a bright smile talking to Parker. "That was really nice of you to help Parker. Mr. Lucas is still learning how to cook so I bet he really needed your help." I glance over my shoulder at the two of them with a glare which causes both of them to giggle. I am just finishing up the pancakes. "Alright ladies now it's time to test out these pancakes. I bet they will be the best pancakes in the whole world." I wink at Parker and she smiles and jumps down from the barstool.

Me and Sage dish up the three plates and carry them outside. It's a beautiful fall morning and Aspen will love being able to run and play. I run back inside for some cups of milk and then we dig in. Once she has finished her food Parker asks, "Ms. Sage, can I go play with Aspen now?"

"Yeah go ahead but only for a little bit. We need to get ready for the birthday party soon." Parker takes off running "come on Aspen! Let's play!" We both laugh as they sprint around the yard. "Aspen's life was changed when Parker entered." I look over at Sage, "all of our lives changed because of that little girl."

Sage smiles and glances back out to where Parker and Aspen are running around. "Yeah, I can't imagine life without her now." Sage lets out a heavy sigh.

"Hey, nothing will happen to her." She slowly

shakes her head. It frustrates me that there is even a potential of Parker getting taken away. I know Sage doesn't want to push Parker to adoption but that is the best way to make sure she is never taken away. Wanting to lighten the mood and get Sage smiling again, I reach over and cup her cheek, turning her head so she is looking at me. "Did you wear these pajamas because you know how much I love them on you?"

Sage blushes and bites her bottom lip. She better be careful or I will be the one biting that lip. "Maybe I felt a little left out from the sleepover last night."

"Blue you can sleep next to me the rest of my life if that's what you want." Her eyes get a little big at that. I drop my hand from her face. "You should have crawled in last night and joined us. But Parker told me I took up too much of the bed." Sage chuckles, "well you are a pretty big guy compared to her."

"You know what they say about big guys with big hands" Sage smacks my arm and I wink at her with a laugh.

Before I can see if I can taste the syrup on Sage's mouth, Parker comes running back to us with Aspen. "Can we go to the party now?" Sage laughs, "well first we need to go clean up the kitchen and get ready. Then we can leave." Parker nods her head. "Can we take your police car Mr. Lucas?"

I smile at her, "absolutely." She pumps her fist. "Do you wanna help me get all these dishes inside first?" She nods and grabs the cups while I grab the plates and Sage trails in behind us.

"Alright, since you two cooked I am cleaning." I go to say absolutely not but Sage continues. "Parker how about you go watch a show for a little bit while I clean up? That way Mr. Lucas can go over to his house and change out of his pjs." She smiles and heads to the living room "come on Aspen let's watch Bluey. It's about dogs so I know you'll love it." I head to the sink even though I heard what Sage had planned. The dishes are my thing.

"No way Lucas. Go over to your house and get ready. I got these." Knowing I'm about to get Sage's teacher voice if I don't listen I reluctantly step away from the sink. "I'll just pop over and shower real quick then head back." Sage nods her head and heads to the sink. I sneak in behind her and love when I feel her lean into my front as I whisper in her ear. "Or I can join you in the shower here." I'm not at the best angle to see her face but I can still see pink enter her cheeks and she bites her lower lip glancing up at me. "But maybe next time. If we did that, we would miss the party."

I kiss her on the cheek, then head to the back door and rush over to my house. Maybe I should take a cold shower. How am I supposed to spend the afternoon with the Calloway's when all I can think about is alone time with their daughter?

I took a cold and quick shower, got dressed and now am back at Sage's house. I found Parker in her room picking out some bows that match her outfit while Sage is in her bathroom getting ready. What do you think she would do if I just slip in there? Parker breaks up my thoughts, "Mr. Lucas, can you do my hair today?"

"Yes ma'am. I also have a surprise hairstyle for you." We head over to her bathroom and I spin her away from the mirror so she can't see. It takes me a little longer than I would like but I want it to be perfect, just like I practiced. Once I'm done I add in the bows at the ends and have her spin around so she can look in the mirror. "You did braids Mr. Lucas! They are so good!" Pride swells in my chest. Those YouTube videos and practice were so worth it. "Thanks Parker. You look beautiful." Parker looks up at me through the mirror, "just like Ms. Sage?"

"Just like Ms. Sage, baby girl" she beams and grabs her toothbrush. I lean against the bathroom door as she brushes her teeth and think about how much these two girls have changed my life. When she finishes up and is ready to go, we head downstairs to wait for Sage. Parker asks if we can watch bluey together. Not really sure what that is but remembering that was what she was watching earlier I agree.

Alright so bluey may be a kids show but I feel like I need to watch it and learn from the dad. That guy is the type of dad Parker deserves. I'm trying to not panic about if I am good enough for Parker and Sage when Sage comes downstairs. I'm sure my jaw is on the floor. Sage is in a forest green sweater dress that hugs her body so perfectly with some little boot heels. She has her long blonde hair curled and you can tell she is wearing a tiny bit more makeup than usual. It's official, she has complete control over me. If she told me to jump I would ask how high.

"Wow babe. You look stunning." She doesn't think I noticed how she reacted yesterday when I called her babe but I definitely did. Now I can't decide which one I like more blue or babe.

Sage blushes and looks down with a smile. "Thank you." Parker nods her head. "Yeah Ms. Sage you look like a princess." Sage's smile gets even bigger. "I don't know Parker I would say you are the one that looks like the princess. Look at how great your bows look with your outfit."

"Mr. Lucas did my braids! He told me that I looked beautiful just like you." They are both truly beautiful inside and out. My heart may burst as I watch my girls. "Alright princesses, your carriage awaits." I stand up to walk them out the door. Parker covers her hand with her mouth and giggles. "Mr. Lucas, you have a car not a carriage."

I shake my head and smile, "oh that's right." Sage is helping pick out shoes with Parker but turns to me and winks "yeah Mr. Lucas, don't be ridiculous." Her and Parker stand up ready to go and we head out the door. I smack Sage gently on the butt on the way out and whisper in her ear "I can show you ridiculous if you want me to." She glances over her shoulder, "oh trust me I'm sure you can. But I can handle it"

As we get to the car, I open Parker's door and she crawls in after putting her present for Miles in. Then I open the door for Sage, "one of these nights I will have to call your bluff" she blushes and smiles as she climbs in before I round the car and hop in.

On the way to Stanton's house Parker requests my favorite song and Sage puts on Tim McGraw by Taylor Swift. Whenever she talks about blue eyes I look over at Sage and wink. I love making this girl smile. Once the song is over Sage turns to me, "Okay so what is the plan?"

"Well it's a birthday party so we will probably open presents, sing songs, and Miles and Parker will probably play while the adults make lunch." She rolls her eyes and shakes her head, "no I meant what's the plan with us?" I look over confused. "You know... they have probably heard that we have been seen around town and now we are showing up at the party together." Ah got it. How are we going to break it to them that we no longer can't stand each other but quite the opposite. "Blue, I will go about this in whatever way you would like but I will never deny that you are special to me. I'm sure all of them will know that the second we walk into that house with your hand in mine." Sage doesn't say anything for a second but nods her head like she is processing. "The yummiest bachelor of Pennystone really does want to be off the market huh?"

We are at a red light so I turn to her, "we both know I was off the market the second you moved into that house." The light turns green so I return my focus back to the road but caught a smile starting to spread on Sage's face. I glance back to Parker who is in the back through the rear view mirror. "Parker you are going to love Stanton's house. He has a loft where we watch movies and tons of toys for Miles with a big backyard." She looks excited and I love that she feels so comfortable with Sage's family. "I'm so excited! Plus we get to eat cake! Are we almost there?"

"Yep baby girl, almost there." I don't miss the way Sage turns to me at my nickname for Parker, but she doesn't get the chance to say anything as we pull into the driveway. I hop out of the car and open the door for Parker who grabs the presents. Then I open the door for Sage. I'm a man of my word. I grab Sages hand and interlock our fingers as we walk to the door. She glances down at our hands and then looks up to me. I smile and give her a wink as Parker rings the doorbell.

Stanton is the one that opens the door. He says hello to Parker and then realizes that I am there holding hands with his sister. "Well shit. Took y'all long enough."

# CHAPTER 30
# - SAGE

"Hey Stants." I smile as I feel heat rise to my cheeks. I'm not sure what I expected his reaction to be but that wasn't it.

Parker grabs my other hand, "Ms. Sage, Mr. Stanton just said a bad word." Lucas smirks at him, "Yeah Mr. Stanton, watch your language".

Stanton rolls his eyes at him, "Come on in guys. Mom and dad are in the kitchen with Miles." We all step into Stanton's home and walk to his kitchen with him. My dad sees us first and his smile grows, then my mom looks over and lets out a gasp. Quite dramatic honestly. "Yep so this is happening" I whisper to Lucas.

Parker races over to where Miles is sitting in his high chair at the table with my dad. "Happy birthday Miles! We bought you the coolest toy ever!" We all watch the interaction and smile. Parker would be an amazing big sister. Woah. Too fast there Sage. But when I look over at a smiling Lucas, I wonder if he is thinking the same thing.

My mom looks back at the two of us and of course Lucas hasn't dropped my hand but tightened his grip like they are going to take me away from him. "So y'all gonna break the news or just keep us to our assumptions" Lucas looks at my mom and smiles, "your daughter is one of a kind ma'am. A fool would let her slip through his fingers." My dad looks at Lucas with a stern look. "You be the man that we know you to be and we will have no problems." He then comes over to me and wraps me in a hug. Lucas reluctantly lets go of my hand so I can hug him back. "I'm happy for you baby girl. He's a good man"

My heart swells at the love my parents not only have for me but also Lucas. He lets go of his hug and then claps Lucas on the shoulder, "how about you and Stanton come help me outside on the grill?"

"Yes sir". Lucas gives me a quick kiss on the forehead before following my dad and Stanton out the door. I watch them leave with butterflies in my stomach. I know Lucas was a little hesitant about that conversation with Stanton. It's not everyday that you have to explain to your best friend that you are seeing his sister.

I glance over at Parker and Miles who are still sitting at the table. Miles is giggling as Parker tells him all about her teacher and friends at school. I walk around the island where my mom is making a salad. "Need any help mom?" She looks at me and smiles, "what I need is to know how my daughter is now dating the boy she couldn't stand a couple of months ago."

I let out a little sigh and look out the back window where the boys are out by the grill. Lucas is wearing a black Henley again today and some light blue jeans. I'm partial to his cop uniform but love this look too. It surprises me that he can look so delicious no matter what he is in. Maybe the ladies of Pennystone were right about him being the yummiest bachelor in town. My mom breaks up my thoughts, "earth to Sage. Spill." I shake my head and smile, "it kind of just happened. We found out we lived next to each other and then he sort of just kept coming by for dinner. It started as a friendship and then I got Parker. I mean watching him love that little girl, it would have been impossible to resist. He slowly became my best friend and now I think we both want something more."

She looks up from her salad and gives me a big smile. "You look really happy Sage. If Lucas is the one making you look this happy, he can definitely stay." I chuckle, "yeah he's alright." My mom laughs at my sass but we both know he is more than alright. "Well I would like to say that we are all shocked but honestly we aren't. You know what they say there is a thin line between love and hate." Love? That's a big word. The last man I loved ended up betraying and embarrassing me. Do I love Lucas? Can I get there again with the scars on my heart?

My mom must see on my face the internal battle my heart and head are having. "There is no rush or pressure Sage. But promise me that you will let your heart lead on this one. I know you have some walls because of Matt. But Lucas is not Matt." I nod my head, Lucas has already started breaking down the walls that I built brick by brick. "But if he does end up a loser like Matt, then he will have hell to pay." I laugh at the kindest woman in the world threatening a man that she sees as another son. "I'll make sure he knows you said that."

She smiles, "oh honey, do you know your father? Lucas is probably getting that conversation right now. Plus it's not just your dad. Stanton hated seeing you so hurt last year." Stanton and I have been through a lot this past year with me returning to Pennystone and Jessica leaving him and Miles. I glance at the door and back to my mom, "how do you think Stanton will take it?" This is one of the things that made me the most anxious about coming in together today. My parents already had a suspicion but I'm not sure where Stanton stood on it or what Lucas had already told him. Stanton is the best brother in the world but I don't want him to feel pushed out by this or upset that we didn't talk to him sooner.

"Your brother will be just fine. His two favorite people are happy." I nod slowly but still feel anxiety at how the conversation is going outside.

## Lucas

I follow Mr. Calloway and Stanton out to the grill in unbearable silence. Stanton reacted a lot better than I thought he would honestly. I mean it can't be easy to see your best friend with your sister and it doesn't seem like he is upset at all. Once we get there, Mr. Calloway turns to me "Lucas are you going to take care of those girls in there? You know Sage is my world and Parker is soon becoming part of that." I look Mr. Calloway in the eye and with confidence give him the answer we all know. "I will protect them with all that I am." I just hope that is enough.

He nods, "Good because I don't know a better man that I would want for my baby girl." Pride blooms in my chest. I told the Calloways and Stanton about my dad after he died. They know how much work I have done to recover and grow. I just hope it is enough.

Stanton speaks up finally, "anything is better than that bump on the log Matt." I can feel my jaw tighten at the thought of Matt with Sage. How can a man be so disrespectful and dumb? Stanton must see my jaw tighten, "anytime you want to make a trip to Knoxville to make sure he knows what he missed out on, count me in" I shake my head, "as much as I would love to give that dick a good left hook, I can't get involved now that Sage had a restraining order against him. I wouldn't want to be a liability if anything ended up in court."

Mr. Calloway whips his head to me from where he is grilling. "Sage put a restraining order against him? Why?"

Unsure how much of Sage's business I should tell them, I let them in on what's been going on with caution. "Sage has gotten some gifts and messages from Matt. At first she brushed them off thinking he was just continuing to apologize. But the last one mentioned Parker and was gifts for her. Sage was uncomfortable with bringing that around Parker so she came to the station and filled a restraining order."

Now I am really unsure if Stanton will be making that trip to Knoxville. He looks like he needs something or someone to punch. "Stanton, you can't go to Knoxville and tell him to back off. Trust me I would love to be there with you for that. But Sage doesn't want to do anything that makes him escalate. She wants to make sure this is handled through the law." His jaw is also hard and for that I'm grateful. Those two girls deserve all the protection and love in the world. Mr. Calloway speaks up, "well then I am extra grateful that you finally decided to man up and tell Sage how you feel. It's obvious that she feels safe with you considering she came to you and not us about this."

"Of course. She has become my best friend." I cringe and look at Stanton. "Sorry man."

He smiles, "don't apologize for caring for my sister. She deserves that kind of love." Love? Woah. Are we there yet? I mean she's my favorite person by far and I hate when I'm away from her and Parker. But love? Does she deserve more than me? Stanton must see the war going on in my head, "Lucas, you are the best man I know outside of my dad. And she is my favorite person in the world. You *both* deserve to be happy." Mr. Calloway smiles and nods.

"You aren't mad that I am dating your sister?" Not that he ever gave any indication that he was upset about me and Sage living next door to each other and spending time with each other. "Why would I be? You two are my two best friends. You have always been part of the family."

"No protective big brother?"

"Nah man. You know that if you hurt those two girls you will have me and my dad to speak to. I'm not worried. Plus I pretty much caused this to happen when I convinced Sage to buy the house next to yours. So really you're welcome." We all laugh. He isn't wrong. One of the best days of my life was when I found Sage out back with Aspen.

Mr. Calloway shuts the grill, "alright boys it's time to go spoil my grandson. Lucas, we love you and as long as you treat my baby girl with respect and love we will have no issues."

I shake my head, "yes sir. Those two girls are one of a kind." He nods his head with a smile and we head inside. Once we get back to the kitchen we see that Miles and Parker are now in the living room playing with some of his toys and Sage and Mrs. Calloway are finishing up some of the food for lunch.

Sage looks up as we enter and looks at me with questions. I'm sure she is wondering how the conversation went with her dad and Stanton. I give her a smile and a nod and you can see her visibly relax and smile back. Man, to be on the receiving end of a Sage smile feels like I won the world. Stanton looks back and forth between us, "ugh okay so we now have to get used to you guys looking at each other like that." Sage blushes and sticks her tongue out at him.

"Stanton Joseph, you let them be happy." If I didn't love Mrs. Calloway before, I do now. Safe to say I have her vote of confidence too. I give her a smile and a nod and get a big smile back.

"Alright kids, time to get this birthday party started for our Miles." Mr. Calloway heads to the living room and scoops up Miles then holds out his hand for Parker who grabs it with a smile on her face. In that moment I realize that my mama needs to meet this little girl and I need to update her on my relationship with Sage.

Everyone heads up the back yard where Miles

party is all set up. Stanton begins opening presents with Miles. I walk over to stand next to Sage and whisper, "Hey do you and Parker have plans next Saturday evening?" She looks up at me at her side and shakes her head. "Nope all we have next weekend is gymnastics Saturday morning and then the police banquet on Sunday."

"Good. Will you come over to my mamas house with me on Saturday night for dinner? I need her to meet Parker and see my two favorite girls." My heart leaps at the thought of the three of them together."I would really like that, Lucas. Mama Walker is one of my favorite people. Parker will love her." Sage scoots in closer and I loop my arm around her shoulders to pull her into me. "My uncle will also be there. You guys will love him."She looks up at me and smiles, "I'm looking forward to it."Noticing that everyone is busy watching Miles with his presents I sneak a quick kiss in.

The rest of the birthday party goes great. Parker was so excited when Miles loved all the balls that came with her gift. They have been playing together this whole time with Miles crawling after Parker around the yard. Parker then thought it was the silliest thing watching Miles smash into his birthday cake. We are now about to head out the door to return home. Everyone seems exhausted but happy.

Before we head out Stanton pulls me to the

side. "Hey man, I truly am happy for you and Sage." He seems hesitant to continue but does with caution, "have you told her about your dad," a weight drops in my stomach. "No." I sigh, "and before you tell me that I need to, I know. I just worry that it'll change things." He nods and gives me a small smile. "Lucas you aren't your dad and I know my sister, it won't change the way she sees you."

I nod and we join the others again. We say our goodbyes to everyone and I don't miss how Mrs. Calloway gives me an extra squeeze when she hugs me goodbye or the smile that Mr. Calloway gives me as we are leaving. I grab Sage's hand as we walk to the car and she waits by her door as I get Parker in and then I open her door. "What did Stanton want to talk to you about at the end?" I cringe inside, now is not the time. "Oh just big brother stuff. Make sure I treat you well and don't lose my mind dealing with your sass."

She rolls her eyes as she climbs in, "please he should be telling me to stay strong". I laugh as I shut her door and round the car. On the way home Parker is chatting away about how delicious the cake was and how much she loves playing with Miles. There is such a feeling of contentment as we are driving with Parker chatting, my hand resting on Sage's thigh , and Sage listening and smiling along with Parker's stories. I have found the family I have always dreamed of having. Now I need to make sure I don't lose them.

Bedtime routine was a team effort tonight. After we got home, Parker ran around outside with Aspen until dinner was ready. Parker needed to run off some of the effects from the sugar and Aspen loved the attention after having to miss the party. It became obvious after dinner that Parker had a long day and was feeling sleepy so Sage took her upstairs to get ready for bed while I stayed to do the dishes. I finished the dishes and wiping down the kitchen before Sage made it back downstairs so I snuck into her office downstairs.

Sage finds me at her desk flipping through our old yearbook. She smiles as she realizes what I'm looking at, "that seems like a lifetime ago doesn't it?" I've gotten to the picture of the two of us together as the valedictorian and salutatorian. Sage looks pretty much the same as she did in high school with her long blonde hair and big blue eyes. I knew even then in my gut that she was always going to be special to my life. I just didn't realize then how much. "Yeah who would've thought that these two kids would be here today." She laughs, "back then I thought you hated me and only put up with me for Stanton."

I pull her into my lap, "Blue, I don't think I could ever hate you. I just hated the fact that I could never be good enough for you."Before she can make out a response, my hand is cupping her face bringing her lips to mine. Kissing Sage is like riding a rollercoaster, right when I think I am steady she does something that makes my heart leap in my chest. It's a ride that I hope to never get off of.

She slides her tongue against my bottom lip and I happily open for her. I tilt her head slightly so that I can get better access. I could go my whole life savoring this woman. "Lucas" I love it when she moans into my mouth. A growl comes out from the back of my throat. She swings her legs around and I help guide her hips so that she is straddling the chair with me under her. As she sits there is no doubt she can feel the hardness under her.

"Blue, you better not start something you can't finish." That last time I used that line it led to the kiss that changed my entire world. I move my kisses down to her favorite spot, the spot where her neck meets her shoulder and squeeze her butt to pull her flush against me. She tips her head to the side to give me more access. "Mmm... who said anything about not finishing." This girl. I hate myself for doing it but I stop kissing her and rest my head against hers. "Babe, I want the whole night to discover your body and what makes you scream my name. But you have an early morning tomorrow with school." My dick probably thinks of me as its worst enemy at this point.

"Can I just have a little taste?" She looks up to me with her big blue eyes. She knows I would burn the world for her. "Blue, don't do this to me. You and I both know that if we start, there is no way in hell we stop." I can feel the strain against my zipper and I am about to cave. But I want to tell her about my past before we cross that line. If we go there and she chooses to walk away, it will crush me.

Sage sighs dramatically. "Fine. But just remember you had your shot. Next time, I am going to make you work for it." I have absolutely no doubt that I will love every second of it. "Trust me, I will be begging on my knees if that's what it takes." She seems to like the thought of that as she giggles and stands up. She looks down at where I am sitting and smirks as I adjust myself.

"Can I walk you out?" I nod, stand up, and start walking to the door before she stops me by grabbing my hand. "Or we could just walk right upstairs?" She is really testing me now.

I turn to her and lift her chin with my finger, "Sage. You are literally killing me. There is nothing more that I would love to do than to crawl into that bed with you and wake up next to you."

She gives me a wink, "Maybe one day. If you are lucky." She then turns and heads out of the office. A man can only dream. One day.

# CHAPTER 31
## - LUCAS

I wake up the next morning with an ache for Sage unlike anything I have felt. Maybe I should have given in last night. I remind myself that I am not willing to take that next step until I open myself completely to her. If we go there and then she learns about my past and doesn't want a future with me, I don't think I will be able to handle it.

Needing to work through some emotions and having the day off, I head to J&S Mental Health Services for an appointment with John. I started therapy with John after my dad died. Honestly it would have been good for me if I started as a kid but I am glad I did when I did. I run into Stanton as I am walking into the building and he doesn't look shocked to see me. "Hey man, you have a meeting with John today?" We agreed early on that it would be best for me to go to John and not him. We have too much history. He wouldn't be able to remain unbiased and I wouldn't be able to open up as fully. "Yep, figured it was time to check in again."

Stanton gives me a smile and a nod, "it's good to see you. I better get to my office, I have a client coming in." He heads off to his office and I sit in the waiting room. Once I am called back, I sit in a leather seat across from John. He has a couch along the wall but that seems a little too much for me. This way it feels like I am talking to my friend and he always tells me to sit wherever I am comfortable.

"Good morning Lucas. I am glad you called and decided to come in today. It has been a while since we last talked."

I used to come weekly at the beginning and then it faded into monthly sessions but progressed to only popping in when I feel triggered or need to work through things. "What brings you in today?"

I cross an ankle over my knee before diving in. "Well I bought a new house and it turns out my next door neighbor is Sage, Stanton's twin sister." He nods. He obviously knows Sage well. "We started spending more time together. She would cook me dinner and I would help her with things around the house."

"So you two developed a friendship?"

"Yeah it definitely started as a friendship."

"Okay it started as a friendship, but I know you pretty well Lucas and I don't think you would come in today if it was just a friendship. I am assuming it has developed into more."

"You could say that. I crave just being with her and around her. She also has Parker who is the sweetest little girl." He nods his head, "Parker is the Reynolds girl right? The one that Sage is fostering now?" I am sure he has gotten those updates from Stanton. "Yeah and Parker is great. She really is such a bright and happy little girl. Her and Sage were meant to be together. You should see them together. They are a perfect little family."

"And if you are seeing Sage, as I am assuming that your relationship has now developed to that, how does it feel to be part of their family?"

I look down at my feet thinking that over before looking back up at him. "It scares the hell out of me that I am not good enough for them or what they deserve."

"You don't feel like you can be the man that they deserve, how come?"

"Well we know that 40% of children that are abused become abusers themselves." I can see the connections forming in John's face. "Lucas, the abuse that you went through with your father was awful. No child deserves to ever go through it or see the abuse you saw with your mother. But you are not your father. You have the power to choose how you react to situations and to anger."

"I know that. I can't even imagine laying a hand on either of them. But his blood runs through me. There is a chance that when Sage finds out about my childhood that it will scare her and she will run. It may not be the risk she is willing to take for herself and for Parker." I look away from John as I feel my eyes getting watery. I can't lose them. "It is obvious that you haven't told Sage about your past and that fear is preventing you from getting further into the relationship."

"Of course it scares me. I could easily lose her because of my past." I let out a heavy sigh. "I wouldn't even blame her either. Her and Parker deserve the absolute world, not to live in fear that the person that is supposed to be protecting them is the one that can hurt them." John pauses allowing me time to process what I am feeling. "I know I would never intentionally hurt them. I don't think I could. But what if that anger comes out and I end up doing something I regret? What if I end up just like my dad? I can't even say that once you start you can stop because we both know he didn't. He had to die for the abuse to stop."

John nods, "unfortunately this seems like it will be a constant fear due to your past Lucas. It was a fear eight years ago when you first started coming to me and continues to be one." "I just want to know if I will ever be able to push it aside and allow myself to have the family I want. Will I ever get to be a dad? Or will this fear of becoming the father I had hold me back?" I swipe at my cheek where a tear has fallen.

"Let's do an exercise. I want you to close your eyes." I close my eyes as he instructs. "Now imagine yourself in a year from now. What do you see?" I smile at the image in my head. "I am at home with Sage and Parker. I just got off duty and Sage is making dinner while me and Parker help."

"Okay now imagine that Parker accidently bumps the cutting board and all the chopped veggies fall to the ground." He pauses and I imagine the scene in my head. "Now how do you see yourself reacting?" I see it all happen in my mind. "Sage and I both go over and help Parker pick up the veggies off the floor and throw them away. Sage goes to the refrigerator to get more while I tell Parker that it is okay and accidents happen."

"Okay Lucas go ahead and open your eyes." I open my eyes and look at home. "Now tell me what stood out to you in that situation." I take a deep breath. "When Parker had an accident I did not lash out at her or at Sage like my father would have. I remained calm while Sage and I worked together to fix it." John nods at me and I continue, "I know I am not the man that my father was. I have worked really hard to make sure I am not. I just worry that the fear will hold me back or that Sage will choose to not take the risk with me."

"Neither of us can say how Sage will react until you tell her. But knowing the both of you, it sounds like it is a conversation that needs to happen. Let's work through some of the coping skills that have worked in the past to combat those fears."

The rest of the session we work through coping skills that I know will help me push past the fear of becoming the man my father was. The first thing that needs to happen though is to tell Sage about my past.

I stop by my mama's house after my session with John and tell her all about Sage and Parker. She is over the moon happy for me and is excited for this upcoming weekend to meet Parker. When I get home later that day, I notice that Sage and Parker are already home so I run into my house and get Aspen before jogging over to Sage's house.

We are standing outside the back door when Aspen lets out a bark and I can hear Parker inside yell to Sage, "They are here!" I guess they just assume we will be here each night. I love that. Parker slides the door open and gives Aspen a big hug which causes Aspen's tail to wag about a million miles an hour. "Hey baby girl. Did you have a good day at school today?" I follow her inside with Aspen right at her side. "Yep! Today we had art class and I got to paint a picture. Come look at it! It's on the refrigerator." Parker grabs my hand and drags me to the kitchen where Sage has started making dinner. I wink at Sage and she smiles as she sees where Parker is leading me. "See!" Parker points to the picture on the refrigerator. "It's us. There is me and Sage and you and Aspen." We are all stick figures in front of what I am assuming is Sage's house. We all have big smiles.

"That is one of the very best pictures I have ever seen Parker. Do you think after dinner we can make another one so that I can have one on my refrigerator at my house?" Parker looks up at me and nods excitedly and then turns to Sage. "Ms. Sage, can we please paint after dinner so Mr. Lucas can have a picture too?" She looks at the two of us and smiles "Absolutely. That sounds like the perfect plan." Parker looks back at me with a smile and gives me two thumbs up before running off to the living room where Aspen is.

I turn to Sage and lean a hip on the counter, crossing my arms. "How was your day at school today babe?" It really does something to my ego when Sage looks down at my arms and then back to my face while biting her bottom lip. "It was good. We had a little trip to the library so the kids could see the new treehouse section. It was great until little Tommy refused to leave." I laugh and make my way over to her. Since she is chopping vegetables, I use my finger to turn her chin so I can give her a kiss. "I missed you girls today."

She looks at me with hooded eyes before she

gets a small blush across her cheeks. "We missed you too."

"Alright Chef, can I help you tonight?" She glances back to the oven to check her timer. "Uh, could you make some rice since you are a pro at that?" I head off to the pantry, "Anything for you babe".

We finish making dinner and decide to eat outside. It is getting closer and closer to the middle of fall where it will start to get a little more chilly at night so we want to take advantage of the time we have. Parker ate quickly and is now running around with Aspen. "So Lucas, what did you do today on your day off?"

I look over to Sage and smile. She is sitting on her outdoor sofa next to me in sweats and a lightweight hoodie. She has a blanket across the both of us and after finishing off her meal kicked her feet into my lap. Now that I am done eating, I reach under the blanket and start rubbing her feet. "Mmm... that feels really good Lucas." I smile at her and try to ignore the blood that rushed towards my lower half.

"Today was a good day. I ran into Stanton before I had a session with John and then went and saw my mama. She is really excited to see you and Parker on Friday." She doesn't call me out on nonchalantly throwing in there that I had a therapy session today. "And don't worry I already told my mama that you and I are officially together so she won't be shocked like your parents. But honestly with all the talk around Pennystone, she probably wouldn't have been anyways."

"Oh we are "officially together" are we?" She smirks over at me. "You seemed to think so last night when you were on my lap begging me to take you to the bedroom." You can see the redness deepen in her cheeks, "But we can do this formally if you want. Sage will you do me the honor of being my girlfriend?"

Sage rolls her eyes at me, "You're such a dork. We aren't kids anymore, you don't have to ask me. But I am glad to hear you are on the same page as me." I chuckle, "Sage if you don't know how much I want you to be mine by this point, I am failing. Don't worry I will step up." Sage shakes her head with a smile, "Lucas, Parker and I are lucky to have you."

"I am the lucky one." As if on cue, Parker runs up. "Mr. Lucas, we need to go paint!"

"How could we forget?! We need you to make another masterpiece." Parker giggles as she takes both of our hands and we head inside. We spend the next hour painting. Parker looked over at me every so often and giggled. Not too sure what that is about, I thought my pictures looked pretty good. By the end we had lots of pictures for both Sage's refrigerator and mine. "Alright Parker girl, it's time to head upstairs and get ready for bed." Sage stands up to clean the paint supplies and I stand to help as well.

Parker looks up from her paintings, "Already? Can Mr. Lucas read my book tonight?" I smile and glance over at Sage. She gives me a smile and a small nod to go ahead. "Yeah Parker, I can read with you tonight. Can you yell for me when you're ready?"

"Yep!" Parker dashes off and heads upstairs. Sage laughs, "That little girl has you wrapped around her finger." Little does she know, they both do. "How can I say no to those beautiful big blue eyes?" Sage smirks, "You did it to me for years."

"Yeah what a waste of time." I wink at her as we continue cleaning up. "I just can't figure out why Parker kept looking at my pictures laughing. Were they that bad?" Sage chuckles, "It wasn't your pictures." I look at her confused, "You have a smudge of paint on your cheek."

I go to wipe at my cheek but Sage grabs my hand and pulls me to the kitchen, "Come on, let's get the paint off your face." I stand by the sink as Sage grabs a paper towel, wets it, and then wipes the paint off my face. Standing this close, I can't help but reach out and hold her hips. "Blue, have I ever told you that you have the most beautiful eyes I have ever seen?" You can see a blush form across her cheeks as she smiles, still getting the paint off my cheek. How much did I get on there? No wonder Parker thought it was funny. "Maybe a time or two, but it never hurts to hear it again."

I grab Sage's face with both of my hands and

point her face up so that she is looking at me. "You always have been and always will be the most beautiful woman I have ever seen. Your beauty is one that comes from deep within and shines so brightly that it makes me weak in the knees."

"I wouldn't mind seeing you on your knees." I laugh before diving in for a kiss. Once we need air, we pause. "Just say the word and I will drop to my knees for you Sage." Before she can tell me to do just that, Parker yells from upstairs, "Mr. Lucas! I am ready to read!" I drop my hands from Sage's face. "I better go up and tuck our girl in." The smile Sage gives me almost does make me go to my knees. "I am not planning on sleeping this time around." I pause as she nods, "and I would like to talk to you about something when I come back down."

She gives me a worried look that I instantly feel bad about but nods and I spin heading for the stairs before she can see how anxious I am about that conversation.

We only made it through one chapter before Parker fell asleep. I gently crawl off her bed and make sure all her blankets are pulled up around her. I lean forward and kiss her forehead, "goodnight baby girl." When I get to the hallway I take a deep breath before making my way downstairs. I will never be ready for this conversation but it needs to be done. It is wrong for me to not give Sage my everything when I want her to be everything to me.

I look around when I get to the bottom of the stairs and find Sage outside with Aspen. She is sitting on her couch with a blanket over her lap as Aspen is sniffing around the yard. I step outside and shut the door behind me. "Hey babe." She looks over at me with tentative eyes. "Hey, she go down okay?" I smile, "Yep. We read one chapter and she was fading pretty hard at the end. She should be out for the night."

Sage nods and picks up the blanket beside her to invite me in. I happily join her and pull her legs into my lap. I look out towards the trees collecting my thoughts and wondering where to begin. "Lucas, I am going to need you to talk before I start to panic and think of worst case scenarios." I glance over at her with an eyebrow raised, "what is the worst case scenario going through your head right now?"

She looks down at her lap, "That Parker and I are more than what you bargained for and you are about to tell me that you want to take a step back and only be my neighbor." This girl doesn't realize how lucky I am to even be invited into her home with her and Parker. "Sage, that is definitely not what is happening. I feel like the luckiest man in the world to have you. And that little girl? I didn't think my life could be so full before you two." I pause and she nods for me to continue. "That is why I am struggling. I am worried that I am about to lose the best thing that has ever happened to me and I wouldn't blame you if you choose that." She looks at me confused. "Lucas, I am sorry to tell you but I think you are stuck with us. We aren't going anywhere." I nod and look back out to where Aspen is rolling around in the grass. "Is this about your visit with John today?"

I nod and she remains silent waiting for me. I continue looking out, "I was seven the first time I saw my father hit my mama. He thought I was upstairs asleep but I came down for a drink of water. They were arguing in the kitchen and when I saw him slap her, I was so confused so I came in and told him to stop. He was so angry that he turned and slapped me. I remember crying because my nose was bleeding and my mama holding me as he left the room." I can't look at her to see her reaction. Not yet.

"The next day he bought me a new toy car and told me that he was sorry and that it would never happen again." I let out a sigh, I really believed him then. "The next time was a few days later. My mama let me go over to your house to play after school and she didn't start dinner as early as normal because she needed to pick me up. He got home from work and noticed that dinner wasn't ready. He shoved her against the wall and held her throat as he told her that her only purpose in life was to make his life easier. He then turned to me and shoved me down telling me that I needed to remember who the man of the house was." Sage reaches over and puts a hand on my arm but I don't look at her. I can't see the pity on her face. My eyes well up with tears at the thought of that little boy being so terrified of his father.

"From then on it was like he didn't care if I saw the abuse. He soon learned that my mama would listen if he hurt me instead. If my mama tried to jump in to stop him, he would hit her even harder. I saw him knock her unconscious once and I almost called 911 that day but he locked me in my room so I couldn't." I remember that day all too well wondering if my mama was going to wake up.

"He loved the day I joined football. It was a way for my bruises to be blamed on something else. As I got older and grew stronger, he went back to hurting mama instead of me. There were countless times that I would step in to take the beating for her even as she screamed at me to stop." I take a deep breath as the memories wash over me. I can still hear her crying my name and begging my father to hurt her instead. "He knew it would be easier for me to hide the bruises than her so he would happily let me take her place." I can feel tears start to spill onto my cheeks.

Sage grabs my cheeks in her hands and makes me turn to her, "Lucas I had no idea. I am so sorry you had to live through that." She wipes the tears from my cheeks and I look to see she has her own tears. "Did my parents know? Did anyone know or try to stop this?" I shake my head, "I didn't tell anyone until after my father died. He would threaten to kill my mama if I said a word about it. I think your parents had suspicions. There was once where I am pretty sure someone reported something but since my father was on a councilman nothing ever happened and all suspicions disappeared."

Sage lets her tears fall on her cheeks, still holding mine. "No child should ever go through that trauma. It may make me a terrible person but I am glad that your dad died. I hope he rots in hell." My little spitfire would do anything for her people. She drops her hands from my cheeks and becomes hesitant, "Why did you not want to tell me about this Lucas?" I look away from her. This is the part that terrifies me. "I may never be the man that you deserve Sage. What is even worse is that I could end up like him. That is something I don't know if I am willing to risk with you and Parker."

From the corner of my eye I can see Sage shaking her head, "No Lucas. You are nothing like him. You will never be him." I look down at the ground, "There is a cycle with those that experience abuse. The abuse victims can later become abusers themselves. His DNA lives in me which means there is a chance that could be my future." Sage grabs my chin and pulls my face to look at her. "Absolutely not Lucas. You are kind and patient. Your heart longs to protect and serve others. You are one of the best men I have ever met. You. Are. Not. Your. Father."

I let the tears fall and can feel them drop from my chin. She scoots over and into my lap hugging my neck. "I don't care about the cycle. Parker and I lives would be bleak without you in it. I want you in it Lucas." We sit in silence and Sage lets me cling to her as my emotions take over.

After a few minutes, Aspen jogs over and sits at my feet, putting her head in Sage's lap. Sage loosens her hold on me and turns to see Aspen, "Hey girl, we are good over here. Thanks for checking on us." I take the opportunity to cup Sage's face and put her forehead against mine. "I will never be deserving of you and Parker. But I would really like the chance to try." She closes her eyes and sighs, "Lucas you are more than enough. Like I said earlier, you are kind of stuck with us." I kiss her forehead, "Thank you."

She cuddles into my chest, "Thank you for letting me in. I want to know every part of you and how you became this amazing man. But I am truly sorry you had to live through that." I nod my head and we sit in silence as we look at the stars. Realizing it is probably getting late and Sage has to wake up early tomorrow we say our goodbyes with a kiss that makes me want to head inside but instead I make my way with Aspen across the yard. We watch as Sage heads inside and lock her door. I am left wondering how she will feel tomorrow after she has processed everything and hoping that she doesn't change her mind about keeping me around.

# CHAPTER 32
# - SAGE

It's been 4 days since Lucas told me about his father. My heart still breaks for him. No kid should ever live through that abuse. I never did like his dad. Never really interacted with him thank goodness but he gave off this attitude that he was better than everyone else. I would see him at the football games and remember watching his interactions with Lucas and cringing.

He was always so aggressive about what Lucas needed to be doing better. Someone on the outside, like me at the time, just thought he was passionate and wanted his kid to be successful.

Now it makes complete sense why he chose to stay close to home for college, probably to protect his mom. Then his father died suddenly. I can imagine that it was a relief for the two of them but with that came the grief of reality. Lucas has come by for dinner on the nights that he isn't at the station but seems hesitant with Parker and I. He leaves back to his house as soon as dinner is cleaned up like he is worried that if we have too much alone time that I am going to end things.

I woke up that next morning with a clear head knowing that Lucas's past was not going to prevent our future. He is a great man and a wonderful influence in Parker's life. I am hoping that dinner with his mom tonight will help him see a future with us. I call Stanton while getting ready for work.

"Hey sis. What's up? It's pretty early for you to be calling."

"Hey Stants. I hope I didn't wake you up."

"Nah, little man woke up early because his teeth were hurting him. We are in the theater watching some Mickey Mouse clubhouse."

"Little man just needed a show and some cuddles."

"Yep. So what's up? Everything okay with Parker?"

"Yeah Parker is great. Uh, this is about Lucas." I'm hesitant on how much to say.

"Okay…. Has he done something to upset you?"

"No. I, uh, just learned more about his childhood."

"Ah. He finally told you about his father." Oh good he already knows.

"Yeah he did. Stanton, did you know?" Stanton sighs, "I didn't know until after his dad died. Lucas started seeing John and that's when he told me and dad about it." I nod my head. That makes sense. I'm sure if my parents knew when he was a child, they would've done something to stop it. "Why didn't you ever say anything? I always treated him like he had it all."

"Him telling you about it is a big deal, Sage. You needed to hear about it from him. It wasn't my story to tell."

"I'm really glad he had our family growing up. My heart breaks for what he had to go through."

"Yeah I know. I don't know how I didn't notice the bruises. I saw the way his father talked to him at games. I just honestly thought his dad was a jerk. I didn't realize that I was right plus some until later." I nod as I process. "Sage, I'm really happy for you two. You both deserve happiness and I am so happy too found it together."

I smile, "thanks Stants. He's a good man."

"I would only accept the best for my baby sister." I roll my eyes, "alright I better go and get Parker and I out the door for school. Love you Stants."

"Love you too Sage. Have a good day at school." I hang up, continuing to think about the man Lucas grew to be as I get myself and Parker ready for school.

My students have music class at the same time that Julie's students are at lunch and Michael doesn't have any classes coming in at that time so we all agree that lunch needs to happen together today. It's been a while since we have been able to check in with each other. I head down to the library with my lunch. We will only have about twenty minutes before we have to head to our classrooms but it feels good to take a break and eat with friends. "Hey Sage." Michael is behind his desk grabbing his lunch when he sees me.

"Hey Michael! Has Julie popped in yet?" He shakes his head, "no you're the first to arrive. I'm shocked you guys didn't pass each other in the hall."

Julie comes barreling into the library. "Sorry guys! My students decided they wanted to play leap frog on our way to the cafeteria and it took a little longer than usual." She shakes her head and laughs. "Where should we eat together Michael?" He looks around at the empty library. "Honestly wherever you guys want. There aren't any classes scheduled to come in until later in the afternoon. We could eat at the alphabet rug, the tables by the mystery section, in the treehouse, or just up here at the desk."

I look over to Julie who is weighing her options. "Hmm let's do the tables. I sat on the floor this morning for circle time and my butt is now not too happy." I laugh as we head over to the tables and start diving into our lunches.

"So Sage, Parker is always talking about how

much she loves living at Ms. Sage's house to her friends in my class." My heart warms and I smile at Julie, "honestly I am so lucky to have her. She has changed my life in the best way possible. I honestly can't imagine life without her now." Dread sits in my stomach at the thought. We still haven't heard if there was any progress with the uncle.

Michael must see the anxious look on my face because he puts his hand on mine, "she is really lucky to have you Sage. Have you thought about adoption?" He takes his hand back and we continue eating.

"Yeah I have. But I don't want to pressure Parker with it. She had two amazing parents and I never want to make her feel like I am pushing them away. I would love to keep Parker forever and adopt her but I think I may wait until she is a little older so she can make that decision."

Julie nods her head with understanding. "That makes sense Sage. I bet she knows you aren't replacing her mom and dad but I can tell you this, she loves you." My heart feels so full. I love that little girl with all that I am. "She also talks about Mr. Lucas often." Julie raises her eyebrows up and down at me. I can feel heat rising up my chest and across my cheeks. Michael visibly tenses next to me, "do you mean Lucas Walker? The one that was in our AP classes with us? Wasn't he Stanton's best friend?"

I continue eating my food and try to act

casual. "Yep that's the one. Turns out he bought the house next door to mine and he pops in for dinner." Michael puts down his sandwich, "wow I didn't see that coming, yall hated each other in high school." I chuckle a little, "Yeah that seems like a lifetime ago. We have both changed so much since that time. Parker loves his dog Aspen."

Julie thankfully changes the subject, "oh my gosh guys speaking of dogs, did I tell you guys the story about Melanie's dog?" We both shake our heads. Julie goes on to tell us about how one of her students told her that their dog was having puppies and then the next morning they heard a little bark from the backpack cubbies and they found a tiny puppy in Melanie's backpack. Thankfully it was early and the puppy wasn't away from the mama dog too long before Melanie's mom came and got the puppy.

We are all laughing by the end of her story. Sometimes these kids do the funniest things with their naive and innocent minds. "Alright guys, I better head back and go pick up my kids from music. You know how Mrs. Garcia is about picking them up late."

"I better head out too. My students are probably out at the playground now for recess." Julie and I both stand, clean up our lunch, and head out the door saying goodbye to Michael and going our separate ways.

The next day, Parker and I are waiting in the living room for Lucas. We are all ready to go for dinner at Lucas's moms house.

You can tell Parker is a little nervous. She changed her outfit when she got home from gymnastics saying she needed it to be really nice and special, which also meant that we needed to switch her bow to match the new outfit. I am a little nervous too, not going to lie. I have met and spent time with Julia before but never with the idea that I am now dating her son. Parker had me change my outfit too so that we could match. She even convinced me to wear a matching bow.

We are in the living room waiting for Lucas when Parker looks over at me from the spot where she is coloring on the floor, "do you think Lucas is nervous too?" I shake my head and smile, "probably not. I don't think he is ever nervous. Plus his mom is one of the nicest people ever." Parker smiles, "yeah you're right Lucas is really brave."

My heart hurts as I think about how brave he really is for the life he was given. At the same time I am immensely proud of him for becoming the man that he is. I get a notification that there is motion at the front door and a second later the doorbell rings. Parker jumps up, "that's probably Lucas! Can I get it?"

"Hold on, let me just make sure it's him on the camera." You never know and I would be so disappointed in myself if I ever put Parker in danger. "Yep it's Lucas. Go ahead and open it for him Parker." She nods her heads excitedly and takes off to the door. She swings it open "hi Lucas! We were waiting for you!"

"Hey baby girl. Wow you look beautiful!" My heart. I don't know when he started to call her baby girl but I can't help but think of my own dad whenever he says it to her. My dad has called me that nickname since I was a baby. "Me and Ms. Sage match! You should see her. She looks so pretty!" I smile and stand up from the couch to join them at the door.

Lucas sees me walking over and tracks my every step. My core heats as I watch his eyes roam down my body and then back to my face. "Hey babe. You look stunning as always." Lucas is so freaking yummy all the time. He is in a button up short sleeve navy blue shirt with some jeans. His hair is just the way I like it but tonight he has a little scruff on his face as if he didn't have time to shave this morning. My ovaries are screaming at me.

"Look Ms. Sage, Lucas has flowers!" She is looking at me with a big excited smile before she turns about to Lucas. "Are they for Mama Walker?" He nods his head, "yes ma'am. One is for my mama. But one of them is for Sage." He hands me a beautiful bouquet of red roses. "And one of them is for you." He bends down and hands a smaller banquet of pink roses to Parker. She takes her flowers and hugs them to her chest. "I love them. Thank you Mr. Lucas." He looks up at me, "anything to make my girls smile." My cheeks are starting to hurt with how big of a smile I have on my face. Parker grabs my hand and I look down at her. "Ms. Sage can we take these to dinner?"

"I think we should put them in water here at home so they live a long time." She nods her head, "yeah I want to keep them forever!" We all step inside and head to the kitchen to put them in vases. I head to the cabinet of cups where the vases are at the very top. Lucas must see them as I open the door because he comes around the island and I can feel him behind me.

"Here babe. Let me get them. There is no way you can reach these." I don't move out of his way while he reaches up to grab two vases. I have missed his touch these past few days when he has been hesitant and distant. Once he has them on the counter I turn to him. "Thank you for the flowers Lucas. They are beautiful." He stays close to me and holds my cheek with his palm. "You should be spoiled every single day Sage."

I take advantage of the closeness and fist his shirt with my hand and pull him to me snagging a quick but effective kiss. I then grab the vases and fill them with water. As I turn back around I can see Parker with her hand over her mouth giggling, "you just kissed Mr. Lucas." Lucas laughs, "isn't Ms. Sage so silly?"

"Yeah, but that's okay. My mom would kiss my dad too. She said that's what you do when you love someone." Lucas doesn't seem phased by her comment but I have a little freak out inside. I know I care so deeply for this man but I am not sure he is ready for that quite yet. "Alright Parker girl, the flowers are perfect. You ready to go have dinner with Mama Walker?" She jumps down from the barstool, "yep!"

"Alright ladies, let's go." We head out the front door and Lucas makes sure I lock up before we head across the yard to his garage. Once we are all in his car and ready to go Lucas grabs my hand and pulls out of his driveway. Seems like the old Lucas is back. Good I missed that guy.

"Well aren't you two the cutest thing I have ever seen" Julia opened the door with a big smile. "Lucas, you look great as well." He rolls his eyes, "thanks mama."

"Come in come in." Lucas lets us go in before following and shutting the door behind him. Julia gives me a big hug and whispers in my ear "thank you for taking care of my boy". I can feel my cheeks heat as she pulls away. She doesn't notice as her attention is now on Parker. "And you must be Parker. Lucas has told me so much about you." Parker grabs Lucas's hand, "Mr. Lucas is the best."

"Well isn't that the sweetest thing. Parker do you think you can come help me with our pizza?" Parker nods excitedly, "yes ma'am. I am great at making pizza!" Parker holds Julia's hand and they head to the kitchen.

Lucas takes the opportunity to spin me to him and gives me a kiss that has my toes tingling. He then puts his head on my forehead. "Hey Blue." I laugh, "Hi Lucas. It's not like we haven't been together for the past 30 minutes or anything." He smiles, "I didn't get to give you a good kiss earlier. I wasn't sure how comfortable you were about it around Parker or where you were at with that." He has never questioned my parenting with Parker and has always made sure to let me take the lead on things. "Thank you Lucas. But it's safe to say that she knows we are a little more than friends."

"Well good. I want her to know that I think you are the most beautiful woman in the world." He then kisses me again before we hear a throat clearing. We break apart and look over to see an older gentleman, probably in his 70s smiling at us.

"Sorry for interrupting Lucas but I need to meet this pretty lady that you can't shut up about." I look to Lucas and then back to him with a big smile, "hello I am Sage. It is nice to meet you." I hold out my hand to him which he shakes.

"Hello Sage. I'm uncle Jerry." This must be the uncle from Aspen that Lucas adores. "Come on in kids. Or do you want me to give you some more privacy to continue?" Lucas rolls his eyes. "Nah old man, you already ruined the moment."

They both laugh and we follow him into the kitchen where Julia and Parker are making pizza. While the pizzas are in the oven, we head out back. Lucas turns to Parker, "hey baby girl, do you want to go see my old treehouse? My mama and I built it when I was a kid." Parker nods excitedly, "my dad was building one for me before he died." Parker grabs Lucas's hand and they walk out towards the back corner where there are a few thick trees. "You are doing an amazing thing for that little girl Sage." I turn my gaze back to Julia and Jerry.

"She has changed my life." I smile as I think about how much has changed. "So has your son. It's pretty special to watch those two." Julia nods her head and looks out towards the treehouse, "Lucas has the biggest heart. But sometimes he lets fear hold him back. Please Sage don't let him do that with you and Parker. I have seen a change in him since he moved next door to you. You brought back the happy little boy he once was."

I can feel tears start to form in my eyes and try to blink them away before they fall. "By the look on your face, he told you about his father." She sighs. "Good. He needed to let you into that part of his past. I will always regret letting that man hurt my boy. I hope you don't think that I am a terrible mother now that you know."

I shake my head, "no ma'am. I know that abuse is much more complicated than that. My heart breaks that you both were hurt so deeply. I was with someone who treated me terribly but never hurt me physically, thank goodness. But it is easy to fall into their traps and lies. You did what you could for Lucas." I feel a tear slip out, "you raised the most amazing man I have ever met. Thank you for making him so good." Julia now has tears of her own and nods her head in appreciation.

"Now you ladies are going to make this old man start to cry if you don't stop." I chuckle at Jerry and turn to him. "He named his dog Aspen." Jerry nods his head but I don't know if he ever heard why. "The day I met Aspen, Lucas told me that he named her Aspen to remind him that he could always feel safe when he felt loved." Now Jerry has tears of his own in his eyes. "That boy is a fine man."

I nod and smile as I see Lucas and Parker coming back towards us. Lucas must see all of our teary eyes, "is everything okay?" Julia gives the two of them a smile, "oh yes! Parker I think the pizza is almost done. Let's go check it out."

"Alright! I'm SO hungry" we all laugh at her honesty and head inside. The rest of the night is spent eating pizza and ice cream sundaes hearing all about the adventures of Lucas as a young boy in Colorado with his uncle. It's while we are sitting next to each other on the couch with Lucas's arm around me laughing at a story of him chasing squirrels, that I realize I'm 100% falling in love with this man.

Before we know it, it's time to head home for the night and head to the front door. "Thank you so much Julia for having us tonight." I give Julia a hug and she gives me a tight squeeze back. "You are always welcome in this home Sage. And especially when you bring our Parker girl." Parker gives Julia a hug before giving one to Uncle Jerry.

"Thank you for dinner Mama. We will see you both at the banquet tomorrow right?" Lucas gives his mom a hug and a kiss on the top of her head. "We will be there. Jerry is excited to see what kind of mischief he can pull off at city hall."

I chuckle as I give Jerry a hug. He gives me an extra squeeze with a whisper, "I've never seen Lucas this happy. He looks at you like you hung the moon. Thank you." I nod as we break our hug. We say our final goodbyes heading out the door. Lucas makes sure to open both of our doors allowing us to crawl in. His mom and uncle wave from the porch as we pull out of the driveway. On the way home Lucas lets me know that he will need to drop us off and stop by the station to pick up some paperwork he needs to finish before his morning shift tomorrow. I nod and ignore the disappointment that we won't have any alone time tonight. But I push it aside. Tonight was a really really great night and the start of the next step for Lucas and I.

# CHAPTER 33
# - LUCAS

Dinner last night with mama and Jerry went as good as I could have hoped. Sage and Parker fit in like they were always meant to be there. I could tell Sage was disappointed when I dropped them off and had to head back to the station. I ended up staying at the station to finish up the paperwork and didn't get the chance to see Sage again. Now all the officers are here this morning getting things ready for the banquet. As much as this banquet is for us, it's more for the families and friends of the officers as a thank you for letting us sacrifice our time to serve the community.

James and I are hanging up some twinkling lights around the entrance arch way when Officer Sandoval walks over. "Hey Lucas, how is Sage and Parker doing?" I ended up getting Officer Sandoval an airline gift card so that she could visit family or take a vacation for herself after she all the help she has been to my girls.

"They are really great." I can't help but smile as I think of my girls. James looks over and gives me a nod and a smile. Officer Sandoval continues, "and Sage hasn't heard anything for her ex again right?"

"Nope, thankfully he hopefully went running away with his tail between his legs." She nods, "that's good. The officer in Knoxville that served him the restraining order told me that he was shocked and irritated. Mentioned that Matt was confused on why he would get a restraining order for only a couple of messages. You know there is always a risk that it makes things worse but I am glad to hear that isn't the case here." I nod as I agree. There would be hell to pay if he ever decided to hurt Sage again. Officer Sandoval heads off towards the food tables to help officer Darrell.

James turns to me, "So things are still good with you and Sage?" I focus on the lights as I respond. "Yeah they are. I told her about my father."

"Well shit. This is getting serious then. You typically refuse to tell anyone about that part of your past."

"I knew that if I wanted a future with Sage, I would need to tell her so that she could make the decision on if it's worth the risk to keep me in her and Parker's life." James stops wrapping lights, "Lucas, one day you are going to realize that what your father did is his issues and not yours.

I know you are worried about the cycle but you have already showed plenty of signs of breaking it." I continue with the lights on my side but look up to him, "I know. It took me a few days to process things after telling Sage but she is really helping me realize that I can have the family that I've always wanted."

James nods and smiles returning to his work, "good. She's the best woman for you then. Now don't mess it up." I laugh, "I'm doing my best. I'm excited for them to come tonight so I can show them off as mine."

I told Sage that I would pick up her and Parker at her house so that we could ride to the banquet together. On the way home I picked up some more flowers for my two girls. Seeing how much they both loved it yesterday makes me want to buy them every day to get their smiles. I quickly shower and get ready in my dress blues before heading across the yard to Sage's house. I know that she always checks the camera before opening the door so I make a funny face right at the camera as I ring the doorbell.

A minute later Parker is opening the door. She has to be the cutest little girl to ever walk this planet. Tonight she is in a blush pink dress that goes to her knees and has a fluffy skirt and glittery top. Her hair is curled just like Sage always has her with a section pinned back by a white bow. "Hey baby girl. You look beautiful, just like a princess." Parker beams up at me.

"Thank you Mr. Lucas. Ms. Sage got me a new dress and it's the prettiest!" Her smile grows as she sees the flowers in my hand. Today we went with some daisies so she can combine them with her roses. "You got us more flowers!" I nod my head and hand hers over. She hugs them to her chest with a "thank you Mr. Lucas". Movement catches my eye from the top of the stairs and when I look up I almost drop to my knees. Think about the moment that Ben saw Andie in her yellow dress and that's how I am feeling and it's not just because of her dress. I'm falling for this woman and fast.

Sage is walking down in a long soft yellow dress with strappy beige heels. Her hair is curled and she is wearing a tad bit more makeup then I know she normally does but it's making her big blue eyes pop even more. I don't know how I got so lucky. When she sees me and Parker she gives me a big smile which causes me to walk over to her, grab her face and give her a kiss. I just can't not. When we break from the short kiss she laughs, "Hi Lucas."

"You're beautiful."

"You look pretty good too." She winks and turns to Parker. "And you look like a princess."

"That's what Mr. Lucas said! He got us more flowers." She is still hugging them to her chest and I hand Sage's over to her. I got her some white lilies tonight. She smiles up at me, "thank you. Alright Parker let's put these in our vases before we leave."

Parker nods her head and walks towards the kitchen, "yeah so we can keep them forever". I don't have the heart to explain that flowers die. Maybe I will just buy her more whenever I notice them dying so that she thinks they last forever.

Once the flowers are added to the vases, we head out the door. Time to go show off the two most beautiful girls. On the way to the banquet I make sure to play the playlist that I made of all of Parker's favorite songs. I sing along extra loud which makes both her and Sage laugh.

Before you know it we have made it to city hall. I open up Parker's door and hold out my hand to help her climb out before I do the same for Sage. With Sage I keep her hand and intertwine our fingers as we head to the front doors. Parker comes to the other side of Sage and holds that hand making Sage smile as we walk inside. "Hello Officer Walker. This must be your family." Billy is in charge of greeting people at the door until the party begins and then he will slip inside with us.

Without missing a beat, "yep Billy, this is them" I look over to Parker and wink causing her to smile. "Enjoy your night guys!" We say thank you and I lead the girls into the main ballroom where all the tables are set up. "Wow this looks like a castle!" Parker is looking around the room with awe.

"It's a good thing I brought a princess with me then." Parker smiles up at me before seeing James and waving to him. We head over to the table that James is at and join him. "Hey Lucas. Sage as always it's a pleasure, you look stunning in yellow." Sage smiles at him and he laughs at me as my face turns to a glare. "And little miss Parker looks like a princess."

"Thanks Mr. James. Is Trigger here with you?" James laughs and shakes his head, "no Trigger stayed home tonight"

"Aw man. That's okay. Aspen stayed home too." I get a text on my phone from my mom saying that her and Jerry have made it. "Hey, do you two mind staying here with James while I go walk my mama in?" Sage smiles, "of course not" James gives me a mischievous smile, "I will definitely keep them company. Sage you look like you could be a little chilly. Do you want my jacket or maybe just sit really close to me." My partner better be careful or he is going to need a new one.

Sage sees the glare on my face and laughs as she rolls her eyes. "Lucas, go get your mama. We are fine here" I head back to the front and out to the parking lot where I find my mama and Jerry. "Hey guys. You both cleaned up well." I give them both a hug. "Your mama took forever to get ready tonight." She rolls her eyes at her brother. "Oh please you took just as long tying that tie of yours."

This is exactly how I imagine Stanton and Sage will be in 50 years from now. I chuckle and loop my mama's arm around mine walking them inside. Once my mama sees Sage and Parker she bolts away to say hello. Jerry shakes his head, "you better keep that woman over there. She's good for you. I've never seen you happier and we really like seeing you happy."

"She's definitely one in a million." I look over to him. "But you need to stay alive long enough to marry us one day." He wacks my arm playfully, "you and your old man jokes. I swear. I could still run circles around you." I laugh as we make our way to the table where my mama has claimed the seat next to Parker. James is a smart man, he made sure I had a seat in between him and Sage.

The night is going great. We began with dinner and a toast from the captain thanking the family members of the officers for the sacrifices they make. We have mingled around to say hello to other officers. Parker made sure to drag us over to the table that Officer Sandoval and Officer Darrell were at to say hello. Jasmine and Chief Harrington came over to say hello to us, but mainly to Sage. Jasmine had stars in her eyes when seeing Ms. Sage in her pretty dress. I'm right there with ya Jasmine.

As the night is winding down, music begins to play for anyone that would like to dance. Jerry asked Parker to dance with him and you can see her giggle as he tells her to step on his shoes. I turn to Sage who is watching the two of them with a smile. "Blue, will you dance with me?" She takes the hand that I have waiting for her, "I thought you'd never ask. I was about to ask James to dance with me." James looks over with a smirk, "I'll dance with you any time Sage."

"No way in hell man. Only one man is dancing with the most beautiful woman here and I am that lucky one." I stand up and lead Sage to the dance floor where I pull her in close and we sway to the music. Everyone else in the room seems to disappear. "You are truly the most beautiful woman in this room Sage." She lays her head on my chest and I know she can feel it beating for her.

"I mean, I am the lucky one that is with the yummiest bachelor of Pennystone." I laugh as we sway to the music, "hopefully by now they have stopped referring to me as that." She lifts her head off my chest and looks up at me with her big blue eyes that I get lost in. "Is that what you want, Lucas?"

"Damn straight that is what I want. I want everyone to know that you're mine." There has never been any doubt about that. She nods her head but doesn't look convinced. "You have just been a little distant lately since telling me about your father. I wasn't sure if you regretted letting me in." I stop us swaying and grab her hand leading her to the hallway for some privacy. She instinctively follows me but you can tell she is still feeling nervous.

Once alone in the hallway, I spin her towards me and have her back tracking. She lets out a quick breath when she feels the wall at her back. I cup the side of her face with my hand. "Blue, I have absolutely zero regrets about letting you in. I wanted to give you time to process the information to make sure you had that space to make the best decision for yourself and Parker. Plus that time gave me some time to realize that I can do this. I can be the man you both deserve, if you let me"

Sage puts one hand on my chest, "Lucas I don't need time because I know exactly who you are. You are the best man I have ever met. You are my best friend. You are kind, patient, and loving. I feel like the luckiest girl to have you by my side." I know I should give her a response explaining that she and Parker are my world and everything to me but I can't help myself and dive in for a kiss. I wrap my hand around the back of her head and angle her head up towards mine.

I hope this kiss is telling her everything Sage needs to know. She fists my shirt and I step in closer to her so that our bodies are flush together. I step one leg in between her legs and pull her closer to my body. She teases my bottom lip with her tongue before I open up. She bites my lip and lets out a moan as she feels my extremely hard dick pushed up against her thigh.

I drop my mouth to the spot between her shoulder and neck that I know she loves so that she can let out those moans that I love to hear. She wraps her hands in my hair just the way I love keeping my head there. I angle my leg to hit her center causing her to tense a little and groan "Lucas".

I lift my lips from her neck, "yeah blue?" I give her a smirk, "are you worried about getting this gorgeous dress wet?" She smirks back at me, "no i'm just worried that you aren't going to finish what you start."

"Babe I will drop to my knees right now and throw one of your legs over my shoulders to finally get a taste of you." Sage's eyes grow big and she looks around the hallway. I can tell that she is hesitant and I don't blame her, anyone could walk in on us right now.

"Maybe later Blue. I know how much you want me on my knees for you." I wink at her, steal another quick kiss and step back holding out my hand, "let's head back in. I need to steal Parker away from Jerry and get a dance with our girl."

Sage nods and takes my hand as we walk back inside. When we get back to the table my mama is looking at me with a big smile and James is giving me a smirk as if he knows exactly what happened in that hallway. I leave Sage at the table and sneak off to snag Parker from my uncle. "Alright old man, can I steal a dance with the princess?" Parker looks over at me with a big smile. "She's all yours Lucas. She is quite the little dancer."

He heads back to the table and I take his place with Parker on my feet.

The rest of the night goes by in the blink of an eye. We are all at the table when James tells me that we have been asked to help clean up after. Seeing a yawning Parker, my mama offers to drive her and Sage home. "That would be great Julia. Thank you. We can just snag the car seat from Lucas's car."

Disappointed that I don't get to take my girls home, I walk all of them out to my mamas car and make sure the car seat is installed for Parker. I open the door for Sage and Parker to crawl in before opening my mamas. "Thanks for coming mama. Make sure those two get home safe." I give her a hug and she climbs in. How fast do you think I could help clean up? Hopefully fast enough that Sage is still awake.

Clean up wasn't too terrible, thank goodness. I may have broken multiple speed limits getting back home but I finally made it. I rush into my house, change out of my dress blues, let Aspen out to go to the bathroom, and head to the kitchen to get a quick drink of water while contemplating if I should text Sage or not. My decision is made for me as I look across to Sage's house and see her staying at her kitchen window now in her light blue pajamas that she knows I love with a sign.

*Not seeing you last night was kind of the worst. Come over?*

I don't even grab my whiteboard as I bolt from the window, out the back door, and across our yards. I see her laughing as she walks over to the door to let me in. "A little excited are we?"
I show her just how excited I am as I grab her by the waist and pull her to me bringing her lips to mine. When we are both breathless we come up for air. "Is Parker asleep?" Sage looks at me with desire in her eyes and nods her head.
"Sage I will never push you to do anything that you are uncomfortable with. We don't have to cross that line if you aren't ready." She lets out a sigh. "Lucas I really am going to need you to finally finish what you started." Say no more.
I dive in for another kiss and walk her backwards until we find a wall. I scoop her legs up and she wraps them around my waste. We both groan as our centers connect with each other. She pants, "take me upstairs Lucas." I will literally do anything this woman tells me to do.

We spin off the wall and I keep her in my arms as we quietly make our way up the stairs and into her room. I slowly let her down as we shut the door.

Her room is exactly as I remembered it from the night she fell asleep on the couch. I don't get the chance to look around much as she grabs my face with both of her hands and brings my lips to hers. Within minutes both of our clothes are stripped off and we make our way to her bed never breaking apart.

It could be ten minutes, could be thirty minutes, could be hours later when we both are lying in her bed next to each other exhausted. I roll over on my side, "Sage I don't know about you, but it's not usually like that for me." She smiles and nods, "yeah that felt special didn't it."

"Hell yeah it did. I'm going to need a lot more of that too. I'm pretty sure I'm addicted to you." She chuckles as I stand up, go into her bathroom and get a warm wash cloth.

When I make it back to her room she goes to sit up, "Lucas you don't need to do that." "Blue lay back down and let me take care of you." She bites her lip and lays back down. "Good girl." I go over and make sure she is all cleaned up and pull the covers up over her so she doesn't get cold.

Once I make it back to her bedroom I go to put my clothes back on but Sage shakes her head. "Come here." Because she has me wrapped around her finger I don't even hesitate as I crawl into her bed with her and wrap her in my arms. She glances over her shoulder at me, "please stay." I smile and cuddle in closer, "there is no where I would rather be."

# CHAPTER 34
## - SAGE

My alarm goes off before the sun is up. Lucas grumbles and pulls me into him. I can't even make myself feel bad for waking him up because I'm just so happy that he is here. Last night changed everything. Turns out sleeping with your best friend is the best experience. I've never had someone treat me with such care while making me see stars. I roll over so I'm facing Lucas. He slowly blinks and opens his eyes. "Good morning Blue" I smile as I place a kiss on his chest, "good morning."

He envelopes me in his arms. "Call out sick today?" I laugh, "you know how much Parker loves school. But she may agree because she loves spending time with you." I wiggle out of his arms and rolls out of bed. His eyes darken as he looks over my body. I feel heat swirl into my core and clench my thighs together feeling soreness from last night. "Ugh. Babe you can't seriously look this beautiful in the morning and not expect me to pull you back into the bed." His dramatic self throws on arm over his eyes.

I laugh and head to the bathroom to get ready. I step into the shower avoiding getting my hair wet. I should have enough curls leftover from last night that I won't have to redo them. I smile as I think about the events of last night. I look over and see Lucas come into the bathroom. He smiles when he sees me and opens the shower door to join me. "I am definitely not dumb enough to miss this opportunity." I shake my head and laugh, "just don't make me late for work."

We take longer than I usually do but Lucas wanted to wash my body and I couldn't say no to having his hands all over me.

While I'm doing my makeup and brushing out my hair he heads out of my room and tells me he is going to help Parker.

I'm a little nervous on how she will react with him being here early in the morning. I check my phone for the time and see that I have some missed text messages.

Brooklyn: oh my goodness that picture you posted on social media is precious!

Before Lucas came over last night I posted a picture that Julia got of me, Parker, and Lucas. Lucas and I were dancing when Parker decided to join us. Lucas scooped her up and we were all dancing together. Parker had her head resting on Lucas shoulder and I'm smiling at her while Lucas is looking at me with such a look of contentment.

Gracie: y'all are just the cutest little family! We need updates on all of that asap!
Brooklyn: you've been holding out on us Sage.

I laugh and send them a text telling them I will call them after school today and give them all the updates. I make my way down the stairs and find Parker in the kitchen with Lucas and Aspen. Lucas must have ran home and got Aspen this morning while we were getting ready. Parker is at the island laughing as Lucas is asking her which cereal she would like. He will learn that she only ever eats one cereal, fruit loops.

"How about cinnamon life?" Parker shakes her head, "nope. That's what Ms. Sage eats."

"Alright, we have captain crunch?" Parker shakes her head. "No you can eat that one."

"Yes ma'am." Lucas winks at her before he sees me with a shrug and a smile.

"Good morning Parker girl." I give her a kiss on her head as I walk by to grab the bowls. Her hair is in braids again this morning and she looks overjoyed about our morning visitors.

"Good morning Ms. Sage. Lucas did my hair again. Isn't he so good at braids now?" I glance over at him and he looks like he won a playoff game with that comment. "They look really great." I grab the bowls and place them on the counter. "Now you ready for some fruit loops?"

"Yep!" She laughs as Lucas comes out of the pantry with them. "I should've guessed those first." He pours us each a bowl of our different cereals and we eat at the island.

"Alright Parker, head upstairs and brush your teeth then we need to leave." She shakes her head and jumps down from the island taking off upstairs with Aspen following after her.

Lucas grabs the bowls and takes them to the sink. I sneak in behind him and hug his back, "thanks for getting her ready today. She always talks about you braiding her hair." I can feel his laugh. "I love doing it. Now go finish getting ready so my girls aren't late to school." He glances over his shoulder and I take the opportunity to give him a quick kiss before heading upstairs. This may be the best morning I've ever had.

Today was one of those Mondays. All of my kids are so ready for fall break and so am I. They are becoming restless while also looking exhausted each day. Only two more weeks and then we get a week off. Parker and I are headed to the car when I notice something on the windshield. I head over there before getting Parker in the car and grab the note.

YOU WERE SUPPOSED TO WAIT FOR ME.

WE WERE GOING TO BE A FAMILY LIKE YOU
ALWAYS WANTED, WITH THE BIG HOUSE AND A
TREEHOUSE IN THE BACK. -M

I slowly the thick lump in my throat and look around the parking lot feeling on edge. Parker looks around too. "are you okay Ms. Sage?" I slowly nod my head and put the note back where I found it. "Yeah I just need to call Lucas to come look at something."

"Yes! That means he is going to come in his police car. Do you think Mr. James will have Trigger?" I pull out my phone from my back pocket, "probably. Hopefully they aren't too busy." I dial Lucas and he answers on the second ring. "Hey babe."

"Hey Lucas." He must hear the slight shake in my voice. "What's wrong? Are you two okay? Did someone get hurt?"

I take a deep breath. "We are okay. I found a note on my car in the parking lot." I glance over at Parker. I don't want to scare her. "Could you come by and look at it?" He must realize the meaning behind this call because I hear the sirens in his car click on before he says "we are five minutes away."

Parker and I are waiting by the car when they pull up. They made it in three minutes and I may need to talk to Lucas about his speeding. Thankfully he turned off his sirens before pulling in. I really don't want to scare Parker with this or cause a huge scene. "Good afternoon Sage." James looks over to Parker. "And good afternoon Miss Parker. I have someone who would love to see you." He opens up the door and Trigger pops out with his tail wagging.

Parker gets super excited and runs over to pet him. This gives Lucas the distraction I'm sure he was hoping for as he comes over to me and pulls me into his arms. "You're okay." I instantly feel safer and nod my head, "I know. I just didn't know what to do with the note. I assumed it needs to be taken as evidence with the restraining order." Lucas grabs the note with gloves on his hands, reads it, and looks up at me. "He's escalating by leaving this on your windshield." I nod my head, "I know. I don't even know how it got there. Did he drive down here from Knoxville? Does he have someone here that would do it for him?"

Lucas shakes his head. "I'm not sure but we aren't taking any chances." He puts the note in an evidence baggie. "We will turn this into the station and see if there are any prints on it." He looks at Parker with James and Trigger and then back to me. "I'm moving in Blue. You might fight me on it but I need to know that my girls are safe. At least until we get the print report back and know that Matt isn't in town."

I know I should feel fear in this moment because of the possibility of Matt in town but I feel excited. "I'm not going to fight you on it." I walk back into his arms. "We both feel safer when you are with us at home." He lets out a breath and I can feel him relax. I'm not sure why he was nervous about my reaction to him staying with us. After last night, I want him in my bed every night. "Alright Blue I'm gonna run these to the station and get them expedited. Then my shift should be over around 5 and I'll head home for dinner." I smile up at him. "Perfect. I'll get Aspen to join us."

"Just be careful Blue. And don't you dare open your door for anyone but me." I laugh, "not even my parents or Stanton?" He shakes his head, "they can wait outside until I'm home." I laugh even though I know he is being serious. Parker says goodbye to James and Trigger and then climbs into the car. I give James a smile and mouth thank you and his tips his head down. Lucas waits until I have climbed into the car before going back to his own. They follow us out of the parking lot and we head home.

Could Matt really be here? The thought makes me shiver and I try to brush it aside.

When we get home I first call the girls and give them the updates that they were desperately needing. They are excited for me and really happy with how happy Lucas makes me. Brooklyn tells me that we are romance movie worthy and Gracie seems happy for me but was distant tonight. Hopefully everything is going well with her and Jonathan. They recently moved in together which she seemed excited about the last time I talked to her.

I then call both my dad and Stanton to tell them about the note. Both of them go into super protective mode and try to convince me to come stay with them. I'm a little worried that they will secretly head to Knoxville to find Matt but I emphasize that it would hurt my case if they did anything rash.

I let them know that Lucas is going to be staying with us to keep an eye on things. To my surprise they both agree that it is a great idea and that he better take care of us girls. I smile as I hang up with them. Lucas told me about their conversation by the grill at the birthday party. I'm not sure why he was shocked that they would be happy for us. I love that my family already loves him like he's one of their own.

Lucas comes to the back door while I am making dinner and Aspen barks at him. I laugh because usually Aspen is on the other side of the door barking. Parker slides open the door and Lucas comes in with a duffel bag over his shoulder. We are really doing this. "Hey baby girl. Did you get all your homework done?"

"I am right now. Ms. Sage helped me with my math facts before making dinner. Do you want to help me with my spelling words Mr. Lucas?" He smiles down at her and places his bag by the door. "I would love that. Let's go sit at the island so Ms. Sage can hear too." Parker nods her head with a smile and comes into the kitchen climbing onto a barstool. Lucas gives me a smile and a wink before he joins her at the island.

For the next ten minutes they practice her spelling words for the week. Since it is Monday she doesn't know them quite yet. My heart warms as I watch Lucas be patient with her and help her spell them out correctly. "Alright guys, dinner is ready. I'm thinking we eat outside tonight?" It's a little chilly but we can put on some jackets. I'm sure Parker is wanting to run around with Aspen.

"Yes! Come on Aspen girl. Let's go outside." Parker hops off the barstool and Aspen follows after her with her tail wagging.

Lucas looks back to me and rounds the corner to help me grab the plates. He comes in for a kiss first. "Hey blue." I laugh, "hi Lucas. Thanks for doing those spelling words with Parker." He looks back towards the back door. "She's pretty freaking brilliant." I smile and collect two plates while Lucas grabs the other and the drinks. We are so biased but she really is pretty freaking great.

We take a seat outside and call Aspen over. We eat dinner as Aspen tells us all about how they had a competition in class to see who could read the most words in two minutes and she was the winner and Amanda got second. She is so proud and it's the cutest thing. Once she's done eating she takes off into the yard with Aspen to play.

Lucas turns to me, "are you still okay if I stay here for a little bit? I have a couple of evening shifts this week so I won't be home until late." I nod my head and place my feet into his lap, "yep. It'll be nice to have you here. I'm sure Parker will love having braids every day." He laughs and smiles as he looks out to her. "Any updates from her social worker about that uncle?"

A weight drops into my stomach. Things have been so exciting with Lucas that I haven't even thought about it. I shake my head no and he squeezes my thigh with the hand that he has there. "No news is sometimes good news." I nod my head and then think of something else. "Wait do you think I need to tell Mitchell that you are staying with us? I didn't even think about how that works. I might need to check to make sure that it's okay." Lucas smiles at me, "yeah you could call him but I'm sure he won't be surprised and he will agree that it's fine."

I give him a confused look, "wait why wouldn't he be surprised?"

"Because I have already been certified as a foster parent. I completed the training courses and had the home visit with Mitchell. So honestly if you would feel safer, we could also stay at my house." I can feel my jaw drop. "When did you do all that?"

"Uh probably the same time as you. I got the green light at the end of August." I am in full disbelief now. "Lucas, that was only weeks after I got Parker." Now Lucas turns a little sheepish and gets some pink across his cheeks. He looks out to Parker and Aspen. "I know. I just wanted to make sure she would always be taken care of. You are an amazing mom to Parker, Sage. But I wanted to make sure that I could always be in her life too."

I place my hand on his arm which causes him to look back at me, "you will always be part of her life Lucas. That little girl thinks the world of you." He smiles, "she really does have me wrapped around her finger doesn't she?" I laugh, "oh absolutely."

We stay outside while the sun sets. Lucas and I talk about our days as I explain how restless the kids are getting for the break and he tells me about how Trigger is such an asset that they have been extremely busy and get called to more stops now. At one point Lucas started rubbing my feet and man if I didn't already like this man, he may win my heart with these foot massages. "Lucas please never stop."

He looks over at me and laughs. "Good to know that my girl likes my hands on her body. There are lots of other places these hands would feel good." He winks over at me and I clench my thighs together while biting my lip. He leans over and whispers in my ear, "the best part of moving in is going to be exploring this body every night and figuring out what makes you scream my name." This man. Is it bedtime yet?

He must have the same thought and calls out to Parker. "Hey Parker, do you wanna head inside and watch Bluey before getting ready for bed?"

"Yes! Come on Aspen, we are going to watch your favorite show." I shake my head and laugh as we grab the dishes and head inside. Parker stops in at the kitchen to wash her hands before heading to the living room. Lucas nods his head to the leftover food. "You're on leftover duty babe. I got these dishes."

I nod and smile as we go to our normal tasks. How do I get this man to stay forever?

Parker was pretty tired by the time she got out of the shower tonight. The first day back to school each week always seems to wear her out the most. She asked Lucas to read to her tonight so I am just sitting on my bed anxiously waiting. I can hear them down the hall when Lucas finishes the chapter. He then pops into the room with his duffel bag and his eyes darken as he sees me sitting on the bed waiting for him. He drops the bag to the floor and walks directly to me grabbing my face with both his hands giving me a kiss that I know will lead exactly to what I want. Him staying with us was definitely the safest option.

# CHAPTER 35
# - SAGE

Parker and I both come home on Thursday feeling under the weather. At first I was hoping to blame it on just being tired and ready for the break but now I'm thinking it's a little more.

From the living room I see Lucas pull into the driveway. He's been parking at my house instead of having to go back and forth from his. Aspen also is here full time and I worry about the transition when they go back. He comes up to the front door and opens the door with his key. I can hear as he kicks off his shoes by the front door and make his way to us. I feel my body heat rising as he gets closer. I don't know if I should blame it on how good he looks in that uniform or if I should check for a fever. He walks in to both of us laying on the couch with blankets watching a movie. "Found my girls. How are you two feeling?"

I texted him that we may have a bug and let him know that I would understand if he wanted to stay the night at his house to avoid our germs. Parker lifts her head from the pillow on the couch. "Mr. Lucas, we have a virus in our tummies. Ms. Julie told me that when we get viruses we can get other people sick. I think I got Ms. Sage sick." I sit up on the couch, "Parker we both got sick at the same time. I could have gotten you sick or someone else could have had the virus at school."

Parker nods her head and lays back down. "Mr. Lucas, you should probably stay away from us. We will get you sick." Lucas shakes his head before heading to the couch scooping Parker up in his arms and sitting down where she was laying. "No way baby girl. I'm here to take care of you two." Parker snuggles into his chest and focuses back on the movie. Lucas looks over at me with a smile. "Don't worry babe I'll hold you later." He gives me a wink and kisses the top of Parker's head.

Within the next thirty minutes the movie ends. "Alright Blue, we should get some food in your tummies so you can defeat the virus." Parker giggles and nods. We head to the kitchen and I round the island and open the refrigerator thinking of an easy meal to make. "Sage I have dinner covered." I turn to him and raise an eyebrow which he laughs at, "my mama made you guys her homemade chicken noodle soup. She made so much that we may be eating it for days." My heart warms at Julia's kindness and the fact that Lucas called his mom to make us some soup. "Now you two go sit at the table and I will bring in everything."

Parker and I both nod and walk to the table. Lucas comes in with three bowls of hot soup and some French bread. It smells heavenly and I mentally remind myself to get Julia's recipe. While eating Parker turns to me, "Ms. Sage, are we going to school tomorrow?" I shake my head, "no I told the school that we are going to stay home and rest. We don't want to give anyone else the virus." She nods her head, "can we have a movie day and make the big fort again?" I smile as I remember the last fort that we made. "That sounds like the perfect plan Parker."

"Can Mr. Lucas have a movie day with us?" She looks at him excitedly with her hands clasped under her chin. This girl knows how to get what she wants with him. Before he has to disappoint her I speak up, "sorry Parker but Mr. Lucas has to work." Lucas shakes his head. "No I don't. I called Chief Harrington and took the day off." He sees my shocked face winks and turns to Parker. "I would love to build a blanket fort and watch movies tomorrow."

"Yes!" Parker goes back to her soup and I glance over at Lucas who smiles and shrugs when I shake my head at him.

After dinner, we decide it would be best to have Parker take a bath to get her to relax before going to bed. She is dragging as we head up the stairs.

Lucas breaks for my room to change as I steer Parker to the bath. Parker decides to take a pretty quick bath. I wash her hair as she scrubs her body before rinsing and hoping out. She asks if we can read in her bed. It's a little early but she seems really tired so I agree. We crawl into bed and she snuggles into my side as I grab the book off her nightstand. "I love you Ms. Sage."

"I love you too Parker girl." I kiss the top of her head and begin reading.

Parker only makes it through a chapter and a half before she's asleep. When I look up from the book, Lucas is at the doorway leaning against the frame. He changed into his pajamas, some flannel bottoms and a tshirt. If my stomach wasn't rolling, I would definitely eat him up. I crawl out of Parker's bed making sure not to wake her and pull her covers up around her. Hopefully we will be lucky and she will just sleep this bug away.

I walk out into the hallway and Lucas grabs my hand, "come with me." We walk into my bedroom and I think that we are going to crawl into bed to maybe watch a movie but Lucas leads me to the bathroom. I look over and see my bathtub is filled with a warm bubble bath. I look up at him and he smiles down at me. "It's time for you to be taken care of now." He helps me out of my clothes and leads me over to the bath holding out his hand to help me in. I shake my head, "nope. I'm not going in unless you join me." His eyes spark and he quickly strips out of his pajamas before hopping in. He looks up at me from the tub, "come on blue. Get in here."

I smile and step in, sinking down in front of him. I lean back against his chest and close my eyes as I let out a sigh. "How are you feeling?"

"I'm doing okay. My stomach is a little nauseous and I definitely have some fatigue." I chuckle, "You may have to wake me if I fall asleep in here." He wraps his arms around the front of my body and leans his head against mine. "I feel awful that you and Parker are sick and guilty that it makes me happy because I get more time with you guys tomorrow." I turn and glance up and him with a smile, "next time we call off, let's make it a fun day."

"Come on Blue, tomorrow will be fun in our big movie fort." We both laugh. "But yes, next time we will go on an adventure." We sit in silence for a few minutes and enjoy relaxing. "Hey babe. What do you think about going to Colorado during Christmas break? I know those two weeks can be hectic with Christmas but maybe the week after Christmas and before New Years we can all go and visit Jerry."

"I would love that. See the place that brought us Aspen." My heart fills at the fact that Lucas wants us to see a place that is so special to him.

"Plus I really liked Jerry. He's one of a kind."

I feel Lucas's laugh through his chest, "he really is the best. I promised him that he would officiate my wedding one day. I worry about what might come out of his mouth when that day comes." I laugh as I think of Jerry teasing Lucas at his own wedding. I can't help my mind wander, will I be there too? Lucas breaks my thoughts. "I'll talk with Chief Harrington and James about taking some of that time off."

I nod and settle back. We lay in the tub together for a while longer before Lucas steps out and drys off and then with a towel wrapped around his waist, he holds out his hand to help me step out. He wraps me in my big fluffy towel. "All nice and warm?" I nod and smile. I can't help but let out a small gasp as he scoops me into his arms and carries me to my bed. He places me down gently. "Stay there." I smirk, "yes sir."

He heads back into the bathroom and I can hear the drain get pulled from the bathtub. He comes out a moment later with his clothes back on and with some flannel bottoms and a t shirt for me. "Are we going to match tonight Lucas?" I smirk at him. He comes over to me and slides on some underwear before sliding on the pajama pants. "Mmhmm" Next he puts a shirt over my head and pulls it down. I instantly can tell it's way too big for me. "Is this one of your shirts?"

Once it is over my head and I'm getting my arms through I see that it is in fact one of his old tshirts from college. "Yeah I wanted to see how you look in it." I look up at him standing next to the bed. "What's the verdict?"

His eyes darken, "you may never wear one of your own shirts again" I laugh as I climb under the covers and open them for him. He climbs in next to me and I spin to lay my head on his chest. He starts to tickle my back and no matter how badly I would like to stay up with him, I give up the fight and fall asleep.

I wake the next morning feeling quite a bit better. Not completely recovered but my stomach doesn't hurt as bad. I roll over to find the other side of the bed empty. Seeing that it's super bright in my room I am assuming that Lucas is downstairs with Parker. I reach over and pull my phone off the charger. I'm shocked when I see that it's 10am. I haven't slept this late since I was in college. Before I decide to crawl out of bed I notice that I have a text from Julie.

**Julie**: Girl you are so lucky to be home today. Three kids in my class ended up throwing up. I heard from your sub you had two kids over there that got picked up feeling sick. It's a pandemic over here!

I laugh and text her back.

Me: just woke up! Sounds like a hot mess. I'll pray for your sanity today. Happy Friday!

I roll out of bed and hit the bathroom to empty my bladder and brush my teeth before heading downstairs. This is the first chance I get to see Lucas's shirt on me and I think I agree with him. I'm never wearing my shirts again. I head downstairs to walk straight into a massive fort. I can't even see half my house it is so enormous. They built a tunnel to the stairs so I crawl on in. I find the two of them in the center watching Bluey together with Aspen laying at Parker's side. "Good morning guys."

Parker looks over at me with so much excitement in her eyes. "Ms. Sage I woke up and Lucas had already made this HUGE fort! Isn't it so cool!?" I nod my head and smile. "He told me we were going to let you sleep so the virus goes away. We ate breakfast without you. Lucas made pancakes and some eggs. They were so good! He added cheese to my eggs and I love it!" Well it's safe to say she is feeling better. Lucas laughs, "alright baby girl, slow down a bit". He shakes his head with a smile then turns to me, "how are you feeling?"

"I'm feeling good. Still have a little fatigue but my stomach is doing much better. How are you feeling? Did you get the virus?" Parker speaks up for Lucas, "no way. Mr. Lucas doesn't ever get sick. He told me he is too strong for viruses." I roll my eyes at him as he laughs. "Too strong huh?"

"Yep! I'm gonna be strong and brave like Mr. Lucas when I'm older." Lucas turns his head to Parker in shock and she smiles at him before turning back to her show. He then turns back to me, "are you ready to eat? We saved you some breakfast. You need to get some food in your stomach." I nod and start to crawl to where I am assuming the tunnel to the kitchen is before he stops me. "I got it babe. Just hang out in here and I'll be right back."

I take his spot next to Parker and she snuggles into my side. "Today is the best day ever." I smile and squeeze her, "the best".

Lucas comes back shortly with a couple pancakes and scrambled eggs. I smile when I see that he added peanut butter to my pancakes just the way I like it. My stomach growls once my nose smells the pancakes and syrup. Parker laughs, "sounds like you need to eat Ms. Sage." Lucas nods and hands me the plate, "here you go. Time to feed that beast." I gladly take the plate and try my best not to scarf it down. The last thing I need is for it to come back up.

Parker told me at least ten times today that today was the best day ever. We stayed in the fort almost all day. We watched two movies after

I finished my breakfast then Lucas made some sandwiches for lunch. After lunch we colored some pictures and played board games together.

Now we are in the kitchen warming up leftover soup for dinner. "Ms. Sage, do you think the virus is out of my tummy so that I can go fishing tomorrow?" It's the last weekend that my dad and Stanton are going to make it to the lake before it gets too cold. They invited Lucas and Parker to join them at Miles' birthday party.

I think it over for a minute before answering, "you haven't had a fever since yesterday and you never threw up. I think you should be able to go. But you'll have to make sure to keep your warm jacket on okay?" Parker nods her head with excitement. "I will. I'm SO excited. I've never gone fishing. We are going to catch SO many fish. Are you excited too Mr. Lucas?" Lucas laughs and nods his head, "yeah baby girl I'm excited to go fishing with you. But sometimes you don't catch many fish."

"That's okay Mr. Lucas, you can't be good at everything. I'll catch lots of fish for you." She dives into her soup as Lucas and I both laugh and shake our heads.

Once we finish eating, Lucas tells us to get back on the couch to rest telling us to pick out our favorite movie. Turns out he gets bossy when he takes care of people. I like this side of him. He took down the blanket fort before we played games this afternoon when it got a little too stuffy in there and Parker was worried about Aspen not being able to easily get out to go to the bathroom.Parker snuggles into the couch with a blanket and Aspen jumps up to join her. I sit down on the other side and grab a blanket. "Alright Parker girl, what should we watch next?"

"Hmm..." she turns her head to the side. "I picked last time. You should pick Ms. Sage." I nod my head, "what about my favorite when I was your age?" She nods her head excitedly. "My favorite was beauty and the beast because she loves to read just like me."

"I love to read too!" I smile at Parker and nod my head, "you are the best reader. Does that sound like a good movie for tonight?"

"Yep! I love this movie. Except when Gaston fights the beast. That part is scary."

Lucas joins us, "are we watching a scary movie tonight?" Parker laughs, "no Mr. Lucas. We are watching beauty and the beast. But when Gaston fights the beast it's a little scary." Lucas sits down next to me and pulls a part of my blanket over his lap, putting his hand on my thigh. I have to tell my lady parts to simmer down. "I'll always keep you safe Parker. Promise" I look over at him noticing how serious he is.

"Thank Mr. Lucas. I love you." Parker turns back to the screen to wait for the movie as if she doesn't realize that she just dropped a huge bomb on Lucas. He turns to me with a shocked face and

I nod my head and smile."I love you too Parker."

If I wasn't already falling for this man, I definitely feel it at this moment. I put my head on his shoulder as I start the movie. I'm stirred awake as I feel Lucas lifting me off the couch. I blink awake and Lucas smiles down at me in his arms. "Keep sleeping babe. I'm taking you to bed." I nod my head and notice Parker is already gone. Lucas must have carried her up to bed as well. We get to my room and Lucas gently puts me down so that I can use the bathroom and brush my teeth.

When I get back Lucas lifts the covers to let me crawl in. He then comes around to the other side and crawls in himself.

I roll to my side and bite my lip. "Blue, do you know how badly I want to kiss you right now?" I shake my head and he rolls over and sighs. "I would love to taste every part of your body right now until I memorize every freckle." My core heats and he continues "I've never seen a more beautiful woman Sage. You radiate light and I'm lucky enough to be in your presence to feel the warmth."

I inch closer to him and tuck one of my legs in between his. He sighs again, "but babe, if I wake up tomorrow sick and have to cancel on Parker for that fishing trip, she will be devastated." I can feel myself frown and look down. Lucas pulls my chin up with his hand, "I'm not rejecting you. I don't think I ever could. I'm just letting you know the reason why you will feel my lips everywhere but your mouth." I chuckle and look up at him with a smile which encourages him to do exactly what he promised.

# CHAPTER 36
# - LUCAS

I wake up to a little hand on my face and Parker whispering, "Mr. Lucas is it time to go fishing yet?" I blink my eyes open and turn my head to Parker trying not to disturb Sage whose head is on my chest. I whisper back to Parker. "Morning baby girl." I look over at my phone and notice it's 6am. "Not yet. We have a couple more hours." She nods slowly trying to comprehend what I told her and lets out a big yawn.

"How about you crawl up here with us and try to get a little more sleep? I'll wake you up when we need to get ready." She nods her head and climbs into the bed snuggling into my other side with her head on my shoulder. Parker falls asleep within a few minutes thankfully. But me? I lay there for the next two hours holding my girls and feeling extremely grateful that the girls next door ended up becoming my everything.

Sage's alarm goes off two hours later, waking both of them.

"Good morning babe." She smiles, "good morning" and looks over finding Parker who is slowly waking up. "When did she join us?"

"Around 6am, excited to go fishing. I was lucky enough to convince her to go back to sleep." Parker sees that Sage is awake, "good morning Ms. Sage. Mr. Lucas let me come in here and sleep for a little bit."

"I can see that." Sage smiles as she looks at the both of us then smirks at me. "I'm gonna need a bigger bed since Mr. Lucas takes so much of it." Parker giggles, "yeah we are going to need a HUGE bed for all of us to fit." I laugh as I shake my head grabbing them both and tickling their sides. They erupt in laughs that has me joining them.

Once we all have watery eyes from laughing so hard, I stop. "Alright ladies, it's time to get ready. Stanton should be here in the next hour." Parker jumps off the bed, "it's fishing time!" Sage and I laugh at her excitement. "Mr. Lucas, can you braid my hair?"

"Of course baby girl, go pick out some clothes first and I'll meet you in the bathroom." She runs out the door to her room down the hall. Sage laughs, "she is definitely excited for today. Hopefully she isn't disappointed at how slow it can be to catch fish." I laugh and pin Sage to the bed under me. "How are you feeling Blue?" Her eyes spark, "feeling completely better."

"Oh thank goodness". I lean down and give her the kiss we were both desperate for last night. Before it can go anywhere else we hear Parker from down the hall, "Mr. Lucas, I'm ready for my braids!" I reluctantly break from Sage and whisper, "I'm going need a minute."

She laughs and gets off the bed heading to the bathroom, she turns before she heads in with a wink, "it may take more than a minute to go down." I sigh and sit up. She's right, it takes more than a minute.

I head down the hallway and find Parker in the bathroom on her step stool brushing her hair. She smiles when she sees me walk in. "Mr. Lucas, can we try the Dutch braid this time?" We were watching tutorials on it together when we made the fort yesterday morning. "Let's try it! If it looks bad we can do the other ones." Parker nods as I get to work on her hair.

They don't look too shabby by the time I finish both sides. "Thanks Mr. Lucas. Can you add these bows to the ends?"

"Yep." I grab the two blue bows that she had already picked out and tie them off at the ends before we head out the bathroom and downstairs. As soon as we get to the bottom we both smell bacon and Parker smiles at me, "Ms. Sage is making a yummy breakfast."

"Aren't we the luckiest?" She nods excitedly and speeds up to the kitchen. When we get to the kitchen we find Sage making breakfast burritos. "Babe, it smells amazing in here." Sage beams back, this girl loves when people love her cooking, "thanks! I figured you guys need some protein before you're out on the lake all day."

Parker climbs up onto the barstool and I walk around the island to see how I can help. "Ms. Sage, what's protein?" Sage looks up to where she is cutting the bacon, "it's food that helps give you energy and build your muscles."

"Oh yeah we definitely need protein before we go fishing." I slide in next to Sage, "alright babe how can I help you?" She looks around the counter, "uh, could you warm up the tortillas with that pan over there?"

"Got it" I grab the pack of tortillas and warm up the pan before warming up three large tortillas for us. I finish with the tortillas right when Sage finishes with the egg mixture. We scoop out enough for each burrito and eat outside so Aspen can run around with Parker before we leave.

Before we know it Mr. Calloway is ringing the bell for us to join him, Stanton and Miles in Mrs. Calloway's SUV with the boat on the trailer behind it. Sage walks us to the door and hugs Parker, "be good today okay Parker girl? I'm gonna miss you so so much."

"I'll be good. I'll miss you too Ms. Sage". Parker skips to the car where Stanton helps her climb into the car seat they have for her. I turn to Sage and tuck a stray hair behind her ear, "don't miss us too much Blue."

"I actually don't even know what to do with myself." She looks so sad and I need to fix it. "I bet your dad and Stanton wouldn't mind if you join us." She shakes her head, "no this is their thing. Plus I want you and Parker to have this memory. I will probably call the girls and check in."

"Make sure they know your hot cop neighbor is living with you now." I smirk and she rolls her eyes. "I'm sure that's the first thing they will ask me about." I laugh and cup her face bringing her lips to mine. I forget that her dad and brother are watching as I get lost in the kiss. Sage is the one to bring us both back to the realization of the audience. "Have fun Lucas. Keep our girl safe out there." I steal another quick kiss, "you know I always will." turning I head to the car, ignoring Stanton being dramatic and gagging. I laugh and climb in to the car next to Parker. "I'm so excited Mr. Lucas!" She is bouncing in her seat as we head out.

"Alright Parker girl, here is your fishing pole."

"Its pink! Thanks Mr. Shawn!" I smile as I watch Mr. Calloway explain to Parker how to reel in the line if she feels a tug on the pole. "If you feel like you can't do it by yourself, just tell us and one of us will help you, okay?"

Parker nods her head and smiles, "I'll ask

Lucas. He's worried that he won't catch lots of fish so I'll let him help me." Stanton and Mr. Calloway both laugh and glance over at me.

"I may have tried to explain to her that sometimes you don't catch many fish on these trips." Parker smiles, "so I'm gonna help him since he isn't very good at fishing." She sits down next to Mr. Calloway and he helps her cast her line.

Stanton turns to me while holding Miles, "you guys are going to have your hands full with that one in a couple of years." I laugh and nod, "she's a lot like Sage in that way, very determined." I smile as I think about the two of them as Parker continues to grow up.

"Just be grateful that you missed the teething stage. Little man is getting four more teeth all at once and he has been miserable." Miles is munching on his hand as we speak.

"I do not envy you for that but I do wish I saw Parker at that age. I bet she was very cute." He nods his head and smiles looking down at Miles, "yeah I would take it all and do it again for this little guy. It may be stressful at times and I am terrible at balancing everything but I wouldn't change it for the world."

"You're a great dad Stanton. Miles is a lucky little guy. I would've loved to have a dad like you. Well I guess I kind of did, with yours." Stanton gives me a small smile and nods his head towards Parker, "you are also a great dad to that little girl." I shake my head, "I'm not her dad but man I would love that title. I love her more than I thought was possible. Makes me confused on why there are terrible fathers out there."

Stanton face grows concerned, "you told Sage about him right?" Knowing he is talking about my father, I nod "yeah I told her. She's helping me realize that I have the choice to break the abuse cycle. John and I have been working through coping mechanisms as well just in case."

"I'm proud of you Lucas." Stanton puts Miles down on a towel with some of his toys. Miles looks adorable in his little swimsuit, and lathered up in sunscreen. He is perfectly content playing with his toys in the sun. Stanton turns his attention back to me, "how are things going between you and Sage? I'm assuming pretty well with that kiss earlier. Which by the way, I'm okay with you dating my sister but maybe don't eat her face in front of me." I laugh and Mr. Calloway, who I know has been listening, turns our way as Parker continues holding her pole and waiting for a bite. "Things are going really great. As you know after the note on her windshield we decided it would be best for me to stay at her house for extra protection."

Mr. Calloway and Stanton both clench their jaws at the mention of Matt's note. They tried their best to convince Sage to move her and Parker into their houses but reluctantly agreed that it would be best for me to go to them. "Plus I always get home cooked meals." They both laugh at that, "and Aspen loves being there with Sage and Parker. I'm worried she may never go back to my house." I smile as I think about this little family that has fallen into my lap. I don't know how I got so lucky.

Stanton and Mr. Calloway both look at each other with a smile. Mr. Calloway gives him a small nod and Stanton turns back to me, "so have you told her that you're in love with her yet?" My jaw drops. I mean I have been falling in love with Sage for a long time now, probably since the first night she met Aspen in her yard. Maybe even before that. Hell I could've been in love with her my whole life.

"By the look on your face, I would assume you have not." Stanton shakes his head and smiles. "Son, you better tell her how you feel." Mr. Calloway gives me a smile and a nod.

"Yeah Mr. Lucas, you can tell Sage you love her. I tell her all the time and she always says it back. She will tell you she loves you too." Mr. Calloway squeezes Parker in a side hug while she continues holding her pole, "we all love you Parker girl. You are such a blessing in our lives." She looks at him with a big smile "I love you too Mr. Shawn. And I love you Mr. Stanton." Stanton looks a little shocked at first but quickly recovers "love you too Parker girl."

Parker then turns to me, "see Mr. Lucas it's not that hard. You have to tell the people you love that you love them before it's too late." A melancholy silence falls over us but is broken when Parker yells "I got one! I got one!"

Mr. Calloway helps her reel it in and pulls out a 12 inch bass. Well I'll be damned, maybe she is going to catch lots of fish. That is exactly what she did. By the end of the day Parker caught eight fish and I caught one.

We were on the lake for 4 hours before we decide to head back in, which gave me more than enough time to think about what everyone said. In my heart I know Sage is it for me. Now I just need to tell her and it needs to be the perfect moment. This could be the start of our forever.

# CHAPTER 37
# - SAGE

We made it y'all. It's the Friday before fall break and it's been a doozy of a week. With each day getting closer to the break the kids got more and more anxious and restless. Lucas and Parker came back from their fishing trip with big smiles. Turns out that little girl can catch some fish. She was very proud and Julie told me that she had been bragging about it all week.

Now it's Friday afternoon and I am wrapping things up before leaving for the break. Parker skipped off with Amanda to her moms classroom to play while I clean up my classroom. I'm sure they are down there talking about the books they have been reading. Once I finish up and am ready to head out I call down to Mrs. Gardner's room for Parker to come back. It rings and rings with no answer. That's weird. I pull out my cell phone and call her cellphone number.

"Hey Sage, happy break. Are you and Parker back home now? We should schedule a playdate this week for the girls."

"Uh wait. Why would Parker and I be home? She's still with you in your classroom isn't she?"

"No, we just pulled into our garage. Parker said she was going to walk back to your classroom when we were leaving."

A terrible feeling starts to build in my stomach.

"What time did you guys leave?"

"About ten minutes ago. Is everything okay? Did she not make it back to you?"

"No, I haven't seen Parker...I gotta go. I need to go see if she's in the bathroom maybe."

"I'm sure she's okay, Sage. She must be in the bathroom. Call or text about that playdate okay?"

"Will do. Enjoy your weekend." I hang up the phone and head to the hallway. Something doesn't feel right. I check two bathrooms that are in between my classroom and Mrs. Gardner's and both are empty. I head to the front of the school and tell Mrs. Brown what is happening. She makes an announcement over the school's intercoms for Parker to come up front.

After three minutes of waiting I know she isn't coming back.

"Mrs. Brown, can you please call the police station?" I'm trying to stay as calm as possible but I'm losing it inside. With shaky hands I pull out my phone and dial Lucas while Mrs. Brown is talking to the 911 operator.

"Hey babe. Happy last day. Are you two excited for the break?"

"Lucas, something is wrong." My voice breaks as I try to hold in tears.

"What is it? What happened?" I can hear over the phone his radio go off "we have a reported missing child at Pennystone Elementary School. We need all available officers on route."

There is no way to prevent the tears now. That missing child is mine. "I'll be there in three minutes tops Sage." I nod my head and realize that he can't see me, "okay I'll be here."

I hear the sirens turn on as he disconnects the call. I'm stunned in silence for a couple of minutes. "Everything is going to be okay, Sage." I turn to Mrs. Brown, "my gut tells me that someone took her. Parker is smart and a very good kid, she would never run off. Can you check the cameras for me?"

She looks hesitant and I feel my anger rising as Lucas comes in the door with James and Trigger. Lucas runs up to me and envelopes me in his arms, "we will find our girl Blue. I promise." I nod and turn back to Mrs. Brown, "do you have access to the cameras?"

"Y-yes. But I'm so sorry the cameras were shut off after the students were picked up for maintenance to work on them over the break." I immediately feel guilty for snapping at her. "I'm sorry Mrs. Brown, I'm not trying to be rude." She shakes her head, "I would do the same if my baby girl was lost."

Mrs. Applewhite comes out of her office and

we fill her in on what's happening. Her eyes get big as we explain that there are no cameras to see what occurred. James speaks up, "she could still be in the school somewhere. Sage, do you have something of Parker's that Trigger can sniff?" I nod my head, "yeah she keeps a jacket in my classroom in case it's cold or it rains."

Our entire group walks quickly to my classroom where I grab Parker's jacket and hand it to James. He allows Trigger to sniff it and then leads him into the hall. "Her scent is probably all over your classroom so it's best if we start out here. Where was she last?"

"She was in Mrs. Gardner's classroom playing with her daughter Amanda. I called her and she said that Parker told her she would walk back to my classroom when they left." James nods his head and I lead him to the hallway that her classroom is in. Trigger sniffs around in the hallway, seems to catch a scent and follows it. He leads us right to the exit door that is right down the hall from Mrs. Gardner's room. We only use this exit for fire drills but some teachers use it to leave campus after the day is over. James is the one that is brave enough to speak up and say what all of us are thinking, "anyone could have slipped in when someone was leaving." I nod my head and Lucas grabs my hand. "Are you okay? We will find her. I promise."

I nod my head again and glare at the door, "I'm fine. But when I find out who took our little girl there will be hell to pay."

Lucas drives me home with James following behind us in my car. I am going through every scenario in my head on where Parker could be, who could've taken her, and why her? "Blue look at me." I look over from the passenger seat. "We. Will. Find. Her."

I feel my eyes filling with tears. "She's already been through so much and she is just a kid. She's such a light to everyone even after everything. This isn't fair Lucas. Why her?" He grips the steering wheel until his knuckles are white. I lean over and touch his forearm causing him to glance over at me. "We will find her, Lucas. It isn't fair but we will not rest until she is found." He nods his head and we pull into my driveway finding the cars of my parents and Stanton already there. When we get inside we also see that Chief Harrington is there as well.

My dad is the first to get to me and wraps me in a big hug. Something about a dads hug is so comforting and I feel tears spill out of my eyes. When we break he grabs my shoulders, "no one messes with my family and doesn't receive justice. We will find her Sage." I nod and my mom hugs me tight. "It's going to be okay."

Stanton comes over next with Miles crawling after him. He gives me a hug that's extra long. If anyone knows how I am feeling right now it's my twin brother. "She's okay Sage. I can feel it. She's okay and we will find her." We all head to the living room where Chief Harrington sits down with us.

"Sage, I have chosen to run lead on this case." I see Lucas go to say something but she cuts him off, holding up a hand to stop him. "As far as I can tell, Parker is as much of your daughter Lucas as she is Sage's." I nod my head. She is right. Lucas is her dad in all sense of the word except the title. "You can't pull me off this case Chief. If this was your little girl, you would be working it." She nods, "you're right, which is why I'm allowing you to work it, but you can't run lead and I can't have you on documentation. When we catch the perp nothing can sway the court's decision to put them away for a long long time."

Lucas nods, "thank you Chief." He grabs my hand and pulls it into his lap, interlocking our fingers. "Now Sage give me the rundown of what occurred with as much detail as possible." I explain everything that I remember down to checking the time that I called Mrs. Gardner and her report of leaving ten minutes prior. "Okay that gives us a good foundation and timeline for when the kidnapping occurred."

My stomach drops at the word kidnapping. Lucas squeezes my hand and my dad puts his arm around me from my other side. "I am going to head to the station and start outlining the case. If I get any updates, you will be the first to know." I nod my head and Lucas and James both stand with chief Harrington. "Babe, I'm gonna go with Chief to work through this. Are you going to be okay here?"

"Go. I need you to be there getting more information and being our eyes. Go find our girl." Lucas nods, gives me a quick kiss on the forehead, and stops when passing Stanton. "Please stay with her." Stanton nods, "of course man. We aren't going anywhere."

Lucas, James and Chief Harrington leave out the front door. The room is sitting in silence. Miles breaks it when he crawls over to me and tries to pull himself up to stand using my legs. "Hey big guy. Look at you. You're going to be walking before we know it." I pick Miles up and he snuggles into my shoulder. "He always knows when someone needs a little extra love." I nod and close my eyes as I hug him. We will find her. She's okay. She's going to come home safe.

My parents stayed until after dinner and then headed home. Stanton refuses to leave and told me that Miles can sleep in the portable crib tonight. We are sitting in the living room watching Miles crawl around the floor with Aspen. "Stanton, what will I do if we don't find her?"

Stanton looks at Miles. "I don't know what I would do if this was Miles." He looks to me, "you are going to find her. You are the smartest person I know. What are some of the theories you have come up with?" I sigh, "well there's the obvious one that it could be a random person. But this doesn't seem like that's it. Someone would have had to watch the school to time getting through the side door."

He nods his head and I continue, "no this seems like it could be connected to something. It could be the mysterious uncle that wants access to her trust fund." Stanton sits by to analyze, "I agree that it doesn't seem random. There were too many convenient timings. So let's start with the uncle. Have you heard more besides that first call from the social worker?" I shake my head, "no I asked Mitchell a couple of times and he said that the uncle was still reviewing logistics."

"Okay so that one seems like a stretch. People will do a lot for money but it would be easier for him to just go through the state for custody if he wanted her." I get up from the couch to pace as my brain continues turning. "That makes sense. But he could be wanting to avoid the hassle of that process." Stanton fixes one of Miles' toys before responding. "Yeah but the only way to access that trust fund would be through the state so taking Parker would not get him any closer to the money." I stop walking and think it over. He's right, the only way to have access to the trust would be to be granted guardianship over her. He would completely ruin his chance if he took her. He's off the suspect list.

"What other theories do you have? We both know you can't only have those two." I nod my head and resume pacing. Miles is watching my movement and giggles when I spin once I get to one end of the room. "The other theory would be Matt. He has mentioned Parker in the notes and last time it was left on my windshield so he could have been scoping out the school to see the best way to get in."

Stanton contemplates that, "do you think Matt would go to this extreme though? I mean I never loved the guy but to kidnap a kid is pretty serious." I stop and look at Aspen laying in her dog bed, "I'm not sure. Before the notes I would say there was no way. He has too much to lose with his career."

"But now?"

"Now I don't know. The notes were escalating and the officer in Knoxville reported that he was agitated when he was given the restraining order. If his boss found out about it, it could look really bad for coaching opportunities so he could be acting out of anger." He pulls out his phone from his pocket, "we need to call Lucas and see if that officer in Knoxville can drop in and see if Matt is there in Knoxville." I nod my head as Stanton dials Lucas.

"Hey man, everything is fine. Sage is okay. We

have been considering a theory. We are worried that the kidnapping is connected to Matt's notes to Sage. Can an officer in Knoxville drop in and check to see if Matt is still there?" There's silence as Lucas is responding to Stanton.

"Okay thanks Lucas. Keep me posted." Stanton hangs up the phone. "He's going to have Officer Sandoval contact the officer she originally spoke with about the restraining order and see what she can find out."

"Okay great. At least now it feels like we are doing something." Stanton nods his head, "sadly now we just have to wait and see."

Ugh that's the worst part. Give me a badge and let me go search the entire city. In that moment I realize that when we find Parker she will be shaken up by all this. "Stanton I know you don't take family as clients but when we come out on the other side of this, will you talk to Parker and see if she needs to be referred to someone?" Stanton gets up from the couch and pulls me into a hug, "of course Sage. I will do everything I can to help her when she gets home. And she will get home."

"Thank you. I just need her to be okay." We hear my phone ding and I pull out my phone out of my pocket hoping it's from Lucas with an update but find a text from an unknown number.

Unknown: it was always meant to be us at the end. Now we can be the family we both dreamed of. -M

My face must go white because the next second Stanton is looking over my shoulder to read the text. "We need to call Lucas back." He dials Lucas and I am stuck looking at the text as he is explaining what happened. "Yeah, that sounds good. I'll bring her down to the station. See you soon."

I finally break from my state and look up at him. "We gotta go. They are hoping to trace the number to its owner. They also want to document the message into Matt's file." I nod and follow him as he heads out the door with Miles on his hip.

I feel like I'm on autopilot as we head to the station. The only thing that snaps me out of it is Lucas coming up to us once we are at the station. "Sage, this is good. This means we have a lead. The text very much implied that he has Parker. Now we confirm the owner of the number and that will lead us to find her." I slowly nod my head but don't look him in the eyes. He lifts my chin with his fingers, "you gotta let me into your head Blue." I let out a heavy sigh, "This is all my fault. Parker was taken because of me. She already has gone through so much trauma and now this? She's going to hate me." I can feel my heart getting heavier and heavier and eyes filling with tears.

Lucas grabs my head with both his hands, "Sage you are an incredible mother to Parker. She will not hate you. This is not your fault. The only one to blame is Matt. No one else. He will pay for this. I promise." I nod my head and shake off the tears, "let's figure out where he is at and get our girl."

Regaining my confidence I head into Chief Harrington's office and tell her about the message. Officer Sandoval has contacted the officer in Knoxville for an update on if Matt is there. She is still waiting to hear back. "This is good, guys. We will get the number into the system and see what it pulls. We may also be able to track the location from where the message was sent. It could take a little longer to track the location but I have a contact at the county office that is excellent with that type of stuff. I will contact him now."

James is standing next to Lucas and looks like he could punch a wall. I forgot to think about how much this could be impacting him. He has a special relationship with Parker too. On our way out of the office I pull James to the side. "She's going to be okay James. We will find her." He nods his head, "I know Sage. We just need to do it soon. I've seen how fast human trafficking can happen." Dread settles in my stomach. He must see it in my face. "We will find her Sage. Lucas and I aren't going to leave the station until she is home."

"Thank you James." I give him a quick hug and he heads back into Chief Harrington's office.

Lucas walks us back to Stanton's car and Stanton goes to buckle up Miles. Lucas gives me a tight hug, "are you sure you don't want me to come home with you?" Home. Is my house a home without Lucas and Parker? No.

"Yes I'm sure. I need you here working with Chief Harrington to get as much information as possible. We have to find her, Lucas. I trust you more than anyone to help find her and bring her home." We say our goodbyes with a quick kiss and him telling Stanton to make sure he takes good care of me.

Once back home Miles starts getting fussy. Stanton has him on his hip walking in the door, "sounds like it's bath and bedtime for this little guy."

"I'm gonna take Aspen outside to go to the bathroom then I'm gonna head to bed. Today has been a really long day. Maybe in the morning Lucas will have some news for us."

"I want you to stay inside though Sage. Let Aspen out, shut the door and don't open it again until she is back at the door. We aren't taking risks." I reluctantly agree and head to the back door. I watch as Aspen hurries out the door, do her business, and come straight back. Lucky for me she didn't want to run and play. I take Aspen upstairs with me. I'm not used to sleeping in my bed alone anymore. Aspen will have to do tonight.

I quickly get ready for bed putting on one of

Lucas's shirts that still smells like him. But even that doesn't settle my heart. As I'm laying in bed with Aspen snuggled into my side, I think back to all the notes I have received from Matt for clues. The first note was when I started at the new school, then there was the gift basket when I bought my house, the note for the new school year, the presents for Parker, the note on my windshield and lastly the text message tonight. There has to be something there right? I sit up in my bed and the sudden movement has Aspen immediately on guard.

Oh my gosh. I know who has Parker. Not only that. I know where he took her.

# CHAPTER 38
# - LUCAS

James and I follow Chief Harrington outside Sage's front door and to James's patrol car. The ride to the station is silent as we think about how the next 24 hours will go. We both know with a kidnapping, the first 24 hours is the most important. After that, details become fuzzy and the chance to find the child becomes harder.

James knows this first hand more than I do with his tours in Afghanistan. He was on a special forces unit and has told me of some of the rescue missions he went on. I am assuming that today could be triggering for him and could bring back some memories. I look over at him in the driver's seat and see the tension in his jaw, "Hey man, you doing okay?" James gives a small nod, "yeah I'm okay. Just worried. I am trying not to let my brain go to the worst case scenarios but sometimes that is hard to do." I know how he feels. Staying busy is the only thing that is keeping me from going crazy. If I stay busy, then

I won't have time to think about where Parker is or how scared she must be. "If you need to take a break tonight and take a breather, just let me know."

"I'll let you know but that won't be needed. Tonight's focus is finding Parker." We get to the station and head straight to Chief Harrington's office. Officer Sandoval and Officer Darrell are already there waiting for us.

Chief takes a seat behind her desk and Officer Sandoval hands over some documents. She lays them out on her desk and we look over them. We have witness statements from the people at the school, a statement from Mrs. Gardner, and a description of what Parker was wearing today.

She was so excited for the last day before break. She asked to wear her sparkly skirt with a purple shirt. Sage put her hair in a bun on top of her head with a big sparkly bow. She has white vans that match Sage's and she wears them almost every day.

I can see her smile as she climbed into the car this morning. I have to remind myself that wasn't the last time I would see her. I shake my head and focus back on the task at hand. "Alright Officers, here is what we know. Parker was abducted between 3:40 and 3:50pm today at Pennystone Elementary School. Almost every teacher was gone for the day resulting in no one witnessing her leave the building or in the parking lot. The cameras at Pennystone Elementary were turned off an hour before, after all the students were picked up for the day. Trigger tracked Parker's scent leaving the building out of the side door."

We all nod solemnly. We need more information than just that if we are going to catch the person that took Parker. "Let's brainstorm some theories. Who has one?" James speaks up first, "the perp could have scoped out the school, knows that the students were about to be on break, and saw teachers leave out of the side door. He or she took the opportunity to slip in when someone left for the day and waited in the bathroom for the perfect moment. Parker left Mrs. Gardner's room stopping at the bathroom. The perp took the opportunity and left out of the same side door with Parker." Chief thinks it over for a minute. "Did Trigger follow Parker's scent to the bathroom? James shakes his head, "No he stayed in the hallway until he got to the exit."

"Your theory makes sense James. But if Trigger didn't follow the scent to the bathroom, it is safe to say that Parker never entered the bathroom." Officer Sandoval looks up from the documents, "Wait so the prep was able to take Parker directly out of the hallway? How? They would have no place to hide while waiting for Parker."

I look at her, "Unless they perfectly slipped in when Mrs. Gardner slipped out." that would have been the most impeccable timing. "Do we have a map of the school? Is there a janitor's closet or stairwell near that hallway?" We spend the next thirty minutes to an hour looking over the school's blueprints thinking of every possible entrance and spots that the perp could have used for the abduction.

"Alright everyone. We all need to take a break for dinner. If we burn ourselves out, that does no good. Take at least thirty minutes and then we will meet back here." We all agree and head out of Chief's office. James and I decide to head across main street to the bakery for some quick sandwiches. We eat in silence as we continue thinking about the most important case we have ever had.

When we get back to the precinct, we head straight back to Chief Harrington's office. Right before we step inside I get a phone call from Stanton. "Hey, this is Stanton. I'm gonna take it and make sure everything is okay with Sage."

"Of course man. Take your time." James slips into the office as I step aside."Hey Stanton, is everything okay? Is Sage okay?"

"Hey man, everything is fine. Sage is okay. We have been considering a theory. We are worried that the kidnapping is connected to Matt's notes to Sage. Can an officer in Knoxville drop in and check to see if Matt still there?" Freaking Matt. "Yeah I will have Officer Sandoval check into it. There is a chance that there could be a connection. It's definitely worth looking into. I will let the team know."

"Okay thanks Lucas. Keep me posted." I hang

up and head into the office. James looks over as I walk in, "Is Sage okay?"

I nod, "Yeah she's good. Her and Stanton were talking and they think that Parker's kidnapping could be tied into her notes from Matt." I think about it for a second, "Actually the last two notes did mention Parker didn't they?"

We pull out the documents that we have collected for Sage's restraining order and review them. I turn to Officer Sandoval, "Can you contact the officer in Knoxville that served the restraining order and see if he can drop in to see if Matt is currently in Knoxville?"

"Yeah I will step out and call him now." She steps out towards her desk to get the number and to contact the officer. Chief Harrington is looking over the notes, "He talks about them having a family together fairly often." My jaw tightens. He wants *my* family. "In the package for Parker he talks about wanting to complete the family Sage started. Then on the note left on her windshield he mentions that she was supposed to wait for him to be the family she's always wanted. My gut is telling me that if the person writing these notes also took Parker, they aren't harming Parker. They are wanting to use Parker to get to Sage."

My phone begins to ring and everyone looks at me. "It's Stanton again. I'll step out and take this." I step out in the hallway as they continue to analyze the messages from Matt. "Hey Stanton, what's up?"

"Hey man, Sage got another message from Matt." My heart drops. "He texted her from a random number. It says 'it was always meant to be us at the end. Now we can be the family we both dreamed of. -M'." He definitely implied that he has Parker. We found our guy. "I need you to bring her down here. We need to document the text message and we may be able to track the number."

"Yeah, that sounds good. I'll bring her down to the station. See you soon." I end the call, take a deep breath, and head back into the Chief's office. Everyone is looking at me with concern.
"Sage received a text message from Matt." I fill them in on what the message said and that Stanton and Sage are on their way to the station to document it.

By the time Stanton and Sage leave the station, I am feeling beat. This day has felt like a never ending nightmare. It's getting late and I have been at the station for over 12 hours now but I told Sage I wouldn't leave until we get Parker back home. I head back into the precinct and find everyone back in the office. I am not the only one looking exhausted.

I look to the Chief who is sitting behind her desk staring at all the documents then look over at Officer Sandoval, "any updates from the Officer in Knoxville?" She couldn't get through earlier and had to leave a voicemail. She shakes her head, "No but let me try again." She heads out to her desk. James is pacing around the room causing Trigger to pop his head up every few minutes. Officer Darrell is sitting in a chair across from Chief Harrington staring at the desk unblinking. It's been five hours since Parker was taken.

5 hours of being scared. 5 hours of wanting to go home. 5 hours of wondering if anyone was coming to save her. "Okay guys I finally got through to the officer in Knoxville." Officer Sandoval comes back in and everyone snaps their head to her. "He told me that he got the voicemail and drove to Matt's apartment. There was no answer at the door." James's eyes snap to mine. This is our answer. Matt is the one that took Parker. "However, he did mention that he talked to neighbors and they saw him earlier this week. They reported that he is typically out each evening and especially on Friday nights."

Chief Harrington stands up and rounds her desk looking out the window. "Let me check in with the technology specialist at the county office to see if there is an update on that text location and owner. It may be our best lead to confirm Matt's involvement and where he is keeping Parker." She walks back to the desk and dials the county office.

"Hello Officer Thomas, we are hoping you can provide us an update on that phone number."

"Good evening ma'am, I was just about to call you. Unfortunately I don't have the news you were hoping for." You can see everyone in the room shoulders drop.

"The number was a temporary number from a burner phone or a restricted line."

"With that, were you able to track the location of the message?"

"No ma'am. It seems like your perp is intelligent enough to prevent that." This was supposed to be our break and now we are back at square one. "I'm sorry I don't have any more information for you. I know you were hoping for some direction from this."

"I appreciate you staying late, Officer Thomas."

"Of course ma'am. Best of luck finding the little girl." Chief Harrington disconnects the call and leans back in her seat. We all stay silent for a good five minutes, shocked and defeated.

"Okay everyone, I know that we all were hoping that was our breakthrough but we have to keep pushing ahead." Chief Harrington turns to Officer Darrell. "Did we get any hits since we put out the Amber Alert?" Officer Darrell shakes his head, "no but I know everyone in this town is on the lookout." She nods her head, "you're not wrong about that. This town protects their own. It is safe to assume that there is a high chance that Parker is still somewhere in town." Not if he took her directly from the school back to Knoxville.

"Chief, can we contact gas stations in a 50 to 100 mile radius to be on the look out for a male with Parker? He will need to stop to get gas at some point if he has left Pennystone." More eyes equal a better chance at finding her. James nods his head and adds, "we also should contact hotels in that same radius and see if they have records of Matt checking in. If he doesn't plan on leaving immediately but to bait Sage out, he would need somewhere to stay."

Officer Darrell looks up from where he was staring at the desk, "we could also contact close family and friends of Matt to see if any of them know of his current location. We could use his social media to gain contacts and see what responses we receive." Chief Harrington nods, "these are great tactics everyone. Let's all break and complete those various assignments. Officer Sandoval check back in with that officer in Knoxville and see if he has an update as well." We all head out to our desks and get to work.

I've called about 20 gas stations and each of the employees agreed to be on the lookout and make sure the next shift is aware of the situation. I rub my eyes, grab my phone, and I see that I missed a call from Sage an hour ago. This late at night? She should be sleeping. I listen to the voicemail she sent.

"Hey Lucas, looks like I missed you. You're probably crazy busy. I think I figured out where Parker is. I'm going to go save our girl. Maybe it's better that you didn't pick up because you would've stopped me. But I have to go now. I can't let her be away from home all night when I know where she is. I may be able to stop all of this. I am going to text Chief Harrington where I'm headed. This is probably not the best timing but just in case, I love you Lucas Walker. I've been in love with you for a while now. Parker told me to tell you before it's too late and I can't let our girl down."

James looks at me with concern from his desk as I'm sure he can see the tears forming in my eyes. If something happens to my girls before I can tell Sage I love her, I will forever regret it.
I jump up from my desk and storm into Chief Harrington's office. "Where is Sage?!" She looks up from all the documents laid out on her desk of all the evidence we have from the kidnapping. "What do you mean Lucas? I haven't seen her since she came in with Stanton."
"She left me a voicemail saying that she texted you her location. She figured out who has Parker and is probably there now trying to save her."
Chief Harrington grabs her phone and reads the message before looking up at James and I. "She

went to Parker's old house."

# CHAPTER 39
# - SAGE

I have been to Parker's old house one time before tonight, when we came together and packed up more of her things to take to my house. It was a little awkward and you could tell that Parker was hesitant to come inside. She stopped and looked at pictures of her parents in the hallway before she skipped off to show me her room. As I pull onto the street leading to her house I notice that the treehouse is now complete. He must have finished building it before he took Parker.

I park down the street. I don't want him to know I'm here until I confirm that Parker is in a safe place. If this goes sideways I don't want her to witness it. This little girl has already been through way too much. I sneak across the front yard and hope that I am being more sneaky than the time I put the gift basket on Lucas's doorstep.

My mind drifts to Lucas. I hope he listens to my voicemail and doesn't hate me for doing this. Tonight there is no room for silly mistakes. Thankfully I know they don't have a doorbell camera. I type in the door code and hear the door unlock. I turn the knob as quietly as I possibly can, take a deep breath, and walk into the foyer of the house. The house is completely dark except for the living room. Hopefully Parker is upstairs asleep.

Walking in the living room, I find him sitting on the couch. "Sage, you finally came."

"Hello Michael." The hairs on the back of my neck stand and my gut is telling me to get as far away as possible. Sorry gut, we have a little girl to save tonight.

"We have been waiting for you. We had dinner without you." He looks towards the kitchen and backyard. "Did you see that I finished the treehouse for us? Now Parker can say that her dad finished it." Her dad? He will never be Parker's dad. She had an amazing one before he died and now has one in Lucas.

I've seen enough movies to know not to agitate a psychopath so I nod slowly. "It looks nice Michael. Just like the one in the library."

"I knew my girls loved treehouses. I just had to finish it before we could be a family." I look out back towards the treehouse. It does look really nice. It's almost sad that I will have to destroy it after all this is over. Parker does not need a constant reminder of today in her backyard. Speaking of Parker, "Michael, where is Parker?"

"Oh our girl is just sleeping in her bed. We ate dinner together and she said she was super tired, which is weird because she didn't look tired. She didn't even want me to read her a book or anything just said she wanted to sleep." Parker was probably so scared and wanted to get away from him. If I find out that she cried herself to sleep tonight I will do everything in my power to make sure this man never sees the light of day outside of a prison. "Come sit by me Sage. We have so much to discuss."

I walk over slowly checking my surroundings for anything that I can protect myself with. There is a lamp on the end table by the couch, the tv remote on the coffee table, and a glass of some type of drink next to Michael. Michael must see me looking around and frowns, "I'm not going to hurt you Sage." I sit as far away from Michael as possible on the couch making his face turn even more angry. Before he can say anything I jump in, "Michael, why are you doing this?"

His forehead creases as his eyebrows come together, "what do you mean? We are a family Sage. Families are supposed to be together." I shake my head slowly, "we aren't a family Michael. We are friends. We both work at the school and are friends." He is getting agitated. I need to be careful. "No Sage. We. Are. A. Family."

He's now getting louder and I worry that he will wake up Parker. I speak quietly, "when did you start feeling like this Michael?"

"We were meant to be together in high school. We had a special connection. I know you felt it. We were always partners in class. You were always so nice to me. You would sometimes touch my arm or give me a special smile. We just weren't ready back then." I think back, trying to remember. I guess we were partners on projects but I don't remember it being more often than any other person. What he remembers is definitely not what I remember of our time in high school. "Then you chose to leave for college so I waited and waited. The day you returned to Pennystone was a day I knew that we were always meant to be."

He takes a deep breath and I remain silent. "I played the long game trying to let you heal from your ex. I am so grateful he was dumb enough to let you go. Then you got Parker and it was perfect. I wanted to give you enough time but she jump started my plans. The day I heard you got Parker, I bought all the supplies for the treehouse and the box of things for Parker. But it's weird because I never saw her wear any of the clothes that I bought her." I swallow the lump in my throat. Luckily he doesn't seem to notice and continues. "Things were going great until I found out that you were spending more time with Lucas. Then you went to the police banquet with him and posted a picture of the three of you." He laughs manically, "it's kind of funny. The one guy I never thought I would have to worry about, became my biggest competition. I knew I needed to do something before it was too late to save my family." It's official, this guy is crazy. Crazy enough that he may plead insane when this ends up in court.

"Michael, did you hurt Parker?" He shakes his head aggressively, "no Sage. I would never do that. You should know that."
I mean the Michael I thought I knew would never, but this guy?
"I heard her and Amanda in the library talk about playing in Amanda's mom's classroom after school. I was conveniently in the hallway when Mrs. Gardner left for the day and Parker left her classroom. I told her that you were putting things in the car and asked me to walk her out for you. She was nervous at first and confused when I told her she needed to get in my car to find you. By the time we got here she wouldn't speak."

I'm going to kill this man. He terrified Parker to the point where she didn't speak. I can't help but think of the trauma she went through today. "She didn't even want to see the tree house." He looks disappointed but I sure as hell am not going to feel a twinge of empathy for him. "We will just have to show her together in the morning." Little does he know my plan is to get Parker out of here as soon as possible. I need to distract Michael until Chief Harrington shows up.

"Can I see Parker? I didn't get to tell her good

night." Michael contemplates it and you can tell he is hesitating. "Please Michael. I have missed her today. I always tell her goodnight" He nods and stands up. "Yeah but we have to be quiet. She needs her sleep." He motions with his hand for me to go ahead towards the stairs. I walk ahead of him and can feel his presence behind me. I don't know how the guy I thought was such a good friend to me when I moved here is this same person. Michael puts his hand on my lower back and I fight my body's reaction to stiffen and pull away. Keep it together Sage. We don't want to wake up Parker, just make sure she's okay.

I head towards her old bedroom and take a deep breath before walking into her room. Thankfully Michael stays at the door watching us. I sit down on Parker's bed and am thankful she is asleep. You can tell she went to sleep scared with how she is clutching the blankets around her. I lean down and kiss her forehead trying to keep my tears in.

Parker stirs a little and blinks her eyes open. "Ms. Sage? Are you really here?" I lean down to whisper so Michael can hear, "I'm here Parker. I'm gonna get you out of here but I need you to go back to sleep for a little longer" She nods her head and glances over to the doorway before looking back at me. "I want to go home." Her eyes start tearing up and I contemplate walking over to Michael and kneeing him in the balls to be done with this. But I don't know what type of weapons this crazy man has on him.

"I know Parker girl. We will. Lucas is going to come and save us, I know it. I love you." Parker nods her head, "I love you too mom" and closes her eyes again. I watch her breathing even out as my heart feels like it is about to burst. I raise my voice so Michael can hear, "Goodnight baby girl." I stand up from the bed and walk back out of the hallway with Michael following behind me.

"Isn't our girl just perfect? She was meant to be ours Sage." Nausea rises in my stomach. I need to get this man away from Parker. If he loses his patience with me, I'm not sure what the explosion will entail. I stop walking and turn to him, "Michael can you show me the treehouse?"

"No, we will see it in the morning with Parker." I shouldn't push it but I shake my head, "you should show me tonight so that we can surprise Parker together in the morning." Michael contemplates and then grabs my hand interlocking our fingers. I choke down the nausea as it rises. If I can get him out of the house and away from Parker, she will be safer when the police show up. As we walk out to the backyard and up to the treehouse he tells me all the things he did to the treehouse to make it perfect for Parker.

I don't want to give him power but I may never look at a treehouse the same way without a cringe. "It looks great Michael." He looks at me with a big bright smile. Somewhere in his mind he truly believes he did this to become a family. A part of me feels sorry for him. I get it. To have a desire for a family of your own is real. But the problem? He wants *my* family.

I'm contemplating if I want to get him up in the treehouse before I figure out how to knock him unconscious or if it's safer on the ground when he interrupts my thoughts. "We can build a library up there with all her favorite books. It will be like she never lost anything at all. We will adopt her as soon as we are married. I'm sure she will call us mom and dad in no time. Then we can give her siblings." I've been really good about hiding my real emotions all night but he gets a peek at the disgust I feel when envisioning that future with him.

He lets go of my hand and grabs me by the shoulders. "This is your family now Sage. We finally have our dream." I shake my head and try to wiggle free. "This is not my dream Michael."

"Yes it is! You have talked about wanting a family to raise and a partner to do it with. I got you a home and now we have Parker. You just now have to stay. You. Will. Stay." I can feel tears enter my eyes. "Michael you're hurting me."

"Say you will stay Sage and I will let go. We will go inside and start our forever." We can't go back inside. Parker needs to stay away from this lunatic."No."

"No? What do you mean no? I did this all for you!" A tear falls down my cheek and I turn away as Michael tries to wipe it off, avoiding his touch. He drops his arms and grabs my hand again pulling me to the house. I try my best to stand ground but he has at least 75 pounds on me and a few inches. "No Michael. I don't want this. You don't know what you're doing. This isn't right."

He stops and drops my hand. I walk backwards in the yard as he stalks after me. "This is our family Sage." We both hear sirens coming in the distance. I breathe out in relief, "Lucas".

Michael looks back at me with fire in his eyes. "Lucas?! Lucas never deserved you. Not when we were kids and definitely not now. I will just need to get rid of him. Matt was lucky, you know? When I saw him sending you messages on your social media I almost had to create a little accident. But then you went ahead and took care of it for me with your restraining order. Honestly if I knew that you thought those packages and notes were from him I wouldn't have made them so nice."

This man has been watching me for over a year, hacked into my accounts, and threatened the lives of multiple people. My gut and instincts are screaming now to get away. The sirens are getting louder as they get closer. "Now listen Sage, this is simple. You are going to tell those officers that you gave me permission to take Parker home today and this was all a misunderstanding then no one gets hurt. No harm no foul."

I shake my head and regain my confidence. "No Michael. We are not your family. We will never be your family. We already have our own family." I step to make a break to the front yard but he is too angry and too fast.

He grabs my throat with both hands. "No Sage. We are a family. You, me and Parker will be together forever." I'm starting to see black around the edges of my eyes and am starting to lose gripping on my feet as I rise to my tiptoes. I do what any woman in distress knows, I shove my knee as hard as humanly possible into his balls. Michael's hands break from my neck as he crumbles to the ground.

I take the opportunity to dash off to the front yard. About five police cars pull up as I make it around the corner. Lucas is out of the car before James has the chance to park running at me. He scoops me in his arms. "You're okay Blue. I got you."

# CHAPTER 40
# - LUCAS

The moment I see Sage running from the backyard, I am filled with such relief. I can't help but jump out of the car and meet her in the front yard. I take her into my arms immediately, "You're okay Blue. I got you." Sage breaks. I have never seen this girl cry so hard. I walk her to the ambulances that pulled in behind us. I see James with Trigger, Chief Harrington, Officer Sandoval, Officer Darrell, and others take off to the backyard. I trust them to deal with Matt.

Once we get to the ambulances, I set Sage down on the gurney and two paramedics step up. I see red marks on her neck in the shape of fingers. He tried to strangle her. "I'm going to kill him."

Sage snaps her eyes to mine and grabs my arm before I storm off. "You have to go get Parker. She's in her old bedroom. Please Lucas, I promised her you would come." I kiss her forehead and jog to the house. The front door is unlocked so I swing it open and rush upstairs. There is only one bedroom that is shut so I head to that one. I quietly but quickly open the door. Parker sits up immediately sees me and launches off her bed. She runs over to me and I squat down as she flies into my arms."I got you baby girl." She nods and I feel my shirt getting wet from her tears.

She looks up to me with her big blue eyes, "Mom told me that you would come save me. Then I had a dream and my mom and dad in heaven told me that it was going to be okay and I just needed to be brave a little longer." I hug her close to my chest, scooping her up, and walk down the stairs to the find Sage.

Once Sage sees Parker she lights up. I place Parker next to Sage who is now sitting on the gurney. "Parker girl are you okay?" Sage pulls Parker into a hug. Parker snuggles into her and lets out a breath. "Yeah mom. I went to sleep like you said until I heard the sirens then waited for Lucas to come get me like you told me to." My heart swells hearing Parker call Sage mom. Their bond will never be broken.

I breathe out in relief. This is my family and they are safe. My thoughts are interrupted as we all watch James come from the backyard with Michael in handcuffs.

Wait Michael? Where's Matt? Sage must see the confusion on my face. "It was Michael this whole time. The flowers, the packages, the notes, the text, all of it was him." I have so many questions, but I know we will discuss those things later. We all watch as they put him in the patrol car.

He has the audacity to look over at my family. I fold my arms in front of my chest and step in front of them blocking Michael's view.Officer Darrell jumps in with James as they head to the station. Officer Sandoval comes running up. "Sage, Parker are you guys okay?" Parker nods and Sage squeezes her, "yeah we are okay."

Officer Sandoval gives her a small smile. "I'm sorry Sage but we are going to need your statement. We can do it now or we can wait until the morning. It's been a long day for you two so whichever is better for you." I look at my two girls. They both look exhausted. "Let's do it tomorrow morning, Officer Sandoval. Could you come by the house in the morning and get it from them?" She nods her head at me. "Of course. Take your family home, Officer Walker."

I turn to my girls, "you ready to go home?" Both of them look at each other, smile and nod. "We just need to make sure we get an all clear from the paramedics first." The paramedics come over and check out Parker. She tells them that Michael didn't hurt her or touch her besides trying to hold her hand. Sage sees my hands go into fists as Parker talks to them and grabs my hand, interlocking our fingers.

I look down at Sage and she looks up to me

with a small smile. I see the red marks on her neck and touch them gently with my other hand, "you sure you're okay?" I try not to imagine how she got these markings, knowing they will bruise. Not wanting to push Sage to talk before she is ready I don't ask questions. She nods, "yeah I'm fine. I'm just grateful you came when you did."

If I would have answered my phone I could have been here with her to save Parker. I wouldn't have been here so late if I was paying attention. Sage must read my emotions and regret on my face. She stands from the gurney and grabs my face with both her hands. "You saved us Lucas. A crazy man targeted Parker because of me. Because of *you* we are okay."

"No Sage because of *you*, you are both safe. Michael chose Parker to get to you but none of this is your fault. You can't take blame on any of this." She nods and I wrap her in my arms. Once we get the all clear, I load up the girls in Sage's car and we head home.

I wake up the next morning before Sage and Parker. I lay in bed next to them feeling grateful that they are okay. Last night when we got home Stanton looked torn between being angry at Sage for sneaking out and being grateful that everyone made it back safely. He gave us all hugs before letting us head upstairs. He could tell that everyone was exhausted. Parker went straight to our bed and crawled in. I convinced Sage to jump in the shower with me to help her relax. I could tell she wanted to tell me I didn't need to when I started to wash her body for her but she was too tired.

We got out of the shower, put on our pajamas, brushed our teeth, and crawled into bed with Sage in the middle snuggling Parker and me snuggling Sage. Everyone was asleep within minutes.

Parker begins to stir next to Sage. She looks over and notices I'm awake. I smile at her and give her a little wave which makes her giggle. She puts her hand over her mouth and I nod towards the door. We both slip out of the bed and head downstairs. We find Stanton and Miles in the kitchen with Mr. and Mrs. Calloway making breakfast. "Good morning guys."

Everyone snaps their heads to us as we walk in. Mr. Calloway is the first to make it to Parker. He pulls her in for a hug, "we are so glad you are home Parker girl." The doorbell rings and everyone looks to me. "Do you know who that would be Lucas?"

"It could be Officer Sandoval. She was going to come over for Sage and Parker's statement today." I jog off to the front door pulling out my phone to check the camera. I smile when I see who is on the other side. I open the door, "good morning mama". My mama storms into the house. "Is Parker and Sage okay?! Mrs. Calloway called me this morning and told me what happened." She gently swats my arm. "My son should have called me to tell me that his family was back home."

Yesterday during the madness she would call once an hour for an update. "Sorry mama, we got home so late last night and went to bed. I was planning on calling you first thing this morning." I give her a smile. " I promise." She nods her head and starts walking to the kitchen. "Are the girls awake?" We make it to the kitchen before I can answer.

"Mama Walker! Are you eating breakfast with us?" Parker goes over and gives her a hug looking overjoyed that all her family is here. "Yes ma'am. Can I help with anything?" Mama walks around the island and starts helping Parker and Mrs. Calloway with the fruit.

Mr. Calloway looks up from flipping pancakes, "thanks for saving our girls Lucas." I shake my head, "honestly that was all Sage. She figured out where Parker was and texted the chief the address. I don't know where we would be without Sage." He shakes his head with a smile, "we just need to talk to her about making sure she's not alone next time."

Next time? No way this ever happens again with my family. I plan to make sure no one can ever take away Sage or Parker ever again. "Good morning everyone." Sage comes down the stairs with a smile. It takes everything in me not to grab her and show her how much she means to me. Knowing we have an audience, I control myself and only pull her into my side. She leans her head on my chest and I lean down and whisper in her ear, "good morning babe. Did you sleep good?" She nods and looks up to me with a smile. Damn this woman with big blue eyes has my entire heart and soul.

"Alright everyone, breakfast is ready!" Mr. Calloway walks over to the table with a large stack of pancakes and syrup. Mrs. Calloway and mama bring over the fruit while Stanton takes over the bacon he was working on and sits down by Miles who is in his high chair munching on some smashed up strawberries. Sage gives hugs to everyone and I can see the tension in both Mr. Calloways and Stanton's face when they see the bruising on her neck.

Parker sits in between Sage and my mama. I take the seat on the other side of Sage and we all enjoy breakfast as a family. This. This is what I have always dreamed of having one day.

## Sage

The last 24 hours have been a whirlwind but

in the end I'm at home, safe with my family. After breakfast, the boys told us that they were on clean up duty so my mom took Miles into the living room. Julia, Parker, and I followed and now are all sitting in the living room as Parker and Miles play on the floor with some toys, with Aspen glued to Parker.

We are discussing some holiday plans when Lucas pops in and sits down next to me. "Hey babe, officer Sandoval just called. They need yours and Parker's statements. Are you okay if she comes by here or would you rather go into the station?" I look down at Parker, "let's just do it here so Parker can stay here." He nods and shoots Officer Sandoval a text saying to come by whenever works for her.

Officer Sandoval, Officer Darrell, James and Trigger show up in the next ten minutes. As they walk into the living room they all give small waves. I stand up to hug each of them telling them thank you for their help. I hug James extra long. "I hope it's okay that I came along. I wanted to make sure that you and Parker were okay. Plus Trigger really wanted to see everyone."

I give him an extra squeeze before pulling away, "of course it's okay James, you're family. I was going to tell Lucas to call you for you to come for breakfast but I wasn't sure if you guys were able to go home and sleep." He nods, "after we booked Michael last night Chief Harrington told us to go home and get some sleep. We all met up again this morning at the station before coming here." Lucas comes in behind me and nods at James, "hey man, thanks for coming by."

"Of course. I'm glad your family is safe and home." Lucas looks to Parker and smiles. Officer Sandoval comes up, "Alright Sage, I know that you probably want to enjoy your day with family but we need to get these statements filed so that details aren't lost."

I nod, "of course. Do you mind if we start with Parker and then let her go out back with the dogs? There are details from my side that she doesn't need to know about." Officer Sandoval nods, "of course. Whatever you feel comfortable with. As her legal guardian, you can also decline her statement. However it will help the case when it goes to court." Lucas told me this last night and we agreed that we would let Parker choose what she was comfortable with.

I walk over to Parker and kneel down next to her. "Hey Parker girl. Officer Sandoval needs you to explain what happened yesterday with Mr. Jones. Are you okay with that? If you don't want to talk about it you don't have to." She thinks about it for a couple of seconds then nods, "I can tell her what happened." She stands up and sits with me on the couch.

Officer Sandoval pulls in some kitchen chairs for her and Officer Darrell. "Hey Parker, I just need you to tell me what happened yesterday and everything you remember." Parker grabs my hand, interlocking our fingers. Lucas is sitting next to her and she also grabs his hand. I nod to her and she tells her story. "Yesterday I was playing with Amanda in Mrs. Gardner's classroom. They told me that they needed to go home so I was going to go back to my mom's classroom." I can see my parents eyes widen slightly hearing Parker call me her mom. My heart still swells each time. "When I was walking Mr. Jones was in the hallway and told me that we needed to go to the parking lot to see my mom. We got outside and he told me to get in his car and he would take me home." Lucas's eyebrows drop and I can see his jaw tighten.

"We went to my old house. He told me that he wanted me to see the treehouse but I said no thank you. When we got out of the car he tried to hold my hand as we walked to the door but I crossed my arms. We ate dinner and then I went to my old bedroom and stayed in my bed. Mom came in and told me that everything was going to be okay. I went to sleep and woke up when I heard the sirens. Then my dad came up and got me." My eyes jump to Lucas. He is staring at Parker. I can see water welling up in his eyes. "Then my mom and dad brought me home."

Officer Sandoval gives her a small smile, "thank you Parker." I turn to Parker and squeeze her hand, "hey Parker girl you did so good. Do you want to go outside with Aspen and Trigger now?"

"Do you think Trigger likes to play with the sticks like Aspen?" James steps up with Trigger, "he loves that. Do you want to show me where the best sticks are?" Parker nods and hops off the couch, "come on Aspen, let's go play!" My mom scoops up Miles and follows them out trailed by Julia.

Lucas slides over next to me and grabs my hand putting both in my lap. "Alright Sage. Are you ready for yours?" I nod. "Last night I was thinking over all the notes and gifts I have received from 'M'. Some of the phrases and wording didn't sound like Matt the more I thought about it. They kept mentioning the 'family we always dreamed of'. Matt and I talked about a future together but didn't dive too deep into a family. That's when I remembered the note about the treehouse. Only someone close by would know that Parker's dad didn't finish hers before he died. That made me remember a conversation I had with Michael in the library about him living down the road and seeing the treehouse. Michael started acting weird after I got Parker and especially when he found out about my relationship with Lucas." Lucas squeezed my hand and I can tell his jaw is very tight. I squeeze his hand back to encourage him to relax.

"Once I figured out it was Michael and knew it had something to do with the treehouse I figured he took Parker back to her old house. I drove over there and used the code to get in. Michael was in the living room when I got to the house. I convinced him to let me see Parker so I could see that she was safe. After I checked on Parker I knew I needed to get him away from her in case he exploded. We went out back to see the treehouse. He kept trying to convince me that we were meant to be a family." I pause. They don't need to know all the details. I'm sure I'll talk them through with Lucas later.

"When we heard the sirens, Michael told me to tell them that everything was a miscommunication and that I gave him permission to bring Parker to her house. When I refused he grabbed my neck and started lifting me off the ground." I see my dad and Stanton both fist their hands. "I didn't have many options so before I lost all footing, I lifted my knee as hard as I could into his balls. That made him drop his hands and crumble, giving me the opportunity to run around front. That's where Lucas found me." I have never seen so many people look murderously angry in one room.

"I'm okay guys. Michael will go to prison for a long time for kidnapping Parker and assaulting me. We are okay."Lucas grabs the side of my face with his palm, turning me to him. "You are incredibly brave Sage." He puts his forehead on mine. "But I am struggling. Everything in me wants to go to that station and kill him for touching my girls."

I let out a deep breath, "he isn't worth it. He wanted our family but can't have it. That's torture enough for him." Lucas nods, kisses my forehead and I turn back to the officers. "Thank you Sage. We are going to head to the station and get this to the chief." I stand up and shake their hands. "Thank you for all your work."

"Thank you for saving that little girl out there. She has touched a lot of hearts." I smile and nod thinking of how many lives Parker had changed for the better. Lucas walks them to the front door and my dad and Stanton give me a hug before they head out back to join the kids.

Lucas comes back in, locks eyes with me, and stalks towards me. He takes me into his arms and I lay my head on his chest hearing his heartbeat. I close my eyes and let out a sigh. This is home. "I love you Lucas Walker."

I can hear his heart rate increase before he pulls away. He grabs both sides of my face with his hands. "I am so completely in love with you Sage. I'm pretty sure I have been my whole life. You are my best friend, my world, my everything. And one day I will make you my wife. I will never forget the fear I had driving over to that house not knowing if my girls were safe. You two are my family and no one will take that away from me."

I lean up while grabbing his shirt, pulling his lips to mine. If I could go back in time, I wouldn't change a thing because all roads led me here.

# EPILOGUE

## Lucas

Six weeks ago one of the worst day of my life occurred. Now I'm hoping that today is one of the best days and one we always remember. Michael was sentenced to 25 years in prison for kidnapping and assault. The court case was pretty seamless and the jury had no question or dispute. I'm so proud of Sage and Parker for being willing to testify in court about what occurred. That was and will be the last time Michael ever sees either of them.

We made it to Aspen two days ago. Parker has been obsessed with the snow and is constantly outside with Aspen running and building snowmen. Uncle Jerry and my mama have loved showing Parker and Sage the town and all the places that we always visit when we are here.

I told Sage to get dressed up for our date tonight. I am adjusting my tie when Sage comes down the steps with Parker holding her hand. Sage is wearing the yellow dress from the police banquet. Just like the first time, I go weak in the knees. Once she gets to the bottom step I step up to her and tuck one of her blonde strands behind her ear, "you're beautiful." She smiles, "you look pretty good too." I smile, lean down and give her a quick kiss.

"Dad, where are her flowers?" I smile and look at Parker. "They are in the kitchen in a vase, do you want to go get them for me?" She nods and races off to the kitchen. This gives me time to take all of Sage in. She has her hair curled with half of it pinned back. She is wearing her strappy heels again. She sees me eye them and I chuckle, "later tonight you will only be wearing those."

Her cheeks pinken just the way I like and my heart swells. I will never be good enough for this woman but damn do I know I am lucky. Parker comes back a minute later. "Here you go mom. Dad got you roses with lilies. He got me roses and daisies. And got Mama Walker roses with baby breath." Had to make sure all of my girls felt special tonight. Sage turns to me, "they are beautiful. Thank you"

"Anything for my girls." Sage and I head to the restaurant. Sage is telling me all about the story Parker was telling her earlier of Parker wanting to try to snowboard after hearing that what I did growing up. I smile, that little girl can do anything she wants. Sage sees my smile, shaking her head with her own smile.

Once we get to the restaurant I park the

car and walk around the front to open Sage's passenger door. I hold out my hand for her as she steps onto the snowy ground. I loop my arm around her waist as we walk in. She gasps when we get inside. I rented out the entire restaurant. There is a single table in the middle of the room with red roses and candles all around the room. She looks at me and chuckles, "what's going on?"

"We are having dinner babe." She rolls her eyes, "yeah okay." I laugh as I walk us to the table, pulling out her seat for her. We enjoy our three course meal with conversation flowing from small things to big things. The day she got a note on her windshield I moved in and neither of us have talked about when I plan to move out. I think we both know that I don't plan to.

Once both of our stomachs are both full, I grab Sage's hand and stand from the table. There is quiet music playing and I pull her into me, swaying to the music. "Blue, you have changed my life in so many ways. You made me realize that my dream of having a healthy and happy family was not only possible but could be better than I could ever imagine." I take a deep breath trying to control my emotions but know there is no use as I feel my eyes start to water.

She stops us from swaying. "Lucas, we are so blessed to have you. Who would've thought the two of us would be here today." I chuckle, "from pulling on your pigtails in middle school to you bringing me to my knees." I wink at her and she bites her lip. "I love you Sage. More than I ever thought was possible. You are my best friend, my partner, and soulmate. You are the person I long to go home to after a long day and the person I am desperate to see the world with. You are an incredible mother, sister, daughter, teacher, and friend. The list could go on forever. I also love Parker with all that I am. You two are my family. It's time we make it official." I drop down to my knee and her hands fly to her mouth. "Will you marry me?"

## Sage

"Yes! Of course I will marry you." I can feel tears on my cheeks as Lucas slips the most gorgeous ring onto my finger. I pull on his suit coat as he stands and bring his lips to mine. I hope that the kiss shows him how happy he makes me. I can't believe I am lucky enough to marry my best friend.

We break our kiss when we hearing clapping and cheering. I look over to the kitchen to see all our family members file out.

Parker flies out and runs at us. Lucas picks her up and pulls me into a big hug. My parents are the first to come to me giving me hugs and saying how happy they are for us. "When did you guys get here?"

"Baby girl, Lucas has been planning this since the day you brought Parker back home. We flew in last night but didn't want to ruin the surprise." Stanton is next to pull me in to him and Miles. Miles giggles as I tickle his tummy. "Happy for you sis. There isn't a better man out there for you." I give him a good squeeze, "thanks for letting me steal your best friend"

He shakes his head with a smile, "nah he was never mine. I was just there for the in between." I see Lucas hugging his mom and Uncle Jerry and overhear Jerry, "you better plan this wedding fast. I gotta marry you before I die." Lucas rolls his eyes, "you aren't going anywhere old man."

My parents pull Lucas away while Jerry and Julia come to me. Julia pulls me into a hug, "thank you for giving my son a family." I nod, "thank you for raising such a good man." You can see tears in her eyes as she pulls away. Jerry pulls me into a hug, "you sure you want to deal with that guy forever?" I laugh, "yeah I think we can handle him." He laughs, "you definitely can. But if you ever need a break, you are always welcome here."

Lucas comes over and gives Stanton a hug. Parker, who has been holding my hand, drops it to tug on Stanton's arm. "Oh right. I almost forgot, Parker girl." He hands over some papers to her. She turns to us, "this is for you." You can tell she is very excited. Lucas takes them, looks them over and then looks at me with a shocked look.

I take the papers from him and scan them over. Tears well up in my eyes. "Are you sure Parker?" She nods her head with excitement, "yep! Uncle Stanton helped me get those. I want you to be my mom and dad forever." I can feel tears coming back as I look down at the adoption papers. "Of course we will adopt you Parker." I squat down and she throws her arms around me. I see Lucas bend down and kiss the top of Parker's head.

I found my forever and no one can ever take them away.

# ACKNOWLEDGEMENTS

It's hard to convey how much this book means to me. Thank you for being part of this journey. Have you ever had a bucket list item that seemed out of reach? This book was one of mine. After months of wondering if I could turn my ideas into reality, I finally took the leap. Not only did I find a deep love for writing, but I also uncovered more stories waiting to be told. What began as a "let's see what happens" turned into a full-blown passion.

To my husband: This dream would have been nothing but an idea without you. You have always inspired me to chase my dreams and held my hand as we watched how far they go. The countless nights listening to my ideas and helping me bring this story to life or driving across country listening to the final project are some of my favorite memories from this book. You brought depth to the story in a way that I never could and inspired so many of these characters with your selfless love and devotion to our family. Everyone wants a forever love and I am beyond lucky to have my own.

To my daughter: Your birth inspired me to strive for my best and follow my dreams. You showed me that pursuing dreams is worth it, and I hope my example encourages you to chase yours. The love I have for you as your mom is unmatched and boundless.

To my sister: My love for books began with you. What started as an attempt to become more like you became a source of light in my darkest days. Without our shared passion for reading, I might never have discovered my desire to write. As my number one editor and advocate, I am profoundly grateful for your support.

To Amanda and Gabby: You inspired many of these characters and gave me the confidence to turn this story from a mere document into a published book. Your impact on my life is immense, and you will always be part of who I am today.

Lastly, to my readers: Thank you for embracing the story that transformed my life. Initially, this book was for me alone, a way to fulfill a dream. Your support has made this journey even more special, and I'm excited to share that this is just the beginning. Many more stories are on the way!

# ABOUT THE AUTHOR

## Sierra Hebdon

Sierra was born and raised in a small town in northern Arizona, where her love for reading sparked a desire to bring the stories in her to life. When she's not writing, she enjoys spending time with family and friends, supporting others in pursuing their dreams, and working on her own personal growth. Passionate about mental health, Sierra's books emphasize the importance of understanding and advocating for mental well-being. She aims to make readers experience a full range of emotions, encouraging them to embrace their feelings while leaving with hope and a smile.

# BOOKS IN THIS SERIES

## *The Pennystone Series*

The Pennystone series delves into the intertwined lives of three inseparable best friends as they embark on individual journeys to discover their true selves and find their soulmates. Each character confronts unique personal struggles and battles, from grappling with past heartbreaks to navigating career challenges and self-doubt. As they face these trials with resilience, they ultimately uncover joy and fulfillment in their own stories of lasting love. Through triumphs and tribulations, the series beautifully captures the transformative power of true and unconditional love and the enduring quest for happiness.

## Choosing My Forever

Brooklyn and Stanton both carry the weight of their pasts, yearning to move beyond the shadows that have shaped their lives. Their paths cross in an unexpected and dramatic way when their office buildings are positioned right next to each other, causing their worlds to collide in ways neither could have anticipated.

Stanton, juggling the overwhelming responsibilities of being a single father, a dedicated business owner, and a committed family member, finds himself trapped under the immense pressure to be everything to everyone. The anxiety and weight of his multiple roles have built emotional walls around him, making it difficult for him to open his heart to new possibilities. As his world intersects with Brooklyn's, Stanton faces the challenge of overcoming his fears and letting go of his past, seeking a way to balance his personal and professional life while allowing himself to be vulnerable again.

Brooklyn is presented with a once-in-a-lifetime career opportunity that could potentially change the course of her life. However, this golden chance comes with a significant dilemma: it requires her to make a difficult choice between her professional aspirations and the deepening connections she has formed with Stanton and his family. As Brooklyn grapples with the decision, she must weigh the value of the new opportunities against the love and sense of belonging she has discovered in Pennystone.

As Brooklyn and Stanton's lives become increasingly intertwined, will they have the strength to confront their pasts and choose each other despite the obstacles they face?

## Loving My Forever

After fleeing an abusive relationship, Gracie arrives in the picturesque town of Pennystone, yearning for a fresh start and a chance to rebuild her life on her own terms. She hopes that this new chapter will offer her peace and the opportunity to leave behind the shadows of her past. However, this quest for a new beginning is abruptly challenged when she receives news that is both unexpected and life-altering. This revelation shakes her foundation, casting a pall over her dreams of recovery and making her question whether she will ever truly be free from her past.

In the midst of her turmoil, Gracie finds herself grappling with the uncertainty of her future. Feeling isolated and overwhelmed, she finds herself relaying on James, a kind-hearted stranger who has unexpectedly become a supportive friend. Seeing Gracie's distress and the profound impact of the recent news on her well-being, James offers a solution he never imagined he would propose: a marriage of convenience. His proposal comes from a place of deep concern and a desire to protect her from further harm, even though it means making a significant personal sacrifice.

James himself carries the weight of his own past traumas, which complicates the situation further. As they enter into this unconventional arrangement, their shared living situation quickly becomes a minefield of emotional hurdles and unspoken pain. The daily challenges they face together are compounded by their individual histories, testing their ability to navigate their new life as a couple.

Will Gracie and James be able to confront their challenges, complicated by their individual histories, and navigate the obstacles together? Will they discover that they don't have to settle for a life of compromise and unfulfilled dreams, but can instead find a life they truly love?